Netta Muskett was born in Sevenoaks,
College, Folkstone. She had a varied
teaching mathematics before working as a secretary to the then owner
of the 'News of the World', as well as serving as a volunteer during
both world wars – firstly driving an ambulance and then teaching
handicrafts in British and American hospitals.

It is, however, for the exciting and imaginative nature of her writing
that she is most remembered. She wrote of the times she experienced,
along with the changing attitudes towards sex, women and romance,
and sold millions of copies worldwide. Her last novel 'Cloudbreak' was
first published posthumously after her death in 1963.

Many of her works were regarded by some librarians at the time of
publication as risqué, but nonetheless proved to be hugely popular
with the public, especially followers of the romance genre.

Netta co-founded the Romantic Novelists' Association and served
as Vice-President. The 'Netta Muskett' award, now renamed the
'RNA New Writers Scheme', was created in her honour to recognise
outstanding new writers.

FLOWERS FROM THE ROCK

Netta Muskett

This edition published in 2014 by House of Stratus, an imprint of
Stratus Books Ltd, Lisandra House, Fore St., Looe,
Cornwall, PL13 1AD, UK.

www.houseofstratus.com

Typeset by House of Stratus.

A catalogue record for this book is available from the British Library and the Library of Congress.

ISBN 07551 4281 0
EAN 978 07551 4281 1

Chapter One

Verne sat on the park bench and stared bleakly into space, her hands gripping her handbag in which lay Robert Grimtree's ring. The huge, blatant diamond seemed to send its icy coldness through the cheap plastic to her fingers just as the memory of it, and the way he had flung it across his office table at her, struck its numbing chill through her mind.

'Better take it and think it over,' he said when she made no attempt to pick it up, backing away from it as the evil thing it was, and he had taken it up again, opened her bag and pushed it inside and shut the clasp.

Why had she not snatched it out and given it back to him then?

Sitting there in dumb misery, she knew why she had not done so.

She shivered.

She was going to marry Robert Grimtree.

It was not marriage which he had suggested the first time, a week ago.

On that occasion, in his private office since they had never met anywhere else, he had made his proposal clear, and in it he had offered her just the same as he had offered today, except for the eventual wedding ring.

'You can get anything your mother needs, including the winter at this place in Switzerland, all the best doctors, this new treatment—and all you want for yourself as well. I'm not mean.'

Her small, bitter smile had shown him her thoughts.

'You're thinking of that fool Gorner?' he asked harshly. 'He didn't give value for my money. He robbed me. I sacked him. He killed himself. So what?'

She did not speak but continued to look at him with that look of scorn which infuriated him. She, his paid employee, daring to be contemptuous of him, the great Robert Grimtree with his millions!

He was tempted to fling at her the evidence of his weakness in having sent Mary Gorner, the young widow, his personal cheque for five hundred pounds, but it still galled him that the cheque had come back to him the next day, torn in half.

'Well?' he asked angrily, glaring at the self possessed girl whose face showed the strain and weariness with which she was meeting yet another winter in the small, airless Fulham flat, the mists from the river and the November fogs draining away the life of the one being she loved, loved with the utter, selfless devotion of her heart.

Everything possible had been done in England for Mrs. Raydon, the hospital treatment, the long stay in the sanatorium which had only prolonged her life and sent her back to London to die – unless by some miracle she could go to the expensive sanatorium high up in the Swiss Alps to escape the English winters.

As well try to reach the moon – until Robert Grimtree had come out with his stupefying proposal.

There had been no offer of a ring of any sort then, and Verne, after another contemptuous glance at him, had left his office, tapped out on her typewriter the bald words of resignation of her job, put on her coat and hat and, passing through the hall of the monster block of offices, had dropped the envelope in the private box of which only Robert Grimtree himself had the key.

Frantically, and too late, she had known a moment's panic, for she could not recall it. Inevitably he would read it, possibly tonight before he left. He often unlocked the box and took home any late contents of it.

But what else could she have done?

It would, anyway, be easier for her to get another job than it would be for Grimtree to fill her place adequately. During the two years of her service to him, she had become most of the things a busy man of affairs could ask in a private secretary. She was capable, trustworthy and discreet, worked long hours without complaint and was never ill nor temperamental – an efficient machine.

Whatever she had expected the next day, it was not the silence and complete ignoring of the situation between them, but a week later he had called her into his office just as she was leaving, and had made this second, amazing proposal.

'I'll marry you,' he said abruptly, glaring at her with his cold, piercing blue eyes, his voice like that of an enraged bull. 'Here!' and he flung the diamond ring across the table to her.

She backed away from it, staring at it and then at him.

'Are you mad?' she asked, giving him neither his name nor the 'sir' which he liked his employees to use.

'Probably, but it seems it's the only way to get you,' he snarled.

'Why should you want me?' she asked curtly.

'I want to get married and have a family and you're the only woman I know,' he said.

Her lip curled.

'You know dozens of women.'

'I said *know*. Idiots, morons, women after my money—any amount of them for the lifting of my finger and for much less than that,' with a jerk of his head towards the ring, winking and sparkling on the dark wood.

'What should I be after, if I married you, but your money?' she asked scathingly.

His big, hard face creased into what passed with him for a smile.

'Quite,' he said; 'but you'd give value for it.'

'In what way? You don't love me,' said Verne, her smile flicking him on the raw.

He laughed, a harsh, mirthless sound.

'Love? Storybook stuff? Who's talking of love? I'm making you a business proposition, and I'm making it to you rather than to any other woman because I know you, Verne Raydon. I'm a lonely man, but I'm not asking for sympathy for that. Loneliness suits me. There's only room for one at the top. I've got a big house and a lot of money, and I can make a lot more. But I've decided I need a wife and someone to leave my money to.'

'Someone to hang your diamonds on?' asked Verne mockingly. 'I'm sorry, but I don't like diamonds and I'm not for sale.'

He looked at her with a new interest. He had told her that he 'knew' her, but realised now that his knowledge had not been complete. He had not been prepared for her to turn down his offer of a week ago, when he had made it clear that she was to be his mistress.

But it really amazed him that she seemed prepared to refuse an offer of actual, legal marriage.

She stood there, quite composed, a tall, slight girl with nut brown hair kept short and very neat in spite of its tendency to curl upwards where the deep waves ended. Her features were well cut, her mouth perhaps a thought too generous for beauty, and he saw now that her eyes, usually cast down at her book when she was with him, were brown and very steady.

He noted these unimportant details unconsciously and remembered them afterwards. The important thing now was that she was defying him, refusing an offer which seemed to him stupendous – refusing to become his, Robert Grimtree's, *wife*!

'I'm offering you a good price,' he said.

'I'm aware of that, but I'm still not for sale, Mr. Grimtree,' she told him, head in air, two spots of colour coming into her too pale cheeks. 'May I go now? I will finish the Allen report tomorrow morning.'

'You don't come in on Saturday mornings.'

'I will do so tomorrow as I shall have a lot to do next week.'

'Why specially next week?'

The spots of colour spread.

'It will be my last week,' she said, her eyes cool and steady though her heart was thumping painfully.

She did not want to leave Grimtree's. The work was hard and the hours long, but her salary was good, better probably than she would get elsewhere, and she needed desperately as much as she could earn for all the little extra comforts she was able to get for her mother, and to save enough, if possible, to get her out of London and into the clean air of the country for the worst weeks of the winter.

'Still determined to leave me?' he asked.

'Of course.'

4

'You're a fool, Verne Raydon,' he snarled at her, and then, as she was about to pick up the handbag which she had laid on the table, he snatched it up and thrust the ring inside it.

'Better take it and think it over,' he said, and watched her go.

He was angry at the frustration of his plan, unused to any such thing.

It had taken him a week to decide to marry her and even when he had brought himself to ask her, he had not been quite sure it was what he wanted to do. Now, his offer spurned in that high handed fashion, he knew that it was a thing he both wanted and intended to do.

The impertinence of such a refusal! The effrontery!

And she had dared to bring up that nasty little business of young Gorner, not in so many words but obviously by implication.

He had not wanted to be reminded of that, though he told himself savagely that the young fool's suicide was no fault of his, Robert's, but the cowardly weakness of a man who, found out in his criminal robbery of his employer, could not 'take it'. And he, Grimtree, had not actually said in so many words that he intended to prosecute. He had dictated the letter himself, avoiding a second glance at Verne Raydon's disapproving face, and if the young fool had seen more in it than he had actually said, and shot himself the next morning, it was no one's fault but his own.

And had he not made the gesture of that five hundred pounds which the widow had refused? He almost wished he had told Verne about that, flinging the information at her as a reply to that cynical smile of hers.

But why should he justify himself? He was Robert Grimtree. He was a law unto himself. He could do what he liked.

He had intended to stay to do another hour or two's work, sparing himself even less than his employees, but he could not settle to it, rang for his car to be brought to the door, and went home.

Home.

It was a great mansion in a famous London street not yet given over to the flat makers, and it was furnished with all the ostentation on which he had insisted when he had handed it over to a famous London firm five years ago, telling them to spare no expense.

In the huge dining room, at one end of a table which could seat forty guests, looked down on superciliously by portraits of other people's ancestors, a perfect meal was served to him by a butler who might have come straight out of a Hollywood film with a maid in attendance. He pushed most of the food away, however, though as a rule he was a prodigious eater, sat for a while with his final brandy almost untasted and his cigar unlit, and then told the butler in his usual curt fashion that he wanted nothing further of them that night.

Left alone, he wandered through the great, empty rooms, his step heavy, his face grim and thoughtful.

Once he paused before a long mirror and looked at his reflection, his thin lips pursed, his eyes mocking what he saw.

Not a figure for romance, if that was what Verne Raydon was looking for.

The height of his tall figure was disguised by its bulk, his broad shoulders stooping a little, his heavy head with its broad, flattish features thrust forward, his square chin jutting out as if to meet, belligerently, any enemy preparing to challenge him. His thick brown hair was slightly grizzled, and he had been glad of it. It had helped him in his endeavour to appear more than his age. Few people knew that he was only just forty. People who speculated as to his age put it at fifty, or more. He despised youth, his own in particular.

At last he left the first floor on which was the elaborate, never used drawing room and his own luxurious suite and went on up the stairs, past the second floor where the servants slept and at which the main staircase ended, and passed through a door which led to a narrow, uncarpeted passage from which a bare, steep staircase led to the unused attics. At one time the staircase had led right down to the ground floor, but now it had been boarded up so that there was no access to it except by this one flight. Dust lay thickly on the steps and the enclosing walls, but he took no notice of it, not pausing until he reached one of the three narrow, closed doors which led from the upper passage, and this he unlocked with a key from the bunch in his pocket

No one but he had ever been into this room since the removers had placed in it, not without surprised speculation, some odds and ends of furniture vastly different from anything else brought to the house.

He shut the door behind him, locked it and drew a deep breath, the familiar personality of Robert Grimtree sloughing off him.

It was a small room with a sloping ceiling which, in places, would not allow him to stand upright. One small dormer window, set in grimy, faded wallpaper of a bygone taste, looked out over the rooftops and chimneys, a curtain of cheap Nottingham lace stretched across it on a string. The furniture was in keeping with the room, a small iron bedstead which sagged under a faded cotton cover, a lopsided wickerwork chair, an unpainted deal table, a chest of drawers off which the paint had peeled long ago, a small cracked mirror on it, supported by a box. A rusty iron tripod held a chipped hand basin with a spoutless ewer standing in it and a tin pail beneath it, and in one corner was a water tap with a lead lined trap beneath it for the waste.

The room was one of the many secrets of Robert Grimtree's life. It was for him both an escape from the present and a reminder of whence he had come. It was as faithful a representation as possible of the room in which he had spent his childhood. There was only this main difference: that other room had been dirty and foul smelling, but this one was clean, its atmosphere redolent of the strong disinfectant which, at each visit, he poured down the waste trap and sprinkled on the floor.

He cleaned the place himself, even to washing the floor and the curtain, heating water over a small gas ring. Now, his immaculate dinner jacket hung on a nail behind the door, his dress trousers exchanged for old flannel slacks, he heated water in a battered pan, washed the net curtain and hung it up again, and swept and scrubbed the worn strips of linoleum on the floor. When he had finished, poor though the place was, it shone with cleanliness and smelt of carbolic soap.

There had been no cleanliness in his mother's home. She was a drink sodden slattern and his father was seldom out of prison, but some unknown ancestor must have put into Robert Grimtree's being a hatred of dirt in any form so that whilst he had devised this room for some queer reason of his own, he had revolted against the filth which would have made it a more exact copy.

When he had dressed again, he sat in the crazy wicker chair and let his thoughts roam back as they always did in this room but seldom anywhere else.

He saw the small boy of his earliest recollections, dirty, ragged, unloved and unwanted, cuffed out of his mother's way and scurrying from his father's sight during the short periods that unworthy spent with his wife and child. His happiest hours were spent at school, which was clean and where he learned avidly anything which could be taught by one harassed teacher with a class of fifty unruly boys to cope with.

He was always hungry, cadging food as and where he could, for there was little at home and he did not know where even such scraps came from, for his mother seemed seldom to do any work and certainly his father made no attempt to provide for them. At one time he might have been trustful and confiding, as most young things are by nature, but he quickly learned to trust no one but himself, and decided that honesty was usually the best policy, since it kept one out of the grip of retribution. He asked nothing of others, and he gave nothing.

Just once in his lifetime he had failed to observe his own rule of living only to and for himself, and he had been eighteen by then.

He had fallen violently in love and had bought the girl a lemonade, a bag of potato crisps and a near silver ring set with a large glass 'diamond', and had taken her to the pictures.

The next day he saw the ring exposed for sale in a junk shop and the girl had vanished. The lemonade and the crisps and the price of the cinema seats were irretrievable, but the lesson was worth its price.

He had had a grim memory of that ring when he had bought the magnificent jewel to give to Verne Raydon. The near silver had become platinum, and the glass stone a huge, flawless diamond.

His rise from the dire poverty of Bobby Grimtree to the opulence of Robert Grimtree, a name known in the 'rag trade' all over the country, had been due partly to luck, but chiefly to his ability to snatch any opportunity which offered itself and turn it to his advantage.

During one of his father's lengthening periods in prison, his mother had been knocked down by a lorry and killed, and though the insurance company had fought the case on the plea that the woman was drunk, the court awarded damages, and Bobby, just sixteen, found himself in the extraordinary position of having a fortune of two hundred pounds. He was at the time employed in a small draper's shop, and it was his elderly employer who had interested himself in obtaining compensation for the mother's death and in ensuring that the money should go to the son and not the ne'er-do-well husband. It was not gratitude but business acumen which prompted the boy to offer the old man the two hundred pounds in exchange for a share in the business for which, in spite of his youth, he had practical schemes for improving and developing. He hated the war, considering those years a futile waste of time, but he was caught up in its maw and survived it without a scratch if without distinction, though it nearly put an end to the business into which he had put four strenuous years. Bomb damage and clothing coupons left little for Robert to return to, and the old man had lost heart and interest in it, but within a year of his young partner's return, he was obliging enough to die and leave to Robert the freehold premises to be rebuilt under a War Damage claim.

It became the first of the Robert Grimtree shops, and after that early struggle to re-establish himself, Robert never looked back, never took his eyes off the glittering future until now, at forty, he held that dazzling bauble of success within his grasp. His shops were all over the country, the big stores emblazoned in great gilded letters with his own name and selling expensive goods, the smaller shops, filled with cheaper merchandise, bearing other names and serving as an outlet for articles and materials which had not found their market in the big stores. They in their turn had an outlet in the booths of the cheap street markets so that nothing was lost or wasted.

It was of all these things that Robert Grimtree liked to think when, as now, he made his way to the poor little room which not even the servants knew about and which, in his own mind, he thought of as 'upstairs'.

But for once it failed to give him that glow of satisfaction and pride he had formerly experienced there. Instead of complacence, it was giving him a restless sense of something approaching failure.

He left the room at last, locking the door and its secret behind him, and went heavily back into his luxurious home, which had never seemed less a home.

He wandered about the house, appraising the rooms with a new valuation, as if he saw them with someone else's eyes.

He looked into the library on the ground floor, an almost austere appearance having been given to it by the firm who had laid on the floor the thick, tobacco brown carpet which deadened every footfall, had lined the walls with glass fronted bookcases filled with books which no one ever read, and set here and there, on ebony pedestals, a marble or a bronze bust of some famous man of letters, of many of whom Robert Grimtree had never even heard.

Though the whole house was kept evenly warm by the central heating, a fire burned in this grate as in all the others. On the huge table lay, neatly arranged, duplicates of all the newspapers which awaited him daily in his office. He did not glance at them. He had already read all the financial news, and any other item which might be of importance to his business. It was one of Verne Raydon's duties to go through them before he arrived and mark any passages which she thought he would wish to see. He had come to rely on her judgment to such an extent that he rarely thought it worth his while to read anything she had not marked.

He gnawed his lip at the memory. Was she really going to be such a fool as to leave him? What on earth for? Because he had invited her first to be his mistress, and then his wife, and she had refused both invitations; did she think he was going to rape her in the office, or what? Irritably he left the library and went up to the drawing room. He had seldom been into it since it had been handed over to him with the rest of the house, complete. It was not a man's room, and he never entertained women.

It was ornate in cream and gold, the pale yellow carpet specially woven for it, the rich brocade on chairs and couches never sat on. Long curtains of gold satin hung at the windows with cobwebby silk net beneath them. Exquisite watercolours on the white panelled walls were never looked at, no one was ever warmed by the fire in the two great fireplaces, only the man who came at regular intervals to tune the magnificent grand piano ever touched its keys.

Silence there. Emptiness. Solitude.

He was a lonely man, but until this evening, he had not realised the truth of that.

He thought of the alleviations he had found for this 'loneliness', especially of the woman for whom he maintained a small, expensive flat which he seldom visited.

Hermione Veronica.

His lip curled. What use had he really for the Hermione Veronicas? Why had he ever started anything like that? He would not care if he never saw her again, and so long as he made the parting sufficiently advantageous to her, Hermione would not care either.

He spun his mind away from her.

He thought instead of Verne Raydon, Verne with her pale face and fatigue shadowed eyes, Verne in her neat, almost prim office dress, navy blue with touches of always-spotless white. He was remembering her as he had seen her last, with two spots of angry colour in her cheeks and that look of scorn in her eyes, calm and dignified and composed even in her anger.

His mind conjured up another picture of her. He saw her coming into this room, not as his paid employee but as his wife, the mistress of his great house. She would wear a flowered silk, perhaps – or velvet, something rich and soft which swept the yellow carpet as she walked, and his diamonds would sparkle on her hands and her bare arms, at her throat, in her ears.

Brown velvet, since her eyes were brown – or a rich, orchid coloured satin moulded to her slim figure and flaring out at silver shod feet – but whatever she wore, she would be calm, dignified, composed, the fitting mistress of this great house, the fitting wife for Robert Grimtree.

Just to hang his diamonds on?

His mind thrust her gibe aside. No, as his wife, his equal. His thoughts felt for and found the old, outworn word of helpmate.

And he knew that he wanted Verne Raydon desperately, more than he had ever wanted anything else in his life, even success and wealth.

Acting on sudden impulse, he crossed the room and opened a small panel in the wall which concealed a telephone. There were extensions in all the rooms. He was surprised that he remembered where this one was.

'Give me a line,' he said curtly to the servant on duty, and dialled the number of the telephone he had had installed in the Raydons' flat.

He must hear her voice again, and not the one which still rang in his ears, but when she answered, he had to think quickly what to say to her.

'You need not come in in the morning,' he said abruptly, without announcing himself.

'I prefer to, Mr. Grimtree,' she said in her usual tone.

'I've told you you need not,' he said. 'That report can wait.'

'Very well. Thank you, sir,' she said, and as he replaced the receiver, he had a feeling that she used that form of address to him to maintain unquestionably her position as his employee.

Verne had forced herself to recover her customary cheerfulness by the time she reached home, but she stood for a moment outside the door listening to the familiar but always heart breaking sound of her mother's cough. It was starting early this winter, though the river mist was still thin and there was no actual fog in the air yet.

Then she took a grip on herself, put her key in the door and went in with a smile and a bright word.

Mrs. Raydon must have been very much like Verne when she was young, but now the brown hair was dull and lifeless, the slenderness of her body was emaciation, and the brown eyes were set in deep hollows. Verne recognised only too clearly the bright colour in the thin cheeks and the slight huskiness in the voice.

They did not kiss, though the girl longed to take the frail, beloved form in her arms. They had kept scrupulously to both the letter and the spirit of the instructions laid down when Lorna Raydon had come home from the sanatorium. Though they had only two rooms besides the little ill equipped kitchen and tiny, cold bathroom, Verne slept on the divan in the sitting room to give her mother comfort and herself reasonable security of health in the other room. Everything they used was kept apart, and Verne did the cooking. They had had to accept that way of life as the only possible one, though it tore at the mother's heart that it had to be so, and that Verne could not come home to a meal prepared for her by loving hands.

'Any news?' asked Verne brightly, putting on an overall and getting busy with the saucepans.

'Bill popped in to see me,' said Mrs. Raydon.

Verne's face changed a little.

'Oh? What did he want?' she asked.

Mrs. Raydon smiled rather ruefully. She knew that Bill Trailer had come in the hope of seeing Verne, though he had not been able to stay because of an assignment for the newspaper with which he had a good job as a reporter.

'To see you, of course,' she said. 'Verne—'

The girl stopped her with a gay wave of her hand.

'Mum darling, no! Not another treatise on Bill Trailer! I've had a hectic day and I can't take him on top of it. Had *he* any news?'

'Something I didn't much like. The papers aren't being very nice about your Mr. Gorner's suicide.'

'Would you expect them to be? I hope they won't say anything Mr. Grimtree could get them for, though. He wouldn't hesitate to bring an action if they did.'

'I wish you didn't have to work for a man like Robert Grimtree,' said Mrs. Raydon. 'He must be a dreadful person.'

'He is,' agreed Verne cheerfully, 'but his money's as good as anyone's. Better, in fact. I—I might make a change, though,' wondering how she was going to explain to her mother why she was going to leave Grimtree's without telling her the truth.

'I'm sure we could manage on less,' said her mother bravely.

'We're not going to. If I do leave, I'll see that I get the same anywhere else. How have you been today, darling?'

'Oh quite all right,' said Lorna Raydon with her usual optimism.

'If only I could get you away before there's any smog,' sighed Verne. 'Oh, Mum, isn't it beastly not to have any money? That place in the Alps—'

'You worry far too much about me, lovey. I love England, smog and all, and I'm really much better than I was this time last year. I'm not coughing nearly as much,' but they both knew it was untrue.

Verne watched her anxiously as the evening went on, though her mother would not admit she was tired and insisted on sitting up to hear a programme on the radio. Later a knock at the door prefaced the arrival of an unwelcome visitor in the shape of Mrs. Biggin, their neighbour across the passage. Mrs. Biggin, always full of troubles and usually wanting to borrow things ('a spoonful of tea just till tomorrow', 'a cup of flour, dearie. I clean forgot'), was one of the Raydons' minor trials. Mrs. Raydon was always exhausted when Mrs. Biggin had been in 'to cheer her up' with a recital of her matrimonial troubles and the iniquities of her horde of unruly children, nor did she ever return the groceries, the kindling wood, the bucket of coal, which she 'borrowed', to Verne's enraged disgust.

This evening's visitation left the sick woman so tired and strained that Verne kept her in bed over the weekend and went to the office on tire Monday morning still anxious and worried. If only she could get her away! Even the country near London would be better than Fulham just now, but she did not know how she was to accomplish even that. Though her salary was a good one, she found it impossible to save, and week by week nothing was left over when the deductions had been made for income tax, National Health contributions and the amount she must contribute compulsorily to the Grimtree Pension Fund, and the rent of the flat paid.

She thought bitterly of Robert Grimtree's millions. Inevitably, too, she thought of his offer to do everything possible, everything luxurious for her mother – at his own terrifying price.

He did not refer again, by word or glance or any change in attitude, to that proposal, nor to her intention of leaving his service. In fact, from his various projects for future work, she realised he did not expect her to go at all, and she did not remind him, going on doggedly with her job and preparing as best she could for not being there to finish many of the things she started.

One day she met Bill Trailer for lunch at his invitation, but wished she had not done so.

Bill, light hearted, amusing, earning good money, a cheerful and engaging companion, had asked her several times to marry him, but she had refused. He was no more to her than this gay companion, and she knew that she would ask much more from marriage. There was no stability in him, and if there were depths of thought and feeling, she had never been able to find them. Yet now she knew that if Bill could offer her that chance of life for her mother, she would marry him thankfully and make the best of a second best in marriage.

He asked her again, of course, over the luncheon table.

'Have a shot at it, beautiful,' he said. 'If it doesn't work, we don't have to stay married, not in this day and age; and I'd make it easy for you.'

'Sorry, Bill, but that wouldn't be my way,' she said regretfully, for she wished with all her heart that she could feel anything for him beyond this pleasant friendship. 'I'd want to be—well, in love,' with a deprecatory smile, for Bill was not a sentimental person. 'There are so many broken marriages. I wouldn't want mine to be one, and even you don't suggest ours might last. Sorry, Bill.'

He shrugged his shoulders and laughed.

'All right—but I'm still here,' he said. 'Shall we go?'

That afternoon, her mother did an unprecedented thing.

She rang up Verne at the office to ask if she could possibly get home a little early.

'What is it, darling? Are you ill?' asked the girl with a painful lurch of her heart.

'Well—not so well, dear. I—I got the doctor to come, but—well, I don't suppose it's anything much, but—being alone—'

'I'll come,' said Verne at once and went into her employer's office with her request to be allowed to go home.

'I don't expect private affairs to interfere with business, Miss Raydon,' he said curtly.

'I'm leaving at the end of the week, Mr. Grimtree,' she said. 'I will leave now and forfeit my week's salary.'

'Don't talk rubbish. All right. Go, if you must—but don't be late in the morning.'

15

'I'm afraid that may depend on how my mother is,' said Verne, and for the first time since he had known her, her voice shook and her hands which held some papers were trembling.

He gave her a keen glance.

'Worried about her, aren't you?' he asked, and though he had meant his voice to be kind, it came out as gruff as ever.

'Yes. Very,' she said and turned to go.

At the door she paused, stopped by his voice.

'It's in your own hands, you know,' he said meaningly.

She went out of the room without replying.

That was the awful truth which she had to face. It *was* in her own hands whether that beloved being were to be given her one chance of life or not. It was not just gratitude she felt for the long years since her father's death during which Lorna Raydon had worked selflessly, denied herself every comfort, even necessities, to give Verne the kind of education and training which had brought such a job as this within her grasp. Passionate gratitude and appreciation she felt indeed, but they were lost in the deep love she bore to her mother, the one being on earth she had ever loved, for she could scarcely remember her father. Mothers and daughters are often at variance, even at enmity with each other, but not Verne and her mother, and the prospect of Lorna Raydon's death was unbearably poignant, a sword ever at her heart.

And it was clear to Verne that to remain in London, even anywhere in the bitter English winter, was robbing her mother of what little chance she had of combating the deadly disease. Nothing could cure it, but something might be done to give her a longer tenure of life, years of life perhaps, and without this racking, almost incessant pain.

Her mother's life – or hers.

It had come to that.

Mrs. Raydon had had one of the terrifying haemorrhages which left her so drained and exhausted that at one time Verne had thought she could not live through the night, in spite of all that the kindly doctor could do, but by the morning she was still alive, and for that time at least it was over.

Verne got a nurse in, though she did not know how she was going to pay for it, and called to see the doctor on her way to the office.

'Will you tell me the truth quite frankly?' she asked. 'If I could possibly get her away to this place in Switzerland, will she live?'

'That's a question no one could answer with any certainty,' he said gravely, 'but at least it would give her a chance, and she would be well looked after and in clean, dry air.'

'And in England she has no chance?'

He hesitated, but he had known the Raydons for many years and knew the quality of Verne.

'Very little, I am afraid. You asked me to be frank. Isn't it in any way possible for you to get her away? No one who would help you? Your employer, perhaps?' for he knew where she worked.

'Nobody does anything for nothing,' said Verne bitterly; 'but—I think Mr. Grimtree might help me. Will you see whether arrangements can be made for my mother to go there as soon as possible? I'll come in to see you this evening.'

He frowned after she had gone. He knew Robert Grimtree only by repute, as a hard, ruthless man not in the least likely to do 'anything for nothing'. But what price would he ask of Verne Raydon, and was there any price which she would consider too high?

Still, his waiting room was full. He must pass on to someone else's troubles, and during the day he would see what could be done about getting Mrs. Raydon away – if the money were forthcoming.

Verne, her face very pale and her eyes deeply shadowed from her sleepless night and her anxiety, put away her hat and coat and went at once to Mr. Grimtree's private office.

'I'm sorry to be so late,' she said, 'but my mother is very ill and I could not leave her until I had found someone to be with her.'

He grunted, shooting her a keen glance from under his bushy eyebrows. It was obvious that the girl was in great distress. He was not enjoying the knowledge that she found the way out so distasteful to her that she would not even consider it.

But her next words, spoken quietly and steadily, brought him up with a jerk.

'Mr. Grimtree, did you mean what you said the other day? That in return for my—marrying you, you will do everything possible for my mother?'

'And for you,' he said.

'That is not important. I want nothing for myself, but—Mr. Grimtree, she will *die* if she does not go away.'

She could not keep her calm composure. Her voice shook and he heard the pleading, desperate note in it and knew what she was asking of him – something for nothing!

'Yes. I understood that,' he said.

'You—you won't help me in any other way? I'll work for you for nothing, or only just enough to exist on, until it is paid back—'

But she knew even as she started the halting plea that it was useless.

'I don't borrow and I don't lend,' he said harshly, 'neither do I give charity. There's only one way—Verne,' and one big hand tightened on the sheaf of papers which it held. With a sick feeling of impotence she saw herself in that ruthless grip, knew that once in it, there would be no escape.

But she had fought that last battle during the long hours of the night, and now she had laid down her arms. She would not fight again.

'Very well,' she said, her head high, her face a grey mask, her eyes utterly without expression. 'If you think your part of the bargain worth it—yes.'

'You'll marry me, Verne?'

'Yes.'

'When?'

'As soon as my mother has left for Switzerland.'

His thin lips curved in a bitter smile.

'You don't trust me?'

'I must, but there will be so much to do before she goes. I can't think of myself, or of anything else.'

'You're asking me to trust you! What is there to prevent you from refusing to go through with it once she has gone?'

'Nothing,' said Verne, and they eyed each other steadily, two strong opponents aware of each other's weapons and their strength to use them, but forced to trust an unknown quantity in each.

Then he nodded.

'All right. I accept your conditions. Have you got my ring?'

'In my handbag.'

'Get it.'

She came back into the room holding the gleaming thing in her hand.

'Put it on. You need not wear it. I only want to see it on your finger.'

She slid it on her engagement finger and held her hand so that he could see it. It looked big and blatant. It felt like a band of hot iron.

'All right. You can take it off again,' he said with a snarl. 'Now about the arrangements for your mother.'

'The doctor promised to see to them.'

'Give me his name and telephone number. I'll take it over. You can go now, if you like.'

'There is a nurse with her. I'll do my work first,' said Verne.

'All right. Better ring up an agency and get someone to replace you as soon as possible—someone who can at least *spell*,' with a savage curl of his lip.

When Verne went back to the flat, she was wearing the ring. She would not try to hedge or to lie, except in so far as it was necessary, and in any case Robert Grimtree's marriage would make headlines in the papers and it would be impossible to conceal it even when her mother was out of England. There would be English newspapers.

Mrs. Raydon saw the ring at once, but waited until the nurse had gone.

'Who gave you that?' she demanded.

Verne managed a little laugh. She had decided on her course.

'Can't you guess, since it's real? Mr. Grimtree,' she said, and managed to look at the ring with pride, twisting it to catch the light.

Mrs. Raydon gasped. She had made the temporary recovery which followed these attacks, though each one left her weaker and less able to fight.

'Verne! It's on your engagement finger!'

'Yes. He's asked me to marry him and I'm going to. Aren't I in luck? You could have knocked me down with a feather! Of course I've seen for some time which way the wind *might* be blowing, but I could never be sure until today,' said Verne gaily, still looking at the ring.

'Verne, you're doing this for me,' said her mother sternly.

'Darling, as if I would! As a matter of fact, he offered to lend me the money we need,' lied Verne calmly, 'and then to my astonishment, he proposed to me, and of course I said "yes". Don't look so—awful about it! Think what it means to me! No more scrimping and scraping, no more living in this wretched little place—everything I want! You've simply no idea how rich he is. I doubt if even I know the extent of it, but I shall have everything in the world I could possibly want.'

'Everything except the one thing you should marry for,' said Mrs. Raydon, still in that stern voice which had never been used to her beloved child before in all the twenty two years of her life.

'Love, you mean?' asked Verne lightly, though she felt like death. 'Darling, you still live in dreams, in storybooks. Love's an exploded myth to my generation. We call it by its proper name and keep it in its proper place.'

'I married your father for love and it never failed us and we had no money at all, nothing but our love.'

'That was a quarter of a century ago, darling,' said Verne with a laugh. 'We're more practical now—and though I don't pretend I'm in love with Robert Grimtree, I—I like and admire him tremendously, and—well, I've told you. I'm sick of being poor, of going without, of wearing old clothes, of the eternal round of nine till six, and no fun.'

Her voice trailed away and she turned her back on her mother's hurt, bewildered face. She knew how bitterly she was wounding her, breaking into bits the life they had made for each other and for themselves, all the happiness, the quiet contentment, all the little mutual sacrifices, the consideration, the love. She was turning herself, in her mother's eyes, into something she had never been.

'I never dreamed you felt like that,' said Mrs. Raydon dully, and turned her face away and lived through her Gethsemane alone, and Verne knew she must do nothing to comfort her or everything would be undone.

It was difficult to persuade her to go to Switzerland at all, and in the end Verne had to do further violence to herself by telling her mother that if she did not go, it would present her herself with a difficult problem

'I couldn't just plant you in a nursing home, dearest,' she said, 'and Robert would have to pay even for that. And I can hardly cart you off to Wellington Gate with me and establish you there with a nurse! Not as a start to our married life! That would be too much to ask even of Robert!'

'Can't you wait till I die?' asked her mother bitterly. 'It won't be long.'

Verne closed her eyes for a moment and gripped the edge of the mantelpiece, her face turned away.

'Robert's such an impatient person,' she said when she could control her voice. 'He can't see any reason for waiting, and there isn't any really, is there? He's got it all fixed for you, your journey by air, someone to go with you, a nice room, everything.'

'What a hurry you're in to get me out of the way! I'm all at sea, Verne. I realise that I've never really known you at all, and that all these years I've lived with a stranger. All right. If that's the way you want it, take your way. I don't care any longer.'

There was nothing Verne felt she could do. She would not be proof against her mother's reactions to her proposed marriage if she had any inkling of the truth. In time, when this miraculous cure had been effected, it might be possible to let her see her again as she really was. By that time her marriage to Robert Grimtree would be an established thing and herself adjusted to it. Meantime she must live from day to day, from hour to hour.

Grimtree made all the arrangements himself without recourse to Verne, and they were made with his usual practical efficiency.

She continued with her work in the office, and he made no reference, to her infinite relief, to their changed relationship until, a day or two later, he told her of the arrangements he had made.

'Your mother can go on Thursday of next week,' he said. 'I thought you would need that time to get her what she will require. I have provisionally engaged someone to go with her. See her yourself. Here is the name and address. Confirm the arrangement if you agree. The marriage can take place after the plane has left. Here are all the times and places. I take it you don't want a church wedding?'

'No,' said Verne briefly, taking the piece of paper from him. He had written down the information in his own curiously unformed, laborious handwriting, a legacy of his lack of education. He seldom wrote anything but his signature on cheques.

'Good. Neither do I. Let me know if these arrangements suit you, and go to Harrods for anything your mother wants, or that you want yourself. Get the best. I have arranged with them for you to sign the bills. Is there anything else?'

'No,' said Verne again.

'As soon as you've got someone in your place, you can go if you like.'

'I'll stay,' she said unsmilingly, and he nodded.

'Is that all?' she asked.

'Not quite. Do you hate me, Verne?'

Face and voice were hard and grim. The question took her unawares, and in spite of her determination not to reveal to him anything of her secret life, she hesitated, flushing a little.

Then she lifted calm eyes.

'No,' she said.

'Just indifferent?'

'Grateful.'

'You need not be. I'm getting what I want too. You know I shall exact my pound of flesh?'

The colour deepened in her face, but she did not flinch.

'Yes,' she said.

'All right. So long as we understand where we are. That's all.'

She went back to her office.

Did she hate him? She did not know. The whole thing was so fantastic, so unreal, and her heart was so numbed by the estrangement from her mother that it could feel nothing else, not even anything at all for this man in whose ruthless, grasping hands she had laid her destiny. She would not look ahead – but she would pay his price to the uttermost farthing.

Chapter Two

Possibly no girl had ever had a stranger, colder or more bleak wedding than Verne Raydon's to Robert Grimtree.

To begin with, it was a raw November day, with gusty winds bringing rain and sleet which sent shivering people within doors unless their business kept them in the icy streets.

The few days which had preceded that Thursday had passed with nightmare rapidity for Verne. She had engaged a capable looking, middle aged women to take her place at the office, and Grimtree had looked her over and afterwards grunted his grudging approval to Verne.

'What's her name? Bright? Well, let's hope she is. Pick her for her looks, eh?' with a sour smile, for his new secretary was plain to the point of ugliness. 'Not going to risk wondering what your husband's up to with his secretary behind your back, are you?'

Verne found herself smiling for the first time since this incredible train of events had started. Had he, after all, that sense of humour with which she had never had occasion to credit him?

'I think you'll find her efficient,' was all she said.

'She'd better be,' he said.

He went home early on the day before the marriage, restlessly unable for once to settle to any of his business affairs. Besides, there were things which must be done at home, things which rather incomprehensibly he had not been able to bring himself to do earlier. It was still difficult for him to convince himself that this thing would go through, that he would indeed find himself with a wife before the week was out, and that wife would be the familiar Miss Raydon, the girl whom he painfully forced himself to call by her Christian name when they were alone, though he was still 'Mr. Grimtree' to her.

He wandered into the kitchen premises, startling the maids, some of whom had never seen him at close quarters at all, and Mrs. Wise, the cook-housekeeper, was caught in her curlers, to her utter shame, though he took no notice of them, probably did not even see them. It was her evening out, and she had popped down to the kitchen to see that everything was being done.

'I've something to tell you, Mrs. Wise,' he said unsmilingly. 'The rest of you may as well hear it too. I am going to be married. Your new mistress will live here, of course, but unless she wishes otherwise, everything will go on just as usual. If any of you want to leave in the circumstances, you are free to do so after giving the usual notice or forfeiting your wages. You know the lady, by the way. My secretary, Miss Raydon.'

His aggressive stare round the goggle eyed group challenged their disapproval, but all he saw on their faces was blank surprise.

Burn, the parlour maid, in her neat black and white uniform had risen like the rest of them, but she still held a teacup in her hand, its contents spilling over. Parlow, the butler, caught in shirt sleeves and baize apron, tried to look as if he wasn't there, whilst Mrs. Wise began furtively to take out her curlers.

But it was left to Parlow to speak, struggling to maintain his dignity in spite of his undignified appearance.

'I'm sure, sir, we all wish you well,' he said. 'May we inquire when the happy event is to be?'

'Tomorrow,' said Grimtree harshly. 'I shall bring the lady back here. I have no time to be going away just now. See that everything is ready, Mrs. Wise. Prepare another room. The one next to my bedroom which I have used as a sitting room is to be made into a second bedroom. Move some furniture from another room. See that everything necessary is there. That's all,' and he strode out, leaving the excited babble of conjecture and amazement to break out as soon as he had gone.

He walked through the upper rooms and tried to visualise Verne in them, but now his imagination failed him. He could no longer see the gracious figure in velvet or satin, hung with his diamonds, his wife, the mistress of his house. He could see only Miss Raydon, the familiar secretary, cool, detached, utterly impersonal, in her navy blue dress with its touches of white.

What would she make of his house? A home? He realised that he had no idea of the sort of place she now called home, and on one of those impulses, rare indeed but seemingly always connected with Verne, he rang for his car and gave the chauffeur the Fulham address.

He looked disparagingly at the worn stone stairs and the shabby doors as he went up to the Raydons' flat, and then checked himself with a saturnine grin as he remembered 'upstairs' and what it represented.

Well, Verne was finished with this sort of thing, anyway.

He heard her voice from the other side of the door after his knock.

'It'll only be Bill,' she said, and he felt a swift spasm of—what?—as he heard another man's name. Who was this Bill? What place had he in her life?

Well, she had finished with that too, he thought grimly.

Then she opened the door and stood aghast.

This was quite a different Verne. She was in a shabby enveloping overall, and her hair was damp and twisting into little curls over her head, and she had a towel in her hand. Obviously she had been washing her hair, and it gave him a queer feeling of satisfaction that she had been making even that small preparation for her marriage to him. It had appeared to him so far that, from lack of evidence to the contrary, she had made no preparations of her own at all. She had put on his desk without comment copies of the bills she had signed at Harrods, and none of the items had been for her personally.

'Mr.—Grimtree,' she faltered in amazement and then glanced back nervously towards the open door of their living room.

'May I come in?' he asked curtly. I'd like to meet your mother,' which was not at all why he had come. He had no idea why he had come.

She spoke in a low voice, for his ears alone.

'She—doesn't know—why—' said Verne on a note of appeal.

He nodded, understanding. Whatever she had told her mother, he gathered that it was not the truth, not the whole of it, anyway.

'Please come in,' she said, still nervously, and, over her shoulder, 'Mum dear, it's—Robert,' using his name for the first time in his hearing.

Mrs. Raydon, flustered, rose to meet him.

'Oh—Mr. Grimtree—I'm afraid we're very untidy,' she said. 'Verne has been washing her hair and—we didn't expect—'

'That's all right,' he said gruffly. I was just passing and thought I'd look in, just to see if you have everything for tomorrow.'

'Thank you. You have thought of everything, and I am very glad to be making your acquaintance,' said Mrs. Raydon, calm and dignified once the first flutter of confusion was over. 'Will you sit here, Mr. Grimtree? And please smoke if you would like to, though I'm afraid we have no cigarettes to offer you. Verne will make us some coffee. Will you, dear, please?' the request coming with a note of definite authority and he understood from it that the little woman was planning to have a few minutes alone with him.

Verne understood it too and hesitated, flushing and instinctively turning her head to meet his eyes. He saw that plea in them which had been in her voice, and he nodded again.

'Thank you. I should like some coffee,' he said, and sat down in the offered chair and took a cigar from his case.

Verne was left with no choice, and when she had left the room, he got up and closed the door behind her. She was in an agony of apprehension about what he might reveal. Even now, at the last moment, her mother would refuse to accept the sacrifice she was offering once she knew the truth.

But Robert Grimtree realised the position and accepted it grimly. What business was it of his? Verne could explain things as she liked.

'I am glad to have an opportunity of thanking you for what you are doing for me—Robert,' said Mrs. Raydon, using his name bravely.

'Glad to do it,' he said gruffly. 'Hope you'll benefit from it.'

'Mr. Grimtree, I must say this to you. I can't say it to Verne,' said Mrs. Raydon earnestly. I don't think anyone can do much for me, not for long, but I am going because she insists on it, and it makes her happy. I—it is a great surprise to me, this marriage, but if it means happiness for her—you *will* make her happy—Robert?'

'Try to,' he said in his gruff fashion.

'Do you love her? But you must, as you couldn't have any other reason, but—Verne—'

She stopped uncomfortably and he nodded. He did not think that Verne would have gone so far as to pretend to her mother that she actually loved him, but he did not intend to queer her pitch, whatever she might have said.

'Don't worry, Mrs. Raydon,' he said. 'Verne and I understand each other. After all, we've been together, working together, for two years, and I know what she wants and she knows what I want. I'll look after her. I can give her anything a girl can want, as I expect you know.'

'Yes,' said Mrs. Raydon; and then again, almost sadly, 'Yes.'

He changed the too personal subject to speak of the arrangements for the journey the next day, of the trained nurse. Miss Dillon, who was to go with the sick woman and remain with her as long as they both liked, and when Verne came back with the coffee, they were chatting amicably by the fire.

Verne had changed into a dress and done her hair. She had also changed her manner, and now she was bright, talkative, defiantly gay, almost frivolous, someone he had never yet known.

She addressed him by his name, spoke of their marriage the next day and warned him, laughing, that unless the plane took off in good time, the bride might be late.

'I hope you'll wait for me, Robert,' she said gaily, 'though waiting is not your strong point, is it? Don't abandon me and leave me disconsolate at the door of wherever it is!'

He took his cue from her and responded with somewhat heavy gallantry.

'I'm not likely to do that,' he said, 'but if you keep me waiting too long, I shall probably come after you to the airport.'

'Breathing fire and fury!' she laughed. 'Is that enough sugar for you?' handing him his cup. 'See what a lot I've got to find out about you!'

Between them they were able to lay many of Lorna Raydon's fears to rest.

Verne *was* happy about marrying him. Even if it were true that it was only for his money (a hateful, painful thought to the woman who had married for love and had never lost it through the long years of loneliness), she was happy to be doing so, and in spite of her preconceived ideas of Robert Grimtree, this big, ostentatious man gave an impression of equal happiness and satisfaction.

He rose at last.

'Well, Verne my dear,' he said, 'I'd better be going or you'll lose your beauty sleep. Good night, Mrs. Raydon, and—all the best. Going to see me out, Verne?'

'Of course,' she murmured, and when she had closed the door behind them and they stood in the tiny hallway, she turned to him. All the animation had gone from her face, leaving it exhausted and drained of colour.

'Thank you for not making it too difficult,' she said in a low voice.

'I've never wanted to make anything difficult for you,' he said. 'You put up a good show, by the way,' his lips compressed in an ironic half smile.

'I had to,' she said briefly. 'She wouldn't go if she knew the real truth.'

'I know,' he said almost brutally. 'You don't have to point out what is the real truth. I'm quite well aware of it. Not going to let me down tomorrow, by the way?'

'Of course not,' she said, her eyes meeting his in a level gaze.

'Right. By the way, I think I'll change the plans. I'll pick you up at the airport after the plane has left.'

Her lip curled.

'Don't you trust me?' she asked bitterly.

'Yes, but I'll pick you up at the airport just the same,' he said. 'If I don't come myself, I'll send the chauffeur,' and he left her.

Verne had pleaded in vain with her mother to be at the wedding and to leave after the ceremony, but Mrs. Raydon had been adamant.

'It's no use, Verne. I couldn't stand there and watch what cannot seem to me anything but a tragedy,' she had said. 'You don't love this man, and I refuse to be present at what is merely the sale of yourself for money. We won't speak of it again.'

Nor had they done so, but when Verne returned to the living room after Robert's visit, she broke the silence imposed on her.

'Mum dear, you can see now that ifs quite happy, this marriage. Robert and I understand each other and have a much better chance than people who marry just for—well, the sort of emotions that are bound to pass. Won't you come to my wedding? I can ring up Robert as soon as he gets home. He'll alter the time, make it earlier, before the plane leaves.'

'No, we'll leave things as they are,' said her mother. 'Verne—dear child—'

Verne dropped on her knees by her mother's chair and held the frail hands in hers. It was the first time since she had broken the news of her plan to marry Robert Grimtree that she had heard the old, tender note in the voice which until then had never spoken to her with anything but love and understanding. In her heart, Verne was grateful to Robert for the odd impulse which had brought him here this evening and supported her in the gay pretence at satisfied happiness which had been her determined role throughout.

'Mum darling, you do see now that we're going to be happy, don't you?' she asked. 'We're both sensible, unsentimental people, Robert and I, and we know what we want of life. You could see that, couldn't you?'

'It doesn't seem much of a basis for marriage, and I still strongly disapprove of your reasons for it, but—I shall pray for your happiness, my darling, always.'

And there they left it.

The next day, she handed her mother over to Miss Dillon, a pleasant, capable girl whom already Mrs. Raydon liked. The nurse had her own thoughts about Verne Raydon and the marriage to Robert Grimtree which had been announced in that morning's papers. Still, it was not her affair and she took up her appointed task with cheerful competence.

To her relief, Verne found that Grimtree had not come himself to the airport after all, so that she had the big car to herself, and during the journey to the registrar's office, she could struggle alone for composure and fight back the tears which she was determined should not show when Robert saw her again.

It was over. He had done with the utmost generosity all she had asked him to do. Now she would pay the price and shed no tears over it.

Through a long traffic jam, the car arrived a few minutes later than the time estimated for her arrival, and Grimtree was standing on the pavement, a frown on his face. In spite of all she had promised, in spite of his precaution of sending his car and chauffeur to the airport, he had had the niggling fear that something would happen, that she might evade and cheat him after all. His relief at sight of her showed in his grim face and surly voice.

'You're late,' he said.

Verne by now was completely composed.

'I'm sorry, but you should have had the street cleared and the traffic held up,' she said serenely, and Jeffery Templar, Robert's solicitor and friend of many years, a straight dealing man who thoroughly disapproved of this marriage in spite of having known Verne for those two years, could not forbear a smile.

So the big, blustering man was not going to get it all his own way! He might even have caught a tartar as well as a gold digger. It was a pleasing and amusing thought. No one but himself had ever stood up to Robert Grimtree.

The business of turning Verne Raydon into Mrs. Robert Grimtree was suitably cold blooded and business like, Robert still surly and testy, Verne cool and composed, and when the wedding ring was on her finger, she looked down at it and smiled cynically. Instead of the plain gold or platinum band which lesser mortals used, this was a circlet of diamonds.

Jeffrey Templar offered formal congratulations, his keen little eyes telling Verne unmistakably what he thought of her, but she met them with unconcern. She did not care what anyone thought of her now.

'Just about time for a glass of champagne,' said Robert, hustling them out. 'Any further business to do here, Templar?'

'No I've paid all the dues. She's yours now,' said the solicitor.

'All right. I've ordered the champagne. Hope they've chilled it properly. Get in, man. Get in,' and Templar followed Verne into the car.

She had been painfully aware that on the pavement there had been a crowd of reporters and cameramen, and amongst them she had caught sight of one familiar figure.

Bill!

Their eyes had met for an instant, scorn and anger in his. Then she was in the car. She had not seen him during these last hectic days, as he had been away from London on an assignment, and she had been glad of it. She did not love him nor want to marry him, but he had been her good friend and she did not relish the thought of the contempt with which he would undoubtedly view her marriage to this wealthy man.

By the time the three of them had made a pretence at eating the light meal and drunk the champagne in the hotel where it had been ordered, the reporters and cameramen were at their heels again, and it was Bill Trailer who detached himself from the group and came forward, an impudent smile on his face for Verne, though he did not address her.

'Mr. Grimtree? May I offer my felicitations to you and the bride?' he asked.

Robert glowered at him.

'Why the hell should you? Who are you?' he asked roughly.

Bill proffered a card.

'The *Evening Sun*' he said, still smiling. 'It would be interesting if—'

'It would be interesting if you would mind your own business,' snarled Grimtree. 'Hi, you!' to the waiter, 'tell the manager to get rid of these people. I said this was to be kept private. See that it is!'

They dwindled away regretfully. Bill amongst them, but when the wedding party left the hotel later, there they were again, the newshounds with pictures they were determined to get, and a story which they would make up if there were no other way.

Bill contrived to be nearest to the waiting car, and as Verne had to pass close to him, he spoke to her, though no one else heard what he said.

'Happy is the bride the sun shines on!' he said sarcastically, for the rain was now heavy and pitiless. 'Congratulations on dreams come true, *Mrs. Grimtree*!'

Verne, her face averted, got quickly into the car.

Grimtree, following her, spoke to his solicitor.

'Better get in, Templar.' he said in the curt tone he always used to anyone who was in any sense in his employ. 'I want to see you about that Grandison matter. We'll go to my office.'

Verne gave him a quick glance of dismay.

'Me as well?' she asked.

He frowned.

'I could do with you,' he said, 'but—oh well, better not, I suppose. You can go on home. I'll tell Johnson to take you. Tell them I'll be in to dinner.'

She stared at him, colouring.

'You mean I am to go to your house? Alone?' she asked.

'Why not? Oh, you don't like the idea? Well, go and amuse yourself for an hour or two. Go to the pictures or something. Tell Johnson where to pick you up. I should be through by about six. Here,' taking some notes out of his wallet and pushing them at her.

Her head went up. She disdained the notes and, with a shrug, he put them back.

'All right. Have it your own way. What are you going to do?'

'I'll go back to the flat and finish tidying up,' she said as calmly as she could, though she was painfully aware of Jeffrey Templar's eyes glinting with ironic interest.

'As you like. Johnson can call for you there and bring you to the office,' and Grimtree proceeded with his talk with the solicitor on the Grandison affair and ignored her, leaving her with a nod when they reached the familiar office building and telling the chauffeur to 'take Mrs. Grimtree to Fulham'.

Verne realised how unwise she had been to choose to go back to the empty flat, with all its memories, but she set about putting the place into meticulous order without allowing herself time for futile misery, wondering who would be its next occupant.

She had not had time to do anything about the furniture, and the flat was still in Lorna Raydon's name as its tenant, so all Verne could do at the moment was to make it clean and tidy, all their small personal oddments packed in boxes, and leave its final disposal for future consideration.

When the chauffeur called again for her, he brought a message from Robert.

'Mr. Grimtree says he may not be ready for half an hour or so, madam, so he wants you to wait.'

'Very well. I'll wait in the car,' said Verne, who could not have faced the curious stares and furtive grins of her former colleagues, who must be staggered by this marriage of which they had had no inkling until the announcement in the morning's newspapers.

Johnson sat, stiff and formal, with his back to her whilst she tried to relax against the soft cushioning of the car, waiting for her husband.

Her husband!

She could feel the unfamiliar hardness of the diamond ring on her wedding finger and for almost the first time began to think of herself and of this strange, frightening marriage which, until now, had been merely the prelude to her mother's bid for life.

What did she really know of Robert Grimtree as a man? What was he like when he was not working, not evolving and carrying through, with ruthless determination, the schemes which made him richer month by month and year by year? What did he do with his money? With his spare time, if he had any? Who were his friends? What were his tastes, his outside interests?

She realised that after the two years of her close association with him, she knew nothing of any of these things.

One small personal and quite unexpected thing had stirred her oddly that day.

Before her mother and Miss Dillon had boarded the plane, a messenger had arrived with a box of flowers, magnificent orchids under their cellophane cover.

'They're for you, Verne,' Mrs. Raydon had said at once, though the messenger had had her own name called.

But the attached envelope had borne the name of the mother, not the daughter, and Robert's card inside had a message on it in his own writing.

Wishes for a safe journey and resuming health. R.G.

Verne had been oddly touched by it until she reflected that probably it had been actuated by Miss Bright.

But would Miss Bright not have meant them for her, the bride? She felt that only Robert himself would have chosen to send them to her mother.

She sat up with a jerk when she saw the ornate entrance doors open and Grimtree come out and cross the pavement. Every thought and feeling fled but panic. There was no escape now. There would never be an escape.

He shot a searching glance at her as he entered the car. At least she had not been crying! Most women were anathema to him, but a woman in tears was not to be borne.

'We may as well dine out,' he said. 'We can go to the house and change.'

'I haven't an evening dress,' she said, gulping.

'Why not? I told you to get what you wanted.'

She began to recover. This was the familiar employer again, the tyrant who gave orders.

'For one thing I haven't had time,' she said quietly. 'Also I could not buy things with your money until—now.'

'All right. Get things tomorrow. We'll go somewhere without dressing,' and he gave an order to the waiting chauffeur and they were driven away.

She forced herself to eat, for she had had nothing all day, and it was a relief that they had at least one topic on which they could talk without embarrassment. He told her of the progress of the business he had been discussing with Templar, and she could comment on it with knowledge and intelligence.

But towards the end of the meal, she forced herself to speak of more personal things.

'My mother will be writing to you herself,' she said, 'but I would like to thank you for sending the orchids. It was a very kind thought.'

'Huh,' he grunted, and left it at that.

'Finished? Want anything else?' he asked, and when she refused, he rose.

'Might as well go then,' he said and called for the bill, checked over the items with the menu card open in front of him, crossed off one of them and paid the rest with an adequate if not generous tip.

'We didn't eat the smoked salmon,' he said brusquely, and the waiter knew Robert Grimtree well enough not to argue the point that it had been ordered and would, in the ordinary way, be charged on the bill.

The Italian proprietor saw them out himself, smiling obsequiously, but Verne walked past him head in air, not returning his smile.

She felt sick with dread but she had to go through with it. She fixed her thoughts on her mother, who must by now be arriving at the end of her journey, if she had not already done so. She would be in the clear, cold air of the mountains, cherished, waited on, cared for as in no other way could she have been cared for. It was worth the price she had to pay. It was worth everything she could possibly have paid.

When they reached the house, Grimtree hurried her up the stairs and out of the view of the interested servants, Parlow, urbane and expressionless as ever, Burn, the parlour maid finding some excuse to be in the hall, little Mrs. Wise hovering anxiously in the background but not daring to come forward to express the hope that everything would be found satisfactory in the room which, by the superhuman efforts her employer always expected of them, had been transformed according to his instructions. She knew there was no need to express such a hope, for if everything were not satisfactory, they would very soon learn of it.

He threw open the door of the room that was to be Verne's.

The tobacco brown carpet had vanished, and in its place lay a thick white square into which the feet sank softly. Into her mind, absurdly, came the memory of a girl she had known who was angling avidly for a rich husband.

'If I get him, I'll have carpets so thick that they'd have to use a mowing machine for it instead of an electric cleaner,' she had remarked.

How ridiculous that at such a moment she could think of such insane trivialities!

The heavy furniture had gone, and in its place was a bedroom suite of bird's eye maple, a wood which she particularly disliked, and a double bed covered with quilted satin with a fat eiderdown in the same sumptuous ivory – definitely a bridal bed fit for a princess.

Verne turned her fascinated, appalled eyes from it. How had such a thing got into Robert Grimtree's house? Had he bought it specially for her? For tonight? She did not know that Burn had been sent rushing off in a taxi to buy such things and that this was the choice of Robert's parlour maid, in Verne's eyes both ludicrous and grotesque.

But her bridegroom's eye approved it and went forward to touch the satin texture with furtive fingers which made Verne feel sick. The cold night air, even so little of it as had met them as they got in and out of the huge, too warm car, had completed the effect of the champagne on him, and the sight of that ornate double bed, and the consciousness of Verne in that room beside him, his *wife,* made his senses reel.

'No point in going downstairs again,' he told her thickly. 'They'll bring your luggage up. Might as well get to bed,' and he crossed the room to the second door, went into the adjoining room and left the door open behind him.

Verne could see at a glance that it was his own room on the other side of the door, and she went to it precipitately and closed it and stood with her back against it, leaning there weakly, her heart pumping horribly, her head swimming, her whole being filled again with that sick horror of what she had done, her reason for such action no longer able to bring her any comfort or encouragement.

A knock at the other door brought her to herself and she moved away as Burn came into the room with her small overnight case, the only luggage she had brought with her and which had remained in Johnson's charge in the car.

'Is there any other luggage to be brought up, madam?' asked the woman with formal courtesy, though Verne was aware of her curious eyes.

'No, nothing else, thank you,' she said.

'Would you give me your keys, madam, and I will unpack for you.'

'It isn't locked and I'll do that myself,' said Verne.

'Is there anything you would like, madam? Mrs. Wise told me to ask you. Or would you like to see her? She is the housekeeper.'

'Nothing at all, thank you, and I will see Mrs. Wise in the morning,' said Verne in the decided voice she had used for years in her business life. It was, she felt, a defence at this moment against the maid's obvious, speculative interest.

'I will tell her, madam. Goodnight, madam. There are two bells. The top one rings in the kitchen and the other in the housekeeper's room, but that one can be transferred to your personal maid's room later. Mrs. Wise wishes you to use the one into her room meantime if there is anything you need tonight.'

'Thank you, but there will not be anything,' said Verne firmly, and the maid withdrew.

No, thought Verne tragically, there would be nothing she would need – except rescue or death, and the one was as unlikely as the other.

Since there was no help for it, she undressed, found a bathroom on the opposite side of the corridor and was in bed under the enormous eiderdown when the communicating door opened to admit her husband, unfamiliar in a thick, padded dressing gown.

She shrank down under the covers and looked at him with wide eyes which made no attempt to conceal their fear.

As he prepared himself for going to her, Robert Grimtree had let his passionate anticipations inflame him. She was there in the next room, Verne Raydon, his wife Verne Grimtree, and nothing now stood between him and his possession of her. His thoughts were a strange mixture of all the experiences he had ever had with women, but not one of them with a woman like Verne, dignified, cool, and fastidious about herself, utterly self possessed. There had been no triumph in taking these other women, women like Hermione Veronica.

Hermione Veronica! What a name! She had never told him her real name, which was probably Maggie Bloggs or something like that, and certainly he had never cared.

Hermione!

He conjured up the memory of her, golden haired with a dark line sometimes showing near the roots, voluptuous, greedy, generous of herself for her own enjoyment, always ready for lovemaking, with no reticence, no reserves.

Hermione – and now Verne.

By the time he opened the door into her room, he was on fire for her, an eager lover though love had never touched his life.

And then he saw her, strangely small in the huge white bed with the covers drawn up to her chin and her eyes with that frightened, wide look in them.

As if a cloak had been stripped from him, the eager lust of the last half hour left him. He saw not a woman waiting for him to ravish her, but a child, a frightened child, a trapped thing at his mercy.

His face grew grim and his small, beady eyes hardened and his mouth tightened.

'Well?' he asked, throwing the syllable at her roughly.

Verne did not speak. All she could do was to look at him with that trapped, helpless fear.

'You hate me, don't you?' he flung at her. *'Don't you?'*

'No, I–I–'

She could frame no words, but she turned her eyes from him with an effort, wishing he would not talk but that it would soon be over.

He put out a hand and wrenched at the covers, pulled them back until her breasts, small and firm and virginal, showed beneath the prim, closely buttoned pyjama jacket, a clean but an old one of much washed blue. Even if she had had time, she could not have brought herself to buy the sort of thing he probably expected and wanted, some frothy, frilly thing of transparent nylon.

She did not move, and for a few unbearable moments he stood there, looking down at her, his wife, his chattel, brought with his own good money, bought for – what?

As abruptly and roughly as he had dragged the covers away from her, he pulled them back over her and turned away.

'What do you take me for?' he shot at her angrily – and left her.

She heard him go, knew in every fibre of her being without the sound of the banged door behind him, that she was alone, that he had gone away, gone without so much as touching her.

She lay with closed eyes, her figure tense, unbelieving, unable to grasp the fact of her release. Why had he gone? Would he come back? She began to long for the door to open again, for him to return so that it might be over, so that the horror might be behind her instead of still to come.

But he did not return.

Though she lay there, motionless save for the painful intake and exhalation of breath which shook her, for what seemed hours, the door did not open again, and after a time she heard his step in the passage outside, the unmistakable step she had heard for years.

He went down the stairs, his heavy tread audible in spite of the thick carpets, and then the massive front door closed behind him.

She sat up in bed, staring across the room unbelievably.

He had gone out! He had dressed again and left her alone!

Her mind was confused with amazement. It was so entirely out of character. She had never known him voluntarily yield up the accomplishment of his slightest desire – and yet, if he had not desired her, why had he married her?

She waited, but there was no sound of his return, and presently she slipped out of bed and turned the key in the lock of the communicating door, which she had not dared to do earlier.

She was alone.

On her wedding night, and married to Robert Grimtree, she was alone!

Chapter Three

Robert Grimtree had flung himself out of his house on his wedding night in a storm of rage and disgust – rage and disgust at himself for what, as soon as he had left Verne's room, he told himself was his own, unprecedented weakness.

She was his, wasn't she? Hadn't he bought her and paid at least part of the price already? And wasn't he prepared to pay more? To see that this mother of hers had everything she needed? To lavish money on Verne, on clothes and jewels which would make her the envy of all other men's wives?

And what had he taken for himself? Nothing. Nothing, Not even the touch of her hand or her cool, firm lips, when he had the right to take everything.

He could not recognise in himself the thing which had made him leave her, untouched and virginal. Some sort of spell had been laid upon him by the sight of her lying there in that ornate bed. She had changed for him completely. Miss Raydon, the tall, self possessed, efficient secretary, had in that instant changed into a small girl, wide eyed, defenceless, helpless, afraid – and he had not been able to take her.

Storming down the stairs and out into the street, he could find no excuses for himself. He, the great Robert Grimtree, had been cheated out of his rights by the girl who owed him everything – and yet of what could he accuse her? She would not have resisted him. He knew that. He could have had his will with her, slaked his now consuming thirst for the long limbed, perfectly proportioned body whose naked whiteness he had not even glimpsed, perhaps now never would. He lashed his seething mind with fresh pictures of her pale, soft skin, felt in imagination the suppleness of her thighs, his hands cupping firm, round breasts, his lips tasting the young fragrance of her.

Furiously he tried to cast out the unprofitable, tearing fancies, and suddenly hailed a slowly passing taxi and gave the man an address he had thought never to use again, certainly not on his wedding night.

He had not given back the key of the flat, as he had meant to do, and he stalked straight into the over furnished, over scented bedroom, his face strangely pale, his eyes hot with misery and frustration.

Hermione had started to undress, but had got no further than her lace trimmed satin slip when she turned to see him there, stared at him for a moment in incredulous astonishment and then opened her arms wide to him.

'Why, honey lamb! Of all things!' she said, and her opulent, eager mouth was crushed into silence beneath the hard cruelty of his.

'Didn't expect me tonight, did you?' he asked, and the overtures of something approaching the cultured accents for which he had striven for years slipped away from him and became coarsely natural. 'Well, I'm here and don't ask questions if you expect answers. Don't struggle. I'll do all that,' and with rough hands he tore the flimsy shoulder straps away and sought greedily the voluptuous body so responsive to his violence.

At least this woman could never look like a frightened little girl, never flaunt her virginity's touch-me-not defences before him.

Hermione knew all the answers. Her light, uncaring mind did not need to ask him anything or to know anything. It was enough for her that, through whatever queer circumstances, he had come to her on the night of his marriage to another woman, and that she could give him whatever it was he needed.

After the first turmoil of his bitter passion had been calmed, she rose from the bed and shook the mane of pseudo-golden hair about her shoulders, veiled her big, soft breasts in it and laughed at him in lazy enjoyment through its meshes.

'Well, big boy, you certainly came to the right place tonight!' she said. 'After all that, I want a drink, and so do you. There's no whisky, as I didn't expect you, but there's brandy and that'll have to do.'

But when she came back with two generously filled tumblers and put one into his hand, he held it and looked through its clear amber without putting his lips to it.

For the first time in his life, he felt debased and lowered in his own estimation. Whilst he had fondled and taken his fill of Hermione's desiring body, with its voluptuous curves of soft, yielding flesh, he had been able to forget his cool, virginal wife in her white bed. Now that the rage of passion was over, he was filled with a nauseating disgust.

He pushed the glass back into Hermione's hand, spilling the brandy over the bed, and rose and started to put on his clothes.

'Not going yet, are you?' she asked, amazed and realising that, in spite of the mad orgy, she had not got him back after all.

'Yes,' he said, and pulling on his coat as he went and stuffing his tie into his pocket and leaving his shoes unlaced, he went out of the room and banged the door of the flat behind him. Only after he was in the street again did he remember that he had left his wallet on the dressing table and probably had not even the price of a taxi in his pockets.

He shrugged his shoulders. She would clear the wallet of its contents, of course, but he could not care. She was welcome to what she found. However much it was, it was a cheaper price for him to pay than having to go back for it.

He went back to his house by underground and bus and walked the rest of the way, his shoelaces still dangling and his tie hanging out of a pocket, but no one gave him more than a casual glance which he did not even see.

The front door would be locked and bolted now, for it was past midnight and Parlow would have gone to bed, never dreaming for a moment that his master would be out of the house on this night of all nights, but there was a side door which no one but himself ever used, and fortunately he had not left his keys with his wallet amongst Hermione's jars and bottles and spilt powder.

He fitted the keys into the two locks, let himself in and went noiselessly up the stairs, paused for a brief moment outside the door behind which Verne would now be sleeping, serene and inviolate, and crept to the room 'upstairs', locked himself in and, without putting on the light, sat down on the edge of the hard little bed, his elbows on his knees and his head in his hands.

Verne – Verne –

Over and over again his mind repeated her name as if it could in some way restore her image to him, but all he could see was the cool, calm Miss Raydon looking at him with contempt in her eyes and with lips curved with scorn. He remembered vaguely that he had once actually seen her like that. It had been after that young idiot Gorner had committed suicide and she had come to tell him of it. As if it had been his fault that the man first stole from him and then sneaked out of paying for his crime by the coward's path!

Damn it, what right had she to look at him like that? Practically accusing him of murder? And what right to come to him in his imagination now to torment him with her disdain because he had gone to Hermione, the woman to whom he had the buyer's right, gone to her from the very bedside of his wife who had lain there, white as death, looking like a holy martyr waiting for torture?

His thoughts raged on and on until at last he threw himself down on the hard, lumpy mattress and fell into a series of snatches of uneasy sleep from which he wakened finally to creep downstairs into his bedroom, take a bath, dress and go down to breakfast at his usual time.

Verne was already down. She wore the familiar office dress with its always spotless white collar and cuffs and it seemed fantastic that she should be there at all, having breakfast with him.

'Sleep well?' he grunted without other address.

'Yes, thank you, Mr. Grimtree,' she said mechanically and then felt her face flush. 'I mean—Robert,' she added, bungling the name.

Burn always served breakfast, and she did so with her eyes going curiously from one to the other. So this was how newly married people looked and acted after their first night together? No joy there, though they both looked pale and tired and had dark shadows beneath their eyes – which, of course, was how it should be, to Burn's informed though not experienced ideas of such things.

The two did not speak again during the meal. Newspapers lay beside each plate, but Verne did not touch hers, and Grimtree studied the financial columns of *The Times,* making a few notes on the margin of the paper.

Then he rose.

'I shall lunch in the city,' he said, to Burn rather than to his wife.

'Yes, sir,' said the maid and lingered, hoping to see the interesting spectacle of her employer kissing someone, but she was disappointed though intrigued. Grimtree merely nodded to Verne, scarcely even looking at her, and left the room.

It was a vast relief to Verne to hear the front door close and to know that at last she was alone again. How was she going to fill her day, though? For the first time in her life, she had nothing to do and she was not of the type to enjoy the prospect.

What on earth *was* she going to do with these long, empty days? If she had thought about it all beforehand, she had vaguely supposed that she would 'look after the house', but it was obvious that that would not be her job. She wished she had stayed in bed, if only to make the day shorter, but she had been glad enough to leave it, still afraid that if she stayed there, Grimtree would come to her and perhaps fulfil the intentions of the night before which he had so strangely left unfulfilled.

As she was preparing to leave the table, Mrs. Wise knocked at the door and came to her.

'Would you like to give any orders, madam?' she asked obviously as ill at ease as Verne, her eyes anxious and wishing to please.

'What sort of orders, Mrs. Wise? I'm afraid I don't know in the least what I am supposed to do about everything.'

The girl's voice was friendly and she smiled as she spoke. At once the tension between them relaxed, and the housekeeper ventured to return the smile.

'I wondered if perhaps you would—wish me to go, madam,' she said.

'Go? You mean leave?' asked Verne, aghast. 'Oh, no! No, please don't do that. As Mr. Grimtree's secretary I could manage that job quite well, but as for running a house of this size—I shouldn't know where to begin! Please don't think of going, will you?'

Mrs. Wise sighed with relief.

'I don't want to, madam. It suits me very well here, and I have tried to give satisfaction, but of course, you're the mistress here and I'd like everything to be as you like it now.'

'I shall like it if it's the way Mr. Grimtree likes it,' said Verne, trying not to let her feelings about that become evident. 'The only thing is that, as far as I can see, I shall have nothing to do. If you would let me help in some way—?'

Though I don't know in what way,' with another of the friendly smiles which endeared her to the heart of the housekeeper forever.

Mrs. Wise had a tragic background, though it was only gradually and over a period of time that Verne learned of it.

Married young, she had endured ten years with a drunken ne'er-do-well for a husband until, reeling home one night, he had given her her release under the wheels of a lorry and left her with a son and daughter dependent on her. In order to keep the home together for them, she had taken daily jobs, 'charring', and after her heavy day's work had scrubbed and cooked and washed and mended for the growing children who thought nothing of her in return and gave her endless anxiety by their shiftless ways and, when they left school, by their inability to settle at the jobs she found for them. George eventually drifted into the army and out of it again into a shoddy firm which sold second hand cars and, getting mixed up in one shady deal after another, eventually landed himself in prison for fraud. His mother saved every penny she could so that she could help him with a fresh start when he came out, but he took the money and disappeared, and left her at least in ignorance of what he was doing. She had not heard of him for three years.

Sybil, her daughter, showily pretty in a flashy style, left the office job in which her mother had felt thankfully that she would be 'safe' and joined the chorus in a cheap, unsavoury suburban theatre whose lurid playbills offered, as their chief attraction, girls wearing as little as possible and suggesting by their antics that they wore even less.

Little Mrs. Wise, who throughout her troubles had always prided herself on remaining respectable, was shocked to the soul so that inevitably she quarrelled with the girl, who took herself off, to reappear some months later, obviously very ill. The dreaded 'polio' was diagnosed, and Mrs. Wise nursed the girl devotedly and slavishly, receiving in return not only no thanks but the bitter, quite unfounded accusation that it was her fault that the girl had lost not only her trivial good looks but also the power to use her limbs in other than jerky, graceless movements, every one of which gave her pain so that she refused to do the exercises which might have effected, if not a complete cure, at least some measure of comfort.

In the end, unable to maintain an idle, ailing girl by daily work which was becoming more difficult to get as housewives' resources were strained to the uttermost by the high cost of living, she had in desperation answered Robert Grimtree's advertisement for a resident housekeeper, had been stupefied with astonishment when she got the job, and moved into his house, putting Sybil into a home for such cases as her, a place where she could be cared for efficiently and was amongst others similarly handicapped.

Most of her substantial earnings went to the upkeep of the girl in the home, and though her employer had told the staff casually that all of them would 'probably' be retained, the news of his marriage had been a bad blow to her. Though she had taught herself by strenuous efforts to satisfy him in her capacity as cook and housekeeper, she knew that another such job would be difficult to get, so that Verne's assurance that she was not to be displaced was an enormous relief to her.

Together, on that first morning, they worked out a rough scheme which would give them both something to do, though Verne was dismayed at the prospect of the long hours which, for her, would be unoccupied. She would discuss the day's meals with the housekeeper, and also take over the care of the huge stocks of linen, most of it unused, but apart from that, she would have little or nothing with which to fill her day.

By eleven o'clock, she had finished, for everything was in good order and she could not count piles of sheets every day.

She decided to do at once the job she had in anticipation feared, which was to go back to the flat she had shared with her mother and see to the sorting and giving away and packing of their personal belongings, and make arrangements to give up the flat. When

Mrs. Raydon returned to England, she must not remain in London but be installed somewhere in the country with someone to look after her.

She hated the task as much as she had feared she would. Every familiar object gave her a fresh stab, reminding her of the happiness she had lost, but she went on stoically. She had chosen her course. She was not going to regret anything.

She had just finished packing a case with her own clothes in it, ready to be sent to Wellington Gate, and had sat down to the sandwich lunch which she had bought on the way, when the bell rang.

It was Mrs. Biggin, large and voluble and untidy as ever, but with a new ingratiating coyness which made Verne feel sick. Why had she been such an idiot as to answer the bell?

'Well, and here's the bride!' gushed the visitor. 'I could hardly believe my ears when I heard you about, today of all days! "That surely can't be Verne?" I asked myself, but then I knew it couldn't be anyone else, with your poor mother gone off to Switzerland—fancy that! Some folks have all the luck! It's just what I should like, getting out of all this rain and fog and what have you, but there! I wasn't as sensible as you, going as secretary to a rich old man and getting him to marry you! Well, I suppose I oughtn't to have put it like that, but between such old friends—I mean to say—'

'Did you want something, Mrs. Biggin?' Verne interrupted her icily.

'Oh, nothing for myself, dear. I'm not that sort, as you know. I thought "there's dear little Verne in there all by herself, with so much to do and such messy sort of things too, and I don't mind betting she hasn't even got a cup of tea for herself" so I just popped in to see. Now what about a nice cuppa? I've got one all ready, and I nipped up to the corner and got some of their special cakes. None of your old biscuits, I thought, now! Not for Mrs. Grimtree!' with another maddening little giggle and more coy glances.

Actually Verne had been longing for a cup of tea, but she had found herself without a shilling for the gas meter, and though she had tried to boil a kettle, the gas had died on her before the water was even hot. Since Mrs. Biggin was unlikely to go away and leave her in peace again, perhaps the best thing was to get her out of the flat by going with her, having the longed for cup of tea (without the special cakes, which would be sickly things filled with mock cream) and then firmly take her departure and get on with her work in solitude.

On the way to Mrs. Biggin's flat, that lady confided to her in a loud, aggrieved whisper, that 'something else had happened to her'.

'It's the old lady, Biggin's mother,' she grumbled. 'Planted herself on us, if you please! Of course it was Biggin's idea, with not a thought for me in my state of health! Says that since the old man died, Grannie can't manage on her own and must have someone to look after her, and of course it has to be *me*, though what I say is, why can't one of the others have her? They haven't got husbands like Biggin, *and* they've got their health and strength, which I shall never have. So there she sits, and there I suppose she'll go on sitting till the day she dies, and if I know anything about the Biggins, that'll be a long way off! Just as I've got Lola settled in a job, too, and could have had a bit of time to myself. It makes me mad.'

The strident whisper, which had more carrying power than most people's ordinary voices, went on until after Mrs. Biggin had unlocked her door and ushered the guest into the untidy hall, and Verne glanced nervously at the open door of the room in which someone could be seen sitting over the small, smoky fire, a basket piled with mending beside her. If this were the unwelcome visitor, she could scarcely fail to hear what her daughter-in-law was saying.

Old Mrs. Biggin struggled apologetically to her feet as the two entered. She was a frail looking old lady, white haired, with a delicate pink and white skin, scrupulously neat and clean in her widow's black, with touches of snowy white at neck and wrists.

'Sit down, dear,' said 'young' Mrs. Biggin to Verne effusively. 'Sit here near the fire,' indicating the chair which the old woman had vacated. 'The kettle's just on the boil and I'll have that cuppa for you in two shakes. Oh, Grannie, do you *have* to have all your sewing all over the room?' her voice changing on the instant to one of irritation.

'I'm sorry, Flo dear, but I thought I'd just go through these socks and things, and Lola will be wanting her pink blouse and I was looking for some buttons for it,' said the grandmother with a nervous, apologetic glance at the younger woman and a shy smile for Verne.

'Well, for heaven's sake keep it to yourself then,' snapped Mrs. Biggin without introducing the two. 'Place is like a pigsty.'

From the look of the rest of the room, hopelessly untidy and oven dirty, Grannie's corner with her mending basket was the least unappetising spot, but Verne hastened to help the old lady gather together the socks and the tangle of coloured wools.

'Do sit down in your chair again,' she said. 'I'd rather not be too near the fire anyway. I'm Verne, you know. Verne Ray—Verne Grimtree,' she corrected herself with a little grimace.

The old lady smiled and hesitatingly sat down again when Verne had taken another chair.

'Oh yes, I know,' she said. 'You were only married yesterday, weren't you? Flo was talking about it. I'm Lola's grandmother. Jake's my son, you know, my youngest boy. He's a good boy. A good boy. So kind and thoughtful,' her wistful voice and smile suddenly turning the unknown 'Biggin' into something quite different from what his wife had always represented him to be.

'It's nice for you to be able to come to stay with your son and Lola for a little while,' said Verne gently.

Grannie Biggin sighed and picked up another sock and peered at a huge hole through her old fashioned, steel rimmed spectacles.

'Yes,' she said. 'Yes. Very nice—though I am afraid it makes extra work for Flo, and she doesn't have very good health. It's rather sad to get old, especially when one is alone. Nobody wants you when you're old!' though there was no self pity in the gentle, tired old voice.

Verne's heart, occupied as it had been for years with the care of her mother, contracted a little. Yes, it was sad, sad to be old and alone and unwanted, to feel oneself a burden on younger people, to have to accept services given grudgingly and with little ability to return them – though from the look of the overflowing basket, Grannie was going to find some of that ability. Verne wondered if she ought to be straining her eyes under the old spectacles and in the smoky dimness of the room whose grubby curtains kept out what light might have come in from the dull winter afternoon.

Mrs. Biggin returned with a laden tray of chipped, unmatched china and the 'special cakes'.

'Grannie, I told you to give that chair to Mrs. Grimtree,' she said shrilly, but Verne, hastening to help her to set the tray on a cleared space on the table, said at once that she had refused the chair.

'As I haven't a fire in my own flat, I don't want to get too warm here,' she said, and handed the first cup of tea and the plate of cakes to the old lady, who glanced apprehensively at her daughter-in-law and then took a plain biscuit.

Verne carried back to her flat a depressing memory of the Biggin home and the frail, sad old lady who would never for a moment be left in ignorance of the fact that she was there on sufferance, a recipient of grudging charity. It helped her to accept her own position. She and her beloved mother would never have to endure that. If Robert Grimtree's money did nothing else, at least it would save them from poverty and this soul destroying dependence on others.

But how much more that money could do!

During all her association with him, she had never known him do a completely disinterested kindness. Even his gifts to various charitable organisations had 'tags' to them. They publicised his name, got him elected to various boards where he would meet influential people, and she suspected that at the back of his mind was the thought that some day, if he gave enough and in the right quarters, he might even be knighted.

Sir Robert and Lady Grimtree!

Her lip curled at the thought, but she knew it was not beyond the bounds of possibility. Such things did happen.

She toyed with the thought of what his money might do in matters which would not redound publicly to his credit. For instance, there must be a great many old people like Mrs. Biggin, poor and alone and unwanted, who would be utterly happy to the end of their days with some tiny home, a place for the treasures of a long lifetime, some place to call their own and some kindly people paid adequately to look after them and see that they were comfortable and happy.

Robert could do that, establish a home for old people like Mrs. Biggin, good, decent, kindly people who through no fault of their own were alone and poor, struggling to keep themselves independent, but forced at last to swallow the bitter pill of the charity of their children, who had enough cares and problems of their own – and some of whom, at least, had wives like Florence Biggin.

She wondered whether she could ever propose such a thing to Robert, later on when he – when she – when she was really his wife and had paid her debt.

That thought sent her back, most of her task finished, to the place which did not even remotely seem 'home' to her.

To her surprise, she found Robert already there, considerably in advance of his usual time. Parlow, who opened the door to her, had told her gravely that 'the master is at home' and had indicated the door of the library.

She hurried in, still in her coat and hat, ready for a breathless apology.

'You're home! I'm so sorry—'

He cut her short with a wave of his big hand.

'No matter. You're not a slave, you know—nor an employee. Take off your hat and coat and tell me how you've spent your day,' and as he watched her hand her outdoor things to the assiduous Parlow, quite naturally and as if she had been waited on all her life, he reflected with some satisfaction on the easy way in which she seemed able to accept her new position. It had taken him a long time to get used to servants and even now there were moments when he felt uncomfortable, almost overawed, by Parlow.

'Bring in something to drink,' he told the man in the curt voice he habitually used to his employees.

'What will you take, madam?' asked the man.

Before Verne could answer, Robert forestalled her by an impatient wave of his hand.

'Bring in everything,' he said, and the butler withdrew imperturbably.

He disliked his employer but knew where his bread and butter lay.

'I don't know what to have,' said Verne, when the heavily laden silver tray appeared and was set on a table at her side, Parlow waiting by it. 'I'm not very well up in these things, and this is such an array.'

'The dark sherry, madam?' suggested Parlow. 'Or would you prefer something dry, or a cocktail?'

'I'll take your suggestion of the sherry,' she said with a smile and the butler who, like the rest of the staff, had been expecting the much elevated private secretary to 'throw her weight about', found himself endorsing his first impression that there was nothing high hat about the new mistress.

His face relaxed into the faint ghost of a smile which was the most he ever permitted it to do, and when he had poured out the sherry for her in an exquisitely hand cut wine glass, he set the whisky decanter with soda and a tumbler beside his master and silently disappeared.

'I've got an awful lot to learn,' said Verne, sipping the sherry and liking it.

Her husband grunted, busy with his own drink.

He had been annoyed to find she was not in the house when he arrived, annoyed and vaguely alarmed, especially when he had learned that she had been out all day and had not had lunch at home. Was it possible that she had let him down after all? Had run away without the fulfilment of her bargain, which was to be his wife?

When, soon afterwards, she had appeared, his relief had been so great that his irritation had vanished and he was prepared to be magnanimous.

'Well, what have you been up to today?' he asked.

'I went home—I mean, to the flat,' she said, checking herself.

'What for?'

'Clearing up, sorting out, packing things. Mother's and my own.'

'What do you want to pack yours for?'

'Well, I've got to have clothes,' she said with a little smile.

'I told you to get them. Why didn't you?'

'Well—for one thing, I haven't any money,' she said, colouring.

'What do you want money for? Isn't my credit good enough? Go anywhere you like and buy things, all sorts of things, and charge them to me. They'll recognise you by now in all the big papers this morning. See 'em?'

She nodded.

'Pretty awful, weren't they?' she said.

'Of you, yes. Get some decent photographs taken. They'll be wanted. Go to the best people for them. Tell them you'll want shinies for the Press as well.'

'Surely the newspapers won't go on being interested in me?' she demurred.

'Of course they will. You're news, as my wife. And we're going to entertain, make a splash, get important people here, dinner parties and so on. That's why you must have clothes, plenty of them, all sorts—dinner dresses, low gowns, cocktail things, the sort of clothes other women wear, rich women. I'll buy your jewels myself, but you get the clothes. I don't mind what the bills are.'

She stared at him, fascinated by this new aspect of him.

'That doesn't sound like you,' she said.

'You don't know much about me,' he grunted, feeling that he was making himself slightly ridiculous in her eyes.

'No. No, I suppose I don't,' she said thoughtfully, after a moment. 'I thought I did, after working for you for so long.'

'Tell you some day,' he muttered, and had an instant's wild impulse to do so then and there, to take her 'upstairs' and show her that most secret place in his life, let her get under the skin of him, the hard, tough, protective skin which hid him from the world.

Then he checked himself. It was his initial mistake. Had he obeyed the impulse, who knows how differently their course might have been set, that vague, undefined, scarcely discernible path which they must tread to find their way through the wilderness in which now they wandered as strangers, alone though so near?

'Well, see to the shopping tomorrow,' he said.

'I can charge all those things to your account, if you wish,' she said, 'but—I shall still need some money, shan't I?' loathing the necessity for asking, but the Raydons had never been able to have anything left over after the week's necessities had been paid for. At least she had no debts.

'What for?' he asked, further confusing her.

'Well—bus fares and things like that,' she stammered.

'You don't have to travel by bus any more. I'll buy you a car. Matter of fact, I saw one today that would suit you and told them to bring it round in the morning. That will make you independent of my Rolls, and I've told Johnson to engage another man to drive you.'

'I—that's very—generous of you,' she murmured, wishing she did not feel so acutely embarrassed.

'You don't imagine I want people to see my wife standing in a bus queue, do you?' he asked roughly. 'Well, anything else?'

'There's—there's the rent of the flat. Mother's flat,' she said, though until this moment she had decided to give up the flat, seeing that her mother was quite unlikely to return to it. Now, suddenly, she knew she did not want to give it up. It was the one place that remained to her as 'home', the one place where she could be herself, Verne Raydon again, doing bits of housework, cleaning, even cooking, so long as she had a shilling for the gas! She could write her letters to her mother there as well, hoping that in that atmosphere, she could make her words sound natural and the story of her happiness with Robert credible.

He considered this point and then nodded.

'Yes. She may want to come back to it later. All right. Keep it on if you like. How much is the rent?'

'Twenty seven and six a week.'

He made a note of it, asked her for the name and address of the landlord, and put the piece of paper in his wallet.

'I can't be bothered with piffling little weekly sums,' he said. 'I'll tell the Bright woman to send them a cheque for a year's rent and see that it is renewed after that if you still want it. Bright! She should be called that!'

'Isn't she getting on very well?' asked Verne, glad to change the subject, though so far the discussion had not produced any of the needed ready money.

'No brains,' he said, quite untruly. 'Looks at me as if I was a Nazi torturer or something.'

Verne laughed a little.

'You used to look at me like that,' she reminded him.

'You stood up to me, didn't you? This woman takes everything lying down, waiting for me to kick her, I suppose,' disgustedly.

'She'd probably rather you did than just glared at her,' said Verne with another little chuckle. 'You'd better keep her. It isn't easy to find you what you want in that line, you know.'

'No, and when I do find what I want—dammit, look what I've done about it!' with an expression more nearly approaching real amusement than she had ever seen on his face so far.

'Regretting it?' she asked, unwisely.

'You know I'm not.'

He set down his glass and rose from his chair and came to stand in front of her, staring down at her with the smile vanished.

'You know I'm not,' he repeated. 'Verne, may I kiss you?'

'Of course,' she said at once, though some of the colour and all the laughter left her face and her two hands gripped the arms of her chair.

He put his hands into her armpits and lifted her bodily from the chair and held her there, looking into the face near his own. Then he brought his lips hard down on hers, firm, strangely cold lips to which she made no response, standing passively within his hold, her body frozen into immobility by that first contact with his.

Abruptly he released her and she almost fell back into her chair, her pulses hammering and her limbs trembling though her eyes still held his, steadily, proudly.

He seemed about to speak, but he closed his lips again and went back to his chair, took out a cigar, pierced and lit it carefully and then spoke as if the kiss had never happened.

'As soon as you've got something decent to wear, we'll give a dinner party,' he said.

Her eyes widened but her pulse was steady now and she was no longer trembling.

'Shall I be able to manage it?' she asked.

'Of course you will. That's one of the things you're for,' he told her rudely. 'I've been working up to this for years, making money, getting a position, this house. Now I'm ready to start spending—on the things I want, of course.'

'Of course,' acquiesced Verne in a low, calm voice, and though he shot a suspicious glance at her, he saw nothing to which he could take exception, nothing to which he could even put a name.

'I'll make out the list. You'll know most of the men from meeting them at business, but you won't know their wives and the wives don't know me, or you, but they're going to. By golly, they're going to! You'll set 'em all by the ears. Buy something good. Expensive.' (They were synonymous words to Robert Grimtree.) 'Knock 'em flat. You're going to have the best dress and the biggest diamonds of 'em all.'

'Will that be in the best possible taste?' inquired Verne calmly. 'For the hostess to outshine her guests is not exactly the thing, is it?'

'Well, maybe. Maybe not. We might let up on it later, but to start with, it's going to be done my way. You get yourself a dress. Gold or silver or red, anything but black. Can't stand women in black.'

'You don't mean *solid* gold or silver, do you?' asked Verne with a malicious grin. 'Why not solid platinum? It costs more than gold, and I could have a breastplate of diamonds to go with it.'

He chuckled, that wheezy, rusty sound of an old gate rarely opened.

'I'd even make it solid platinum if it was possible,' he said. 'I want to show you off, Verne, make 'em all see what I've got.'

'What you've bought?' she asked with an acid touch.

'Huh,' he grunted noncommittally. 'Let's have some music. Like music?'

'Some of it,' she said warily, resigning herself to a session of 'hot jive' and saxophones.

He went across to a resplendent piece of furniture which she had taken to be some kind of sideboard, but which he revealed as a superb radiogram, and she watched him sorting over a stack of records and fitting them on, one by one, above the turntable. He seemed to have a job finding all the ones he wanted, and she wondered if she could make it one of her woefully insufficient jobs to sort and file them.

When the music started, she had a surprise, for instead of the cacophonic blare she had anticipated, the sweet, solemn beauty of Beethoven filled the air.

She let her head drop back against the chair and, after that one surprised glance at Robert, settled her mind to the enjoyment of the music.

The records changed automatically until the first half of the concerto had been played, and Robert moved for the first time to change the pile of records over and then settled down again, his eyes closed, a look of peace on his heavy face.

When it had finished, and the set switched itself off, he opened his eyes and met the speculative gaze of hers.

'Like that?' he asked.

'Yes, I did. Very much. What was it?'

'Beethoven. The Emperor concerto.'

'It would not have occurred to me that you went in for classical music,' she said.

'What did you think I'd like? "Dancing all night with my baby", eh?' with so passable an imitation of the accents of the usual pseudo-American crooner that she broke into an irrepressible little gurgle of laughter.

'Something like that, perhaps,' she said.

'Well, I don't, and I hope you don't either, because you won't get any of it here. If I'm listening to the radio or watching television and those morons start wailing at me, I turn 'em off. Like to hear some more? They're mostly Beethoven, and that fellow Brahms, and I've got one or two things that Chyko something or other wrote.'

'Tchaikovsky?' supplied Verne.

He nodded.

'That's it. Hell of a name. Like to hear some?'

'I shall like to hear anything you put on if your taste's people like Beethoven,' she said frankly, and he actually flushed a little and looked embarrassed, like a pleased child unexpectedly commended.

And that was the second evening of her married life, sitting with her husband at the side of a huge fire constantly and silently replenished by one of the maids from time to time, their only talk being occasional comments on the music.

'Your records seem to require some professional attention,' she observed once, when part of a concerto was missing.

'Never let anyone else touch 'em,' he said.

'Not even—your ex-secretary?' she asked.

'Know how to handle 'em?' he asked suspiciously.

'I could find out. I'd like to put them in order for you, Robert,' beginning to be able to speak his name without hesitation, though it still seemed odd not to be calling him Mr. Grimtree. 'I really shall have nothing to do here!'

'No need for you to do anything,' he growled. 'My wife, aren't you?'

'I—yes. Yes, I suppose so,' she said slowly, and though she saw his hands pause for a moment over the sorting of the records in their paper covers, to her relief he made no rejoinder except to say that if she liked to give herself a job, she could take it on.

'There's a big case for records in one of the other rooms,' he said. 'Never been used. Too complicated for me but you might be able to fathom it.'

'After your filing system in the office, I feel I could handle anything,' she laughed, 'but it may take me time to find them again.'

'Well, you'll be there, won't you?' he said, not waiting for an answer.

He was remembering the unpleasant moment he had had when he thought she had left him.

After dinner, which had been served to them in the dining room with its enormous table and array of high backed chairs, he muttered something about having work to do.

'Isn't it something I can help you with?' she asked.

'I've told you once that your job now is to be my wife, not my secretary,' he said gruffly, and went back to his library without discussion about what she was going to do nor where she was going to do it.

She went slowly up to her room to find everything in readiness, the pyjamas she had worn the night before washed and ironed and laid out on the monstrous eiderdown and a cheerful fire burning in the grate.

Knowing that Robert would by now be immersed in his work (he would have more of it to do, she thought grimly, now that she was not in the office), she opened the door into his bedroom and went in, looking round with mixed feelings at the huge room with its massive furniture and one single bed. Mrs. Wise had told her that her own room had been specially prepared for her, all its original sitting room furniture replaced by articles from one of the guest rooms, so she knew that, as far as his personal life in his own home was concerned, she had had no predecessor. There was certainly no provision for a mistress in this room, which was severely masculine in its appointments.

She went back to her own room, hesitated for a moment, and then left the door unlocked. Though the prospect of having Robert Grimtree in her bed still made her shiver with fear and dislike, she would not resist him if and when he came to claim that as his right.

But she went to sleep before he came upstairs, and by the morning he had not come near her.

'You don't have to get up to breakfast if you don't want to,' he told her curtly, all the *camaraderie* of the evening before gone from his face and tone.

'I'm used to getting up early,' she said. 'It would bore me to have to stay in bed, but I will if you like.'

'Please yourself,' he said shortly, and returned to his study of the markets.

Chapter Four

Verne's first dinner party was an unqualified success, and except that she did not wear brown velvet, the sight of her at the opposite end of the elaborate dinner table fulfilled Robert Grimtree's first dreams of her.

She had felt, as she so rarely felt, uncertain of her capabilities in this new role. Even had it been possible, she would have made no attempt to hide from her husband's guests the fact that so recently she had appeared before them as his secretary, but she had made up her mind from the beginning that it would be as the mistress of the house and their hostess that she would receive Robert's guests that night.

Since such a function was beyond the powers of Mrs. Wise, a famous chef had been engaged not only to cook the dinner, but also to select the menu and the wines, and the only instructions Robert had given Verne were to buy herself a gown that would 'knock 'em all flat'.

With slightly mocking amusement at herself, she had proceeded to do so, and when she had finished dressing, on a sudden impulse she crossed her room and tapped at the door which led to his.

'Do you want to inspect the finished product?' she asked. 'May I come in?'

He was struggling with his tie, and a little heap of white wrecks on the floor testified to his difficulties.

'Of course come in,' he growled. 'Can you tie—' and then he broke off, dropping his hands and staring at her.

'Oh,' he said, and then again, in a strangely softened tone, 'Oh!'

'Like it?' she asked, and excitement edged her voice for she knew that, over elaborate as she felt her gown to be for a mere dinner party, she had never looked as beautiful as she did now.

The dress was of pale gold brocade shot with threads of green which glistened as she moved. Her shoulders and arms were bare, and the gown, moulded to her figure, swept to swirling folds about her feet in their high heeled golden sandals. She had had her hair dressed for the occasion, feeling that her usual severe style did not suit so elaborate a toilette, and the outline had been softened so that the hair lay in loose waves about her head.

He was startled; for once in his life even nonplussed. She was no longer Miss Raydon, his secretary, and he was quite unable at that moment to think of her as his wife. She seemed a creature from another world, unknown, undreamed of.

'Well?' she asked, her breath coming quickly.

'You're—beautiful,' he said thickly, and turned his eyes from her and began to fumble amongst the things on his dressing table, his gold mounted toilet articles, a few more wrecked ties, and at last picked up a flat leather case which had been lying there and without looking at her again, pushed it unopened into her hands.

'I—I thought this might do,' he mumbled, so much out of character as she knew him, that at first she could only stand there and stare at him with the case still unopened.

'Well, open it. Open it.' he said testily, beginning to recover himself, but though he made a pretence of dealing with his tie again, he was covertly watching her, waiting for the exclamation which, when it came, was touched with something like fear.

'Oh—Robert!' she breathed, and stood staring at the open case, at the necklet of diamonds which winked and caught a million lights as they trembled in her hold.

'Put it on,' he told her, now completely master of himself again, and he moved aside so that she could stand in front of the mirror to fasten the glittering thing round her neck.

'It's—much too wonderful,' she said shakily. 'It isn't like me at all.'

For the life of her, she could not say thank you to him. Bitterness had welled up in her heart at the sight of the magnificent bauble, at the cold touch of it at her throat. It was not a gift of love but of pride, not to give her pleasure but to enhance her value in the eyes of others. She was Robert Grimtree's and must therefore outshine and out value everybody else's possessions. If she had doubted the Tightness of that conclusion, the look of gloating pride that now gleamed in his eyes would have dispelled such doubt.

'That'll make 'em sit up,' he said, and completed the picture for her.

She took another look at herself in the long mirror and her eyes grew hard, the excitement and pleasure in her appearance a burnt out flame.

'I certainly look expensive,' she said curtly.

He drew back and flinched as if he had felt a whiplash. Now why in the name of all things holy had she to speak like that? As if she didn't care what he had made her look like? As if she despised the gift that had cost a prince's ransom?

His anger mounted. Ever since he had first conceived the idea of buying her a diamond necklace, he had been enjoying the thought of her surprise and delight, the anticipation of seeing her unbend and express her gratitude. Surprised she might have been, for that first moment, but where were the delight and the thanks?

'Isn't it worth saying thank you for?' he growled.

'Is it mine?' she asked with a cynical twist of her lips.

'Whose else would it be?' he demanded angrily.

'Robert Grimtree's,' she said. 'Another of his possessions,' and she turned and left him, her golden gown whispering as it swept the carpet and leaving behind it the subtle fragrance of her perfume after the door had closed behind her.

He rang the bell for Parlow and got him to tie his white tie, growling at the man for some quite imagined inefficiency, his thoughts still with that remote and lovely vision of his wife.

His wife!

Would she ever be that? What a fool he had been to let her escape him, as if in some strange way he knew she had. She was his, wasn't she? Hadn't he bought her? Wasn't she wearing his clothes? His diamonds? Sleeping in the soft bed his money had provided for her?

And not even a thank you! Just that infernal, proud disdain of him and all that was his!

Well, he'd show her. He'd show her who was master, and what he was master of!

Yet, though the evening had started off wife that strain and anger, it was an undoubted success. When he saw Verne again, standing with him in the flower filled hall to receive his guests, nothing remained in her demeanour to suggest that those few minutes in his room had ever passed.

As Robert had boasted, none of the bidden guests had refused the invitation, and the men, most of whom were known to Verne, had brought the wives and daughters who must, she thought, in their hearts despise this rich, arrogant, self made man who was so obviously flaunting before them his possessions, including his bejewelled wife in her golden gown, who outshone them all.

Yet she showed no consciousness of her position, treating her guests, especially the older women, with deferential courtesy which made them feel they were conferring an honour on her by being there.

Robert, watching her with covert pride, realised the effort she must be making, remembering the position and the modest home from which he had taken her, but no such effort was apparent. She might have been used all her life to such a gathering, and if she depended to some extent on the watchful care of Parlow and his hired staff, it was not discernible. She seemed to know exactly what to do, what to say, and his pride in her swelled. How right he had been to choose her, when it came to choosing a wife! But then he, Robert Grimtree, never made mistakes.

Had it not been for that little scene in his bedroom, he might have brought himself afterwards to express some measure of his satisfaction, but his tongue was tied by that new hardness and disdain which he could not understand and which had the power to enrage him whenever his mind recalled it.

When they parted at her door that night, she unfastened the necklace and gave it to him. She had left the case on his dressing table.

'It's yours, not mine,' he said angrily.

She met his eyes with a level gaze.

'Isn't it the same thing?' she asked, and turned and went into her room and closed the door.

Inside, she stood quite still except for the involuntary clenching of her fingers on the folds of her gleaming gown. She had not hated him when she married him, had been merely indifferent to him as a man, had felt that, however distasteful to her was the prospect of yielding her body to him, she would be able to do it without any more than that distaste. Now, without being able to find any reason for it, she hated him, loathed unspeakably the thought of his touching even her hand.

All the evening she had been aware of his gloating eyes which had declared, to her at any rate, his possession of her, and she had feared unspeakably that tonight he would claim her.

Yet he had not done so, and though she had forced herself to leave unlocked the door between their rooms, he did not come to her.

Why? In the morning, she felt she would almost have been glad had he done so, so that the unspeakable sacrifice would be over, its torment no longer still ahead of her.

She would have been amazed and incredulous had she known that on the other side of the closed door, Robert Grimtree lay sleepless, longing not for the easy conquest of her body but for the yielding of herself, willingly and gladly. He no longer wanted to take her by compulsion, forcing her to his desires. His body ached for hers given in love.

Love?

He turned his face into the pillows and knew that the thing he had despised had come to him. Verne was no longer a woman to be decked out by his wealth and displayed as his bought trophy. She was a woman to be loved and desired – and somehow, in some way his mind could not begin to understand, he had turned her into a woman who hated him.

What more could he do? How else could he show his feelings for her than by heaping possessions on her? How else could any woman be won?

The next morning, to her relief, she found that he had gone away for a few days, leaving her a stiff, formal note to that effect.

'If there are any invitations, accept them,' he had added, ending the note as he had always ended notes to his secretary, merely 'R.G.'

He was away for three days, in which time she got a grip of herself again. This was her life, the life she had chosen deliberately, and if her feelings for him had changed for the worse, that was just one of the things she must accept and endure, since she could not change them.

But on the morning of the day on which he had told her to expect him back from the tour of country branches which she did not suspect had been used by him as an escape, she had a letter from him which surprised her.

For one thing, it was a novelty to see herself addressed in his unformed handwriting as 'Dear Verne', though she could scarcely have expected him to write 'Dear Miss Raydon'!

It went on to tell her, with unfamiliar touches of humour, of the things which had occupied him, and then it said:

I find I am missing you. Does that make you smile in your superior fashion? As I am not giving you time to answer, I am saving you the necessity, for which I am sure you will be thankful. If you miss me, it will probably be to the good in your view. By the way, I am sending you a present. It is not one you have to give me back to put in the safe. – Yours, R.G.

The letter was followed immediately by the 'present', which was a magnificent coat of blue mink, sent by special messenger from a famous London furrier.

She stared at it when she had taken it from the box, and, oddly, it gave her none of the feeling of aversion she had felt for the diamond necklace. Was that because he was not there to gloat over the gift? She would not have been woman, nor human, had she not felt a thrill at such a gift, and she was still handling it when Mrs. Wise came in for the day's orders.

'Oh—madam!' she breathed, at the sight of the coat.

'It's lovely, isn't it?' said Verne. 'It's just come.'

The master dotes on you, madam,' said the housekeeper. 'Seems as if nothing's too good for you. It must be wonderful,' with a note of envy arid a flash of memory of her own experiences as a wife. 'You're very lucky, madam.'

'Yes,' said Verne briefly, and let the coat fall softly back over the chair and turned her attention to Mrs. Wise's business with her.

When she was alone again, she picked up Robert's letter and re-read it.

It was not like him at all, she thought. Why, it was almost human!

In what way exactly was he missing her? She smiled involuntarily, and then saw what he had written about that smile, its 'superior fashion'.

Was that how she seemed to him? Was it how she felt? Superior?

The thought made her uncomfortable. After all, what had she really given to Robert, that she should feel in any way 'superior'? He was as he was made, or as he had made himself, and how was he in any way different from the man as she had always known him, arrogant, self satisfied, and vulgar in his pride at his own achievements?

Yet when, later in the day, he came back, she found it more than a little difficult to be gracious in her thanks, and he brushed them aside with a brusqueness which rendered them useless.

'Why do you give me these things, Robert?' she asked him. 'Is it for your satisfaction, or mine?'

She found herself wishing she could understand him, could see if only for a moment the man himself.

'You do what I want and you can have anything you fancy,' he told her roughly.

'I don't often know what you do want,' she said.

He stared at her out of his small, expressionless eyes, seemed about to say something, and then turned away and picked up his letters.

'I'll tell you when I want anything,' he said morosely. 'You'd better open letters when I'm away. This is an invitation—and this—' throwing them down on the table.

'Accept them—and you'd better get yourself some more clothes.'

'I've got a lot already.'

'Never mind. Get some more. Don't wear the same dress twice. And ring up my tailor and tell him to come. Must have more dress clothes.'

A little smile flickered across her face. Beneath the studied casualness of his manner, she detected the satisfaction he felt in these invitations, the pleasure of a small boy with a treat in store. Why could he not let her know his satisfaction? Share at least his pleasure in the social ladder she knew she was helping him to climb? It would be something personal which they could share, surely?

'We are going up in the world, Robert,' she said. 'This one is from Lady Viewley,' picking up the invitation card.

'I always meant to get there,' he said brusquely, glaring at her.

The suggestion of the flattered small boy had gone, and the man was there again, pushful and grasping, to be denied nothing. The moment of softness passed and her smile faded.

'Then isn't it a pity you didn't marry somebody higher up in the scale than your secretary?' she flung at him.

'I know why I married you,' he said.

'Then your knowledge is considerably larger than mine,' she told him tartly and picked up the invitations and left him.

He stared after her. Now why on earth had she to take the huff like that? What had he said or done *now*?

Verne felt the prick of her conscience. She had never been ill tempered or irritable, and yet it seemed that the merest contact with him brought out her prickles.

Though she had now an extensive wardrobe, the least she could do for him was to obey him in the matter of a new dress for Lady Viewley's dinner party, something quieter and, she felt, in better taste than the elaborate golden gown she had worn for her own party, but on the day before the accepted date, Robert came home to find her in a state of distress, with strained face and tear reddened eyes.

'Hullo, what's the matter with you?' he asked.

She went into the library and he followed her.

'Oh, Robert, it's Mother. She has been so much better, but I've just had a telegram from Miss Dillon to say that she's had a bad haemorrhage and they think I ought to come. I've tried to get a plane passage tonight, but the earliest I can get is tomorrow morning, so I've asked them to hold it for me.'

'Go tomorrow? But you can't,' said Robert. 'We're going to the Viewleys' tomorrow night. You can go the next day.'

'But Robert, Miss Dillon says at once! I think she's going to—to die,' on a note of anguish. 'She'd never have sent for me like this if it hadn't been urgent. I *must* go tomorrow.'

'Well, you can't,' said Robert decidedly. 'I'm not going to have the Viewleys upset, and that's flat. Now don't bother me any more. I've got some work to get through that can't wait.'

'Don't you realise, Robert, that my mother's *dying*!' she asked him. 'You can't put an invitation to dinner before that?'

'Why can't I?' he asked roughly. 'I do my job. Now you do yours, and if it doesn't turn out to be convenient for you to do it, that's just too bad. We're going to the Viewleys tomorrow night and you can go to Jericho the day after if you want to. Now clear out.'

She gave him an incredulous stare. She had heard him speak to other people like that many times, employees at the office, even his servants in the house, but it was the first time he had used such a tone and such words to her.

'Robert, I'm going to my mother tomorrow,' she said, and turned and walked out of the room.

He resisted the impulse to call her back, to tell her she could go and to hell with the Viewleys. He was remembering her coldness and the way in which, saying nothing, doing nothing, she had held him in check, kept herself inviolate, a wife but no wife.

He was right, he told himself savagely. She owed him something, and if she were not prepared to pay it in the way he had expected and had the right to expect, she could damn well pay it in another.

He opened his file of papers, but could not concentrate on them. He was seeing her affronted face, her incredulous stare, her reddened eyes.

He thrust the papers aside and flung himself out of the house.

'I shan't be in to dinner,' he told Parlow roughly.

Verne, in her bedroom, wondered wretchedly what she was going to do, for in spite of her declaration that she was going to take the plane the next morning, the fact remained that she had literally not the money for the fare. That had been a source of private and maddening annoyance to her throughout these weeks of her marriage. Robert would apparently give her everything but actual money. She had her car, or she used Robert's, but even petrol was charged to his account, and she could buy anything she wanted, but always on his credit. He had never given her one penny in hard cash, and she had already used up the very little money which she had had left when she was married.

How then was she to pay her fare to Switzerland unless Robert gave it to her? And she knew him too well to have any hope that he would change his mind, having stated it in so many words.

Finally, hating the necessity but seeing no other way since she was determined to go, she rang up Bill Trailer, who she knew would be in his office at this time.

'Bill? It's Verne,' she said when she heard his voice.

'Good heavens, what's this? Royal command or something?' he asked with a dry facetiousness.

'Bill, I'm desperate or I wouldn't be doing this. It's something really serious, so don't turn it into a joke, will you?

He could hear the strain in her voice.

'All right, my queen. I'm serious. Fire away,' he said.

'Bill, it's Mother. I've had a telegram. She's desperately ill. You know she's at that place in Switzerland?'

'Yes. I had a letter from her. I'm terribly sorry, my dear.'

His voice was linking her with the past, that dear, safe, familiar past which was lost to her forever. She strangled the sob that rose in her throat.

'I know. Thank you, Bill. I'm going, of course. I can get a plane in the morning, but—Bill—will you lend me some money? Enough for my fare?' desperately.

He gave a low whistle.

'What's all this? Don't tell me Grimtree's gone broke?'

'No, but—he doesn't want me to go and he won't pay my fare and—Bill, I'm desperate. I've got to go.'

'Of course you have,' he said soothingly. 'How much do you want? Never mind. I'll find out. Do they want the money tonight?'

'No. Tomorrow when I pick up the ticket.'

'O.K. Don't worry, sweet. I'll get it all laid on and meet you at the airport with the ticket. What time's the flight?'

'Nine thirty from London Airport. You mean you'll be there, Bill?'

'Of course. Now don't you worry—and take something to make you sleep tonight or you won't be fit for the journey tomorrow. Bye bye, honey. See you in the morning.'

'Oh—Bill. Bless you,' she said and replaced the receiver, blinded by her tears.

Bill sat for a few minutes considering the surprising situation in which Robert Grimtree's wife had to borrow a few pounds from another man. Was anything happening to that marriage? And so soon? Because if so –

He broke off with a speculative smile and rang up the airport to arrange about picking up her ticket.

Verne, unable to face Robert again that night, asked for some dinner to be sent to her room, saying that she had a headache and would go to her bed. Her lip curled at the thought that he was not likely to be much concerned about a headache when he could contemplate a heartache so callously, but it was a relief to be told that he had gone out and would not be in for dinner.

Her thoughts and her prayers were all for her mother. She could not doubt the urgency of the summons. Miss Dillon was not the type to send the telegram, worded as it was, otherwise. If only she had been able to go today instead of wasting all these hours! Even though she herself had failed to get a passage, she felt certain that Robert could have managed it had he been so inclined, and that certainty added to her bitterness against him.

She undressed and sat by the fire, knowing she would not sleep without a drug, and afraid that if she took one, she might sleep too long. She was not yet accustomed to the reliable service she could command.

She heard Robert go into his room very late, and, feeling that she must get it off her mind and let him know definitely, once for all, how far he could go in his domination of her, she knocked at his door and opened it.

He looked at her in some surprise, and his glance reminded her of something she had forgotten, namely that she was in pyjamas and dressing gown. She brushed it aside as of no moment just then.

'I think you ought to know,' she said deliberately, 'that I am going to my mother tomorrow. I will ring up in the morning and give a message to Lady Viewley, or you can do so yourself if you prefer.'

'You're going, are you?' he asked, his look darkening dangerously. 'May I ask what you are going to use for money? You can't have an air passage on credit, you know.'

'I have borrowed it,' she said, meeting his eyes steadily though her heart was thumping uncomfortably. She had never before seen Robert Grimtree being defied.

'Who from?' he snarled.

'A friend,' she said. 'I shall find some means of paying it back, even if I have to sell something. Yes, perhaps my ring, if that is the only way,' interpreting his quick glance at her hand.

'Who is this friend?' he demanded. 'A man?'

She was silent, and her obstinate refusal to answer him sent his anger to boiling point, for always beneath whatever he felt for her was fear – fear, which was an unknown quantity in his life. His mind would not diagnose the source and meaning of it. He only knew that he was afraid, and that this slip of a girl who owed him so much (in his own estimation) was the only human being in the world who could do this to him.

She saw the red flush mount in his cheeks, saw it fill his piercing little eyes, saw him clench his hands and for a moment she thought he was going to strike her.

'So you've got some man somewhere who gives you money?' he snarled.

'Who has lent it to me, since you refuse to give it to me,' she said steadily, her outward coolness increasing with his anger and serving further to madden him.

'Refuse? When have I ever refused you anything, until this?'

'I have never asked you for anything, until this. What you have given me has been for your own satisfaction, to see me dressed up and hung with diamonds so that you can parade me before your—friends,' the pause before the last word making her interpretation of the word unmistakable and contemptuous. She knew he had no friends as she understood the word.

He made a great effort to control into a less hazardous course the situation which was getting out of hand.

'Verne, be reasonable. You know as well as I do the importance I attach to this affair tomorrow night—perhaps not quite as well as I do, but I'll tell you now. I want Viewley on my board in this big scheme I'm putting through in Scotland. The Scots are cautious people and his name in connection with mine will give them the necessary confidence in it. I am not going to risk offending him at this critical point. I am not asking you not to go to your mother, but only to postpone it for one day. You can go on Thursday. I'll see that you get a passage, have a car waiting for you at the other end, make everything smooth and quick for you. That's all I am asking of you—just one day. Is it too much for you to give me?'

In any other circumstances, she might have yielded to the unprecedented pleading in his voice, but nothing at this moment had power to move her.

'With my mother dying, it is too much, Robert,' she said.

His anger boiled up again more fiercely than ever.

'Everybody's got to die,' he shouted at her brutally. 'You knew she was dying when she went.'

'I hoped she was going to live. That's why I married you, the *only* reason why I married you. Are you going back on your word now that you've got me?' she asked scornfully.

'Got you? Got you?' he raved at her. 'What have I got? A blasted, cold virgin content to take everything and give nothing? Haven't you gone back on your word? You're no wife to me.'

She was very pale, but she stood there motionless, her head high, her eyes coldly hostile, her lips curling, entirely mistress of herself as he lost his own self possession.

'I have never refused to be that, Robert,' she said.

'Refused? Refused? Lying there like a bird fascinated by a snake? With loathing of me in your eyes? A Christian martyr flung to the lions? I wasn't so besotted with you that I could take you with that look on your face, but by God I'll have no more of this! You're mine, and I'm going to make you know it!' and the last thread of his self control snapped and he reached out for her, caught her savagely in his arms, fastened cruel lips on hers, picked her up bodily and threw her across his bed, clawing at her like an animal with its prey.

It might have been hours afterwards; it might only have been minutes. She had lost all count of time when she stumbled from his room, dragging her gown about her, weeping though she hated herself for showing him her tears, her shoulders shaking, her whole body trembling so that she could scarcely walk. She did not know whether he was watching her or not, and no longer cared. His heavy body lay half on and half off the narrow bed and his breath came in uneven gasps. He made no attempt to detain her, having had his will of her, and when she reached her own room, she turned the key in the lock and somehow reached her bed and lay on it face downwards, the tears dried up now at their source, her loathing and anger too deep for such superficial relief.

She was not aware of the wounds of her body, her arms crushed by his ferocity, her lips bruised and bleeding, every limb tortured by his savage onslaught which had spared her no degradation. Her spirit was beaten and agonised. She no longer knew herself or her pride. She had become a different creature, Robert Grimtree's creature, a captured and beaten animal.

Gradually, lying there with her face in the pillows, some sort of calm returned to her and her mind began to assert itself again. She told herself with what reasonableness she could that this was what he had married her for and that she had counted the cost and decided it was worth it. If she had not reckoned on such ferocity and lustfulness, it was because she had been ignorant of men. This was what marriage meant to them.

But at the core of her being was a bitter hatred and disgust. Perhaps if he had taken her on that first night instead of coming to her and then so strangely leaving her alone, she might have been able to accept it with less loathing. These weeks of her marriage had brought her a feeling of false security, a faint belief that she was to be allowed to repay him in other ways. Now, at the moment of her anguish over her mother when she needed tenderness and kindness, the whole thing was revolting and brutal.

Well, if that were the price she had to pay, she had paid it. Nothing in the future could ever be as bad again. He had had what he wanted of her. She wondered, in her bitter humiliation, what satisfaction it could possibly give to a man so to degrade another human being. The iron had entered into her soul, nor could she have any idea that her own sense of humiliation and degradation were as nothing to that which filled the whole being of Robert Grimtree in that hour.

As soon as she heard him leave the house in the morning, she rang up for a taxi to take her to the airport. She was in a fever of anxiety to be gone, but she dare not risk his following her, either to make a scene in public or to manage somehow to prevent her from going.

Bill was waiting for her and she had a sense of relief at sight of him.

'Pay the taxi, Bill, will you?' she asked, avoiding his glance as she did so. 'This is the only luggage I've got.'

'I was afraid you were going to be late,' he said. 'I've got a Customs wallah laid on, but we'll have to run.'

He was appalled by the look of her, her face pale, her eyes sunk in deep, purple shadows. Poor kid, what a devil that man must be to let her look like that!

He expressed nothing of this to her, however, surrounding her with his considerate care, leaving her to do nothing but accept it, and there was time for no more than a few words at the last minute.

'You'll let me know, Verne?'

'Yes.'

'Give her my love.'

She nodded, incapable of more speech. She could not even say thank you.

'If you want me to meet you when you come back, you've only got to wire. Goodbye, my sweet.'

Again she nodded, touched his hand for a second and went.

She did not know, and would not have cared just then, that sitting in his car where he could watch everything with jealous, misery filled eyes was Robert Grimtree himself. He did not know who the young man was, though he had a vague idea that he had seen him somewhere before, perhaps with Verne in the old days, or waiting about the office for her.

He had not at first believed that she would defy him and go to her mother, but after what he had done to her last night, he could no longer believe that she would stay. He had been mad, a raving lunatic, a wild animal with the mark of the beast on him. And nothing would now undo it. Nothing would now bring her close to him in spirit. Perhaps he had even cast her from him altogether so that she would never come back even in body, the lovely, desirable body which he had ravaged and outraged and from which he had drawn not even any satisfaction other than that of mere physical conquest.

He saw Bill standing there until the plane had left, and when he turned away, Grimtree spoke to Johnson, whose wooden face had been allowed to express nothing.

'Follow that man,' he said. 'If he takes a bus, keep behind it.'

'Yes, sir,' said the man imperturbably and he did not even have to ask which man. He had seen as much as his master had, but his thoughts were his own. He knew, too, who the man was. He was an ardent football fan, and Bill Trailer covered some of the matches and his reports in his paper had sometimes been headed by his photograph. There was no need for him to tell Grimtree that, however. Good servants kept their own counsel.

Bill had brought his own car, a ramshackle two seater which he used for his work, and when Grimtree had seen it parked outside the office in an offshoot of Fleet Street and watched him run up the steps into the building, he nodded to his chauffeur.

'I'll go to the office now,' he said in a surly voice.

Whatever there was there, he would find it out and deal with it. If he had lost Verne, it was not going to be because some other man, some shoddy little man in a newspaper office, had taken her from him.

When Verne reached the sanatorium in the high Alps, Lorna Raydon was dead.

She accepted the news with a stoical calm which frightened the pitying Miss Dillon, for she knew that this was no sign of indifference.

'Won't you lie down now and try to get a little sleep, Mrs. Grimtree?' she asked gently. 'The doctor will give me something for you. It will at least give you an hour or two's unconsciousness and you'll feel stronger after it.'

'I don't want to sleep,' said Verne, but she let herself be led away after a time from the still, utterly peaceful figure of the woman for whose sake she had given everything she had, without avail.

The piercing tragedy of it was that her mother had never known, had lived the final weeks of her life believing her beloved daughter the poor, cheap thing which Verne had made herself out to be.

That was life.

She did not want to bring the body back to England, even if she had had the means. Bill had raked up in the short time at his disposal enough money for her to do what was necessary, and also to get home again, and when the simple funeral was over, she left the sanatorium alone.

She had offered to send Miss Dillon's passage money to her as soon as she reached England, but the nurse shook her head.

'No, please don't do anything more about me, Mrs. Grimtree. You forget that I have already been paid for a much longer time than this, and I could pay my fare out of that easily, but I have decided to stay here. They are short of nurses, and I understand this type of work and am glad to have been offered the opportunity. If you would like me to come back with you, though—'

'No. No, I shall be quite all right, but thank you. I—I'd rather be alone,' and because Faith Dillon was strong and self dependent herself, needing no prop, she understood and let her go.

She did, in fact, understand a lot more about the situation than Verne supposed, and her quiet, unexplaining championship of the girl had done much to sweeten and comfort the mind of the dying woman during these past weeks.

Verne sent a telegram to her husband before her plane left.

My mother died Tuesday morning. - Verne.

That was all she told him, not when she was coming back nor even if she were coming at all. He tore the telegram into shreds with his thick, strong fingers and wished he could destroy in the same fashion that thing that was devouring him, his passionate desire for Verne which had turned into love, though for him love would never be the selfless thing which seeks another's good rather than his own.

He was determined to get her back, though how and when he could not yet visualise. She was his. His she must and would remain. He would have given much to wipe out that night when he had taken her, but nothing would avail him there. He had to accept the fact. She must accept it too. He had only taken what was his right, and that was the price she had known she was agreeing to pay. It was tough luck that her mother had died after all, but that made no difference to their bargain. She could not expect to cry off because her share of the winnings had been less than she had anticipated. That was one of the things that might happen to anyone.

Verne had not telegraphed to Bill. She did not want to find him waiting at the airport. She had yet to make up her mind just what part he was to be allowed to play in her life, if any part at all. She was deeply grateful to him and the very thought of him was a warmth at her heart, but her feelings towards him had not changed. Even if she were still free, she had nothing to give him to match his faithful love, and she would cheat no man with less.

With no actual plans, when she landed in England again, she went instinctively to the flat like a wounded animal seeking the silent darkness of its lair. It was not quite eleven when she climbed the stairs, all the familiar sights and sounds of Sunday morning about her, children playing raucously outside, women gossiping at their doors, an occasional husband in weekend undress and braces bringing in his newspapers with which to fill the day.

At her own door she paused, feeling for her key, and the new loneliness of her life henceforth struck her afresh like a physical blow. It had never occurred to her that her mother would die so soon. She had believed so intensely in the healing power of the Alpine air, and the care she would have. Now her whole life seemed to have been laid waste. There was nothing left.

She could scarcely bear to enter the well known place, even though all their personal belongings had been packed away and only the bare bones of their home remained, but she steeled herself to meet the desolation, automatically took wood and coal to make a fire, and was kneeling before it for the inevitable coaxing it required when she heard a timid tap at the front door.

Her first thought was of Mrs. Biggin, but she had never announced herself in this fashion, either pressing the bell vigorously or giving a resounding rat-tat on the knocker, so she straightened herself and went to the door.

To her surprise, it was old Mrs. Biggin, 'Grannie', who stood there with a timid smile on her face.

'Why—Mrs. Biggin,' said Verne doubtfully.

'My dear, I hope I'm not intruding, but I heard you in here and I—I thought perhaps—I didn't like to think of you alone, no one even to get you a cup of tea or—or anything.'

Her faded old eyes were kind and gentle, with an appeal in them which found its way through the close armour of Verne's self concern, and she smiled reassuringly.

'That was so kind of you,' she said. 'Won't you come in for a moment? I'm just trying to get the fire going, but this grate is a brute.'

'I know. My son's is just the same, but I think it's going to burn up, don't you?' giving it a critical eye as she followed Verne into the room. 'Are you all right, my dear? You look very tired.'

Verne turned her head away. She felt that kindness would be unbearable just now.

'I have just flown back from Switzerland,' she said unsteadily. 'My— my mother was buried yesterday.'

'Oh, you poor, lonely child!' said the old lady, and at that the walls of Verne's defences broke and for the first time since she had learned of her mother's death, the tears came.

Mrs. Biggin put her frail old arms about her and drew her close, smoothing her hair, speaking to her as a mother does to a suffering child, murmuring old fashioned, tender words which had come so readily and so often to her children in the long ago when they had wanted her.

'There, there, my pretty. Cry then. Tears will do you good now. I'm here. It's the tears we shed alone that are so bitter. There, my little love. Cry all you want. Nobody will know but old Grannie, and she won't tell.'

Gradually the tears subsided and Verne lifted her head and scrubbed her face with her handkerchief, making both of them grubby from her coal dirty hands.

'Thank you,' she said. 'I really do feel better now, though I'm sorry to have inflicted it on you. It was just—your heavenly kindness that I couldn't bear.'

'I know. But one need not always keep what they call a stiff upper lip, not when one's with a true friend. Now you go and have a little wash and tidy up, and I'll make us a nice cup of tea. Have you got things here, or shall I run into Jake's place and get them? There's nobody in but me. They've all gone off somewhere or other for the day, but they didn't ask me to go, which was lucky for me because I didn't want to. At my time of life, in weather like this, there's nothing like a chair by the fire.'

'I think I've got tea and sugar in the kitchen, but no milk,' said Verne. 'Oh, and I believe I've got a shilling for the gas,' taking out her purse and finding one.

'Well, then, I'll just pop over and get the milk, and we'll have a little picnic of our own in here.'

Over a meal, which Mrs. Biggin had turned into a real meal by the addition of a pork pie and a bag of potato crisps, assuring Verne that she had bought them for herself out of her own money, the girl found herself, to her astonishment, telling the old lady things she had never dreamed she could tell.

Mrs. Biggin had mentioned Verne's husband, expressing a hope that he would not suddenly appear until she had had time to clear away the remains of their picnic, which they had had sitting on the floor in front of the fire.

'He won't,' said Verne. 'He—he doesn't know yet that I am back.'

'Not even that your dear mother has passed away?' asked the old lady, slightly shocked.

'Yes; I wired to him, but—we're not quite normal husband and wife, you see, and I felt I wanted to come here—first.'

Mrs. Biggin had never seen Robert Grimtree, but she had seen his picture in a newspaper, carefully preserved by her daughter-in-law, and Flo had added details which may or may not have been true, though the old lady, after the past hour with Verne, found it difficult to believe her the sort of girl who would marry a rich, horrible old man (again the description was Flo's) just for his money.

Gradually, by the things left unsaid rather than the spoken word, her old mind, astute and pitiful, pieced together much of the truth, even something of that hideous scene of Verne's last night in England.

'I don't know what I am going to do,' she ended, looking away, her mouth tight, her eyes hardening. 'I don't feel I can go back—and yet it isn't his fault that Mother died. He did everything he said he would do, though I didn't know she would die so soon. I didn't knew!' all the anguish she had suffered from the lack of knowledge in her tone, enabling the old lady to complete her own and very true conception of the circumstances of that marriage.

She took the girl's hand in hers and stroked it gently.

'My dear, I'm an old woman and with old fashioned ways and ideas. He is your husband and I think perhaps he cares for you a lot—oh yes,' as Verne made an emphatic gesture of denial. 'Men are not like us, and if we try to think they are, we can't hope to make anything of marriage. I think he does love you, Verne—do you mind if I call you that?'

'I like you to.'

'He is probably suffering a lot of anxiety over you and he may be very sorry—about it all. Try to be kinder in your thoughts. To be unkind never makes one happier.'

'I hate him,' said Verne in a low, hard voice.

'Hate? That hurts you because you're not like that. You're kind and loving in your nature. You're too good in your heart to let hatred change you. He's your husband, dearie, and your duty is to stay with him and to try to make the best of it. If more women did that instead of rushing off to get divorces, everybody would be a lot happier and not so restless and—worried. Give him a chance to show you that he loves you and is sorry. He may not ever say so in words. When we had words, and of course all husbands and wives have them sometimes, my Joe never once said he was sorry but always left me to shoulder the blame, but I knew he *was* sorry, so I didn't worry about the words. Go back to your home, dearie, and let him think you have forgotten even if you know you can't forget. After all, you did promise to be his wife if he would look after your dear mother. That was it, wasn't it?'

'How did you know? I didn't tell you,' said Verne.

'Ah, but you did—not in so many words, you know, but I guessed. You say yourself that it is not his fault that she died so soon, and if she had not died, he would have gone on doing everything he could for her, wouldn't he?'

'Yes. Yes, I suppose so,' she said unhappily.

'Then do your part instead of blaming him because he was not able to do all his.'

'I don't see how I can ever live with him again. He's—like an animal,' with a little shiver of disgust.

'Men are like that, many of them, perhaps most of them. I could tell you things even about my own marriage, which was a very happy one, but I won't. A woman, just buries those things in her heart and remembers that men are made differently, and thinks of the better part instead, and there are always better parts if one looks for them.'

In the end Verne went back, as in her heart she had known from the first she would do. She would not cheat Robert even if she felt life had cheated her.

Parlow's expressionless face relaxed a shade at sight of her.

'Oh, madame, you're back! The master said you might telephone from the airport for a car.'

'No, I had a taxi,' said Verne, who had had just enough of Bill's money left to pay for one. A grim thought that another man had to pay for her to return to her husband's home!

'The master left a message that he would like you to telephone to him when you arrived, madam.'

'Thank you. I'll do so,' said Verne, who had had no intention of any such thing but who felt indifferently that she might as well do so. If she did not, Parlow was likely to get the blame.

She felt cold when she heard Robert's voice.

'It's Verne,' she said curtly. 'I'm back.'

If she could have seen his face, that moment would have revealed to her the truth of what little Mrs. Biggin had said to her. A cold sweat of relief set him wiping his brow with his hand, and for a moment he could not speak.

'I'm glad to know it,' he said at last, and his voice sounded just as usual to her, impersonal, not greatly interested. 'I shall be in about five,' and he rang off.

'That'll be all for the present, Miss Bright,' he said, and the harassed woman slipped thankfully away for a short breathing space. During the past few days, he had been more than usually unbearable and difficult to please. She marvelled constantly not only that Verne Raydon had married him, but that she had even stuck him for two years in any capacity. She wondered how long she herself would be able to bear it, even with the lure of the good salary.

When he arrived at the house, Verne was in the small sitting room on the first floor which had been arranged for her, not in her own taste but comfortably. It was too opulent and over padded for her, and, like the rest of the house, too hot.

He gave her no impression of the turmoil of uncertainty seething within him, but nodded to her as he came in and took a chair on the other side of the fire.

'Well?' he asked. 'Not had a particularly good time, I suppose?'

'Scarcely.'

'I'm sorry, Verne,' he managed to grunt. 'Know that, of course.'

She eyed him calmly.

'You mean about Mother's death?'

'What else?' he asked belligerently, but could not go on meeting her eyes.

'Nothing else, of course,' she said. 'You explained to Lady Viewley?'

'Yes. She was all right about it.'

'She could hardly be anything else in the circumstances.'

'They want us to go next Friday.'

'Very well,' said Verne, and he drew a breath of relief.

So she had come back to stay.

He fumbled in his pocket.

'I got you this thing,' he said ungraciously, and pushed it across into her lap.

It was not wrapped, and she looked at it—a tiny watch set in diamonds, an exquisite and costly thing which she did not want. She wanted nothing from him any more.

'I have a watch,' she said without touching it.

'Well, now you've got another then,' he said roughly, and got up and left her.

He was bitterly disappointed at her reception of his gift. Though he had refused to admit it to himself consciously, he had known that his attitude over the summons to her mother had been harsh and unnecessary, prompted more by his jealousy than by the reason he had given her. He had made a gesture of atonement in the only way he knew, by parting with the price of the watch. Since she neither appreciated the gift, nor understood what had prompted it, he might as well have kept the money in the bank, he thought angrily.

She did not wear the watch, he noticed, during the days that followed, and he would not refer to it. She continued to use the cheap little gold watch that her mother had given her on her twenty first birthday, probably not even gold either, he thought contemptuously.

Though she forced herself to leave the door between their rooms unlocked at night, to her intense relief he did not come to her, and as the days passed, it seemed that they had relapsed into their former state of mutual indifference and tolerance.

It was almost a shock to her when she realised that it was Christmas Eve. She had forgotten all about Christmas, though in the weeks preceding it, she had been working on a gift for her mother, a soft woollen bed jacket for which she had bought the wool before her marriage. It had never been finished and now would not be. There was no one else to whom she wanted to give a present – which was as well, she reflected grimly, since she had no money to buy gifts. She knew she could have bought anything she wanted and have the cost charged to Robert, who never queried any purchase she made in that way, but the idea of buying gifts for other people out of his money was unthinkable.

They spent their usual evening by the library fire, he reading his financial papers and making his endless notes, and she with a book.

Suddenly he spoke.

'I haven't bought you a present, Verne,' he said gruffly, 'since you don't seem to appreciate what I buy you.'

She looked up, flushing slightly. She knew she had been ungracious and even rude over the watch.

'There is nothing I need, Robert, thank you,' she said.

'Nothing you need, perhaps, but what do you *want*?'

What did she want? Most passionately and desperately, her freedom, but she knew she might as well have asked him for the stars in the sky.

'Nothing,' she said.

He grunted and went back to his papers, but presently he spoke again.

'That money. The money you borrowed. Have you paid it back?'

'How could I?' she asked coldly.

'Of course you can. How much do you want?'

She told him the exact amount, and he took out his private chequebook, wrote a cheque payable to her and gave it to her.

'I've made it for cash and opened it,' he said. 'You can get it from the bank in the morning—no, of course, not tomorrow, but as soon as they open again.'

'Thank you,' she said perfunctorily, and slipped the folded paper into her book without looking at it.

'You'd better see if I have made it for the right amount,' he said, and when she did so, she flushed.

He had added fifty pounds to it.

Thank you,' she said again in the same unmoved tone.

'Well? Isn't it enough?' he asked testily.

'For the moment, yes,' she said, 'but, Robert, I am placed in a very embarrassing position, never having any money.'

'What do you want it for? To skip off out of the country again?'

'No.'

'All right then. You can have money whenever you ask for it.'

'Can't you make me an allowance? Even a small one? You cannot expect me to like coming to you for a few shillings now and then. It's—undignified.'

'Well, that's all I am prepared to do. Pay this fellow what you owe him, and never borrow again. Understand?'

'I am not likely to need to,' she said, and rose. 'Goodnight, Robert. I am going to bed.'

'Tomorrow's Christmas Day. Do you go to church, like other holy people?' he asked with an unpleasant jeer in the question.

'I do go on Christmas Day as a rule,' she said quietly, refusing to be drawn into a retort, and left him.

She got up early to go to the eight o'clock service. She was not a professedly religious observer, but she and her mother had always made a habit of going oh this day of the year, and she felt that if there were any afterlife, surely that beloved person would be with her in spirit, knowing and understanding everything at last.

The church, which was within a short walking distance, was already almost full, and she was conducted up the aisle to a pew near the front, and she knelt in the flower scented silence to let its peace steal into her troubled, unhappy mind. She did not consciously pray. It was years since she had been sure that there was anybody to hear and to answer, and it was rather with a stilling of the mind that she knelt there than with any petition.

Before she rose from her knees, she was aware that someone else had entered the pew and was sitting beside her, and when she sat up, she was amazed and confused to find Robert there. She thought that his large form and obvious discomfort at being there would have made his presence seem incongruous even if she had not known him.

After the first startled glance, she did not look at him again as the service proceeded, though she was surprised to hear his voice joining in the old, familiar hymns which most people have known in their childhood and never forgotten. She did not sing. It was not possible in the circumstances, and she felt that even if she had tried, no sound would have come.

He did not communicate when the time came, and though she had intended to do so, again because of the peace it might bring to her rather than from any inner conviction, she could not have passed him without embarrassment, so she remained in her seat. She watched some of the faces as people passed the pew on their way to the altar rail, and wondered what lay in their minds and what this communion would bring them. Were any of them as troubled, as unhappy, as fearful of the future as she was?

At the end of the service, they waited in the pew until the church began to empty, and when she glanced at him to see if he intended to move yet, she was astonished at the expression on his face. He was looking, not at her, but at the Christmas manger scene set within the altar rails, the child in the stall, with the young mother kneeling in the straw beside it, the plaster animals, the three wise men – all of it rather crude and garish, but softened into reality by the dim light from stained glass windows and the one lamp, fashioned like a star, shining down on the scene.

His gaze was intent, absorbed, strangely affecting to her. It was as if all the brute strength of the man's body and mind had for the moment been laid aside, and she saw how he might have looked when he was young, a boy perhaps, a boy who could still dream dreams which were not of wealth and power.

A queer, shaking thought came to her. What if that was the answer to this inexplicable marriage he had made? What if it were really a child he wanted? Needed?

And with that thought, and of what such a thing would mean to her, she felt herself grow sick and faint. She had thought, before there was any idea of her marriage to Robert Grimtree, that some day she would bear children, and it had been a happy thought. It had not been connected with any particular husband. It was just the feeling that some day she would fall in love and marry and have a family, not just one lonely child as she had been, but several children.

But to have Robert's child? Share that mystery of creation with him? Bear something that would have his characteristics as well as hers, perhaps with none of hers? Not the sweet gentleness of her mother, nor the dimly remembered gaiety and joy of life of her father, but this – this hatefulness and lust and greed and harsh cruelty of her husband!

She gave a little involuntary shiver, and it recalled him from that place in which his mind had been wandering, and he glanced down at her and rose.

'Shall we go?' he whispered, and she nodded and followed him.

Chapter Five

It was nearly the end of February before Verne began to suspect that she was to bear a child to Robert, conceived on that night of terror and hatred and disgust before her flight to Switzerland. She had thought nothing of the first irregularity, which had seemed a natural reaction to her grief and mental agony over her mother's death, but now she could not ignore it, and the horror grew in her.

An unknown doctor in a distant part of London, where she had gone blindly and on chance, confirmed her fear, though he refused to consider that to be her reaction.

'Yes, Mrs. Raydon,' he said cheerfully, 'I think that with the usual care, you may confidently expect a little stranger towards the end of the year. I should put it in the latter part of September.'

She was shaking, realising that all the time she had hoped to be reassured that it was not so.

'I can't have it. I can't endure to have it,' she told him, white faced.

He glanced at her wedding ring, an unusual one with its glinting diamonds, but it went with her well cut suit and perfectly shod feet, and with her air of culture and refinement. On another hand, he might not have thought the stones real, and though in his profession he met all sorts of women, he did not take her as other than a wife.

Still, he put the question to her.

'Why not, Mrs. Raydon? You are married? Forgive me, but it is best for me to know.'

'Oh yes, I'm married,' she said, 'and—and it's my husband's, of course.'

'Then why all the distress? Not frightened of it, are you? Because nowadays there's no reason to be, you know.'

'I'm not happy with my husband. I don't want a child,' she said jerkily.

'Come now, mightn't it make all the difference? Turn it into a happy marriage? What about your husband? Surely he would like you to have the child?'

'I don't know. I don't expect so. We've never discussed it, but—please, oh please, do something for me! I can't have it. I can't! I'm not frightened. It isn't that at all. It's just that—I can't have his child.'

'You mean there's someone else?' he asked seriously.

'No. Nothing like that. You will help me, won't you? I—I don't know how much these things cost, but—'

He interrupted her stumbling speech.

'My dear Mrs. Raydon,' he said sternly, 'surely you know that no reputable doctor would agree to any such thing? If that was your real reason for coming to me, I must ask you to go. Go home and have this child and be sure that it will be its own reward.'

'But somebody can do something—surely—'

'No one will do anything of that sort,' he said firmly, and rose to end the interview.

She opened her handbag.

'I don't know how much I owe you—' she began, and again he stopped her with a gesture.

'Nothing. Nothing at all, since I have done nothing for you but offer some advice which you do not appear disposed to take. I suggest you go to your own doctor, or to a hospital, and make preliminary arrangements for the birth of your child. Good morning.'

She knew no one who might help her. She bought pills from a nasty little shop in a side street in the West End; she did everything she could think of which might induce miscarriage. Nothing was of any avail.

She did not know what else to do. She felt trapped and realised that at the back of her mind, ever since the death of her mother, she had had the idea of escape, of leaving Robert and re-making her life as best she could.

Now there was no escape. Robert Grimtree never loosed his hold on anything that was his, and even if his wife could find a means of getting away from him, he would move heaven and earth to keep his child and the mother of his child.

She could not bring herself to tell him. She would not even speculate on what his reaction would be. Until that Christmas morning, when she had seen him looking at the child in the manger and the mother beside it, she would have said that he had no thought or desire for a child. With that memory clearly in her mind, she could not believe that now.

Their relations were what she now considered 'normal', that is they had no arguments or open quarrels, but pursued their own lives with very few points of contact, and he made no attempt to enforce his rights as a husband nor showed her in any way that he remembered that he had ever done so.

Their social circle was rapidly enlarging and increasing in importance. It did not appear to him necessary that she should observe any period of even private mourning for her mother, and since she would not flaunt her grief by wearing black, she made no outward show of it, nor did she attempt to resist the social activities in which he involved her.

Only Lady Viewley, kindly and friendly, appeared to know of her loss, but except for a gentle comment on it when they dined with her, she did not mention it and probably thought it had not been a deep grief. Verne accepted other invitations at Robert's behest, refusing others without asking for an explanation, and was a serene and accomplished hostess when he told her to arrange functions at his own house. She carried out her duties automatically, her trained, orderly mind able to cope with such situations as arose, and though Robert seldom expressed his appreciation in words, she knew that she had come up to his expectations and requirements in that direction.

Fortunately, she was bearing her pregnancy well, with none of the *malaise* or minor ills some women have to endure. In fact, she had never felt so well physically, and in spite of her inner rebellion and inability to feel any pleasure in the position, she seemed to bloom with a new beauty, with added dignity and self possession.

But she knew that she would have to tell Robert, and she preferred to do so before he made the discovery with his own eyes.

The opportunity came when, one evening in late April, he started to make plans for a summer holiday.

'I haven't been away for some years,' he said, 'but I feel I could be spared for a month or so this year, even with that fool Bright to look after things. I thought we might go abroad somewhere, get some sunshine for a change. I might even charter a small yacht, if you would like that. We could leave London about the middle of August and keep going south until we find the sun, and get back, say, about the end of September. I don't know if you have any ideas?'

She hesitated, swallowed, and then looked at him.

'I'm afraid that wouldn't be possible, Robert,' she said as calmly as she could.

He stared at her with the beginnings of a frown. Who was she to suggest that anything he wanted was impossible?

'Why not?' he demanded ominously.

'Because—I am going to have a child in September,' she said, and turned her eyes from him.

For a moment there was complete silence. Then he spoke very slowly.

'I—see,' he said. 'How long have you known?'

'Since about February.'

'Why haven't you told me before?'

'I didn't know how you'd feel about it.'

He got up from his chair and went to stare out of the window, and she could not surmise what his thoughts might be. Suppose he resented the fact of her pregnancy and insisted on her ending it, even at this stage? He could, of course, get something done. She knew that women did have things done, without risk if at considerable expense. She realised at that moment, for the first time, that she no longer wanted to lose the child. She had carried it within her, a living part of her, too long now. She had accepted it, could even begin to look forward to it, for though it was Robert's child, it would be hers as well.

But he had no such thoughts.

When he turned back to her, she saw that he was smiling – smiling with an expression of satisfaction, even of triumph, on his face.

'Well, well,' he said. 'Didn't know how I'd feel about it. How do you feel about it yourself?'

'I am glad—now,' she said in a low voice.

'So you ought to be. Not afraid, are you?'

'Of having a child? No. I am very healthy and normal.'

'Yes, but you must take care, you know. We mustn't let anything happen. Have you seen a doctor?'

'No.'

She was not going to tell him of the one to whom she had gone in her first horror and distress, hoping to get rid of it.

'Well, you must, of course. I'll call up Sir Donald Revere in the morning and get him to come. He's about the best, isn't he? If he isn't, we must get the best. You're sure, I suppose?' his eyes raking her figure in a way that brought a flush to her face.

'Quite sure,' she said quietly.

Their married life had not been such that she could have borne to discuss the intimacies of her body with him.

'Huh,' he grunted. 'Well, well. Who would have thought it? I must say it never entered my head. Don't suppose it did yours, either, eh?' and he gave one of his rare, wheezy chuckles and rubbed his hands together with a dry, rasping sound.

'Well, you're quite right, of course, about not being able to go away in August, but I can probably arrange things to get away for a little while earlier than that, say in June. If we get any decent weather, we could have a week or two in Devon or somewhere, take the journey easily so as not to tire you, have a lazy time on some quiet beach, eh? Like that? Mustn't risk anything going wrong, you know, not with *my* son.'

'Don't count too much on its being a son,' said Verne drily, and he chuckled again.

'Well, a daughter perhaps, though naturally a man wants a son first. Now what about your going to bed? Want a lot of rest now, you know.'

It was the first time he had expressed any consideration for her welfare, but it was not for her, of course, but for the precious Grimtree heir which was housed in her body!

'With two dinner parties here next week, and an evening at the opera, and Mrs. Buchanans big crush for her daughter's twenty first on Friday, there's not likely to be much rest this week,' she reminded him with an enigmatical smile.

'Oh, confound it, yes. Ought to have told me sooner, you know. I'd have eased off. Well, this week can't very well be helped now, but no more functions, mind,' as if it were she who arranged them for her own benefit, not he for his.

'We've already accepted invitations,' she said.

'Then they must be cancelled.'

'On what pretext? Do I write and say that Mr. and Mrs. Grimtree regret that they must cancel all accepted invitations on the grounds of Mrs. Grimtree's pregnancy? Or would it be simpler to put it in *The Times*?'

He chuckled again. He was obviously very well pleased, and her slightly acid suggestions had no power to rile him.

'We could say you are indisposed,' he said.

'Since I don't look it, that would amount to the same thing. I'm not made of anything breakable, you know, and until I begin to show, there is no reason why I should not go on leading a perfectly normal life. Women don't retire to their couches for nine months nowadays.'

'Well, so long as you don't risk anything,' he agreed doubtfully; 'but don't accept any more invitations that are not absolutely essential, and no more parties here. Understand?'

She smiled.

'It'll be quite a change to be wrapped in cotton wool and labelled "precious",' she said and went quietly out of the room.

Well, it was over, anyway, and he was pleased about it, and at the moment happier than she had ever seen him. Perhaps it would make a difference to them. Would she be glad if it did?

In the morning, Burn brought up a note with her early tea, and a great armful of flowers.

'Good heavens. Burn! However did those get here at this hour of the morning?' she asked, wondering who could possibly have sent them.

'Oh, madam, what do you think?' asked the maid, who had developed a great liking for Verne, and was not nearly as imperturbable as the stately Parlow. 'The master asked to be called at five, and he went himself to Covent Garden and brought them back in the car. Look, this is a note to go with them.'

Verne opened the envelope, half amused, half annoyed.

Stay in bed for breakfast. These are for you. – R.G.

That was all. A strange note, but oddly expressive of the man. Had she thought about it, she would have expected diamonds. Then she remembered her reception of his last gift of them, the diamond watch, and she realised that it was a quite unusual delicacy on his part to send her flowers instead.

'They're lovely, Burn. Put them in water, will you? Has Mr. Grimtree left yet?'

'Yes, madam. He left early this morning. He said you were not to be wakened.'

Verne lay for a long time without pouring out her tea.

She was thinking about Robert Grimtree, that strange, unknown man with whom she had linked her life. She would have believed that she knew him through and through even before she married him, a hard, ruthless man with not only none of the graces of human contact, but also without the very source of those small, utterly important things which make human contact possible to endure. She had known him selfish to the point of extinction for any other advancement but his own, grasping for his own gain, always grasping for more, never satisfied, looking for fresh gain almost before the one desired was satisfied.

He had no love in his life, no friendship, was utterly independent of others, sitting on the high pinnacle of his own self esteem.

Was there something about him that she had not known? This business of the child. That look she had surprised on his face at the Christmas Day service. The way in which he had left her alone, not even seeking to touch her hand, since that one night which had revealed to her that, cold and ruthless though he was, all a man's physical passions blazed and demanded satisfaction.

What would the coming of their child do to him? For him and for them?

She shrank from the very hint of leading a normal married life with him. She closed her eyes and turned her head away at the thought of his big, square hands with their thick fingers, of his hard lips which had kissed her with no tenderness. Were not even his bodily desires a part of the man as she knew him, helping him to take and grasp and hold what he desired to own?

Burn came back into the room with his flowers, great bowls and vases of them. No mere ordinary sized bunch of flowers for Robert Grimtree!

Even when he had sent flowers to her mother, they had had to be orchids because there was nothing more expensive on the market.

'There, madam. Aren't they lovely? And so fresh! I always say that by the time they get into the shops, half their beauty is gone—but fancy the master getting up at five on a morning like this to go and get himself from the market! Brrh!'

'Just leave them, Burn. They can go downstairs later. I am not fond of flowers in my bedroom,' said Verne, and knew she was being ungracious about them.

Couldn't she even take flowers from Robert without that feeling of resentment and dislike?

Then she realised the source of that resentment. The flowers were not for her, but for the unborn child in her womb—for Robert Grimtree's son, Robert Grimtree's possession.

Meantime the man himself was being absorbedly active in his office, and when he returned in the evening, he showed her a paper, a legal looking document, with something triumphant, almost boyish in the bravado with which he produced it.

'Know what this is? It's a deed of gift. For my son. He's got quite a sizable fortune already. Templar tried to put me off it, said it was absurd, not really legal. Said you couldn't make money over to someone not even alive! I insisted. Not alive? Then what is he? He is alive, Verne, isn't he? Can you feel that he's alive?'

'Not really yet,' she said with a reluctant smile. 'I understand you don't feel any movement until the child quickens, about halfway through.'

'Oh well, you may not feel him yet, but of course he is alive. Robert Grimtree is not likely to have fathered a dead child! Look at it, Verne,' pushing the document nearer to her. 'These shares. You remember when I bought them? You didn't think they would be much good, but I knew. Oh yes, I knew all right. Lucky that idiot wanted money, or if he'd had any sense, he would have hung on to them, and I got them for a song in the end. No one else would look at them. Remember?'

Yes, she remembered. The man who had offered them to Grimtree had been at the end of his tether, a sick wife, a son going wrong at Cambridge, debts mounting up, a writ threatened. He had wanted Robert to lend him money on the security of the holding, had not wanted to part with it, had shown that, with any luck, he should be able to redeem the debt within a few months. But Robert had given his flat. An outright sale or nothing, and after the man had gone away to think about it, Grimtree had reduced his offer and had been gleeful and triumphant when at last the man had been forced to sell, and at the new price.

And her child was going to reap the harvest of that almost broken man, with the despairing eyes, the heart torn with indecision and fear. His son had been killed soon afterwards in a car accident, his wife had died, his business had failed because he had neglected it so that he could stay at her side, night and day, in the last weeks, and he had come back to Robert and asked to be allowed to buy back the shares at their already enhanced value. Possibly in a few months they would have reached a value which, when sold, would have enabled him to start again.

But of course Robert had refused.

'Oh no, old boy. You sold 'em and I bought 'em, and that's just the luck of the game.'

She could have wished his gift to his unborn child had been anything else – but were not most of Robert Grimtree's 'lucky' deals coloured with the same thing? Nothing actually dishonest, but just keeping within the margin. 'Seizing a chance by the forelock', he called them as he rubbed his hands gleefully and added a few thousands to his ever mounting fortune.

He had done something else that day, but of this he did not tell her. It was one of the many secrets locked closely in his heart. Only Jeffery Templar knew of this one, and that was only because without the help of a legal mind, he might not have been quite sure all was in order.

A long time ago, when she was working for him, he had grudgingly been forced to leave her with a small amount of money banked in an account in her name to use for certain eventualities which might have arisen during a few weeks in which he was obliged by a big business deal to be out of the country.

She had used some of it, accounting to him meticulously for every penny of it, and there had been some twenty pounds of it left.

'Draw a cheque for the balance, payable to me, of course, and I'll pay it into one of my other accounts,' he had told her. But he had kept the cheque. He had told himself that the same circumstances might arise again, but they had not, and the money had remained there, though Verne was in ignorance of the fact, if indeed she ever thought about it again.

Since his marriage, he had from time to time paid into the account sums of varying amounts, the results of some of the small deals he made on the Stock Exchange on a whim, not really caring whether they 'came home' or not, though, as he was Robert Grimtree and had an uncanny flair for such things, they very seldom went astray.

He had been inwardly and sardonically amused at himself for parting in this way with such sums. Fancy him, Robert Grimtree, voluntarily parting with his own money, putting it where not even he could touch it! *Giving* it away! He realised the situation the more because Verne had no idea of it. Some day he would tell her, to her surprise and delight, that she was a comparatively rich woman, show her how wrong she had been in her surmise that he never gave her money!

It never occurred to him that, so long as she did not know it was there, she might as well not have had it. What did she want money for, anyway? She knew she could buy anything she wanted, and what woman could ask more of a husband?

Now, when he had learned that she was to give him a child, he added something substantial to the account. It set her balance at more than five thousand pounds.

It gave him peculiar pleasure, even whilst his mouth twisted wryly as he paid in the cheque, passing it casually across the counter of the bank.

'Mind, you're not to bother Mrs. Grimtree with any statement of account or anything like that. They can be sent to me at my office. Have you made a note of that in your ledger, or wherever you keep customer's instructions?'

'Oh yes, Mr. Grimtree. We are very careful about such things,' the cashier assured him, but when he looked at the account, curious about it, he remarked to the ledger clerk that it was odd that Mrs. Grimtree never drew on it but left a large sum, now considerably larger, on a current account without attempting to invest any of it, which would be the normal thing to do.

The clerk grinned.

'I don't suppose she ever wants anything, married to old Grimtree, and what would a few paltry hundreds be to her even if she did invest it? I bet my old woman would soon make ducks and drakes of it! And more power to her elbow!'

Though there had been moments when Robert Grimtree had surprised himself by the thought that he loved his wife, he would never have permitted any idea that he was *in* love with her. He had no use for such limiting emotions. He refused to recognise the source of his pride in her, the sickening anxiety he had felt on the two occasions when he had feared she would not return to him. She had come back, hadn't she? She had too much sense not to know which side her bread was buttered, even though (he added to himself with a chuckle) she had no idea just how thickly it was buttered, nor that it had jam on it as well!

By resolute force he prevented himself from telling the people he met that day that he was to become the father of a son. The only person he told was Jeffery Templar, whose dry, legal mind rebelled against the scheme put up to him whereby considerable property was to be made over at once to that unborn child.

'Don't blame me if this thing isn't legal, or if anything goes wrong,' said Templar, when he had failed to dissuade him, or to wait until the child was born.

'What should go wrong?' blustered Grimtree. 'My wife's young, healthy, and every care will be taken of her. You do it the way I say, and I want it tonight, signed, sealed and delivered. Understand?'

'Yes, in so far as any lawyer could understand such a fool scheme,' said Templar drily.

He wondered if he, or anyone else, would ever understand Robert Grimtree? Who would have thought that the old curmudgeon would have gone all haywire like this over the mere fact of his wife's pregnancy? What really went on in that crafty mind behind the cunning little eyes that gave nothing away?

Verne, a few days later, saw yet another unexpected facet of the oddly fashioned mind, when Robert brought home a puppy.

She had often longed for a cat or a dog, something young and innocent and ignorant of the twisted strands which made up her life, but Robert had never shown any interest in animals, had refused a subscription to the R.S.P.CA. on the grounds that a society which winked at stag hunting was inconsistent and had tossed aside, with a snarl, literature which that estimable body had sent in an attempt to convince him that the 'sport' did not exist in high places.

Verne had sent a guinea of her own money.

Now he came home with a puppy, but not the aristocrat with impeccably long pedigree she would have expected him to choose for his money.

He set it down on the rug.

It was a 'pathetic, bedraggled object of no conceivable origin. It started as a spaniel, with the heartbreaking brown eyes of its kind, but whilst one ear flopped, the other stood up like a Scottie's. Farther down it passed through a variety of breeds, had a greyish body covered with short, stiff hairs broken by brown spots, and supported by long, uncertain legs spindling into large, splay feet, and it ended its insignificant length in a long tail which might conceivably be white if clean, and which drooped until it almost trailed on the ground.

Verne looked from the creature to Robert, speechless.

'Whose is it? And where on earth did you get it?' she asked. 'I suppose it *is* a dog?'

'Can't be anything else,' he said with a sheepish grin, 'and it's mine. I paid a lot for it. Sixpence.'

'Robert!'

He picked it up, dirty though it was and probably full of fleas. The creature shrank against him and put out a furtive tongue to give a half frightened and very tentative lick at his cheek.

'It was down by the river. Some urchins were trying to drown it, but it kept coming back in spite of the stones round its neck. I liked its spirit and its determination not to be cheated out of life, though what sort of life it expected, starting off like that, heaven knows. They said their father had told them to drown it, but they were just as pleased with the sixpence and ran off and left me with it—and there wasn't anything else I could do with it, was there?'

'Are we going to keep it?' she asked, taking in with pitying eyes the pathetic spectacle it presented, ail its bones showing through that incredible grey and brown body.

'Well, I thought if we got it cleaned up and some food inside it, somebody might give it a home,' he said, and turned to Parlow, who had been standing regarding the unusual scene with unconcealed disgust, and stuck the puppy into his surprised and unwilling arms.

'Take the thing away and give it a bath and delouse it, or whatever they do to dogs—oh and tell Mrs. Wise to find out what it will eat and feed it,' said Grimtree. 'I need a wash and change myself too!' looking at the muddy marks on his coat.

'Are we to keep it in the kitchen premises, sir?' asked Parlow, holding the puppy at arms' length as if it were a tray, its long legs and absurd tail dangling down beneath it.

Verne longed to laugh at the expression on the butler's outraged face, but dare not. One did not laugh at Parlow.

'Oh—bring it back when it's clean and fed and I'll have a look at it,' said Grimtree easily.

When, later, Burn brought it to the library, Parlow having inflexibly refused to have any more to do with it, Verne exclaimed with delight.

'Oh, Robert, he's sweet!' she said, enticing the still nervous puppy to come near enough to her to have its absurd ears rubbed.

The coat was not as grey as they had supposed, but it was definitely not white, and the long tail, gradually and fearfully tending to become erect, was snowy and threatened to become an actual plume.

Robert rubbed his hand over his chin and put down two tentative fingers towards the dog, which instantly left Verne and came to him, rubbing himself ecstatically and with no sign of timidity against his trouser leg.

'You see? He knows he's mine,' he said, with quite disproportionate satisfaction. 'Nice feller then. Good feller. *Clean* and unlousy feller, I hope.'

Verne saw that the creature was going to stay, and she was glad. It would be something young and possibly cheerful about the house whose grandeur and incurable gloom had never failed slightly to depress her.

'What are you going to call him?' she asked.

'Bunker,' he said at once. 'A sort of—er—opposite name if you know what I mean, because he stuck to his guns and wouldn't bunk. I thought of calling him Guts, but you might not have liked that.'

She laughed.

'No, I don't think I would,' she said. 'Here, Bunker, come and talk to me for a change,' holding out an inviting hand, but the puppy refused to budge, remaining pressed close to Robert's leg, his appealing spaniel's eyes gazing up at him in utter devotion.

Thereafter, though she would have loved to have the now cheerful and happy animal about the house with her, it would not leave Robert, who even took it with him to the office, where it remained all day either in its basket, an ornate, expensive affair which had its twin at home in the library, or turning out the contents of the wastepaper basket, or relieving the tedium by having an occasional chew at Robert's immaculate shoes. All he did was to move his feet aside and give him a ball, or a rubber bone, or some other doggy toy as a temporary substitute.

Every hour or two, Miss Bright, who disliked dogs, was required to take him down and remain with him for five minutes by the clock in the small, muddy, leafless patch of ground at the offices known as 'the Square', where he scuffled the leaves, chased imaginary cats, hunted for nonexistent rabbits, barked vociferously, and behaved in general like the ill bred young no account dog he was.

Returned to Mr. Grimtree's private office, he became reasonably sedentary again until it was time to go home, and Johnson, who was one of his personal friends, would appear to escort him to the Rolls, where he sat looking out of the window, feeling infinitely superior, though sometimes slightly envious of the common dogs which scavenged in the dustbins put out on the pavements, or engaged in noisy fights with others of their kind.

It never failed to intrigue Verne to see how Robert's manner, however irascible and bad tempered he might be, changed for Bunker. He was never irritable with the dog, never seemed to find him in the way, and even when Bunker had the unexpected happiness of finding an important document which had fallen unnoticed to the floor, and proceeded to sample a corner of it and tie himself in knots with the pink tape, Robert merely took it away from him, gave it a rueful glance and observed that Templar would have to get a move on to produce a copy next morning.

In June, with Verne's figure showing signs of thickening so that all invitations were now refused and there were no more parties at home, Robert carried out his plan of taking her to Devonshire, the weather being for once fine and warm.

They took two days over the journey to spare Verne any possible tiredness, and Robert was constantly pulling back the glass screen of the car to shout at Johnson to go more slowly. Bunker went with them, of course, occupying the back seat next to Verne so that Robert had to occupy one of the less comfortable tip up seats.

'He's used to sitting there,' he explained to Verne, and though she smiled, she made no comment.

The three weeks in Devonshire was a mixed delight and irritation.

Robert had taken a small house in Salcombe, perched high on the cliffs above the estuary, but it meant a long climb down and up again to the beach, where Verne loved to lie and laze in the sunshine, though Robert would not let her put so much as her feet in the water.

'Something might happen,' he told her, and though she smiled unbelievingly, she did not argue against it. If she were not careful, she would begin to see herself as he obviously regarded her, as nothing but the vehicle for the production of the Grimtree son, with no individuality as herself at all.

When, in spite of the earliness of the season, holiday makers invaded their privacy, using the sands and the rocks, which were public, for their fun, their shouting and laughter, even sometimes bringing with them portable wireless sets which destroyed their peace with raucous jazz orchestrations and senseless songs put over in the supposedly American accents which such singers consider the only medium for British listeners, Robert said shortly that they would go.

'These people ruin everything,' he said disgustedly.

'You ought to have bought Salcombe,' observed Verne placidly.

They packed up and went inland a little, decided (that is, Robert decided) to stay awhile amongst the quiet Devon hills and fields, the small farms tucked away in forgotten byways as they had lain for centuries, and looked for a suitable place.

Robert found it, or a place that seemed reasonably suitable, in a small house, little more than a cottage, where a smiling but obviously nervous woman agreed to accept them as guests.

It was not a success, though there were evenings when, sitting alone in the old orchard where King Arthur's knights might well have rested and seen it much as it was still, they would talk – or rather, Robert would talk, for Verne seldom found much to say to him but seemed content to listen, her thoughts in her own keeping.

At first with difficulty, but gradually with more confidence in her silence, he told her things about himself which only he had known, things which had gone in their different ways to the making up of the man as he was now, hard, ruthless, far seeing and prideful of his own achievements.

'What I've done, I've done by myself and for myself,' he told her. 'That's the only one you can depend on. Number One,' tapping his chest as he said it.

She thought of her mother and of the sweetness of their interdependence.

'I wonder whether you haven't missed more than you've gained,' she said slowly, and he gave her a quick glance, but her face revealed nothing.

That, he felt, was the most exasperating thing about her – that she never gave him a chance of knowing what went on in her mind, not even whether she still regarded him with the hatred and loathing with which, on that disastrous night which had had this strange outcome, he had inspired her.

It was never mentioned between them. These months, since he had known that she was to bear his child, seemed a strange pause in their lives, a time when their relationship hung suspended in space, without beginning or ending.

They talked and walked together, drove through the countryside, sat in the evenings in the prim little parlour with its antimacassars and stuffed birds and geraniums in the windows. Verne taught him how to play *besique* and was amused to find he had no aptitude for card games so that she could eerily outwit him, though when he tried to get her to play chess, she was no match for him, not being able to think enough moves ahead.

In some ways she felt she knew him better; in others he was still as great an enigma. It was impossible, even if she had wished it, to keep in her mind the hatred and despair which had once filled it, but nothing came to take its place. Close enough to her to be sharing in the life of the child within her, he was yet a stranger and she would not try to look beyond its birth.

His consideration for her was never tenderness, his unvarying patience never personal. With others, with Johnson, with nervous and inefficient Mrs. Curloe, he was frequently out of temper, giving vent to outbursts of wrath quite disproportionate to their cause. With Verne, even when at times she had the unreasoning irritability which comes to women at such times, he was never out of temper, and when once she flared out at him with, 'Don't be so horribly complacent about me! Say something! Shout at me or something!' he only smiled.

'Why should I? I don't want to upset you any more than you upset yourself. Bad for you, you know,' he said and went into the house.

'Bad for your precious child, you mean,' she retorted just before he was out of hearing.

But there were few of these occasions. She was living in a sort of dream world in which nothing had much reality for her but her child.

How would he be, she wondered, when the child was an accomplished thing, a separate entity? Would it any longer be hers at all? Or would it become just another of the belongings, the achievements, of Robert Grimtree?

They were uncomfortable with Mrs. Curloe, who, with a lazy husband and a brood of untidy children, did her best for them but was left in no doubt about its being a very poor best in Robert's eyes. Verne attempted to help her, but was pulled sharply up by a reminder from him that he was paying to have the beds made for them and the dishes washed and the vegetables prepared.

'But Robert, I must do *something*' she said. 'I've never learnt to be a lady of complete leisure.'

'You've got your job,' he said meaningly, and she flushed with some annoyance and left him.

They were always doing that, she found – just walking away and leaving each other because things were difficult, but they could not keep on doing it. Some day they would both have to face facts, each other and the future. If she could have felt that some of his consideration and extreme care were for her, herself alone, and not herself as the vehicle for the body of the child, something might have grown between them which would in the end hold them together.

But he gave her no sign that he thought of her in any other way, and she found herself resenting it even though she knew she would fiercely have resisted any attempt on his part to make love to her.

She could not know how greatly he longed to touch her, to hold her close, not in passion but in the new, strange tenderness he felt towards her. How would she receive him afterwards, when her body was no longer the temple to be held sacred from his grosser needs and urges?

But the habit of the years was too strong. He could not approach her with that tenderness, and if he had had any doubt as to how any such approach would be received, he could have had none after the evening when, finding the longing to be closer to her unbearable, he had risen from his chair and put an arm about her shoulders, awkwardly and clumsily.

Instantly she stiffened. Her face flushed and then grew pale, and she sat up rigidly, with a jerk which dislodged the tentative hand and left him standing beside her with the blood mounting to his own cheeks.

He flung himself back into his chair and when the little maid, Lucy, came in with their supper, he looked at it and snarled. 'Good God, not that muck again? Take it away. Tell her that if that's the best she can do, we'll eat out, go to the pub or somewhere.'

The child, she was little more, dissolved into tears and Verne, giving him a glance of disdain, went out into the kitchen to do what she could to soften the effect of his rudeness. She knew that Mrs. Curloe had spent the best part of the afternoon preparing the supper, and that it was her misfortune rather than her fault that it had turned into an unappetising mess.

'I think, Robert,' she said when she came back into the room, 'it would be best if we went home.'

'Why?' he growled.

'Nothing seems to please you here, and you can hardly dismiss Mrs. Curloe as you would one of your servants. I'll go and see to the packing. Will you tell Mrs. Curloe?'

'All right,' he grunted. 'Suits me. Been too long away from the office, anyway. That woman Bright!'

Verne smiled ironically.

'Perhaps you made a mistake in getting rid of your former secretary,' she said.

'Huh,' he growled. Then he eyed her sheepishly.

'Mean you were better off then?' he asked.

'Well, I didn't have to put up with your bad temper in the evenings as well as the daytime,' said Verne serenely.

To her surprise, he gave a little chuckle.

'Always did stand up to me, didn't you? Go and get your coat. We'll have supper at the Red Lion.'

'That will upset Mrs. Curloe very much.'

'I'd rather upset her than my stomach,' he said, 'Go and get your coat. Johnson!'

Chapter Six

Robert Grimtree's child was born at the end of a long September day.

In secret, Verne had been studying for months everything she could find in women's magazines and in professedly knowledgeable books on such matters, and had become so imbued with the theory that drugs during labour might be prejudicial to the production of a perfect child that she had persistently refused the alleviations offered her.

But at last it was over and she was still fully conscious, though exhausted, when the nurse showed her the tiny, wizened face, red and angry, just visible between the folds of blanket about it.

'There!' said the girl. 'A lovely boy, Mrs. Grimtree.'

Verne opened her eyes for a moment.

'I wouldn't care—if it were—a rocking horse,' she said weakly. 'It felt like it—anyway—'

The nurse laughed.

'You've been wonderful, simply wonderful, and isn't he a beauty?'

Verne privately thought she had never seen anything more hideous.

'He isn't very pleased with life,' she said, as the baby yelled its protests.

'But what a pair of lungs!' said the nurse admiringly. 'Nobody's going to get *him* down. Now you can settle down for a little sleep, Mrs. Grimtree. Your husband's going to be allowed just a tiny peep at you. He wouldn't leave, you know. He's been here all day, and in such a state! I told him we don't often lose a father,' with a little chuckle.

Robert tiptoed into the room, knocking into things as he came, rather like a nervous and badly trained elephant, but Verne kept her eyes closed. She did not want to see him just now. Her agony was too near.

He stood looking down at her for a moment, his face working strangely. Then he turned to look at his still loudly protesting son.

'He's a fighter,' he said, edging away from the unknown quantity.

'And how!' agreed the nurse. 'So is your wife, Mr. Grimtree. She's been simply marvellous.'

'Yes,' he agreed in an odd tone. 'She is, isn't she? She'll never give in,' and after he had gone, Verne remembered the words and the tone and wondered just what they had meant.

He came the next morning to find her looking remarkably well and sitting up in bed. He had brought a great armful of flowers, and when he had put them down beside her, he took something out of his pocket and tossed it awkwardly into her lap.

'Here,' he said and looked away, furious with himself for not being able to say anything else, though for hours he had been rehearsing the pretty speeches with which he intended to present the gift, speeches which he might have known Robert Grimtree would never bring himself to utter.

Verne looked at it. It was a magnificent emerald ring.

'Thank you, Robert,' she said gravely, not looking at him or touching the costly thing.

'Well, put it on, put it on,' he said testily. 'It won't bite you, and it isn't infectious or anything.'

She slid it on to her finger, but he was angrily aware that it gave her no pleasure. At a moment when they should have been nearest, they had never seemed so far apart.

'It's beautiful,' she said in the same unemotional voice.

'It cost a lot of money,' he snapped and could have bitten out his tongue for the ill chosen and ungracious words.

'Have you seen Adrian this morning?' she asked after a pause in which both looked uncomfortably about the room, never at each other.

They had agreed on the name Adrian some time ago. Verne had suggested it, saying it had always been a favourite name of hers, and rather to her surprise, he had at once accepted it without pressing the claims of John and George and Charles round which his mind had been revolving.

'Adrian Grimtree. Yes. Yes, that's fine. No other name. Just the one people will know him by. And they're going to know him, you bet your life! They know Robert Grimtree all right, but that'll be nothing to the way they're going to know Adrian Grimtree! Just you watch.'

Adrian Grimtree.

So he was an accomplished fact, no longer just a dream kept in the secret fastness of her body.

'He's asleep. He—they say he's like you, Verne.'

She managed a little laugh.

'I don't take that as a compliment,' she said. 'He just looks like a bit of rather red dough at the moment.'

'He won't always,' he said.

Why, he thought, couldn't he tell her that that was what he wanted his son to be, made in her image, looking like her, being like her—a gentler, softer Verne who perhaps would come to understand him, even to love him? He was passionately grateful to her for his son, but he could not tell her so. He could only heap flowers and jewels about her, and she did not even want them.

'I've registered the name,' he said. 'Adrian Grimtree. Sounds fine?'

She nodded.

'I've always liked it,' she said, but it was not until after Robert had gone that she suddenly remembered something for the first time.

Adrian was Bill's second name!

'William Adrian Trailer,' she had said when, years ago, he had told her. 'Adrian's a nice name. Why don't you use it?'

Bill had grinned.

'Too fancy for a bloke like me,' he said. 'Plain Bill Trailer me,' and she had not remembered it until this moment, nor had she connected it in any way with Bill. It was just a name she liked.

They kept her in the nursing home for a full month, though Robert was restless to have her and his son home. An elaborate nursery had been arranged for him, and a highly qualified nurse engaged. Rather to Verne's surprise, it irked him that she was not able to feed her baby.

'Lots of women can't nowadays,' she told him indifferently, giving him no hint of her own disappointment and chagrin.

She too, wanted to take the baby home where, in spite of the efficient nurse awaiting them, she felt he would be more her own.

'I'm sure we should look after him just as well as he is looked after here,' she told the doctor who was keeping them there, and then she gave him a quick, startled glance, seeing the expression on his face.

'There's nothing wrong, is there?' she asked. 'Why do you look like that? And why are you keeping us here? I'm perfectly well.'

He gave her a deep, thoughtful look. There was something that must be said, and it was a thing he hated to have to say, especially to a young mother with her first baby.

'Well—as a matter of fact, we are not completely satisfied,' he said at last, gravely.

She clutched at his arm, alarmed.

'What do you mean, not satisfied? Is there something wrong? Not with me, I know.'

'It may pass, Mrs. Grimtree. We are doing all we can, and babies are wonderfully tenacious little creatures—'

'You must tell me. Don't mince matters. But I must know. What's wrong with my baby?' she asked urgently.

He told her gently, knowing that he had no alternative. There was a condition of the heart, he said, something that might yield to treatment, but—'

'You mean my baby is going to die?' she asked in a whisper, and though he tried to console her with platitudes, she scarcely listened.

Not until she had actually held him in her arms had she realised how deeply the child had grown into her being, had become her hold on life, the only thing that now mattered. It had filled the emptiness of her heart and in some strange way had taken the place of her mother. Even Robert had ceased to matter and her future life with him had been of little moment. She had something to live for, something of her own, something on which to lavish the love which no man had been able to call forth in her. Perhaps she was that kind of woman, she had thought – a mother and not a wife.

In this hour of agony, after the kindly doctor had had to leave her alone at last, confident in her strength, she scarcely thought of her husband nor of what this would mean to him, for from the first moment of the doctor's revelation, she had known that the child would die. She had never really connected her baby with Robert. They were too far apart in mind and in body. The child had seemed all her own.

But when he came to her, she knew that he had been told. She was not prepared for the fury of his anger.

'Something's got to be done,' he raged, pacing the room. 'These people are fools—fools! My son—and they're going to let him die! I'll get someone else. I've told them. There must be doctors who know more than they do! They're not going to let *my* son die!'

She watched him almost as if detached from it. She had lived through her hour alone. She had accepted the inevitable. Now she listened to him, watched him, the great Robert Grimtree having something he owned taken away from him.

'He's my son as well, Robert,' she said with a strange calm.

He spun round at her, his heavy face flushed, his beady little eyes filled with the impotent fury of a caged beast.

'You never wanted him as I did,' he said. 'You never want anything I give you. You're probably glad. You might have done something. You didn't even tell me at first. Perhaps you tried to get rid of it? Was that it? Did you? Did you?' snatching at her arm and shaking it as if by sheer physical violence he could wring from her some admission which would give him something, someone, on whom to place the blame and vent his fury.

She looked down at his hand but did not attempt to move it. Her face was hard. Her voice cold as ice.

'Take your hand away, Robert. You are behaving like a madman,' she said, and he gave her a baleful glance but set her free. 'Of course I didn't do anything, as you put it. Why should I?' but deep in her mind was the memory of those early weeks, of the futile appeal she had made to the doctor, of the pills she had bought at some shoddy chemist's in a back street, of the hot baths and strenuous exercises with which she had hoped, in that first fury of resentment and fear, to dislodge the embryo in her womb.

What if she had done something then? If this could be laid at her door? If all her life she would have to carry the burden of that fear? If she had bereft herself and brought on herself this hour of anguish?

That was a thing which no one, least of all Robert, must ever know. It was her own burden to bear.

'Because you hate me,' he flung at her. 'Because you never wanted to be my wife in anything but name and never wanted the child. Do you think I haven't known all the time? You thought when you married me that you were going to get what you wanted out of it without having to pay my price, didn't you? Didn't you?' glaring at her.

'I never refused it, Robert,' she said with icy calm.

'Not in so many words, perhaps, but when I compelled you to do your part, you behaved as if I were some loathsome reptile crawling over you. How much do you think I enjoyed that, eh? Eh?'

She turned from him.

'What good does all this do?' she asked. 'It cannot—save him,' and in spite of the terrific effort she was making at composure, her voice shook.

He left her and walked to the window and stood looking out, sick with anger and wretchedness and that queer, new, self disgust which she could make him feel. He did not really believe that she had tried to get rid of the child at the beginning any more than he believed she was glad that it might die. Something he did not understand made him want to hurt her even though already he was hating himself for doing so. He wanted to take her in his arms, to have her weep on his breast, to share with her his pain and distress, to be able to find words with which to console her.

He could not. Shut for years within the fortress of his pride and self sufficiency, the soul which he had found could not escape or find the consolation of its own expression.

'Something's got to be done,' he muttered at last as he strode towards the door. 'If not by these incompetent fools, then by somebody else. I'll see them—tell them—find out—' and he went storming from the room, shouting for the nurses, for the doctor, for the august and severe matron even, who was not in the least likely to obey the summons.

The storm raged through the clinic and was heard everywhere. Only in Verne's room was there silence and the stillness which comes after utter desolation. No one ventured to try to console her. Only when she asked for her baby was it put into her arms, and she held it with aching heart and a mind which vainly sought to fight its battle for life.

She did not want to see her husband again, and though she did not put this into words, the nurses kept him from visiting her, an easy task since, after perfunctory inquiry after her, all he wanted to do was to stand in the nursery and stare down at his child.

Since Verne would not go and leave the baby there, she stayed on in the clinic, but she had not to stay for very long. Robert called in the highest authorities, refusing to accept one opinion after another, behaving like a man beside himself, during the last days taking no notice of Verne at all, though she sat there holding the child hour after hour, and when he rushed in to see it, all he did was to stare down at it and rush out again to see if he could summon yet another authority to his aid.

It was of no avail, and the child died when it was six weeks old.

Though Robert had seemed on the point of collapse during the final days after his son's death he seemed as if he had put the whole thing behind him, and returned to his work with unabated fury to make money and yet more money, whilst Verne, paler, thinner, even more self contained, went about such work as she could find to do. If she shed tears, they were in secret and left no trace, nor did she mention the baby to anyone, accepting without a word the well meant condolences offered her and putting aside, after a brief, conventional answer, any letter which expressed them.

She had feared that Robert would invade her privacy again and force her to have another child, but her fears were unfounded, and she could not know that, on the other side of the door into her room, he often lay sleepless, torturing himself with pictures of her, seeing her in imagination as he had never done, coming willingly to his arms, matching his desire with her own, satisfying in both of them the burning passion that consumed him.

During the months after he had known of her pregnancy, he had given up his visits to the flat in Bloomsbury, but now he went back to

Hermione. She found him a changed man, often terrifying her by the fierceness of his possession of her, wreaking his vengeance on her, though she did not know it, because he could not have his wife's love and his child had died.

'You're a brute, Robbie, and I don't know why I put up with you,' sobbed Hermione after one of these occasions, when he had struck her and had kicked her savagely as she lay cringing before him on the floor.

'Because I pay you to,' he told her brutally. 'Here,' and he flung a handful of notes on the dressing table and strode out of the room, leaving her there.

Often his mind and body revolted at the thought of these orgies in which he indulged with the voluptuous Hermione, whose lust matched his own, but he knew that only by such means could he prevent himself from opening that closed door and going to Verne, even begging and imploring her as in some moods he might have done.

'Let her come to me if she wants me,' he told himself savagely, and yet he knew that she would never come, did not and never had wanted him to make love to her.

Chapter Seven

It was a few weeks after she had come home that a visitor was announced to Verne.

'Who is it, Parlow?' she asked listlessly.

'The lady did not give me a card, madam,' said the butler disapprovingly, 'but her name is Gorner. Mrs. Gorner.'

Mrs. Gorner? Verne searched her mind and remembered. Gorner was the man who had committed suicide after Robert had discovered his embezzlement at the Ordborough branch.

She went downstairs reluctantly. What on earth did Mrs. Gorner want with her?

Mary Gorner rose nervously from the edge of the chair. She was a small, thin woman with a pale face and tired looking eyes.

'Mrs. Grimtree, I do hope you don't mind my coming to see you,' she said nervously after Verne had greeted her perfunctorily. 'I—I didn't like to go to Mr. Grimtree after—after everything.'

'No, I hardly think it would have been wise,' agreed Verne. 'Is there something you want me to do for you? I know the circumstances. I was Mr. Grimtree's secretary at the time.'

'Yes. Yes, I know,' said Mrs. Gorner, fidgeting with the clasp of her handbag, a shabby and well worn one. 'You see—I realise now that I did a very silly thing, sending back that cheque—'

'What cheque?' asked Verne.

'The one Mr. Grimtree sent me, the five hundred pounds—'

'Five hundred pounds?' echoed Verne blankly. 'Mr. Grimtree sent you five hundred pounds? When?'

'At the time—the time when—when—'

115

'Yes, I know,' said Verne quickly, 'but I certainly didn't know anything about the cheque. Are you sure Mr. Grimtree sent it to you? Sent it himself?' incredulously, remembering the whole circumstances, and that Robert had indignantly repudiated the suggestion that a month's salary be sent after Gorner's suicide.

'Oh yes, Mrs. Grimtree. He sent a note with it, written in his own hand. I sent it back to him, the cheque. I know it was a stupid thing to do because I wanted it badly. I hadn't anything, you see, but after Mr. Grimtree saying he was going to prosecute and turning my husband off like that—and everything—and what happened—I felt I couldn't, so I—sent the money back, and of course I've never heard from him again. Why should I? But now—it's been very hard for me, and my little girl's never been strong and it's difficult to keep a daily job because of leaving her, and I thought—I hoped—'

She stumbled to a silence and Verne spoke quietly, her mind still stupefied by the woman's revelation. *Robert* had done that? Without saying a word even to her? It was so utterly out of keeping with his character as she knew it that it was hard to believe, and yet of course it must be true.

'You hoped Mr. Grimtree would offer you the money again?' she asked.

'Well, not the whole five hundred,' said Mrs. Gorner eagerly, 'it's not nearly as much as that, but at the shop where I've been working, a little draper's near where I live, they say that if I could put two hundred pounds into the business, I can work there with a share of the profits and live over the shop, which would mean I could still be near my little girl and give an eye to her without neglecting my work. Oh, Mrs. Grimtree, it would be such a godsend to me and I would pay Mr. Grimtree back every penny. I would really.'

Verne knew that, in spite of the extraordinary impulse he had had at the time, Robert was not in the least likely at this date, with the whole episode dead and buried, to have a similar impulse. She could imagine the anger he would have felt at having his gift sent back to him, and he prided himself on never forgiving or condoning an insult.

'I hardly think—' she began slowly, and then an idea occurred to her.

Mrs. Gorner had made a good impression on her. She felt that she was honest and trustworthy, and her love for her delicate child shone in her eyes and coloured her voice, and Verne knew what agony it could be to love a sick child.

When she had straightened out her mother's small affairs, she had discovered that somehow Mrs. Raydon had managed to maintain a small insurance policy on her life, taken out before her illness, and though the tiny pension she had been receiving had died with her, the amount of the policy, a little over two hundred pounds, had been paid to Verne.

She had put it into a bank account, at a branch near her home, and except that it had been a small comfort to her to know that she was no longer actually penniless, she had done nothing with it. It had stayed to her credit, augmenting the fifty pounds overpaid by Robert when he had given her the money for her debt to Bill Trailer.

'Mrs. Gorner,' she said now, 'I will lend you the two hundred pounds myself. There will be no need for you to say anything to my husband.'

The woman's eyes filled with tears and she took Verne's hand and held it against her cheek for a moment, unable to speak.

'I—I will repay it—every penny,' she said presently, whilst Verne stood feeling awkward and embarrassed. 'I can. I know I can. I work hard and I know the business. I was in it when I met my husband, and I know that if I am allowed to do things my own way, as they say I can, I can improve the business quickly. I can't—thank you—'

'Please don't try,' said Verne gently. 'I'll give you the cheque now.'

'But—the security—what shall I do about that? You will want something—'

Verne smiled very sweetly.

'No, I don't want anything but your word,' she said. 'Can't a woman trust another woman?'

'You're so good,' quavered Mrs. Gorner who, since she had lost her beloved young husband, had not met with many kindnesses. 'I would never have asked it for myself, but it's—for my girl—'

'I know,' said Verne. 'I have just lost my son, Mrs. Gorner.'

'Yes, I heard about it. I didn't like to say anything.'

'Please don't. There's nothing to say, is there? If you will just wait a minute, I'll get you the cheque. I'll make it out to "Bearer" so that you won't have any trouble in cashing it. May I offer you something before you go? Tea? Sherry perhaps?'

'No, nothing, thank you, Mrs. Grimtree. If I hurry, I can just catch the three thirty and get back before her bedtime. A neighbour's looking after her for me. I can't tell you, Mrs. Grimtree, how I feel about your kindness—and trusting me—'

'Please, Mrs. Gorner, don't,' said Verne, laying a hand on her shoulder for a moment. 'Let me know how you get on, but don't worry yourself to pay this back before it's really convenient, will you?'

'Thank you, but I shan't have any rest till it is paid back,' said Mrs. Gorner, and Verne wondered what she would have said had she known that the two hundred pounds represented almost the whole of the personal fortune of Mrs. Robert Grimtree.

After the visitor had gone, Verne sat and pondered over his action in sending the five hundred pounds to her, without a word to anyone and after the harsh things he had said about Gorner having made his bed and left other people to lie in it, which was just too bad but no concern of his.

She remembered how angry and disgusted she had been with him for refusing even the meagre month's salary but had insisted on instant dismissal without pay and with the threat of prosecution.

And on top of that, he had sent Mary Gorner five hundred pounds and kept it secret!

Would she ever understand the man? And how could he expect her to, if he hid from her any gratuitous kindness he did? Were there others? Did he go about doing good in secret? The thought was absurd and untenable. She could not believe it for a moment—and yet he had sent that cheque.

When had he ever done a gratuitous kindness to her, not prompted by any self centred motive? The clothes and the jewels he showered on her were to make her resplendent in the eyes of other people as his possession. The little acts of kindness and consideration he had shown her before Adrian was born had been because she was the outer shell covering his child and had therefore to be protected. True, he had given her the fifty pounds, but had she not asked him, as her undeniable right, for much more? For an allowance which would give her a little feeling of independence? The fifty pounds, flung at her, was a sop to his conscience, if he had one, because he knew how unjustifiable was his attitude over an allowance.

She had not seen Bill Trailer since they had parted at the airport when she had gone to Switzerland.

He had written her a brief, characteristic note when she had returned his loan, expressing in it his sympathy for her in the loss of her mother, but there had been nothing in it which she could not have shown to the world.

A short time after the death of the baby, however, she answered the telephone to find him at the other end of the wire.

'Verne? I just wanted to say how sorry I was to hear about—the baby.'

'Thank you, Bill. I don't want to talk about it.'

'I know. Look, Verne, what about meeting me for a spot of lunch or something? I'd like to see you again.'

She was tempted. Bill's voice from the happy past made a little melting point in the barrier of ice with which she had cut herself off from any proffered sympathy and kindness.

'I—don't know,' she said hesitantly.

'Oh, yes you do,' he told her in his cheerful fashion. 'Can you manage today? Where?'

'Let's go where we used to,' she said, burning her boats.

After all, what did it matter? He was only Bill.

He laughed.

'Is that grand enough for Mrs. Robert Grimtree?'

'Oh, Bill, I'm not grand at all. I'm just me,' she said, and he heard the rather forlorn little quaver in her voice. It was certainly time someone did something about Verne, and who better than himself?

'All right. Same place then. Shall I come and meet you?'

'No, I'll go there. Just after one?'

'Fine. I'll be waiting.'

She went in her own car, which Johnson had taught her to drive, and parked it as near the restaurant as she could, hoping she had duly observed all the regulations, the yellow markings, the one way streets, the traffic lights and pedestrian crossings and every other obstacle to peaceful parking she could think of, and went into the familiar place, with the same old odour of oil and garlic and tobacco and perspiring waiters.

And there was Bill as of old, too, in his well worn 'working' suit, his greasy Burberry hanging on a hook beside him, the same cheerful grin on his face.

'Oh, Bill,' she said, and heaved a sigh and smiled at him and dropped into the chair she had so often occupied before.

'You're thin, my queen,' he said. 'Been dieting or something?'

'No, just something,' she said. '*You're* putting on weight, Bill.'

'I know. Frustration,' he said without enlarging on that. 'I've ordered steak and chips for you, with lashings of onions. O.K.?'

'Yes,' she nodded and found herself with a better appetite than she had had for months.

To her relief, he did not speak of the baby and only in passing of her husband, who had recently brought off one of his big deals which had been duly recorded in the Press.

'There's something I want to ask you, Verne. What have you done with your flat? Have you still got it?'

'Well, in a way I suppose I have, though I don't know for how long. You see, Robert took it out of my hands when Mother went away and said he would pay the rent yearly. That was more than a year ago now, of course, but when I called at the agent's the other day to ask about it, I found that another year's rent had been paid, so I suppose Robert had given the order at the office to pay it annually, and had forgotten to rescind it. Why do you ask?'

'I wondered if you would let me have it. Rent it from you, of course. My digs have given me up, and not before time, and I thought that if that flat was not being used, you might consider me as a tenant.'

'Well—of course, Bill, so far as I am concerned, but as Robert pays the rent—'

'You think he might not view the suggestion very well? In that case, is there any need to tell him? I can pay the rent to you, and you can pay it back to him if you want to, though I don't imagine he's feeling the pinch of whatever that costs a week!'

It seemed senseless for the flat to be standing empty and still furnished whilst Bill was without a home, so though she felt doubtful about Robert's reactions to it if he knew, as Bill said, was there any need to tell him? In due course she would remind him that the lease need not be renewed, and Bill could carry on from there.

Bill was delighted.

'Are you in a hurry or could we go along and look the joint over now?' he asked. 'Just to see what I shall need to take?'

She agreed, and she left her car parked, on Bill's blithe assurances that he was known to the police, and went in his.

It was just one of those extraordinary coincidences which took Robert along that very street later in the afternoon, and he tapped at the glass panel.

'Isn't that Mrs. Grimtree's car, Johnson?' he asked.

'Yes, I think it is, sir,' replied the man.

'H'm,' said Robert. 'Well, drive on, man. Drive on. I don't want to stay here all day.'

What on earth was Verne doing round here? Nothing but greasy little restaurants and second hand clothes and junk shops. Though he kept his eyes open, he did not see her anywhere, and when later in the afternoon he sent Johnson home and took a taxi back there, the car was gone.

It looked almost as if she had been lunching there, but if so, who with? She would hardly go there on her own, and with a perfectly good lunch ready for her at home.

A subsequent inquiry satisfied him that she had not lunched at home.

Now who on earth would she be lunching with in that sort of locality?

Robert had never forgotten the young man he had seen at the airport, whom he had trailed afterwards to his newspaper office and who, he firmly believed, must have lent Verne the money for her fare. He had even, in a fit of jealous suspicion, employed a private detective to find out what he could about the young man, and he now knew his name, the nature of his job, where he lived and what in general were his habits.

But there had been nothing even remotely linking him with Verne other than that one episode at the airport, and after a time, Robert had let the matter drop. Now he was remembering it. What if somehow something *had* been going on, and they had managed to elude him?

The thought irked him, but it was not in his nature to go straight to Verne and either question or accuse her. He would bide his time.

Meantime Verne had spent an amusing hour with Bill, going through the flat out of which time had now taken the poignancy of the sting, though she turned her eyes away from the chair drawn close to the empty grate which had been her mother's and Bill, divining it, for he had spent many an hour with the two of them there, had taken an opportunity to move its position.

They had gone through the contents of the flat, the small store of linen, the cheap, gay china with the milk jug shaped like a pig which Bill had bought in a moment of irresponsibility, and they had decided that except for his books and pipes and one or two old treasures, he would not need to add anything to the equipment.

'When the time comes for me to take over the lease, I'll buy this lot from you as it stands,' he said, 'unless you'd like me to do so now?'

'Oh no, Bill, I couldn't think of it,' she said. 'You're more than welcome, and I think I should rather hate to take money for Mother's things,' though afterwards she told herself she had been silly, for whatever Bill paid for the furniture would help to replace the two hundred pounds she had given to Mrs. Gorner without much hope of getting it back, in spite of her reassurances. Two hundred pounds would be a lot of money to make out of a little draper's shop, with herself and a delicate child to keep, and only Verne's appreciation of the little woman's pride had prevented her from calling it a gift rather than a loan at the time.

Still, she could not take it from Bill, and she rather liked to think of him there, using the things and making it his home – Bill, her one link with the old life now so impossibly far away.

The only uncomfortable moment came just before they left the flat, when she was detaching from her key ring the latch key.

'There's another about somewhere, but you'd better take this as well,' she said.

His hand closed over hers and the key ring.

'No. Leave it there,' he said. 'I'd rather you had a key to the place. After all, it's yours—and always will be, so far as I am concerned.'

She looked down at their joined hands, colouring a little.

'I shan't want it, Bill,' she said.

'You may think you won't, but you never know, and I'd prefer to think that you can come here if you want to,' and he took the keys from her and opened her bag and put them into it.

The next moment his arms were around her and though she struggled involuntarily, in the end she yielded, standing still and close to him.

'Bill, please don't,' she whispered.

But he kissed her, gently and tenderly, holding her unresponsive lips with his own until at last, with a little sigh, he let her draw them away.

'I'd say you haven't been kissed for a very long time,' he said. 'Your lips are like a vestal virgin's. What goes on in high places nowadays?'

'I can't discuss my private life with you, Bill,' she said with an attempt at aloof dignity which only made him laugh.

'I can draw my own conclusions. You're frozen, my sweet, and you're afraid of the thaw setting in.'

He had continued to hold her loosely, and now she drew herself away from his arms.

'Bill, please let me go, and—I don't want this at all.'

He smiled and patted her reassuringly.

'All right. All right—but remember that all's fair in love and war, and that this isn't war.'

She turned from him blindly and began to put on her gloves, relieved that he did not attempt to detain her, and when they were in his car everything seemed so normal, Bill the familiar undemanding friend again, that she wondered if she had been silly, turning a molehill into a mountain. They had so often kissed in the past, and there had been nothing in the kiss he had just given her to make it any different from the almost brotherly ones of the old days. It had probably meant nothing at all to him, and she had behaved like an idiot and as if he had actually been making love to her.

A day or two later, Robert told her he was going north on business.

'No point in your coming,' he said. Adding, 'Oh, unless you want to, of course,' indifferently. 'I shall be rushed all the time, meetings and things and you'd be stuck in the hotel.'

Once he would have told her what it was all about, discussed it with her, taken her with him in mind into the hub of things, and she reflected that life had been more interesting for Robert Grimtree's secretary than it was for his wife.

She merely concurred, asking what he would need to take and quite unnecessarily busying herself with seeing that his packing was done, but when he had gone, she did not have the sense of relief and freedom she had expected. His personality so dominated the house and their joint existence in it that it felt empty and too quiet.

'I'm missing my chains,' she thought grimly, wondering how to fill her time now that she had the evenings on her hands as well.

She bethought herself of something she had once tried to do, which was to finish some work her father had begun long ago, a collection of stories of the Victorian era, half fact, half fiction and linked together by the life of an imaginary family.

Her mother had encouraged her in it, liking the idea, but after she had gone to Grimtree's, Verne had put it aside for want of time. It had intrigued her to find that, in the odd way in which heredity makes itself known, she had the same trick of words, the same power to express the gentle, ironical amusement her father had felt towards those favoured, self sufficient Victorians so unaware of the gathering shadows which would blot out them and their ways forever.

She decided to go on with the work, even if it were never to find a publisher, but if it did, the money would be hers, her own earnings again, with just that much independence of Robert. She had never failed to feel humiliated and exasperated by her complete dependence.

Hunting for the manuscript, which was as yet a mass of untidy papers which would, when finished, have to be correlated into some coherent form, she remembered that she had left a considerable portion of it in a box in a forgotten cubbyhole at the flat.

She hesitated whether to ring Bill or not, but decided that it would be better for him to remain in ignorance of the fact that she was going there. She could not even be quite sure that he had moved in.

To her relief, the flat was empty, but there was abundant evidence that Bill was in occupation, for the place was untidy, the bed unmade and the breakfast dishes piled in the sink. She would have to get him a woman to clean up, she thought, automatically setting to work to do it herself.

It was surprisingly pleasant to be working there again, though how she had hated washing up and cleaning in the old days! It was all so familiar here, things going naturally into their right places as she worked, and she even caught herself singing as she swept and dusted.

She realised how unwise she had been to do so when, going outside the door to put out the kitchen refuse for collection, she saw the opposite door open and Mrs. Biggin's head appear. It was too opportune to be accidental, she thought, and that garrulous woman's surprise at sight of her was overdone.

'Why, if it isn't you, Verne! Or ought I to say Mrs. Grimtree now?' with an arch smile. 'I was only thinking about you the other day and wondering whether you had given up the flat, or just let it. Such a nice young man. Didn't he used to visit you when you lived here?'

'He's an old friend—of my mother's,' said Verne.

'Oh? Well, I thought he was yours, being more your age, of course, but it's nice for him to be able to have your flat, isn't it?' with great affability over the barbed words. 'And look at you, in an apron with a duster over your head, doing *housework!* I should have thought you'd have brought one of your servants—but then, I suppose that wouldn't have done. What I mean is, they'd be too grand, wouldn't they?' which Verne knew was not at all what she meant.

'I came to collect some papers I had left here, and thought I might clear up a bit,' said Verne, hating the need to explain anything at all to the woman.

'Men are so helpless without a woman to fuss round them, aren't they? What about me making us a nice cuppa? I'm sure you must be tired after doing housework, and you not used to it now. I'll just pop the kettle on and bring the things across and we can have a nice, cosy chat. We shan't get a word in edgeways with old Gran sitting there, the old nuisance.'

It's very kind of you, Mrs. Biggin, but I've just made myself some tea,' said Verne firmly. 'I shall be going in a minute or two.'

She fled inside, irritated by the occurrence, and when presently the doorbell rang, she did not answer it.

Her search for the papers was successful, and she sat down at the kitchen table to sort them over, as much of the bundle was rubbish which she could burn, but she became absorbed in her task and sat on, reading, automatically correcting and forgetting all about the time until, with a shock of dismay, she heard the key turn in the front door and knew that it was too late to escape.

Bill stopped in the hallway, whistled in surprise, and then came straight to her.

She had not cleaned herself up, the rummaging in the cupboard having been a dusty job, and he looked with amusement at the duster on her head and the apron, discovered in a drawer, over her dress. There was even a dusty smear across one cheek where she had encountered a cobweb.

'Well, well, now isn't this nice?' he said. 'A real homecoming. Any tea on the way? I bought some yesterday, but I'm blest if I know where it is now, it's all so tidy. How are you, poppet?'

'Oh, Bill, I didn't mean you to catch me here,' she said. 'I came for some papers I'd forgotten, and it was in such a mess that I thought I'd better tidy you up a bit,' she said, her first confusion leaving her at his cheerful acceptance of the situation.

'The old lady across the way, tire old one, not the blowsy one, offered to come in and do a bit for me, but I told her I could manage. Can't the other one talk! She seems to live at her front door. Oh, here's the tea. Where have you put the milk, woman?'

'Where it ought to be,' said Verne, showing him. 'Old Mrs. Biggin's a great dear, but as for Flo! She caught me, of course, and had a few things to say about my being here and I had to shut the door in her face. I think I'd better make my exit down the fire escape!'

To her relief, he showed no sign of wanting to take up their relationship where they had left it off a few days earlier, and she felt at ease with him by the time they had made the tea and she had cooked for him the eggs and bacon without which he informed her he could not support life.

She refused to share them.

'I've got to eat an umpteen course dinner when I get back,' she said.

'Well, don't go back. Ring up and tell your slaves you'll be out. There's only you so you won't get beaten and locked up.'

'How do you know there's only me?' she asked, choosing to ignore the last part.

'Grimtree's gone up north, hasn't he?'

'He has, but I can't think how *you* know.'

'All Fleet Street's humming with it. All sorts of rumours, of course, about the great Rag King, and I don't suppose any of them are true, but it's whispered that he's pulling off some terrific deal with Ferrimore's. Didn't you know?'

'With Ferrimore's?' she echoed incredulously. 'Why, we've always been at each other's throats.'

'That's as may be, and of course you know how wild rumours can be, but your old man is an astute one, and if he can get hold of Ferrimore's—'

'But, Bill, it would cost the earth!'

'Well, he's got the earth, hasn't he? Don't let's bother about him, though. Any more tea in the pot? And next time, put a bit more in. I like a bit of colour in mine.'

'It's like treacle now,' she pointed out.

'I like treacle. I must say you know how to cook bacon. This is very jolly, isn't it? Let's do it again.'

'You know it's only an accident, and I didn't mean to get involved in these papers at all, but—they're very fascinating, Bill. Listen to this,' and she took the sheet she had been correcting and read some of it out to him, her father's thin, spidery writing difficult to read but his phrasing so lucid and his choice of words so delightfully apt.

They laughed together, and in a burst of confidence, she told him what she proposed to do with the writings. He was enthusiastic, and discussed the practical side of it, giving her one or two suggestions which she accepted gratefully.

'What's so odd about it, Bill, is that I find I can write in the same style as my father did. The words and phrases just come. The trouble is that whereas he had all his knowledge or facts in his head, I haven't, and I don't know where best to get them. Though he was a generation back, he wasn't a Victorian himself, of course, but he was brought up by his grandmother who used to regale all his young days with tales of her own youth—which must have been a rather lurid one if some of these stories in here are true! Where am I to get my information from, Bill? I suppose I could sit for hours in the British Museum's reading rooms, but the very idea appals me. It's so silent there and out of this world that I feel I should become as dry and dusty as some of their shelves must be.'

'What you really want is some newspapers of the times,' said Bill. 'I believe I could get hold of some for you.'

'Oh, Bill, could you?' she asked excitedly. 'How?'

'Well, there are our own files down in the dungeons. You know we've been running since Adam? Our first flashlight was of the serpent's tail whisking round the tree. Nobody ever looks at the things now, and I dare say I could find a way of boning some so that you could have a look at them.'

'But wouldn't you get into trouble? They must be priceless.'

'Probably be shot at dawn if anyone found out, but I'm prepared to risk it. I don't think I could let you take them away, though. You see, if it *were* discovered, I might be able to rake up a tale so long as the files were still ostensibly in my possession that is on my premises. Would that matter to you?'

'You mean—I'd have to work on them here?' she asked doubtfully.

'Anything wrong with that? I shouldn't be here. As a matter of fact, tomorrow would be a good day as I've got to go off on a job in the afternoon and won't be back till goodness knows when. Have lunch with me somewhere tomorrow—no, better have it here, as I daren't leave the files in the car and we can't hump them around. Will you do that? Meet me here for lunch, and afterwards I'll leave you in peace with the files, and when you go, you can put 'em somewhere safe, in the gas oven perhaps. They usually seem to survive fires! When I come home, I'll dig 'em out and take 'em to bed with me, resting my comfortless head upon them and dreaming, oh my darling love, of thee!'

She could not take exception to his gay quotation from Cyril Fletcher. It was spoken quite impersonally, and for the rest of the short time they spent together, his attitude to her was unexceptional, that of a cheerful companion, almost a congenial brother.

Since she could not miss such an opportunity, she agreed to his plan. Her mind was reasonably at rest. He was not going to try to make love to her, and, after all, she was coming here to work.

She was still working the next day, fascinated and absorbed, when she heard the wireless in the next flat announcing the seven o'clock news, and came back to the Elizabethan age with a start.

Seven o'clock! And she had ordered an early dinner with the idea of working at home afterwards on the material she had gathered during the afternoon! She had said she would be home by seven.

She picked up the telephone and spoke to Parlow, who received with perfect calm her slightly incoherent explanation that she had been delayed and would not be in for dinner after all, but would ask for something cold if she needed it later.

She went back to the files, yellow and faded and incredible, and all thought of food left her mind.

It was eleven o'clock when Bill came in to find her there, bent over the kitchen table where she had been working, tired, hungry, cramped from the long hours on a hard kitchen chair, but with her eyes shining out of their dark rings.

'Hey, what's all this?' he asked.

She sprang up, dismayed.

'Oh, Bill, whatever's the time?' she cried.

'Getting on for midnight,' he said. 'Have you had any food, you gawk?'

'No, I don't think so. No, I haven't. I've been too busy. Oh, Bill, these are simply fascinating! I just couldn't leave them, and even now I haven't half finished with them. They've got everything—the dates, the atmosphere. Just listen to this advertisement!'

'Not now. Food. *And* drink. Where's the hurry? You can get at them again tomorrow.'

'Oh, Bill, can I really? Haven't you to take them back?'

'Might as well be hanged for a sheep as a lamb, and no one has the remotest idea they have left the dungeons. Clear away now, and let's eat. Lucky I brought these back with me,' putting down the parcels he had brought in, amongst them two bottles of beer.

'I ought to dash back, of course, but I really am hungry, and the maids will have a fit if I arrive home at midnight demanding food. I have already cancelled the dinner I'd ordered. What have we got?'

They made merry over a superlative meal of ready cooked food, washing it down with the beer, over which she made a grimace and was twitted by him for having a 'champagne palate'. It was long past midnight when she left, stealing down the stairs with him like a burglar to find, to her horror, that a policeman was strolling watchfully up and down past her parked car.

'This your car, miss?' he asked civilly.

'Yes. Yes, I'm afraid it is,' she said, making frantic signs to Bill to go away.

'Been parked without lights. Mustn't do that here, you know,' said the policeman solemnly. 'Afraid I must ask you for your name and address,' taking out his notebook.

'Oh—must I?' she besought him, but the arm of the law was unbending, and though Bill told him who he was and tried to make out that the lady was working for him, he was adamant.

Verne was tempted to give her maiden name and address and did so, and then, to her horror, the man demanded her driving licence.

'Not the same name,' he observed, 'and not the same address either. Now look, miss—madam—you'll only make it worse for yourself and put me in a spot if you try any funny business. Suppose you tell me who you are? Miss V. Raydon of Beckett Mansions, or Mrs. Grimtree of Wellington Gate.'

She gave him a last appealing glance and then gave up.

'Mrs. Grimtree,' she said. 'Oh, please, please don't do anything about it, will you? It would be—I mean—can't I do something—'

Bill gave her a warning shove, afraid that she might have been going to offer the police officer a bribe – as she probably would have done if she had had enough money in her bag!

'Got to do my duty, madam, and you know you shouldn't have been parked here without lights all this time. The officer I relieved when I came on duty told me it had been here since before dusk, too. Don't worry, madam. They won't make it very hard on you.'

'You mean I'm going to be summonsed? People will know?' she asked, appalled.

'Oh, nobody takes any notice of parking cases these days,' he told her reassuringly, 'and if your gentleman friend is on the newspapers, as he says, he'll probably know what to do. Leaving now, madam? Got your keys?' and she found herself handing them to him meekly and waiting whilst he unlocked the car door for her and held it open.

'Thank you. I—I'm sorry,' she said, and turned on the ignition.

'You haven't got your lights on, madam,' he warned her, and she switched on and drove away, wondering whether Bill, now that he was left with a fellow man, would manage to do anything for her.

What if it got about that she, Verne Grimtree, had left a block of flats at midnight in company with a man, and that her car had been parked outside it for eleven hours!

In the morning, Bill rang her up to reassure her.

'Not to worry,' he said. 'Watch out for the summons coming, and when it does, let me have it. No defence, of course, and no need for you even to appear. I'll go for you and admit the offence and pay the fine, and it won't get into the papers, of course. I'll see to that. How do you feel?'

'A bit better after that,' she said.

'Coming along to lunch?'

'I—yes, I suppose so,' she said.

'O.K. Find somewhere else to park the car this time, and switch on the lights before you leave it! See you later.'

Robert was mercifully still away when the summons arrived. She was fined one pound, which Bill paid into court for her, and he also saw to it that so choice a little titbit did not find its way into the papers.

But it had been an unpleasant experience for her. For one thing, Robert would have been extremely angry at his wife being convicted of an offence against the law, even a parking offence. He was a rigid law abider, as far as the letter of the law was concerned, and he prided himself on never having infringed, either personally or through his chauffeur, any of the many laws set out to snare the motorist, and had Johnson been convicted of Verne's offence of parking without lights, he would have been instantly dismissed.

Apart from that, she was uncomfortably aware of the light in which she would have stood had Robert discovered that she had spent all those hours during his absence in a man's flat, even though it was technically her own, and had not left until after midnight. She could tell herself how wholly innocently those hours had been spent, even after Bill himself arrived, but how would it have looked to anyone else?

So absorbed and excited was she, however, about the work she had undertaken and the access Bill had given her to these invaluable records, that she continued to go to the flat, not only whilst she could retain the riles, but also after Bill had taken them back and even after Robert had returned to London. She did not want him to know about the work, afraid (with reason, she felt) that he would contrive to stop her from finishing it and certainly from publishing it. His ideas on wives who had careers of their own were emphatic, and though she did not dignify her writing by the title of 'career, Robert would take it as such and under his displeasure, even if she had the courage to defy him, the heart would have gone out of it and she would not be able to work with her present absorbed and happy mind.

Bill had 'borrowed' an old typewriter for her from his office, inwardly surprised that she did not buy a new one for herself as one would have expected Robert Grimtree's wife to do, but he made no comment on it, having learnt that the surest way to scare her off and spoil their present relations was to refer in any way to that other existence in which he had no part. Through his good offices, she was able to introduce herself to a publisher who might be interested in the eventual production of *Pantalets,* the title which Herbert Raydon had himself devised for the work. She gave her mother's maiden name, Lorna Derring, under which she concealed her identity, and she was excited to hear from him later, in a letter addressed to Miss Lorna Derring at Bill's flat, that he thought favourably of the part of the manuscript which she had submitted to him, as a fair copy, and that he would be pleased to consider the whole when completed.

It was not as easy to spend many consecutive hours at the flat after her husband returned, but she was helped by the fact that whatever business Robert had done in the north kept him very fully occupied at his office, even taking him back frequently in the evenings, when he would tell her casually not to wait up for him. He was often out until after midnight and even then would remain downstairs in his library for several more hours.

He did not tell her what the business was, and she did not ask him. Though at first, when she was newly released from her position as his trusted secretary, he had discussed business affairs with him, he had long ceased to do so, and beyond an occasional growl at poor Miss Bright's inefficiency, he rarely mentioned the office.

Gradually their lives drew farther and farther apart, and Verne would have been amazed and incredulous could she have known how much she was in his thoughts, nor how often, mentally exhausted by work which he would never allow anyone else to do for him, distrusting everyone, he stood on the other side of that closed door and longed to go to her, not for any satisfaction of his bodily needs but just to be with her, to lie quietly at her side, to talk to her a little about his ever pressing problems, to hold her hand in his and feel the soft sweep of her hair against his cheek.

He realised more clearly than she how far apart they had drifted, they who had never been near except perhaps in the months before their child was born. He did not know how to stop the drift because he was not capable of understanding what had caused it. He was sincerely sorry for the occasion on which he had, in his rage and frustration, compelled her to his will, an act which had resulted in the birth of the child. He had almost forgotten it, however, his mind over occupied with the getting of his wealth, his ruling passion. Until he had made Verne his wife, his relations with women had all been of the type shared with Hermione. He was unable to recognise the difference, physically, between women who could be bought with money, and women who could be bought with nothing else but love. He did not know how to woo a woman. He only knew how to satisfy his physical need of them, and so far in his life those needs, and their satisfaction, had been no more to him than the need of food to assuage hunger, food to be eaten and forgotten.

He searched his mind, but except for the happenings of that night, which he now admitted to himself had been a mistake, he did not know where he had gone wrong with Verne. Had she not had everything any normal woman could want? Had he ever denied her anything? Had he ever questioned her spending or quibbled at them? Had he not given her jewels, furs, and a car of her own? True, there had been that nonsense about giving her spending money, but what did she want it for? She could pledge his credit anywhere, and for anything, without question.

Things were in that state when the anonymous letters from 'a friend' began to arrive.

Chapter Eight

At first Grimtree took no notice of the things. Like most important and wealthy men, he was accustomed to receiving all sorts of communications, begging letters, threatening letters, letters suggesting all manner of improbable ventures, their writers reviling him later for ignoring them.

These, however, were slightly different. They contained vague hints rather than any definite statement, and at first they were so worded that he did not connect them with Verne. Then one came, in the same obviously disguised handwriting, which made him read it a second time and put it into the locked drawer of his library table rather than into the fire or, torn into contemptuous shreds, the waste paper basket.

'Most husbands would be interested in what goes on at Beckett Mansions,' the 'friend' had written, and the 'husbands' had been underlined.

Beckett Mansions? It rang a bell in his mind, though at first the memory escaped him.

Then he remembered.

Hadn't that rubbishy little flat where Verne had lived with her mother been in some place like that?

He looked it up and found that his memory had not been at fault.

But what had Beckett Mansions to do with Verne now? If he had ever thought of the place since, he would have concluded that it had been given up long ago. It was more than a year since Mrs. Raydon had died, and Verne could have had no possible use for it.

When he reached the office, he rang for Miss Bright.

'Do we pay the rent of a flat at this address?' he asked her, giving her the note he had made of it. Find out.'

135

She came back with the information that, on his instructions, the rent for a year had been paid just after his marriage, and again a year later, each time in advance.

'Who paid it last December?' he snarled. 'And what for?'

I authorised the payment under your written authority, Mr. Grimtree,' said Miss Bright, producing the note from her file. 'As far as I know, you have never rescinded the order so naturally I paid it.'

'Well, don't do it any more,' he growled and scribbled 'Cancelled' across the order and signed it.

What on earth did that woman (for of course it must be a woman) mean by saying he ought to be interested in the place? What had Verne done with it? Sublet it as a brothel or something? And why make such a pointed reference to 'husbands'? Was she suggesting that Verne ran the brothel, or what?

He decided that, for Verne's sake, he had better look into it lest, in ignorance, she *had* let the flat to undesirable parties. He did not want to ask her about it in case he had to reveal the source of his interest, and that he was taking notice of anonymous letters. But for a few days the matter slipped his memory, by which time a further note had arrived, this time opening up new possibilities and considerable discomfort in his mind.

If you are not interested in Beckett Mansions, perhaps you would be in Beckett Square. What about the car that was parked there without lights all night on the fifth of December? Ask the police about it.

The note was signed, like the others, 'A friend'.

Whose friend? he thought grimly. Not his, to disturb him like this when he already had all he wanted on his plate—and not Verne's, if the foul thing, whatever it was, were concerned with her.

In whom else would he be personally interested as a husband?

If, as he supposed, the suggestion was that the car parked in Beckett Square was Verne's, how on earth had she come to leave it there all night? And since the police had been concerned, they had obviously found it there without lights.

Growling inwardly at himself for doing so, but unable to thrust the matter out of his mine, he took a taxi to Beckett Square, dismissed it and stood staring up at the grimy outside of the flats. It was difficult now to believe that his beautiful, elegant wife had ever lived there, and not so long ago either, and he found that he could not identify the windows from the outside.

He mounted the stairs to the flat and, with inward misgivings to which he could give no name, he rang the bell and waited.

There was no answer, but when he had given a second loud more peremptory ring, the door of the opposite flat was opened and a small, frail, very clean old lady appeared, looking at him with a friendly smile.

'If you want Mr. Trailer, I'm afraid he's out,' she said. 'I go in and do for him, and he said not to get him anything for lunch today as he wouldn't be in. But he'll be back presently, I expect. Before tonight, anyway,' and she nodded encouragingly.

Grimtree glowered at her and she shrank back quickly, but he muttered something about its not being important and strode off down the stairs again.

Trailer? That was the name of the man who had been with Verne at the airport that time, the man he had always believed had lent her the money which he, her husband, had refused.

Trailer.

And he lived in her. Flat – or rather, *his* flat, since he certainly paid the rent of it! His angry suspicions awoke in full strength and raged through him. He recalled word for word that note which had suggested that, as a husband, he would be interested in what was going on in this place!

He strode round to the local police station to make guarded inquiries about a parking incident on the night of the fifth of December, and was referred to the police court which would have dealt with such an alleged offence, and from there he obtained the information he sought. So it had been Verne's car, and though it had not been there all night, she herself had claimed it after midnight, after it had been parked for a matter of ten or eleven hours. For this, she had been fined a pound, which amount had been duly paid into court, the defendant not putting in a personal appearance but being represented at the court by William Adrian Trailer, of 17 Beckett Mansions.

After the first rush of his fury had subsided, it leaped up again.

William Adrian Trailer. William *Adrian* Trailer.

Adrian!

The name Verne had chosen for their son.

Their son?

He could scarcely walk along the pavement, reeling like a drunken man, and he hailed a passing taxi, clambered in with his legs giving way under him and snarled to the man to drive him anywhere.

'I don't care where you go. I want to think,' he said, and let himself slump in the corner of the cab, his eyes closed, his mouth working as if struggling with words that would not come.

The driver moved off. His fare had had a drop too much, obviously, for all it was only three in the afternoon. Still, he looked as if he could pay all right, and he would probably sleep it off if he drove about for a bit. Might as well run out to Kingston and take a look at a bit of property he thought of buying there. A good chance, and getting paid for it as well.

Still, he hadn't exactly reckoned to drive for four hours, and he had begun to wonder anxiously whether his fare had passed out on him when Grimtree leaned forward and told him curtly to drive to Wellington Gate.

'Mrs. Grimtree in?' he asked Parlow.

The butler permitted himself to look faintly surprised as he took his master's hat and coat.

'Madam came in, sir, but she has gone out again. You are dining with Mr. Templar tonight, so madam said she would not require dinner.'

'Know where she went?' he snapped.

Parlow's eyebrows became actually elevated.

'No, sir. Madam did not inform me,' he said.

'Huh,' grunted Grimtree and shut himself in his library and sat with his head sunk in his hands.

Of course she had gone to that damned flat, gone to that blasted Trailer – *Adrian* Trailer. He realised now that he had seen very little of her lately, that she had often only just come in when he returned, that she had seemed different, brighter, more alert, happier.

Happier because of Trailer!

The thought bit like salt into his torn, bleeding mind.

Another man. All this time. All what time? During the whole of their married life? Right from the start? Had they made that sort of a monkey out of him? What was the word for it? Cuckoo? No, worse than that. A cuckoo was merely an idiotic bird.

Scarcely aware what he did, he seized the dictionary which always lay close to his hand. He was never sure of his spelling and now he hadn't Verne to put him right.

Cubsha. What on earth was that? Here it was. Cuckold: a man whose wife commits adultery.

His face dropped down again across the open book and he knew the bitterness of death – the death of the spirit to which bodily death is a mere passing nothingness.

Verne.

Verne.

He loved her, loved her with all the strength of his being, with depths he had not known lay within him, with that part of him which was not of the body.

He lost all count of time, did not even hear the several knocks at the locked door, the soft trying of the handle, the whispered colloquy outside, did not know that Jeffery Templar had rung up to know where he was, and that Parlow, not venturing to put the call through to him in the library, had whispered back that Mr. Grimtree was not well and might not be able to keep the dinner appointment.

His master's face when he had pushed past him to go to the library, locking himself in, had been enough to make him sure of those facts.

Verne had that afternoon had a second interview with her prospective publisher, and she had excitedly called up Bill to give him her news.

'Oh, Bill, listen! Mr. Garret has seen the rest of the manuscript, and he has offered to publish it! He's going to send me the proposed terms by tonight's post, but he wants me to alter the last chapter, that's all.

You know, the bit about the Prince Consort. He doesn't think it will do, but I can easily alter that. Aren't you thrilled?'

'You bet I am! Congratulations,' said Bill. 'How about coming round tonight to celebrate? I'll bring home a feast. Nicer there than going out, don't you think?'

'All right,' agreed Verne blithely. 'I'm free this evening. Robert's having dinner with his legal crony. In any case, Mr. Garret wants me to think out how I'm going to alter the ending and ring him up about it later in the evening, and of course it wouldn't be so easy to do that at home. I'll be round about seven.'

'Good. I'll go out and get the fatted calf and I think tonight calls for champagne rather than beer!'

She laughed excitedly and rang off.

She had no idea what sort of terms Mr. Garret would offer her, but at the moment that was of little importance. The important thing was getting the book published at all, and she went to her writing case and took out a faded photograph of her parents, standing together with their arms entwined and a look of such utter, confident happiness on their young faces that the picture blurred a little before Verne's eyes.

'You dears,' she said. 'Do you know? Oh, I do hope you do! Surely if you are anywhere, you're with me now, bless you.'

If they were, with a foreknowledge of events, they must have been feeling very sad for happy, unsuspecting Verne at that moment.

Bill had arrived when she reached the flat, and a savoury smell came floating to meet her as she fitted her key into the lock.

'I've moved all your things into the other room,' he called out to her, 'and you can do your work or whatever you want to do in there. The kitchen's all mine for the moment and you're not even to ask what it is.'

'It smells heavenly,' she said, laughing. 'All right. It suits me. I'm full of ideas waiting to be let out.'

They dined magnificently on fried chicken and mushrooms, with a palatial iced sweet just in process of disintegration since there was no refrigerator, and they drank champagne out of tumblers and toasted Lorna Derring and *Pantalets* until they were not quite sure which was which.

And at ten o'clock, the appointed hour, Verne put through her call to Mr. Garret's private residence and read out to him, rather shakily and with many throat clearings, the new ending to the book.

'Yes, I like that very much, Miss Derring,' he said. 'That's just what I want. Send it along to me tomorrow and we'll get that contract fixed up. I don't mind telling you that both my Readers who have had the book are very complimentary about it, and though we may not set the Thames on fire just yet, I think we've got a modest winner.'

She put down the receiver after struggling with her confused thanks, and threw herself precipitately into Bill's arms and hugged him, not in the least because he was Bill but because he happened to be there, and she had to hug somebody.

'Oh, Bill, isn't life wonderful? Aren't you glad you know me? Aren't you proud of me? I'm up and coming!' and she hugged him again, kissing him without any conscious thought of doing so and leaving smears of lipstick all over his face.

And just then the bell rang.

'Who on earth's that? At this time of night?' asked Verne, beginning to disengage herself from his more than willing arms, though he would not let her wholly go.

The telephone was in the tiny hall, so that they were close to the front door.

'It'll only be old Mrs. Biggin,' said Bill easily. 'Let's have her in and fill her up with champagne, shall we?' and, with his arm still closely around her, he pulled back the catch of the door and opened it.

Robert Grimtree stood outside.

Instinctively Verne pushed Bill's arm away from her, her face going red and white by turns, her eyes widening in consternation. She had no idea what Bill looked like, nor what he was doing. The only ones who mattered were herself and Robert.

'May I come in?' he asked curtly, and did so without waiting for a reply, closing the door behind him and standing with his back to it, a huge, square, solid figure which could dominate almost any place, and which in this little flat seemed to fill it.

Verne could not speak, but moved blindly aside, and Grimtree, after a glance at the open door of the sitting room, walked into it and looked round.

The remains of their feast were strewn about the table, the magnum champagne bottle in the middle, and hanging from the light fitting above it were half a dozen coloured balloons which Bill had brought home and insisted on displaying above their heads. They bobbed and floated there ridiculously, the crowning touch of folly and indecency in Grimtree's eyes.

'I seem to have disturbed something,' he said grimly.

'We—I—I can explain, Robert—' stammered Verne, not knowing how and where to begin.

'I've no doubt you can,' he interrupted her roughly. 'I don't want your explanations. I can see them with my own eyes. How long has this been going on?'

'Sir, I think I should—' began Bill, speaking for the first time. 'I don't want to hear what you have to say,' snarled Robert. 'This is a matter between me and my wife for the moment. Your turn will no doubt come later. Well, Verne? How long have you been making a fool of me like this? From the beginning? Even before you tricked me into marrying you and fathering your brat?'

'Robert! You can't know what you're saying?' cried Verne, aghast and ashamed that Bill should hear him say such things to her.

'I know perfectly well,' he said, and by this time the red fury of his anger had burnt to a white hot, still and molten mass. If he could have killed her at that moment, he would have done it by slow strangulation, not by a swift blow nor a shot.

Bill moved in again.

'Really, Mr. Grimtree, I cannot allow—'

'*You* cannot allow? There's no question of what you can or cannot allow, young man. This is between me and my wife,' and put out a hand and pushed Bill aside as if he were no more than a troublesome gnat buzzing about him.

And Bill, to Verne's surprise now that her mind was beginning to function again, seemed to permit and accept the pushing aside, for he stood there, a little in the background, watching and listening as if, as Robert had said, he had no part in it.

'As for you, Verne, what I have to say can be finished in a few minutes. I've done with you. I've given you everything you wanted and denied you nothing, and in return you've been carrying on this dirty business behind my back and using the very flat I pay for to do it. You've hoodwinked me to the top of your bent. Clever girl—but not quite clever enough. You didn't keep it quiet enough, not quiet enough to keep me from getting letters through the post about—you, or from getting yourself into the police court. And but for that car parking business, I might never have known why you named your brat Adrian. Adrian! I thought it was a fancy name at the time, but I didn't know just how fancy! Well, that's all. No one gets a second chance to make a cuckold out of Robert Grimtree. I know what that word means, and if you don't, look it up in the dictionary like I did. We've finished, Verne. Don't come back to my house any more, not even tonight. When I get in, I shall give the servants orders not to admit you. As for your clothes, they can stay where they are until they rot. You came to me in the things you stood up in. You can go in them too. That's all.'

Verne had stood rooted to the spot, listening in silence to the incredible things he was saying, and gradually her first distress changed to an anger as hot and unquenchable as his own. Very straight and still she stood, her face white as parchment except where two red spots burnt high in her cheeks, and her eyes looked black as coals.

'Not quite all, Robert,' she said when he had finished. 'There's my part of it. I might in time have forgiven you for some of the things you have said, even for condemning me without giving me any criminal's chance to defend himself, but what I can never forgive is the wrong you have done to my child, our child, Robert. As for coming back to your house, nothing would induce me to. As you very rightly say, we've finished.'

Bill moved uncomfortably and began to speak again, but in an oddly nervous and hesitant fashion quite out of keeping with his usual gay bravado.

'Mr. Grimtree, you have said some pretty harsh things, and I agree with—with Mrs. Grimtree—about your not giving her a chance to defend herself, to explain—'

It was almost as if he were apologising for Verne even whilst with his words he tried to defend her. He seemed, to her mind, to be making an attempt to patch things up between her and Robert.

She gave him a quick, surprised look and broke in quietly on his stumbling speech.

'There's nothing to say, Bill.'

Grimtree spun round on his heel without another word or look and walked out of the room and out of the flat, banging the door behind him.

They listened to the sound of his footsteps ringing on the stone staircase, heard them for a moment echoing along the street. Then Verne gave a long, shuddering sigh and dropped into a chair and rested her head on her hands amongst the litter of their supper dishes.

She could not speak. The thing was too sudden, too devastating. It was as if the heavens had opened and a bomb had dropped into the centre of her life, leaving nothing whole or recognisable.

She felt Bill move and lay a hand on her shoulder.

'I'm sorry, Verne,' he said. 'The infernal blackguard! What do you want me to do about it? I'll do anything, of course.'

She lifted her head, looking blankly in front of her.

'What can we do, Bill? What can anyone do? I'm—out flat. I can't even think any more. How could he have taken things for granted like that? Simply believed me to be rotten without even doubting it for a moment? He said something about letters, but who could have written to him? And what could they have told him about me, about us? There's *been* nothing, Bill. I almost wish there had! It wouldn't be so bad if I were what he believes me, but I'm not, Bill. I'm not!'

'You don't imagine you have to tell *me* that, Verne? Though I don't mind telling you now that if you'd ever given me half a chance, I'd have made love to you, and to any extent.'

She smiled drearily.

'Poor Bill, you didn't get anything out of it either, did you?'

'What do you think he'll do? Try to divorce you? I don't see how he can, actually, though I suppose if he's determined, he wouldn't be above manufacturing and paying for the evidence.'

'Divorce? Horrible,' she said in a low voice. 'It's unbelievable to be talking like this. I feel—smirched and dirty,' and she stared out again into a space she could not even begin to fill with coherent thoughts.

Could he manufacture evidence against her? Would he? Was that the way things could be done by a man who had enough money to buy everything he wanted?

She thought of Jeffery Templar and longed to be able to go to him, to see his plain, homely, trustworthy face and look into his eyes and make him know that she was not this thing Robert was making her out to be.

But would Templar believe her? He had despised her for her marriage, and his unvarying attitude to her since had been one of utterly cold, impersonal acceptance of her as Robert Grimtree's wife and on many occasions his hostess, but with no interest in her whatever, nor had she ever been invited to meet his wife. No, Jeffery Templar would believe nothing good of her. Besides, as his lawyer, he would act for Robert in any case that might be brought.

Bill spoke again after another uncomfortable pause.

'We'd better think about tonight,' he said. 'Do you think he really means that you are not be go back there?' anxiously.

'Oh yes. Robert never says things without meaning them. I wouldn't go back either. You can't be suggesting I should, Bill?'

'No. No, of course not, but—I mean—it's awkward. What would you like me to do? Shall I ring up and get you a room at an hotel for the night?'

She laughed mirthlessly.

'I haven't any money,' she said.

'What do you mean, no money? Your bag—' looking round for it.

'Oh, I've got my bag. One always carries that! But there's nothing in it, only perhaps a shilling or so. Haven't you realised it? I never have any money. Robert's never given me any. You might as well know the truth of it now. I haven't any pride any more.'

'You mean *actually* none? That he's never given you any?' he asked incredulously.

'I do mean that, yes. Oh, I've asked him for it, though not lately, but he has always said the same tiling, that I don't need any, that I can go and buy anything I like and charge it to him, that he had bought me a car so I don't even need bus fares! His chauffeur keeps it filled up with petrol, and if anything ever went wrong with it, I suppose I should go to a garage, or the police or someone, and get them to telephone for someone to come and fetch me. You see how right Robert is! What do I need money for?' with a curl of her lips.

'But—it's incredible! I simply can't believe it! You've actually no money at all? Nothing even in the bank?'

'I had a little, but—I lent it, or gave it away. I'm not sure which. There was a bit left, about fifty pounds, and—after my baby died, I gave that away too. I gave it to someone who wrote to me for help. They do, you know. I felt sorry. It was for a child, a blind child, and—if my baby had lived, he would have been able to see. Oh, what does it matter now, anyway? I couldn't have lived on fifty pounds, or even two hundred and fifty. So you see, Bill, that if you do book a room for me at an hotel, I'm afraid you will have to pay for it. Funny, isn't it?' with another of those hard, bitter laughs.

For a few moments he did not speak, but walked about the room, aimlessly picking up things and putting them down again. Then he came to her and spoke from behind her.

'You know I'll marry you, Verne, don't you? If he divorces you, that is.'

'Are you being conventional, Bill, since I presume you'll be the correspondent. That's what it's called, isn't it? Or do you really *want* to marry me?'

'I've always wanted to. You know that.'

'You did once. Perhaps I was every kind of a fool not to take you when I had the chance, when you—loved me, Bill. You did, didn't you?'

'I do now, Verne,' he said, but he knew as well as she did that his voice was not convincing.

She rose from her chair and pushed the hair out of her eyes and tried to smile.

'What a mess I've got you into, Bill! Perhaps it's that we've both got older, though it isn't much more than a year. I don't know what sort of things have happened to you during that time, but I've been married, and I've had a baby and my baby—died, and now it seems I am going to be divorced and I feel about a hundred and ninety. I wish I were, because then I'd be dead.'

'Don't, Verne. I know you're feeling rotten about it now, but one gets over everything. You say perhaps I've changed. I don't think it's that so much as that you've changed. You've gone away from me, not only by marrying Grimtree, but—in yourself, your mind. Verne—do you care for Grimtree at all?'

'Care for him? I hate him,' she said fiercely.

'I wonder if you do? I do, but then I'm a man and the circumstances are quite different. I think that in a way he is responsible for the change in you, and again not only because you married him. You've—grown up, Verne, though I used to think you a pretty adult person before. I just thought that—if you care for him—this is even harder on you. I don't know how anybody could be particularly fond of him, but women are queer about men.'

'I'm not queer about Robert Grimtree,' said Verne acidly. 'Let's stop talking about him and talk about ourselves. What *are* we going to do, Bill? Tonight, I mean, or what's left of it? I've told you I've no money and I understand that now nothing belongs to me but the clothes I stand up in, and that means I haven't even a pair of pyjamas to my name. I've got these, of course. He must have forgotten about them!' and she slipped the two rings off her wedding finger, the ring Robert had given her when she promised to marry him, and the diamond 'eternity' ring with which he completed the bargain.

She looked at them as they rolled and settled down on the tablecloth, sparkling with a thousand fires.

'They look valuable,' said Bill.

'Oh, they are. They're the price of Verne Raydon,' she told him in bitter scorn. 'Well, they're not much good to me tonight, so what about those pyjamas? Have you got a spare pair?'

'Do you mean you'll stay here? Sleep here?' he asked, amazed.

'Why not? Since my husband has called me an adulteress, I might as well be one. Don't you want me, Bill?'

She did not know what had taken command of her, nor why she was offering herself to him. It was that she felt lost, betrayed, deserted, utterly lonely and in need of human kindness, and if Bill loved her, as he said he did, why not give him the happiness of possessing what Robert Grimtree had left of her, this empty, desolate, bitter hearted shell of a woman who had never yet known love?

Bill came to her and laid his hands on her shoulders and, after a moment's searching of her fathomless eyes whose meaning he could not read, he drew her against him.

'Want you? You know I do. Darling, you know I do,' he said.

She lifted her arms and laid them about his neck, drawing him closer, her cheek against his.

'Bill, love me. Love me very much. Make me forget. Make me feel I'm wanted—and believed in—and decent again. That's a funny thing to think of at this moment, isn't it? Love me very much. Bill,' she ended shakily and closed her eyes and waited for his kisses and thought that to die at this moment would be sweet.

Chapter Nine

As the weeks went by, Verne Grimtree waited for her husband to take the step that would end their marriage, but she had no word from him or of his intentions.

She had bitterly regretted the impulse which had made her link her life irrevocably with that of Bill Trailer. She did not seek to excuse herself by recounting to herself the story of that evening, beginning with her excitement over the final acceptance of *Pantalets,* followed by the considerable quantity of champagne she had drunk, and ending with the scene with Robert and his appalling accusations of her.

Nothing, she told herself inexorably, could be urged to excuse her for the way she had thrown herself, in her misery and humiliation and anger, into Bill's arms. On that one night, his love and happiness had been a balm to her wounds. For the one man who had spurned and degraded her, there was this man who had valued her, whose tenderness and passion for her had served to restore her. Also Bill's loving of her body had been adoration and respect, easing from her mind the hateful memory of Robert's brutal possession of her.

But inevitably and swiftly, the reaction had set in and by the next day she was appalled at what she had done. She had not even the excuse of loving the man to whom she had now given herself. He was her friend, familiar and long tried and trusted, but he was unable to stir in her that magic of enchantment which she believed, even though she had never yet known it, lay somewhere within her, waiting for release.

Bill had accepted the position with obvious satisfaction.

'This is what I call really wonderful, my queen,' he told her as they sat over their breakfast in the kitchen the next morning. 'The Land of

Dreams Come True. I've half a mind not to go in this morning but stay at home and make love to you all day.'

She had insisted on his going.

'We're not going to start like that,' she said firmly. 'Besides—'

'Besides what?'

'Bill—let's face facts. At the moment you've got me as a liability. I haven't even a change of clothes and no money to buy any until Mr. Garret gives me an advance on the book. I was too excited to take in everything he said over the phone, but I rather think he suggested twenty five pounds advance. When do I get that? Now, or when it's published?'

'When it's published, I think, but why not touch him for a bit? If he's so keen on the book, he won't mind coughing up now that he's got the manuscript and that would see you through for the moment,' said Bill, helping himself to more marmalade.

Verne felt a faint chill trickle down her back. She had wanted him to say that of course she was to get the things she needed, instead of working on a plan for her to get possession of her own money. She would have paid him back, but she wanted him to be generous and thoughtful for her *now*.

'Well, let's think of something else. I know Grimtree said you were not to have any of your things (though what the deuce does he think he can do with them himself?) and you can hardly raid the house and take them, can you? I don't know how you stand legally about that, do you? But you must have things, of course, and he can't have issued orders to all the shops yet, so why not pop out this morning and buy what you want at the shops where you usually deal?'

She stared at him.

'Bill! You mean buy them and have them charged to Robert?'

'Well, why not? He owes at least that to you. He said you were to leave him as you came to him, but I don't expect you went to *him* without even a pair of pyjamas or a toothbrush?' with a little chuckle which did nothing to still the throb of something like dismay in her mind.

Did Bill really mean that? Really believe that she could sneak up on Robert before he had had time to do anything about it, and pledge his credit? *Steal* from the man who had so grossly insulted her and cast her off?

'I couldn't possibly do anything like that,' she said.

'My sweet, we all have our pride, but it doesn't buy the beans! But if you won't do the sensible thing, shall I see Garret for you? I might be able to squeeze a bit more than the twenty five out of him, and don't you go signing contracts I haven't seen. Well, I suppose I've got to go. By the way, we want some marmalade, duckie, and something for supper, and you'll want a toothbrush and things. Wish I could give you a tenner, but I'm on my beam ends at the moment. Can you make do with this?' laying a pound note on the table.

'Bill, I—' she began, flushing and drawing back.

He laughed and kissed her lightly.

'Don't be absurd. We've got to eat,' he said.

'It makes me feel like—like a kept woman,' she said unhappily.

He chuckled again.

'Well, aren't you? I've got you and I'm definitely going to keep you. Give me a kiss. A real one. What a lot I've got to teach you!'

He took her into his arms and held her strained against him in an embrace which he would not have attempted, nor she permitted, yesterday. She tried to draw herself away, conscious of the fact that, whilst he was dressed, she was still in his pyjamas, having left the bathroom free for him.

He undid the buttons and pushed his hand against her soft, reluctant flesh and she felt the excitement surging through him and tried to push him away, but he only held her the more closely, fondling her body.

'Darling, why must you make me go to the office?' he asked thickly against her mouth. 'I want you so desperately and I'm never going to let you rest until you want me as much, my cold fish. Come back to bed, darling.'

She struggled free and moved to the other side of the table. Her breath was coming quickly and unevenly. There was a sort of horror in her eyes. For a moment she almost hated him because she hated herself.

'Of course you must go,' she said. 'You must, Bill. I—I want you to go.'

He made a grimace.

'I could not love thee, dear, so much—and all that?' he asked, but he went.

That had been the first morning, but there were other mornings like it, and on Sundays he could not be persuaded to get up at all but wanted to spend the whole day sleeping in snatches, eating picnic meals and making love to her.

He seemed insatiable for lovemaking, and because she was sincerely fond of him, because he was all she had, because in her weakness and extremity she had given herself to him, and he loved her, Verne tried to do and to be all he wanted of her. He roused in her the capacity for physical passion, but always afterwards she was sick at herself, and felt a nauseating disgust of what she had become – a man's mistress, a 'kept woman' after all her fine regard for herself.

Bill, as good as his word, had seen Mr. Garret for her and triumphantly brought home a cheque for thirty pounds.

'I couldn't get any more out of the old skinflint,' he said, 'out at least you've now got something. What a sell that that rotter Grimtree managed to pinch your car before we could get hold of it! You could have got quite five hundred for it.'

She had not been able to bring herself to go to the place where she had left it parked on that fatal night, and when she did, it was to find it gone, and though Bill had urged her to try to find out whether or not it had been taken away on Grimtree's orders, saying that it might have been stolen by somebody else, she refused point blank.

'If it's gone, it's gone,' she said, 'and in any case, it wasn't mine.'

'He gave it to you, didn't he?'

'For use as his wife, and it was registered in his name, but I should not have taken it. And if it were stolen and the insurance money were payable on it, it was Robert's. Don't let's talk about it any more.'

'I think you're silly to be so proud, my sweet. That five hundred would have set you up for quite a time. You see, Verne duckie, I'm not a rich man. In fact, I'm a damned poor one, and before very long we shall have the rent of this flat to find. How long has it been paid up, do you think?'

'That's another thing, Bill. I don't want us to go on living here. I can't.'

'Now don't be an absolute lunatic, darling! What would be the sense of moving out and having all that extra expense when for the time being we can live rent free?'

'But you surely don't intend us to go on living in a flat for which Robert is paying the rent? *Robert?*' she asked, with the uncomfortable conviction that that was what he did intend to do.

'Look at it sensibly, Verne. The rent's been paid. It's over and done with, and not as if he paid it every week, so much hard cash. He won't miss it, and until we get ourselves settled into some sort of order about things, why burden ourselves with a rent we need not pay?'

'Bill, I sometimes think I've never known you at all, but I don't believe you really mean it. You must have some pride as well, even if you pretend you haven't. I shall go out today and start looking for something.'

He shrugged his shoulders, knowing quite well that it was most unlikely that she would be able to find anything.

'Do what you like,' he said. 'Anyway, if I don't get a move on, I shall miss my assignment. Bye bye, sweet. Be back usual time. If not, I'll ring you.'

Though she had trailed from one house agent to another, searched the newspapers, set off on many a wild goose chase after some flat she'd heard of, she could not find anything offered at a rent approaching what she felt Bill could afford to pay, and until her book was published she would have no more money of her own – and even then it was by no means certain that there would be anything appreciable to come to her.

She very much regretted that she had parted with her mother's two hundred pounds, for that undoubtedly had been her own money and she need have felt no qualms about spending it. But she could not bring herself to write to Mrs. Gorner about its repayment. It would have looked an extremely odd thing for her to do, as Robert's wife, and so far as she knew, the world in general had no knowledge of their parting.

She was restless and worried, feeling that her position as Bill's mistress was unsatisfactory and untenable. Also she was becoming frightened. She realised that the Bill she had known before her marriage to Robert was a different being from the one who was now her lover. It might not be that he had changed, but rather that she had not known him. He became irritable without, she felt, sufficient cause, and though their frequent differences could be and always were made up when they went to bed, they left her with a feeling of insecurity, the basis of their relationship the shifting sands of their emotions rather than the firm rock of understanding and trust.

Some of their disagreements were about money, that terrible pitfall always yawning at the feet of everyday people. Bill was not mean, but he was careless over money, spending lavishly at the beginning of the month on things which she felt were unnecessary, and being harassed towards the end of the month because there was not even enough to buy food.

'What do you *do* with the money?' he asked her once irritably, when she told him he had better have a good lunch at his office canteen because there would be only cheese for supper.

'You know what I do with it. I don't spend it on anything you don't share with me, but don't forget that you bought those lobsters and I had to go in and pay for them, and you also told them to send a whole lot of *scampi* that went bad before we could eat them.'

'Well, good heavens, can't we sometimes have something a bit exciting in the way of food? Not just bread and cheese?'

'That's not fair, Bill. This is the first time I've had nothing but that to offer you, and I'm not used to managing now. I've got out of the way of it and prices have changed a lot, but even I know we couldn't afford the lobsters, or the *scampi.'*

'Even you, you say? Meaning that I am to remember you have been living off the fat of the land, eating oysters and caviar and champagne? I do remember. I never forget it, in fact—that you are used to being Mrs. Robert Grimtree with servants at your beck and call and an unlimited banking account to draw on—'

'Bill!'

In an instant his arms were about her and he was kissing her, ruffling her hair, calling her by all the extravagant endearments that came to his lips.

'Darling—darling princess—we're almost quarrelling, and it's all my fault! Of course you manage marvellously, and I'm a beast to you, and if I could only lay my hands on a million pounds, I'd pour it all out at your feet and let you wade through it. Forgive me, sweetness. Call me every name you can think of. Oh gosh, why have we got to start this when I'm due at the office? Have I really got to go and leave you here, with that little frown on your beautiful brow and all sorts of hateful thoughts about me inside you? Come and let me love you, sweetheart, just for an hour. Brand can go to Chelsea—'

She had to laugh and shake herself free. In this mood, he was hard to resist. The abjectness of his apologies when he had upset her was as wild and deep as the extravagancies of his lovemaking.

'Of course you must go. And don't bother about the canteen lunch. I'll manage something for tonight, not just the cheese.'

'Atta girl. Goodbye, you blessed, heavenly thing—hard hearted Hannah. Give me one more kiss. I could eat you,' pretending to do so.

'Well, at least that would solve the problem of supper,' she told him laughingly and pushed him away.

Dear Bill – so lovable and unstable and so loving! Why could he not kindle within her that fire for which she longed? Why could she not lose herself in him as he could in her, instead of always being conscious of their insecure present, their unknown future?

After he had gone, she wondered how she was going to fulfil her promise to augment the bread and cheese. She had found that, before her coming, he had often run up bills with the local tradespeople, a thing which shocked her. She had never been in debt, and her mother had brought her up on the unbreakable principle that what she could not pay for, she must do without.

She hated asking Bill for money, though when he had it, he gave it to her with careless abandon. She had discovered since that at the time of her coming to him, he had been particularly hard up, the money in his wallet belonging to the office, so that the pound note he had given her that first morning had to come off his next month's salary. That discovery had eased her mind a little, showing that it was not an inherent and unsuspected meanness which had actuated him then.

She had paid up all the tradespeople out of her thirty pounds from Mr. Garret, and had bought actual necessities for herself and now there was none of it left. She realised now that she could have bought more economically, but she had become too well accustomed to buying on Robert Grimtree's credit nothing but the best, and she was having to learn all over again how to contrive on less than the best.

She went to a locked box and took out the two rings which she had never worn since she had come to live with Bill. If she sold them, or even one of them, there would be enough to keep her from worrying for a long time. She could even have paid one of the premiums demanded for a flat.

She put the rings down. She could not do it. To find money by selling something of Robert's would have amounted, in her view, to the same thing as living rent free at his expense.

She picked up the only other thing she had of any value, the pendant and chain which her father had given her. Its proportionate value to the rings was infinitesimal, of course, but at least it would bring in something.

She held it against her lips for a moment.

'Forgive me, darlings,' she whispered to her dead parents. 'It won't be for long. As soon as I get any more out of the book, I'll buy it back.'

Her first visit to a pawnshop was painful and embarrassing, though the little Jew behind the counter made nothing of the business, of course.

'Two pounds,' he said, tossing the necklet down again.

'Two pounds? But—but it's worth at least ten,' said Verne.

'Two pounds. Take it or leave it,' he said laconically.

'Couldn't you make it at least—three?' she stammered.

'Two pounds.'

'I—I shall be able to get it back, shan't I?' she pleaded.

'If you redeem it in time. Here's the card.'

She accepted the two notes and tried not to feel too badly about it, but when she ate the ham and salad and tinned peaches that evening, she felt it would choke her.

Bill did not ask her how she had managed to pay for it. If he thought about it, he would suppose she had had it 'on tick' from the shops.

After that, she decided that she must take a job. So far she had hesitated about doing so because she wanted to be free to go on with her writing if, as Mr. Garrett confidently prophesied, the sales of *Pantalets* proved her to be a money maker with her pen. She had ideas for further writings on the Victoria Era, in which her mind had been steeped for the production of her father's book and this time it would be a complete novel rather than a series of related episodes.

She had started on it, using the old typewriter (whose loss had never been discovered by Bill's firm) on the kitchen table, but to her dismay, she found that the writing did not come easily. Her mind was no longer able to detach itself from the problems of her daily life, and now that she had unlimited time at her disposal rather than the snatched hours, with her eye on the clock, in which she had finished *Pantalets,* she found that the ideas would not flow.

Bill tried to reassure her.

'It'll come, baby. You see,' he told her easily. 'Chuck it up for the moment. Go out and enjoy yourself. I've always understood that to writers, producing a book is like producing a baby. You have to have a little time to recover from the pains of giving birth. By the way, you look a bit peaky. Not by any chance thinking of giving birth to other things than books, are you?'

'Oh no, Bill,' she said, horrified. 'You know you promised—'

'OK. O.K.,' he laughed. 'Trust wily old Bill to know his way about, though I must admit that when I'm with you—'

'Bill, you wouldn't let it happen? Not till we can be married? You wouldn't, would you?'

He kissed her.

'No, my sweet. That would be the end, wouldn't it? We can only just scratch along with two of us, so heaven forbid three!'

She could not bring herself to tell him that, when they were married, she would want a child. She dared not sound him on the subject, but anyway, there would be plenty of time. She was only twenty three, and Bill twenty six. They were both young enough to wait.

She found a job easily enough, giving her name as Verne Weston this time, afraid that as Verne Raydon she might be known, if any business associates of Corbett and Clark happened to be also associates of Grimtree's, and not wishing to be connected at her new office with the name of Lorna Derring, when it appeared on the covers of *Pantalets.*

'I wonder if anybody ever had so many names!' she said to Bill, when she told him. 'I shall soon cease to know who I am.'

'Why didn't you use my name?' asked Bill, for the tradespeople now knew her as Mrs. Trailer, and she had bought herself a cheap silver ring which she hoped looked like platinum and which she wore on her marriage finger.

She supposed that the people in Beckett Mansions knew who she was since the Biggins knew and Flo Biggin was certainly not likely to keep a still tongue about it. Old Mrs. Biggin had gone to make what Flo hoped would be a long stay, possibly a permanent one, with another daughter-in-law and did not know that Verne had taken up residence at No. 17 again.

'I could have done, I suppose,' said Verne, 'but—oh well, I'm not Mrs. Trailer, am I?'

'Nor are you Miss Weston,' he pointed out. 'Where did you get that one from?'

She laughed, though these subterfuges made her feel cheap.

'Off a packet of biscuits,' she said.

'Oh well, what's in a name?' asked Bill with his cheerful disregard of such details.

She settled down to a daily office routine again whilst she waited for her book to appear, but still no word came from any source that Robert was instituting divorce proceedings.

She worried about it considerably more than Bill appeared to do.

'What does it matter, sweet?' he asked her easily. 'You won't be any different and you know I'll never let you down. I'm too darned pleased to have you.'

'Thank you, Bill,' she said, and did not pursue the subject.

It hurt her that he was obviously not interested whether she was his wife or not. It was all very well for him to assure her blithely that he regarded her as such and that the actual legal tie would not bind them any more closely. She could not feel like that about it. She was constitutionally unable to approve of any woman living in what a previous, less lax age called 'sin'. Her mother had brought her up to have an almost prim respect for herself, and she could not rid her mind of the knowledge that here, in the very home in which those ideas had been inculcated, she was doing something which would have outraged that beloved person.

Bill laughed at her and refused to take her seriously.

'Why worry, my sweet? Old Grimtree is bound to come across with a divorce some day and then we can do the thing with bell, book and candle.'

So Bill said – but would he? Would Robert Grimtree ever admit to the world that he had not been able to hold his wife? And if he knew that she wanted her freedom, as of course he must know, that would be enough for him to refuse it.

Other things about her irregular union irritated her as well, smaller things which, if she had loved Bill, perhaps would not have mattered, or at least would be forgivable.

He was careless and casual to a degree, and not only with money. He was untidy about the home and in his own person. He did not even have as many baths as she had been brought up to consider essential. Robert had been meticulously careful and scrupulous in such ways, and she felt that he would have been if he had neither money nor servants. He had never offended her by the lack of care for personal details which Bill showed.

'Great snakes, woman, I don't always have to be washing!' he expostulated one night when he was preparing to roll into bed without even cleaning his teeth. 'It isn't Friday night or Amami night every night!'

'It's bath night every night,' she retorted. 'Anyway, you're not going to make love to me any night that isn't bath night,' and, still grumbling good humouredly, he allowed himself to be pushed off to the bath she had drawn for him.

He was critical of the hours she spent cleaning and tidying the flat after they came home in the evening.

'What's the use? It'll only get like it again. Come out to the pictures and shut the door on it. Bob Hope's on at the corner.'

'We're not going for two reasons,' she said firmly. 'In the first place I let you persuade me not to clean the kitchen last night, and the night before, and by tomorrow, it will *smell*. And in the second place, we can't afford the pictures again. We've been once this week.'

'Well, Bob Hope won't be there next week.'

'I can survive it,' said Verne, tying on her apron.

'Darling, we can't go on without *everything* that's fun,' he grumbled. 'At least, nearly everything,' with an impish grin at her.

'We can go without Bob Hope,' she said firmly.

'Well, I don't intend to,' he said, beginning to lose his temper, as he seemed to do with increasing ease, and since she still refused to go with him, he went alone, leaving her to a miserable, lonely evening which her furious onslaught on the kitchen did little to alleviate.

When he came in, she looked at the clock in surprise.

'Was it over early?' she asked.

'No, I wasn't enjoying it without you,' he said. 'Here. Catch!' and he tossed into her arms a bunch of early chrysanthemums, the tawny, curled kind that she loved.

She knew they must have cost very much more than a seat at the cinema, but he gave them to her with an expression of such boyish pleasure, both as a present and as a peace offering, that she had not the heart to remind him of the fact.

'It was sweet of you, Bill,' she said, 'and I'm sorry if I was a pig and a spoil sport, and if it's any satisfaction to you, I haven't enjoyed the evening a bit and the kitchen doesn't look much better because my heart wasn't in it. It was with you in the two and fours.'

They hugged and kissed and laughed together and presently went to bed and made love.

A week or two later she found she had to pay for the flowers out of the housekeeping money, as he had told the florist to 'chalk them up', but by that time she did not care to rake it up and remind him that it was supposed to be a present. All he would have said, with a gay laugh, was that the money came out of the same trousers pocket anyway.

She hated the disorder he never seemed even to notice. She and her mother had always kept the little place spick and span, and though she had had no work of any sort to do when she lived with Robert Grimtree, she had appreciated and enjoyed the orderliness of the house, and the punctuality on which he had insisted. She knew that Bill could not always be sure what time he would be in in the evening, and she made allowances for that even when she was exasperated over a spoilt dinner, or one which he did not come in to share at all, ringing her up whilst she waited for him, to tell her casually to have a meal without him and he would have 'something cold'. That 'something cold' meant an extra strain on her budget, but they had one of their worst quarrels when she discovered by accident that on many of these evenings he could have got home in time. He had called at the 'local' for a drink, and had stayed there playing darts.

'Darling, I simply can't be bound down by the clock,' he said when she protested. 'When I've finished my work, I need a little relaxation.'

'So do I when I've finished mine, but I get mine coming home to prepare you a meal,' she said tartly.

'My sweet, you don't have to. If I came home to find nothing ready for me, I wouldn't complain, as you know,' and of course she did know it. He would accept the information gaily and say, 'Let's go out then.'

She began to wonder if things would either be, or seem, different if they could be married. Was it this semi detached life that made him feel himself still a bachelor, with unlimited freedom to come and go, to stay or not as the case might be? Would it perhaps give him a feeling of stability and responsibility if she were really his wife?

Now that she was earning, their lives seemed even less inter dependent. They had agreed to put an equal amount into what he called 'the kitty' each month, and out of it they would pay not only the housekeeping bills, but also for any pleasures they took together, such as their weekly visit to the cinema. But as often as not, when they reached the box office he would feel in his pockets and say casually, 'You'd better pay, darling. I'm broke,' though before leaving she had reminded him that, as he had not put the full amount in that month, it would be his job to pay for the seats himself.

There was no avoiding the conclusion that he was thriftless, careless and unreliable, and she found herself bearing more and more of the joint expenditure. It added to her feeling of detachment, and that this was an interlude in her life rather than an established and enduring order.

She found, to her chagrin, that she was actually missing Robert, and though she told herself roundly that it was the luxurious ease of her life in Wellington Gate that she missed, deep within her she knew that it was not so. It was the feeling of security, of course, but it was more than that. Robert was consistent and to be depended upon. Also, in spite of their semi detached lives, she realised now the place in which he had set her in the eyes of other people, his insistence on her importance in his scheme of things, his care that, whatever he did and whether he were with her or not, she should be provided for and protected and planned for.

There was another side to it too, and one which, without her new knowledge of life with Bill, she would not have discovered.

Bill was voracious in his physical demands en her and either oblivious to or indifferent to her own feelings and wishes.

'That's what a man wants of a woman, any man who isn't a moron,' he had told her more than once when she would have been glad to be allowed to go at once and peacefully to sleep.

'Even when the woman is not so inclined at the moment?' she asked him with a feeling of actual distaste.

'You'll be inclined all right!' he told her, and it was to her secret shame that he proved it true.

But what of Robert? He was certainly no moron, and she knew he had all a normal man's appetites from that one experience of Ins need of her, and yet he had never again insisted on that relationship, as he could have done and as Bill would certainly have done.

With her added knowledge of men, she realised that Robert had denied himself such access to her because she had left him in no doubt of her own dislike and fear. Robert Grimtree, who in her long knowledge of him had never denied himself anything he wanted or to which he had a right.

Her mind returned continually to the months before her baby was born. Had he not been almost out of character, as he had assessed it, in his unvarying kindness and consideration for her? Yet she knew now that in his mind and body there had been the desire for her and the resentment and frustration of its lack of fulfilment.

She was beginning to wonder if she really knew him at all, seeing him now in the light of her knowledge of Bill.

And with that wonder came the new, disturbing consciousness of her own part in the failure of their marriage. What if she had insisted on fulfilling her part of the bargain with him? If she had forced herself to subdue and conquer the fear and aversion shown him that she was willing to be his wife in all things?

What if Robert really did love her? His long abstention from the physical side of married life showed her beyond doubt that that had not been, could not have been, the one object of his marriage. And if it were not, why had he wanted to marry her at all? She had had nothing else to give him, and in marrying her, he was losing an excellent employee.

The thought tormented her and she saw it taking its place amongst the confusion of her memories of her life with him, putting a new value on half forgotten moments, setting them in place to make some sense out of the things not formerly understood.

Did Robert love her? And if so, what might not have come out of their marriage if she had known and understood that? If only she could have known him better and got down to the man himself, might she not have found something worth having and keeping?

But it was too late now. Their marriage had gone forever, and she still shivered at the memory of their last interview, his anger and his bitter words. He had flung her off, revealing the fact that he knew her just as little as she knew him, and now there remained only this wreckage and – Bill. Her life and destiny, which had once laid securely in Robert Grimtree's hands, were now in Bill's, for good or evil.

Yet she could not rid her mind of the thought of her husband, alone again in his great, luxurious house, with neither wife nor child and with so pitifully few friends in spite of his host of acquaintances, sycophants most of them, and his great wealth.

Poor Robert.

One day she saw Jeffery Templar in the street, and she crossed over on an impulse, to speak to him.

'Mr. Templar—' He raised his hat gravely and waited for her to speak. He knew, of course, she thought. He must know, even if no one else knew.

'May I come and see you?' she asked precipitately.

'Er—yes. Yes, I suppose so, Mrs. Grimtree,' he said, and it was odd to hear herself called that again. 'When would you like to come?'

'It will have to be during my lunch hour one day. I'm working again now,' she said, colouring.

'Or in the early evening if that would be more convenient for you? I could stay for you so long as I know in advance. Tomorrow?'

'Please. May I do that? I leave at five.'

He nodded.

'I'll wait for you,' he said, and lifted his hat and left her.

She told Bill what she had arranged to do.

'What on earth for?' he asked at once.

'I didn't think about it until I saw him, but—Bill, I must know what Robert is going to do, or if he is going to do anything at all.'

'I can't see why,' said Bill.

'Bill, you know how I feel about it, that I'm not—comfortable leaving things like this.'

'All right, my dear, if that's the way it is, but don't let this Templar chap persuade you to go back to Grimtree, that's all.'

She stared at him and then laughed.

'For a moment I thought you were serious. As if I would! And as if he'd want me back!'

But for once Bill was not laughing.

'Of course he wants you back,' he said. 'I've told you before, Verne, that Grimtree was in love with you. Probably still is. If he hadn't been, do you think he'd have made all that infernal fuss that night and been so brutal, and beside himself with rage? A man who doesn't care for a woman is either Indifferent to her having a little affair on her own, or glad to get rid of her peaceably. He doesn't storm and rave as R. G. did.'

'You're quite wrong, you know, Bill,' she said earnestly. 'Robert Grimtree is not capable of caring for anybody or anything with the one exception of a mongrel dog he adopted, though I never understood that. Everything Robert possesses has to be of absolutely super quality, and yet he acquires an animal of the lowest possible grade in the social scale.'

'You didn't understand that, and I am of the opinion that there were quite a lot of other things you didn't understand about him,' said Bill thoughtfully.

'I worked for him for two years and lived with him for another year and a half,' she retorted.

'Yes, and he gave you a child,' said Bill. 'If I hadn't known that, I'd have said you were a vestal virgin when you came to me. What was it? An immaculate conception?'

'I can't discuss that with you, Bill,' she said, and he laughed and kissed her.

'I don't want you to, my love,' he said. 'The important thing is that I've got you now and he hasn't.'

She approached Mr. Templar's office with a feeling of intense discomfort the next evening, but he set her at her ease by offering her a cigarette and suggesting that they sat in two chairs near the electric fire rather than at each side of his desk. Though it was September, it was chilly and the fire was very acceptable. She hoped Bill would have lit one when she got home.

'Now—Verne,' he said, using her Christian name for the first time.

'Mr. Templar, I'm—so worried,' she said.

'Well, tell me what about.'

'About Robert, of course, and what he intends to do. You know we've parted, don't you?'

'Yes,' he said and waited.

'We parted in April, five months ago, and I expected him to do something about it before now and—well, he hasn't. Or if he has, I don't know anything about it. Mr. Templar, is he going to divorce me?'

'He hasn't suggested it,' he said gravely.

'But—he will, won't he? I mean—he must, mustn't he? I can't go on indefinitely living like this. Do you know—about me?'

'Not very much, though Robert told me just the bare facts.'

She hesitated, and then looked at him very intently with steady brown eyes, eyes which Jeffery Templar felt, against all his previous estimate of her, that he could trust.

'Mr. Templar, if I tell you the truth about all this, will you believe me?'

'Yes, I think I can,' he said and she drew a deep breath.

'Thank you. I didn't actually leave Robert at all. I wasn't unfaithful to him either and, whatever he may have told you, or believed, he was the father of my little baby who—died. Bill Trailer was my friend, an old friend I have known for many years. He wanted to marry me before I married Robert, but I wasn't in love with him. I never have been. Perhaps I can't love anybody. I know it was silly of me to let him occupy my flat, but at the time there didn't seem to be anything in it. He had to find somewhere to live, and the flat was empty and I didn't think anything about it except that it seemed a sensible and friendly thing to do. Then I started to do some work. I had so much time on my hands and I wanted some money of my own, and I decided to try to finish a book my father had started, and for one reason and another, it seemed simpler to go to the flat and do the work there. I knew Robert wouldn't have agreed to my doing it, but I just had to do something to fill my time. I don't know how Robert found out I was going there. He said something about letters, and—there's a woman in one of the flats who might have started it. Anyway, he came there, and I had been having a sort of celebration with Bill because I was going to be able to get the book published—and we'd drunk a lot of champagne, and I lost my head a bit—but I swear to you, Mr. Templar, that Bill did nothing but kiss me, and we had always kissed in the old days. Girls don't think anything of it. I didn't, anyway. I tried to make Robert believe it, but he didn't give either of us a chance to speak. He just—raved at me and turned me off and—that's really what happened. After that, I didn't care what happened to me, and Robert didn't want me and Bill did—and I was there in the flat with him and—I stayed. Do you believe me?'

'Yes,' he said slowly. 'Yes, I do, though it was an utterly foolish thing to do. It appears that at the time, Robert had no grounds against you for divorce, but he has now.'

'I know that, but what's done can't be undone, and so, you see, he must divorce me, mustn't he?'

Templar gave a small, wry smile.

'You should know better than anyone that there is nothing Robert Grimtree *must* do unless he wants to,' he said.

'You mean you think he might refuse, even if I asked him to?'

'I think it's possible.'

'But—I can't go on just living with Bill without being able to marry him,' she said, appalled.

'I'm afraid you're in no position to do anything about it yourself. You see, divorce is supposed to be a punishment for the guilty, not a means of one person getting free to marry another. In fact, under the present marriage laws, it might well militate against the divorce for the guilty party to get what he or she wanted out of it. If you want me to do so, I'll see Robert and suggest his divorcing you, but—you must be prepared for him to refuse.'

'But why? He doesn't want me himself. It would be just dog in the manger.'

He was silent for a few moments. Then he shot an unexpected question at her.

'Why do you suppose he married you?' he asked.

'I've never known,' she said. 'There seemed to be nothing for him to gain out of it.'

'It's so very unlikely that he would strike a bargain if that were true. I suppose it was a bargain of sorts?'

She nodded.

'I might as well tell you everything whilst I am about it. You thought I married him for his money, didn't you?'

'Obviously,' he said drily.

'Well, I suppose I did, but not the way you mean it,' and she told him quite simply about her mother and why she had accepted that sudden and astounding proposal of marriage.

'There was no trickery in it,' she said. 'He knew why I married him. I never pretended it was for any other reason, though I've never been able to make out why *he* wanted to marry *me*. With all his money, I suppose he could have married almost anyone.'

'It didn't occur to you that he might have been in love with you?' asked the lawyer drily.

She shot a look at him and then averted her eyes. There it was, that fantastic suggestion again, and this time not from a jealous lover but from this dry as dust legal man.

'Robert Grimtree has never loved anything but himself and his money,' she said bitterly.

'I wonder how well you know him, Verne?'

'Better than anyone else, probably,' she said, her head high, her eyes defiant.

'Which is not saying much. I've been acquainted with him even longer than you have, but I'd never say I know him.'

'Mr. Templar, I don't know why he married me, except that he has been climbing the ladder of success for years and wanted to launch out in social as well as business life and felt that a wife was necessary. I was just a hostess for his guests.'

'Yet you had a child.'

'Yes. His, but I can't talk about that,' she said, two spots of colour in her cheeks, her eyes still proud and defiant. 'I think the thing that made me most bitter against him, when we parted, was his suggestion that the baby was not his. It was an insult to—my dead child.'

'I doubt if he really thought that. When one is very angry and—hurt—one is inclined to snatch at the weapon that will cause the worst wound.'

'Robert hurt?' she said, her lip curling.

'I think so. He was badly hurt. He's in many ways a changed man since his marriage broke up. To my mind, there's only one thing that can hurt a husband like that and that's the fact that he loves the wife whom he thinks has betrayed him.'

'You're quite wrong, Mr. Templar. There was never any suggestion of love between Robert and me.'

'Or perhaps you didn't recognise it?' he asked and wished not for the first time that Grimtree had not bound him to secrecy about the provision he had made, and was still making, for his wife. Surely for a man like that to show an interest in the woman he had repudiated, whatever the cause or reason, there could be only one explanation?

Verne made no reply, and he rose to end the interview.

'If you're quite sure you want the divorce, I'll see what can be done,' he said.

'I'm quite sure,' said Verne steadily. 'I want to be able to marry Bill as soon as possible.'

'Why, if you're not in love with him? Surely one marriage without love is enough?'

'Oh, love!' she said with a little gesture of weariness. 'Storybook stuff. Perhaps it's that I want to be—respectable again,' with a wry smile. 'Thank you. I'm most grateful to you.'

'I'll do my best, but don't bank on it,' he warned her. 'Robert's a law unto himself and nobody can make him do what he doesn't want to do. Can you get home all right? Shall I get you a taxi?'

She laughed.

'Good heavens, we're not in the taxi class! I can get a bus. Goodbye, and thank you again.'

'How can I get hold of you, by the way?' he asked.

She gave him the address and telephone number of the flat.

'I'm known as Mrs. Trailer,' she said, avoiding his eyes. He wrote down the address with perfect calmness.

On the way home, her thoughts returned again to this extraordinary insistence of other people on Robert's feelings for her. As if she were not the best authority on what they were!

Yet there was that nagging thought again. Why, then, had he wanted to marry her? If, as she had told Mr. Templar, all he had wanted was a hostess for his guests, he could have picked out someone much more suitable, a girl from a higher social sphere who would have added lustre to his name.

And, in the light of her new knowledge of men gained from her association with Bill, she knew that if he had married her merely to go to bed with her, he would not have left her untouched save for that one hideous night, but would ruthlessly and callously have subdued her to his will.

Yet how could he love her? How could Robert Grimtree feel love for anyone or anything – except perhaps for his mongrel dog? For Verne, love must be a tender thing, a gentle thing which did not seek its own happiness before that of the beloved's.

But, if that were so, was it not rather *Bill* who had failed in love, Bill who was always telling her that he loved her? When had Bill sought her happiness rather than her own? And had Robert denied himself the possession of his wife for her sake? It could not have been for his own.

She shivered and drew the collar of her coat more closely about her neck. What had she done, to herself, to Robert, to Bill, to life itself? Was there any way out of the mess in which she felt she was bound and entangled?

She told Bill about her interview with Mr. Templar but he took with equanimity the solicitor's opinion that Robert would not divorce her.

'Oh well, darling, why worry?' he asked. 'We're quite happy, aren't we? Take that look off your face and see what you can do to the welsh rarebit. It doesn't look a bit like yours. It's all runny.'

'Did you do it for supper? That was sweet of you. Bill,' she said gratefully.

Why on earth could she not be content to let life flow on like this? she thought. Bill loved her and was good to her, and Robert had flung her off and certainly didn't want her.

Chapter Ten

It was some three weeks before Jeffery Templar contacted her again, and during that time Verne had made a discovery that made her feel the divorce was urgent.

She had found herself pregnant.

She knew that Bill would not be pleased about it. She was not very much pleased herself, though, remembering the exquisite joy it had been to her to hold Adrian in her arms, to feel that he was a part of her very being magically translated into a separate entity, hers to love and guard and cherish, she could not be wholly unhappy about it. Perhaps, she thought, this was what she really was, a woman born to be a mother and to give all her love to her children, rather than a woman loving a man.

Before she told Bill, Mr. Templar had rung her up and asked her to see him again and since Bill had been sitting in the room at the time, she did not ply him with any of the questions that sprang to her lips but merely made the appointment.

'Is it the news I want?' she asked at once when she was in his office.

'I'm afraid not,' he said.

She went white.

'You mean he won't divorce me?'

'That's what he says. I'm sorry. I did my best. I pointed out to him that he has nothing to gain by holding you legally bound to him when there is no other tie.'

'What did he say?'

'That that was his affair and he didn't want anyone else to tell him what to do.'

She sat in silence, trying to assess her new position, one in which she had never really believed she would be placed. Her thoughts had always been 'When Bill and I are married', never 'if we are', and now there was an urgent need that they should be.

'Mr. Templar, I'm going to have a child,' she said at last, desperately.

His face was very grave.

'There was always that possibility, of course,' he said. 'Do you want me to tell Robert that?'

She twisted her hands together.

'I don't know,' she said. 'I don't know. His refusal to divorce me can only be because he wants to be vindictive, and if he knew this, it would only give him a greater satisfaction in his power to hurt me.'

'You don't think you may be misjudging him?' asked Templar gravely.

'No,' she snapped. 'I know Robert and the way he always gets his own back on people who have—who have come up against him. Do you remember the affair of Gorner, the branch manager at Ordborough? Robert drove him to suicide for cheating him out of some paltry sum of money.'

But as she spoke, she remembered that Robert had tried to make amends by sending Gorner's wife five hundred pounds. To make amends much too late!

Perhaps when she had had her baby, a child who would always be illegitimate, he would send her five hundred pounds!

Her lip curled bitterly.

'Isn't there anything I can do?' she asked in desperation.

'I don't think so. Robert told me something else. I don't know how you will take this, but he did not suggest my not telling you. He probably couldn't divorce you if he wanted to. He's been keeping a mistress all this time, ever since your marriage, I understand.'

She gave him an incredulous stare.

'Robert has? *Robert?*' was all she could find to say.

She could not at first believe it, but then her common sense intervened and she thought that she ought to have guessed it. Denied his right to his wife, as he felt her resistance and disgust had denied him, the most likely thing for him to do was to go to another woman. The queer, unpalatable thing about it was to realise that she minded.

'You see the point?' asked Templar, ignoring her amazement. 'In a case like this, the petitioner for divorce has to ask for the discretion of the court about his own misdemeanours, and as the affair seems to have gone on right through the marriage, it might not be given. The court might well consider that you were justified and that therefore you should not be punished by being divorced.'

'But I want to be!' cried Verne.

'That, according to English law, is the very reason why you can't be,' said Templar. 'Don't blame me. I didn't make the law. I am merely explaining its provisions to you.'

'Would Robert have to tell the court about—this woman?'

'I should certainly advise him to do so, and so would any other reputable lawyer.'

'Does he want to marry her?'

'Oh no, I don't think so for a moment. She's not the sort of woman men marry.'

'I see,' said Verne, wondering whether she did or not.

For Robert to have been going with a woman like that, and all that time! Again, why should she mind—if she did mind?

'I don't know whether I want you to tell him that I am going to have a child,' she said at last. 'May I think about that? And let you know?'

'Of course. I can't advise you there at all.'

She hesitated.

'Mr. Templar, after what you've told me, would it be—be possible for me to take proceedings against Robert and ask for—what did you call it? The consideration of the court?'

'The discretion of the court,' he corrected her. 'I'm afraid that wouldn't be very feasible. For one thing, by the time the case came into court, your—er—condition would probably be obvious and—no, I wouldn't advise that at all. It would be all most unpleasant for you, and I think Robert might defend it.'

'It will be most unpleasant for me to go on living with a man I can't marry and to have an illegitimate child,' retorted Verne angrily. 'It seems that Robert Grimtree is always to get things as he wants them.'

'Most of us try to do that,' observed Templar. 'It's what you're doing, isn't it?'

'I suppose so, but I'm not trying to be vindictive. Mr. Templar, isn't there *anything* I can do?' she asked desperately.

'I can't think of anything, unless—you'd like me to arrange for you to see Robert yourself?'

'Oh, no. No! That's not possible. I couldn't bear it. I'll think about what to do. I must talk to Bill.'

After she had gone, he spoke to Robert on the telephone.

'I've had Verne here,' he said. 'I'd rather like to see you.'

'What for? I've nothing further to say.'

'I'd still like to see you,' persisted Templar, though what indeed was there to say further? No one had ever been able to coerce the man.

His was not a practice for divorce cases and he always refused them, happily married himself and believing in the permanency of the marriage tie, but in this instance he might have to vary his rule. He had hoped that time might effect some sort of reconciliation between Verne and her husband, sure in his own mind that Robert really loved his wife in his own peculiar way, but in the light of what she had told him now, what hope could there be of such a thing?

'All right,' said Grimtree sourly. 'You won't make me change my mind though.'

They met over the lunch table, and it struck Templar again and more forcibly that something had indeed made its mark on the man. He was as difficult as ever, as belligerent and open to no persuasion, but it was as if the spirit had gone out of him and as if this aggressive hostility were a facade behind which the man himself crouched, defensive, at bay.

'If she wants a divorce, let her come and ask me for it,' he said.

'She won't do that. I did suggest it. Robert, what's the use? What have you to gain by keeping her tied to you instead of giving her a chance to make her own life again?'

Grimtree glared at him.

'She made it when she married me,' he said.

'Apparently she didn't leave you of her own free will.'

'Oh no. If I hadn't found her out, she'd have gone on getting what she could out of me and having her nasty little affair with her boy friend at the same time. I quite realise that,' snarled Grimtree, and

Templar saw how deeply it had gone. Was Verne blind that she could not see what was the real root of his anger against her? This was not just the spite of a spoilt child robbed of its toy.

Grimtree parted from him on that note, and to Templar his step seemed slower, his whole body devitalised and lacking its former self assurance.

And it was not only his body that seemed to have lost its alertness.

Lately Grimtree had given him cause for a good deal of surprised thought, for he was speculating heavily and not, in Templar's opinion, always wisely. He had taken risks in the past. Without them, no man could have piled up his huge fortune, but he had seemed possessed of an uncanny power of foresight so that his losses had been very small in comparison with his gains.

Recently, however, either that power had deserted him, or else he had become actually careless whether his deals came off or not, though the sums he risked were often very large.

'What's it matter? Plenty more where that came from,' he had said the other day, when a steep fall in some stocks against which his broker had warned him had lost him several thousand pounds. He had almost boasted about it to Templar over the lunch table.

'There may not always be,' was the quiet reply, and Grimtree had shrugged it off with a laugh, though beneath it Templar had detected a faint anxiety.

Robert had got rid of Miss Bright, who was glad enough to go, and in her place had installed a man, a young man with big ideas of his own and, surprisingly enough, Grimtree seemed to be entrusting to him much more of his business than he had done even to Verne. Templar disliked the new secretary intensely, but he knew better than to say so.

He had told Verne that Robert had 'changed'. What he had not felt disposed to tell her was that, in his opinion, he was going to pieces.

The odd thing about it was that he found himself liking the man a great deal more than he had done before. Could it be that losing Verne in that way had made him more human? Exposed the weakness never before suspected? He seemed a man without either anchor or rudder.

Meantime Verne had gone home despairing. Bill had come in and gone out again, leaving her a note not to wait up for him, but she could not sleep until she had told him.

When he came in, very late and obviously having had a lot to drink, though he always carried it well, all she told him at first was that Robert still refused to talk about a divorce.

He brushed it aside with his usual cheerful unconcern.

'Bill—don't you care about not being able to marry me?' she asked desperately.

'Well, as I've said before, what difference does it make? Why worry?'

'But I am worrying, Bill. And it might make all the difference. What about—children, for instance?'

'I'm sorry if you want them, my sweet, but there just can't be any and you know you can trust me to take care of that.'

'That's just it, Bill,' she said in a low voice, hurt by his casual dismissal of her own feelings about their marriage, and about her possible desire for children. 'I have trusted you.'

He looked at her sharply.

'What do you mean? You can't mean—?'

She nodded.

'Yes, that's what I do mean. I've seen a doctor today, Bill, to make sure.'

'Good Lord! I say, Verne, I'm most frightfully sorry. Can't think how it happened, can you? Have to do something about it p.d.q., shan't we?'

'I don't want to do anything about it,' she said quietly.

'But, my sweet, you must. Can't have a kid when we're not married. Not fair on it. Besides, I can't run to it. I told you that, and of course you'd have to leave your job, which would put us properly in the *potage*. And it doesn't look as though that book of yours is going to do much for us, does it?'

'No,' she said bleakly.

'So you see, darling, we've got to do something. I'll find out how to go about it.'

'I'm not going to, Bill,' she said quite firmly. 'Adrian died, and I shall always believe I killed him in the very early days when I wanted so desperately to get rid of him. I didn't know what to do. But for the first few months my whole mind was set on not having him—and when he was born, he was born with a defective heart, the most vital part of his being.'

'But my dear girl, that's rubbish. Just poppycock. It was nothing to do with you at all, and how on earth could the mere fact of your not wanting it affect his unborn heart? Why, if that were so, none of the horde of unwanted children would survive.'

'I don't care what you say or think. Bill. I shall remain quite certain that it was through that that my baby was born incomplete. I am not going to do anything about this child. If I did, and it failed and I still had it, it might be born with any sort of defect, eyes, hearing, mind—anything. We've created it already, Bill, whether we meant to or not, and I'm not going to risk injuring it. I just couldn't bear—another dead baby,' and she laid her head down on her hands on the table and remained quite still.

For a long time Bill did not speak. When he did, his voice was quite gentle.

'I'm sorry if I've upset you, dear,' he said, 'but I thought you'd see reason. Won't Grimtree change his mind when he knows about this?'

'Probably not. He's trying to punish me.'

'What a brute! Would you like me to see him?'

'Oh no. Bill, It wouldn't do any good either.'

'Oh well. I'm sleepy. How about turning in?'

They did so, but for the first time since she had come to him, they lay apart, and she felt wretchedly that their minds were separated for the moment by an even wider gap than the space between their two beds.

She authorised Jeffery Templar to tell Robert about the child.

For an instant a look of intolerable pain twisted Grimtree's face. Then he drew over it the mask which habitually hid the man from the world.

'She's made her bed. Let her lie in it,' he said harshly.

'You still won't believe that there was nothing between her and this man Trailer until you flung her at him?' asked Templar, who never minced matters with his client.

'No, I won't. What was she doing there, in the flat she's organised him into, if not to have an affair with him?'

'I've told you. She was writing a book. To prove it, the book's already been published. I sent you a copy.'

'Did you think I'd bother with such trash?' asked Grimtree contemptuously, though, sitting alone in his library, he had read every word of it and tried in vain to find Verne in it. 'And in writing a book, is it part of the job to smear a man's face with lipstick?'

'That was foolish but not criminal. She'd known him for years and nowadays girls think nothing of a kiss.'

'Girls may not, but this one was my wife, and I know Verne. If she kissed a man, she was in love with him.'

'Perhaps you don't know her as well as you think you do, Robert.'

Grimtree laughed harshly.

'Oh, I know her,' he said. 'She seems to have got you by the short hairs, though. Well, I won't divorce her. That's flat. Let her have her brat. I fathered one of his for him. He can do what he likes about this one.'

'Isn't that rather unfair on the child?'

'That's my business. I've nothing more to say. If she's got anything to say, let her come and say it. She knows her way to my office.'

'She won't see you, Mr. Grimtree,' said Templar stiffly, reverting to their one time purely business relationship and dropping the more familiar 'Robert'.

'Even if she would,' he added, 'you could hardly expect her to go there, where everybody knows her.'

'Well, she's not coming to the house, and the servants wouldn't admit her.'

'You're very hard.'

'It's the best thing to be. Softness never got anyone anything. Be your own master or everyone else will be it.'

'You're missing a lot in life. Probably more than you think. Well, if this is your last word, I'll get back to my own affairs. You know how to find me if you change your mind.'

'I never change my mind.'

Templar rang up and told Verne. She was not surprised, so received the news almost lethargically.

'I'll manage,' she said. 'Thank you for all you've done, Mr. Templar.'

'Which, I am afraid, is precisely nothing.'

'You believed in me more than my husband did,' she said bitterly. 'I've made a mess of my life, haven't I?'

'Perhaps not irretrievably. If I can do anything for you at any time, let me know.'

What could anyone do for her? she thought wretchedly.

As the months went by, she realised that there was a growing deterioration in her relationship with Bill. He stopped trying to persuade her to get rid of the child, but after that he rarely mentioned it. He might almost not have known she was going to have a baby, she thought resentfully.

Then he came home one evening with a greatly restored cheerfulness, kissed her and asked her how she felt, and without waiting for her to tell him, launched into the cause of his satisfaction.

'I've had a piece of cake,' he said. 'They've given me the Parker Grace assignment. It's a feather in my cap, I can tell you!'

'Isn't that abroad somewhere?' she asked.

'Well—yes, if you call the Commonwealth countries abroad. It's Australia, as a matter of fact.'

'Australia? Oh, Bill, all that way away!' she exclaimed, distressed.

'My sweet, nothing's a long way away nowadays, and you wouldn't like me to have turned this down, would you? What a break for me! I don't know if I'm on my head or my heels.'

'How long will you be gone?' she asked, trying not to show him her hurt resentment. However lucky a break it might be, she felt he should not have accepted it just at this time. It was now January, and with the baby due in May, she must very soon leave the office. Then she would be completely dependent on Bill for both companionship and actual maintenance, for *Pantalets* had not fulfilled Mr. Garret's hopes of it, and she could not expect any further royalties, nor was he now so anxious for her to write the proposed novel.

'Oh, not very long. It only takes about four days by air, and, say, a month or so there. It all depends, but I dare say I shall be back in about six weeks.'

'When do you go?'

'Well—as a matter of fact, they want me to go this weekend. They're getting an air passage by Constellation on Saturday,' he said, looking a little sheepish about it.

'Oh, Bill, so soon?'

'The sooner I go, the sooner I shall be back,' he said cheerfully, to which, of course, she had to agree.

'I'll have to leave the office soon,' she said, absurdly embarrassed, as she always was when she had to mention the coming child. 'Bill, you'll be back well before—before—'

'Oh, good heavens, yes! May, didn't you say?'

'Yes, about then.'

'Oh well, not to worry. I'll leave you some money. I'll arrange for you to have a drawing account on my bank so that you can take what you want.'

'Thank you, Bill. I won't go whoopee with it,' she said, conjuring up a smile.

She did not go to see him off.

'I shouldn't, duckie,' he told her. 'You see—people don't know I'm married—'

'Why should they?' she asked pointedly, and he laughed and kissed her.

'Not still got a bee in your bonnet about that, have you?' he asked.

After he had gone, she felt very lonely. Of necessity, she had made no friends since she had come to live with Bill, nor had she in any way desired to retain any of those she had made as Robert's wife. Now and then, when she could not avoid them, she passed on the stairs or outside in the street other tenants of the flats, and sometimes they murmured a greeting to her awkwardly, though at most times they were as anxious not to meet face to face as she was. Old Mrs. Biggin was still away, but her daughter-in-law was as ubiquitous as ever, her door usually on the latch so that she could pop her head out at the sound of any comings or goings at No. 17.

Bill referred to her as the P.B., which he told her stood for Poisonous Bitch, and Verne had agreed with him that, of all the people who might have known her, Mrs. Biggin was the most likely to have written the letters which Robert had referred to.

Mrs. Biggin was at her door, ostensibly cleaning the letterbox, when Verne returned from her shopping on that Saturday afternoon.

'So you're all alone again, Verne?' she said chattily, but with an obvious undercurrent of meaning.

'Yes,' said Verne shortly.

'Pity! Just at this time too. Still, as I say, women have to put up with everything, don't they? I don't know why we bother with men at all, I'm sure. Though I can't expect you to agree with me there, can I?' with a meaning glance and a nasty smile at Verne's thickening figure.

Verne went in and shut the door and tried not to feel the desolation of the empty flat. She consoled herself with the thought that now she was alone, she could give way to the tiredness and general malaise which were accompanying this pregnancy and which she had tried to hide from Bill. She made herself a cup of tea, cut some bread and butter which she found she could not eat, after all, and lay down on the bed.

Even before she could get the promised cable from Bill to say he had arrived, the office manager called her in and rather curtly suggested that she might like to hand in her notice.

'I don't, of course, know if you are married, Miss Weston,' he said, for since she had started under that name, she had not worn any ring in the office.

'As a matter of fact, I am, Mr. Colby,' she said, her head high, two little spots of colour in her cheeks and her eyes meeting his levelly.

'I'm glad to know that, of course, though it is a pity you did not say so when you came. I understand there is talk in the office, and with a number of young girls on the staff—'

'I quite understand,' said Verne icily. 'I will leave at the end of the week.'

'Yes, I think that would be best. We will give you a week's money, of course.'

She would have liked to refuse it, but common sense prevailed, and she accepted it. She had been buying things for the baby with what she could squeeze out of the joint housekeeping money, to which she contributed considerably more than Bill, and she did not know how much money he had made available to her at his bank.

He had not told her what arrangements he had made for her to draw on his account, and at length she had, very distastefully, to call and ask the cashier.

He disappeared, and then came back to ask her to see the manager.

'Good morning, Mrs. Trailer,' said that official when she had been ushered into his private office. 'I understand you are asking if your husband made any arrangements for you to draw on his account?'

'Yes. He's away from England and forgot to tell me. I hope he didn't forget to make the arrangements too,' she added with a forced smile.

'Well, I'm afraid he did forget, Mrs. Trailer. There is no order to us to enable you to draw on the account, and as a matter of fact, it's in rather low water at the moment,' with an apologetic smile.

Her condition was obvious and he felt sorry for her, but he had no power to help her even if the account had been sound.

'Oh, oh, I see,' said Verne, keeping up a brave front in spite of the sick feeling the news had given her. 'Well, I need not take up your time. I must write to my husband and tell him. I am sorry to have bothered you about it.'

'Not at all. That's what we're here for,' he told her genially and showed her out.

What was she to do now? thought Verne, horrified at the position in which she found herself. Ever since she had come to live with Bill in the flat, she had insisted on their paying the rent, sending the money every week in Bill's name to Robert's office, though Bill had insisted that it was a quixotic gesture and quite unnecessary. Now, with nothing to draw on and Bill thousands of miles away, how was she even to find the twenty seven and six for the rent, let alone keep herself?

She had never been able to redeem her father's gift to her and now, guiltily, but with none of the former sense of personal loss, she paid another visit to the pawnshop and received only a very small proportion of the value of her engagement ring. She had found, on going to the shops, that in spite of his promises and gay assurances, Bill had run up bills and left debts which in her angry pride she settled, so that the money from the ring did not go nearly as far as she had expected. She wrote and told Bill what she had done, also that he had not left her anything in the bank nor arranged for her to be able to draw it.

He wrote back that the tradespeople had cheated her, taking advantage of his absence, and that of course it was absurd for the bank manager to have told her he had nothing, there. He would write to him and make him sit up, he promised, and he would be telling her what arrangements he had made.

The rest of the hastily scrawled letter was an account of his work, its excitement, the thousands of miles he had to travel, and the friendliness of the Australian people.

He did not write to her about the proposed arrangements, and she wrote again, anxiously, asking when he was coming home, but his reply was long in coming, and he made no mention of his return.

Had she been his wife, she thought miserably, she might have gone to his office and explained her position and asked them for help, but she did not know whether they knew the truth and could not bring herself to go to them.

Bill had already been gone nearly three months, though he had told her it would not be more than about six weeks, and the baby was due in a few weeks' time when she happened to meet Douglas Grey, who worked on the same newspaper as Bill and whom she had known in the old days before her marriage.

She saw him hesitate, and then stop, coming towards her with outstretched hand.

'Why, stranger!' he said. 'Where have you been all this time?'

'Oh, I—I married, Douglas,' she said, wondering how much he knew about her.

'Oh yes, of course you did. Went all high hat on us, didn't you? Aren't you married to Robert Grimtree?' though he could not quite disguise the fact that he was surprised to see her on foot, obviously late in pregnancy, and looking almost shabby.

She nodded, wondering what to say.

'Come and have a coffee with me somewhere, for old times' sake,' he suggested. 'That is, if you can come down to a humble tea shop?'

'Of course,' she said with a forced smile. 'I'd be glad to have one.'

Over the marble topped table, they chatted of people they had both known, and inevitably he mentioned Bill.

'You remember Bill Trailer? But of course you do. He and you used to be buddies before you left us for the heights. He's a lucky dog, if ever there were one! Landed himself a very nice job, a very nice job indeed. Had the nerve to go in and ask for it, too! No waiting to see if it would come his way! He's in Australia, special representative there, with the deuce of a long term contract at about double what he'd get here.'

'A—a long term contract, did you say?' she repeated.

'I'll say so! Jonas—you remember him?—was all lined up for it, but old Bill stepped smartly up, suggested to them that it was hardly fair to send a married man out for two years, as he understood accommodation for married people was difficult if not almost impossible out there, and blow me down, he landed the job—pht! just like that. Jonas didn't mind, fortunately, since there was no question of them sending his wife with him and he didn't want to take on a two year assignment without her.'

'You mean that—Bill—has gone for two years?' she asked blankly.

'Two years certain, probably more. Wouldn't have let him go if he hadn't been willing to sign up for duration, but what would he want to come back for? Single man, no ties, good job out there and out of this beastly climate. I'd have jumped at the chance, but I didn't have the pluck to wade in and ask for it as old Bill did. Another coffee?'

'No. No, thank you. I think I'd better be getting along now,' she said and rose to her feet so wearily that he looked at her in some concern.

What the dickens was Mrs. Robert Grimtree doing out and about like this?

'I say, can I get you a taxi or anything?' he asked as they reached the pavement.

'No, thank you. I—I'm being met. I mustn't be late. Thank you so much for the coffee—and everything,' and she hurried away as fast as her burdened body would allow.

She was stunned by what Douglas Grey had told her.

Bill had gone away deliberately, had himself manoeuvred the assignment which he had told her was 'a marvellous bit of luck'. He had left her, knowing that she would be alone and expecting their child, and not for the six weeks he had lied about but for at least two years. The knowledge was bitter to accept.

It was some weeks since she had heard from him, his last letter telling her that as he was 'moving about a lot', future letters might be 'rather irregular'. She wondered now how much truth there was in that.

She lay down on her bed, sick at the discovery of Bill's betrayal, and wished she could die. That would be easy. There was gas in the kitchen and other women defeated by life and by men had taken that way out.

Then she felt the child stir strongly within her and knew she would not take that way. Besides, what if she died and by some miracle of surgery they could make the child live? Her distraught mind could imagine that at such a moment.

As she lay there, she heard a letter fall into her letterbox and mechanically dragged herself to the door to pick it up, staring at the address on the envelope. 'Mrs. Robert Grimtree', it said in a large, ill formed handwriting which she knew.

For a long time she held it in her hand. What had Robert to say to her? The strange, unfathomable thing was that the sight of his handwriting should tug at her heart, could offer her a grain of comfort and make her feel that, after all, she belonged to another human being.

But the letter, when at last she took it from the envelope, gave her little justification for that feeling.

Dear Verne, Robert Grimtree had written in his own hand. The enclosed came for you. I have no idea why you lent this money nor how you got it. There is no need to acknowledge it. – R.G.

The 'enclosed' was a cheque for a hundred pounds and it was signed by Mary Gorner.

The stark baldness of his letter was like the blow of a fist after that strange feeling of comfort. Yet why should she have expected anything else from him? The wife whom he believed had betrayed him and who was at that very moment, as far as he was aware, living with the man who had been party to that betrayal?

Oh, Robert, Robert, if only you could have trusted me and believed in me! she mourned.

Whatever the circumstances, Robert would never have treated her with the callous cruelty Bill had shown her, knowing that she bore his child within her body.

Though he had said there was no need to acknowledge the letter, she was impelled to do so. At least he should know that it was not his money which she had lent to Mary Gorner, though by what means he imagined she should have become possessed of it, she could not imagine.

Dear Robert, she wrote after many discarded attempts,
Thank you for sending me Mrs. Gorner's cheque. She needed the money badly and came to see me at Wellington Gate. I lent her the amount that came to me from my mother's life insurance policy. I hope that all is well with you.
                              Yours sincerely,
                              Verne.

She wanted to tell him that she knew of the gesture he had made after Gorner's death, but knew that if he had intended her to know, he would have told her himself at the time, and also that Mary Gorner's repudiation of the gift must have enraged him and would still be a sore point.

The money could not have been more opportune, but it should have come from Bill and the knowledge made her the more bitter.

She wrote to Bill but could not bring herself to tell him that she knew the truth about his visit to Australia. She merely told him, with none of the endearments she would otherwise have compelled herself to use, that she had made the arrangements for the birth of the child and added that she was looking forward to his being with her before the time arrived. At all costs she must keep up the pretence that she trusted and believed in him. It was her only anchor.

But no reply came as the weeks went by and she did not write again, forcing herself at last to stop looking for the letter, and in the middle of May, her daughter was born.

When they came to her in the hospital for the information that would enable the child to be registered, she hesitated and then, making her face blank of all expression, she spoke calmly.

'I am not married to the father of the child,' she said. 'I don't know how to register her.'

The nurse's face registered no shock, though it had never occurred to her that Mrs. Trailer was 'one of those'.

'You register it in your name, and you can leave the father's name blank,' she said. 'What is your real name?'

'Raydon,' said Verne steadily. 'Verne Raydon.'

'And the child's name?'

'Rosemary.'

It was the name she and Robert had decided upon for their child if it had been a girl. She could not have said why she had decided to give the name to Bill's child, and Robert would never know, in any case.

So, as Rosemary Raydon, the small, perfect thing started on its way through life.

She had told the doctors that this was not her first child, and how her son had died, and she was anxious to be reassured about the health of her daughter.

'Nothing to worry about here,' she was told. 'It's a perfect child, healthy in every way, so you have nothing to fear. Those tragedies do happen and we rarely know why, but they are scarcely ever repeated in a second child.'

When she went back to the flat, feeling little effects from what had been an easy, natural labour, she found Bill's letter on the mat.

Dear Verne, he had written,
I'm not going to find this easy, and I can guess what sort of a skunk you will think me, but we've always been honest with each other and I'm going to be honest now.

The fact is, I am staying out here and not coming back to England. I didn't tell you at the time as I hadn't the face to do it, but I took a two year contract. I thought at the time that perhaps we could arrange for

*you to come out here after the baby was born, but I see now that it
wouldn't have worked out. You wouldn't fit into the life here. We had
a good lime together, but I realised that I couldn't live up to you after
the way you'd got used to living with Grimtree. I'm sorry about the
baby, of course, but I expect you can get it adopted. I don't expect I
shall come back to England. I like it out here, and as a matter of fact,
I have met a girl who is right up my street, and by the time you get this,
we shall be married. She's fond of me and understands what a man
wants. I did love you, Verne. I was crazy about you, but when a man
gets only a sort of tolerant liking in return, it isn't very satisfying. I'm
too much of the earth earthy for you.*

*If I were you, I'd go back to Grimtree. He need never know about
the baby and it's always been my opinion that he's fond of you.
Anyway he can give you the sort of life you really like, which I never
could.*

Thank you for the fun we had. I shall never forget you.

Bill.

She tore the letter slowly into shreds. There was no need to read it
again. Had she not perhaps, in her heart, always known that Bill was
unreliable, unstable as water? Was that perhaps why, when she had so
ardently desired it, she had been unable to give him her love?

She picked up the baby and held it against her heart, closely, with a
hungering, passionately protecting love. Now she was all her own.

'Out of all the mess and folly of my life, you've come, my perfect
thing,' she whispered against its soft cheek. 'Now it's just you and I
against the world, and somehow you're going to get your share of
happiness. Somehow. Somehow.'

She did not answer Bill's letter. There was nothing to say. It would
give her no satisfaction to abuse him. He was as he was made, and now
had no share in her life.

The part of the letter which had wounded her most deeply was his
calm suggestion that she should give up her baby and go back to
Robert. How like Bill, with his easy repudiation of anything he no
longer wanted!

But, with relentless justice, she let her mind go back to that first night with Bill. It had been she who had offered herself, and he who had suggested her going to an hotel. Flung at him by Robert, she had clung to Bill and he had accepted her as any man would have done. Now he was ready to fling her back – an unwanted burden which had served its purpose and outworn its use.

She laid the baby back in its cot and stood up very straight and still.

Well, she had done with men. She wanted nothing more of them. From now on, it was she and Rosemary against the world.

Chapter Eleven

Verne had calculated that, with rigid economy, the money from Mary Gorner could be made to last until Rosemary was six weeks old, after which she must find a means of earning. She could not go into an office again because she would have to leave Rosemary in the care of someone else, and, apart from the fact that she was able to feed this child herself, she could not bring herself to put her in a day nursery. The loss of her first baby had set up all manner of fears and she would trust no one but herself.

She felt that, after managing the housekeeping and work of the flat on so little money, she was now qualified to look after someone else's home, and she hopefully set herself to the task of answering advertisements in the newspapers for housekeepers and mothers' helps. She found, however, that the child was an insuperable objection for even those advertisers who said 'child not objected to' proved not to have included a young baby in their plans.

She stuck to it grimly, denying herself everything that was not essential to Rosemary's well being, and finally she found a Mrs. Briggs-Hallet who, from an address in Surrey, informed her that she kept a 'high class and exclusive residential home for young children', and that she was prepared to accept Verne's services in return for board and lodging for mother and child and a very small remuneration.

Verne had made up her mind from the first that she would not start off with another elaborate fabric of lies, and she told this lady, in her second letter, that she was an unmarried mother who wished at all costs to keep her child with her.

To her relief, Mrs. Briggs-Hallet replied with the gracious intimation that Miss Raydon's 'unfortunate position' would not be an insuperable objection, so would she present herself, ready to start work, on a date three days ahead?

Verne had not expected to start so soon, but she accomplished almost superhuman tasks in the three days, surrendering the flat, selling or storing the furniture, grudgingly buying the 'plain blue dress' and white house overalls which her new employer specified as essential.

'You need not provide yourself with outdoor clothes,' she had added, 'as we have a beautiful garden in which, in suitable weather, you will be able to take your exercise when on duty.'

She did not appear to think it necessary either to interview her new helper or ask for references, which was a relief to Verne, and on the appointed day she set off, with Rosemary in the carrycot which she had bought second hand as an essential.

Her first glimpse of High Clere was not attractive, but it was raining and windy and she told herself that no house would look its best in such circumstances.

It was a tall, old fashioned house which would once have been described by house agents as 'a desirable and commodious gentleman's residence' but had long since ceased to be desirable to any gentlemen seeking a residence, though it was undoubtedly commodious, with a row of huge, flat faced windows at either side of the somewhat dilapidated flight of steps, and above them rows of lesser windows, and above again a series of small dormer windows which were the attics. On a lower plane than the steps was a basement with windows just peeping over the top of a stone parapet and designed to admit the minimum of light to the rooms.

A slatternly maid in an overall fastened with a safety pin opened the door to her and was evidently expecting her, for she gave her a cheerful grin.

'You'll be Miss Rydon,' she said. 'She's askin' for you. In 'ere. I'll look after that,' wresting the handles of the carrycot from Verne and indicating a half open door off the bare, stone tiled hall.

Mrs. Briggs-Hallet rose to meet her, a large busted elderly woman whose obviously dyed black hair in no way concealed her age. She wore a dress of tight purple silk adorned with several rows of improbable looking pearls, and large gold rings dangled from her ears.

'That's right, Miss Raydon,' she said, with a toothy smile and an outstretched hand whose finger nails were not quite clean beneath scarlet varnish. 'I like my helpers to be very punctual, but perhaps the bus was a little late? Well, never mind. Here is a list of your duties, and Margaret will show you to your room. We have twenty seven little ones in our care, and as your own child is very young (two months, did you say?) I am putting you in charge of the babies. Miss Knowle helps with the older ones and will tell you your duties. We are just one big happy family here, Miss Raydon, but of course the comfort of all of us depends on efficiency and trustworthiness. Also as I am a very busy person, with all the care of the home on my shoulders, I do not expect to be worried over small matters for which I pay my helpers,' with another toothy smile.

'I will do my best,' said Verne gravely.

'Yes, we all do that, of course,' and Mrs. Briggs-Hallet rang the bell to summon Margaret, who proved to be the unkempt little maid who had admitted the new arrival.

'Margaret, show Miss Raydon to her room and introduce her to Miss Knowle,' said Mrs. Briggs-Hallet, 'but don't stay there gossiping. You have plenty to do.'

'I'll say,' muttered the girl in an aside to Verne as she escorted her from the room. 'Got any more luggage?'

'Only one other case. I left it at the station to be sent up as I couldn't cope with more than this small one and Rosemary.'

'Well, you won't want much s'long as you've got workin' clo's,' grinned the maid, and Verne felt a vague, sinking feeling against which she resolutely fought.

They passed the first floor and went on to the top of the house and here Margaret opened a door into a large room, made by throwing several of the original attics into one, and at first sight, the room seemed to Verne to be completely full of a confused mass of cots, playpens, strings of washing and small children.

It was a bedlam of noise, and in the midst of it was one adult, a thin, gaunt girl in a white overall with a nurse's linen square on her head, a baby on each arm and two toddlers clinging uncertainly to her skirts.

192

She gave Verne one glance and then, without waiting for an introduction, came towards her and plumped one of the babies into her arms, to receive which Verne hastily set down the carrycot.

'Thank goodness you've come. Take this for pity's sake and feed it. The bottles are over there,' indicating a tin bath filled with feeding bottles.

'It's wet,' said Verne, whose own baby was kept immaculate no matter how much washing resulted.

'I know. So are they all, but it'll be wet again by the time it's had its feed, so it'll have to lump it. We should never get through if we were too fussy,' and she put up her free hand to push back a strand of hair which had straggled from the keeping of her cap.

'Which bottle?' asked Verne.

'They're all the same. Margaret, put that case down and get Bobbie away from the window, will you? The little devil can get it open. And when you go down, tell Hawk he must come up and fix it. For the love of Mike, Iris, stop hanging on to me—and stop that bawling, all of you!' raising her voice to a pitch which momentarily quelled some of the tumult.

For the next hour or so, Verne had no opportunity of talking to her co-helper, whom she knew must be Miss Knowle, but at last all the eleven small babies were fed, changed and put into their cots and she picked up Rosemary who, sweet tempered and patient as a rule, had begun to object loudly to such unusual neglect. It was an hour past her feeding time.

'Where is my own room?' she asked Miss Knowle. 'I simply must feed her.'

'Doing it yourself?' asked the other girl in surprise and some doubt. 'You'll be lucky if you keep it. I should put her on a bottle if I were you. Oh, your room? Here,' and she escorted Verne to the far end of the room where, in the corner, was a bed and a small chest and a cupboard.

'Here?' asked Verne in surprise. 'But—don't I have a room?'

'There isn't one on this floor,' said Miss Knowle, 'and you couldn't keep running up and down the stairs. Miss Parfitt always slept here. It won't be so bad presently when I've got my horde out of the way. Come on, all of you, get in line,' and she marshalled the toddlers and the slightly older children into a long, straggling, giggling, pushing line and marched them out of the room and down the stairs, throwing over her shoulder to Verne the shouted information that she would come up later.

Verne, aghast at the conditions in which she found herself, sat down on the bed and attended to Rosemary, resolutely closing her ears to the yelling of the several babies who had not yet settled down. With eleven to bottle feed and 'top and tail', she had had no time to pat up their wind, and she knew distractedly that the poor mites were unlikely to be able to sleep until this comfort was assured.

She firmly attended to Rosemary first, however, and was settling her down in the carrycot when the door opened and Mrs. Briggs-Hallet sailed into the room, majestic and rustling, the bunch of keys hanging on a chain at her waist jangling as she moved.

'Now, Miss Raydon,' she said firmly, 'though I have allowed you to bring your own child here, you must understand that it is in no way privileged, and you must not neglect your charges to attend to your own baby first.'

'I haven't done,' said Verne, a little indignantly. 'I've fed and cleaned up all the others first.'

'Then why are they crying?'

'I expect they've got wind, poor mites, but I'm just going to see what I can do for them,' leaving the now peaceful Rosemary and picking up the most vociferous of the other babies to hold it over her shoulder and pat its back.

'Well, you seem to know what you're doing,' said her employer grudgingly, 'but another night, I can't have all this noise going on. After my long day's work, I expect to have peace and quiet, and my poor sister rests at this time. She is an invalid, you know.'

Verne didn't know, of course, but it was not necessary to say so, and she was relieved to see Miss Knowle coming into the room, nodding and making faces behind the lady's back.

Mrs. Briggs-Hallet turned to her.

'Miss Knowle, I am sure you have your hands full with your own charges,' she said severely, 'so please don't come up here to gossip.'

'They're all having their supper and Margaret is giving an eye to them, Mrs. Briggs-Hallet,' said Miss Knowle, unperturbed. 'I came to tell Miss Raydon about the arrangements for her own supper.'

'Well, don't stay wasting your time and hers,' said the lady, and sailed out again.

Daisy Knowle grinned and picked up another wailing baby and started to pacify it.

'Don't take too much notice of what she says,' she advised Verne. 'So long as you don't let any of the kids die, or fall out of the window or down the stairs, she won't worry.'

'She must have an awful lot to do, Miss Knowle.'

'Call me Daisy. It's quicker. A lot to do? We do it, you and Margaret and I. She sails about and finds more for us to do, if she can, and makes a lot of business about locking and unlocking cupboards, but that's about all. Rosie does a good bit more. She's the sister, Miss Rose, poor thing. Has to sit on her behind all day and does the sewing and prepares the vegetables and so on. Nice old thing, but of course she can't come up here where we need the help. Gosh, I'm tired!' and she picked up another baby.

'Do I look after all these?' asked Verne, with an appalled glance at the eleven cots. 'Who does the washing?' for by now there was a great heap of nappies on the floor, with another pile of wet sheets and cot blankets.

'You do,' said Miss Knowle. 'There's a scullery out there with a bath and a sink, and a gas stove on the landing for the bottles. I'll come up and show you when I've got my lot down. I shouldn't bother about that one in the corner. It never stops crying whatever you do, though the doctor says there's nothing the matter with it. Just darned bad tempered and cussed. But then it's a boy, so what else do you expect?' and she plumped the baby from her arms into its cot, tucked it in vigorously and departed.

Verne tried in vain to pacify the one she had been advised to leave alone, but finally gave it up, moved the cot as far as she could from the rest, and went back to look at Rosemary, now sleeping peacefully with one chubby arm flung up on the pillow and a soft pink flush on her rose petal cheek. By any standard, she was a lovely baby, and Verne had now seen and handled all sorts of babies.

She bent down and tucked the arm in snugly.

'It looks as though it might be going to be pretty awful, my blossom,' she whispered, 'but so long as I can keep you with me, I'll put up with anything, and after all, all these are other mothers' babies, poor mites—and poor mothers.' She wondered how such a collection of unmothered babies came to be here, and when presently Daisy Knowle returned to give her some advice and help with the stack of washing which she had already carted out to the scullery, her colleague explained the position.

'Most of them are what they call unfortunates, like ours,' she said. 'Mothers but no fathers. They belong to the high ups, though. Girls whose people can afford to pay to keep them out of the way and looked after. Some of them get adopted, but not many. Goodness knows what happens to them when they leave here, which is when they're about six. Goodness knows what will happen to mine.'

'You've got a child, Daisy?' asked Verne, throwing a pile of washed nappies into the rinsing bath and starting on another.

'I have, worse luck. And even worse, a boy. He's four—Georgie, the black headed one. Bit of the tar brush, probably, but I didn't know about that. Sometimes I almost forget which he is. I've got sixteen of 'em at present, but I have had more.'

'And are there only the two of us for all this number?' asked Verne, appalled.

'And Margaret, who is a tower of strength. Can't imagine how she gets through all she does, but she turns up here smiling every so often and gives us a bit of rest, which heaven knows we need. What's your name, by the way?'

'Verne.'

'Queer name, but rather nice. Chuck over the rest of those, the dirty ones, and we'll put 'em to soak whilst we do the bottles for the ten o'clock.'

'Good heavens, do we start the riot again at ten?' asked Verne.

'Too true, but they don't make much racket then and all I've got to do to my lot is to pot them. When we've done the bottles, we'd better go down and have our supper.'

196

'Do we leave the babies then?'

'Oh Lord, yes, or we'd never get anything to eat. Yours can't get out, that's one thing, and if they cry, they won't die of it.'

During the unbelievable turmoil and difficulties and almost unendurable noise of the next few weeks, Verne knew she could never have got through without the cheerful, practical guidance of Daisy Knowle and the willing help of Margaret, in whose breast she had unwittingly aroused a passionate admiration and love.

Their own meals and these of the older children were prepared in the downstairs kitchen, but apart from that, they were entirely responsible for the care and well being of twenty seven children, the oldest of them being a small redheaded urchin named Bobbie, who was nearly six. He was in every kind of mischief and thought out adventures which had never occurred even to the experienced mind of Miss Knowle. He was never clean for more than a few minutes at a time, nor were any of his immediate associates, and there was a constant cry of 'What's Bobbie doing?' because if what he was doing was legitimate, all the rest of the children were almost certainly safe.

But Verne adored him, and his robust courage, his cheerful acceptance of the many threats and punishments that came his way, and above all, his wide, friendly grin with gaps in his gums where his second teeth were almost due to start.

Daisy, who seemed to know most of their histories, told her about him.

'He's not an illegit like most of them,' she said. 'Might be better for him if he were, poor little blighter. His mother bunked off with another man and took him with her, but the father went to the court after the divorce and got him back, and now she's not even allowed to see him whilst they decide what is to be done with him for keeps. The father comes occasionally, but it's my belief that he only keeps him to spite the mother. She came down here once, but Evalina wouldn't let her see him.' (Her helpers called Mrs. Briggs-Hallet by her first name in private, whilst Miss Rose was Rosie.)

'Do you think Bobbie minds?' asked Verne, her heart torn by the thought of any mother being parted from her child.

'Difficult to say. At first he was always talking of her and used to cry at night for her, but kids are adaptable, and he doesn't mention her now and I expect he'll forget.'

'She won't, though,' said Verne.

'Oh, I don't know. She's rather a flashy bit of goods, red haired like him, and she's got her new man, probably married to him by now.'

'What'll happen to Bobbie?'

'What'll happen to any of the poor little blighters? Anyway, better get on. Those old nosy parkers from the Ministry will be coming round this afternoon. It's their day.'

The said nosy parkers were officials whose job it was to pay routine visits of inspection to such homes as this, and in spite of the house being dreary and gaunt, hedged in with high trees and an unscalable wall, the children regimented and allowed little liberty, Verne had to admit that it was well run and that the small inmates were kept healthy and clean. That it was largely owing to the efforts of herself and Daisy and Margaret was undeniable, for she soon realised that Mrs. Briggs-Hallet did very little work herself, but though Verne was over worked and always dog tired, at least she had been able to provide a home and her own care for Rosemary, who probably throve better because she could not have all the attention which Verne felt was her right.

Often at night, after the ten o'clock feed which rarely finished before half past eleven, she was too tired even to undress, but threw herself down on her bed as she was, and rose, weary eyed, at five the next morning to start all over again.

It was after an epidemic of chicken pox which swept through Daisy's charges but fortunately was kept away from the babies, that disaster overtook her. Nobody knew how the infection had started, since the children were never taken outside the garden wall, but it was supposed that Mrs. Lusty, the daily woman who came to help in the kitchen, had somehow brought it in.

Though Verne could not, because of the risk of infection, go down to the lower floor to help the over burdened Daisy, her own work had been greatly increased by the fact that neither Daisy nor Margaret could come up and help her, and one afternoon at the end of a warm, breathless September day, she gratefully accepted Mrs. Briggs-Hallet's reluctant offer to sit with the babies whilst she got a breath of fresh air in the garden. During the two months she had been at High Clere, she had never been outside the garden herself, and she could now understand Margaret's original comment about not wanting anything but her working clothes.

She took Rosemary down with her in her carrycot, and received her employer's instructions to keep an eye on the others whilst she was in the garden, 'the others' being such of the older children as had got over their illness and now were free of infection.

Verne sighed a little. She had been looking forward to a quiet hour, lolling in a chair and perhaps even permitting herself the luxury of cuddling Rosemary in her arms at some other time than her feeding time. With much regret, she had found it impossible to go on supplying the food herself. She was too tired and devitalised by her unending day's work and nights broken by crying babies, but Rosemary had made no complaints, accepting her bottles with complete unconcern.

She found half a dozen noisy little girls and boys playing in the garden, and her heart sank a little when she saw that her favourite Bobbie was amongst them, for where Bobbie was, there was usually trouble.

Still, they seemed to have found a harmless game for the moment, and she settled down in a chair where she could watch them.

A few minutes later, however, she heard a whisper from the bushes at her back.

'I want to speak to you—please,' said the voice, and, wondering who it could be, Verne rose and went behind the bushes to find a woman hiding there, little more than a girl, with a halo of bright red hair above a pretty, tear stained face, an emerald green bandeau round her head matching the brilliant coat and skirt she wore.

Verne guessed at once who she was, even before the girl said in an agitated whisper, 'I'm Bobbie's mother. Do please let me see him for a minute. It's nearly six months now, and I—I can't *bear* it any longer. Please, please let me see him, just for a minute. Nobody will know, and they can't see from the house. Oh please—please!'

The tears were flowing again, and the girl caught her hand beseechingly. Verne's heart turned over for her. The girl's distress was so obvious that she must love the boy deeply, and Verne, who hated to be parted even for a few hours at a time from her own child, could not resist the appeal of this other mother, though she knew quite well that it was against express instructions, Bobbie having been placed there by the direction of the court which was to settle his eventual fate.

'Do please let me,' pleaded the girl again as she stood there, irresolute. 'I'm leaving England tomorrow, and I may never see him again! Just for five minutes. It isn't much to ask, is it?'

Verne gave way.

For heaven's sake keep him behind these bushes,' she said. 'I'll stand here with my eye on the house, and directly I tell you, you must go. You will, won't you?'

'Oh I will. I promise.'

Verne went to Bobbie and disentangled him from the mass of arms and legs of his companions, and led him by the hand.

'Darling, I want you a minute,' she said, and he looked up at her with his uneven grin and made no demur, but when, a moment later, she parted the bushes and let him see who was waiting there, he dropped her hand and rushed with an incoherent, choking cry towards the opened arms.

'Mummy! My mummy!'

So much, thought Verne, for Daisy's impression that he had already forgotten.

With her own eyes not quite dry, she turned her back and let the bushes close in again behind her, fixing her gaze on the only point from which danger, in the form of one of the staff, or Mrs. Briggs-Hallet herself, might be expected.

About five minutes later, Daisy Knowle appeared to call the children in, and Verne turned back to warn Bobbie's mother that she must go.

But the little plot of grass behind the bushes was empty. There was no sign of either Bobbie or his mother, and though she ran frantically from one possible screen of trees and bushes to another, she could neither see nor hear them.

Daisy's voice came to her ears demanding from the others to know where Bobbie was.

'Miss Raydon took him,' said one of them, and Daisy went to where Rosemary lay, knowing that Verne would not be far off.

When Verne appeared, looking anxious, Daisy smiled a welcome. They had scarcely seen each other for the past fortnight

'Have you got that horrible child Bobbie?' she asked.

'Oh, Daisy, something awful's happened. I think he's gone,' said Verne.

'Gone? Gone where?'

'I don't know,' said Verne, really frightened now. 'It's all my fault, too. His mother came and simply begged me to let her see him, said she wouldn't keep him more than a moment, but she was crying—and—and in the end, I did—and now he isn't there, and neither is she. Oh, Daisy, what do you think has happened?'

Daisy looked grim.

'It isn't what I *think*' she said. 'It's what I jolly well *know*. I saw a car standing outside the gate before I came down, and a woman was saying something to the driver before she left him and came in. I thought to myself "that's another of them", but it must have been Bobbie's mother. In a bright green suit?'

'Yes,' said Verne, swallowing miserably. 'I'd better go and look if the car's still there.'

But of course it wasn't. She had known it would not be, and Daisy had known it too.

They stood staring at each other.

'She's pinched him, of course,' said Daisy.

'And she told me she is leaving the country tomorrow,' said Verne. 'Whatever shall we do?'

'Start the hue and cry, I'm afraid,' said Daisy. 'We'll have to tell Evalina.'

'Can't we phone the police or something?' suggested Verne desperately.

'Better leave it to her,' decided Daisy. 'Sorry, Verne, and all that, but I don't see that we can take it into our own hands, not when he's a ward of the courts. There will be all hell to pay if we can't get him back, but she must be stopped from taking him out of the country at all costs. Come on. I'll back you up. Say you didn't know, or something.'

'I can't do that. The children saw me fetch him.'

'Tell her you didn't know she wasn't supposed to see him.'

'But Evalina told me herself she wasn't!' cried Verne, almost in tears.

'That's rather torn it, but let's go. We're only wasting time.'

The upheaval was quite as bad as the two girls had anticipated. Soon the house was buzzing with uniformed police and non uniformed superiors; telephones whirred, Verne was questioned and re-questioned, upstairs all the babies were crying and nobody thought of doing anything about it, Scotland Yard was informed and watchers sent out on the roads and to the railway stations and docks.

Finally, exhausted and utterly overwrought, Verne was sent up to see to the babies.

'You might as well do your work whilst you *are* here, Miss Raydon,' said Mrs. Briggs-Hallet severely, and Verne was thankful to go into the far lesser turmoil of twelve wailing babies, for Rosemary had by now joined in the chorus.

Bobbie was found the next day on board the Channel steamer before she sailed, and brought back, in tearful, defiant, protesting disgrace, and Verne packed her belongings, ready to leave the moment a substitute could be found for her.

'I shall miss you dreadfully,' said Daisy, snatching a forbidden moment on the top floor. 'Evalina is a fool. She'll never get anyone like you again, and you're the least likely person in the world to let Bobbie go again.'

Three days later, Verne and her luggage and Rosemary left High Clere forever.

It was the end of another phase.

What next?

She had saved most of her very meagre salary at High Clere, since there was nothing to spend it on and she had long ago given up smoking, but even so she had not enough to support life for herself and Rosemary for more than a week or two.

Setting her teeth against the necessity, knowing there was no other place where she could hope to eke out her small means better, she went to a Salvation Army Hostel and was given a cubicle to herself. It was rough and bare and comfortless, but it was clean, and after two months of nights with crying babies, seemed a haven of rest and peace.

She wondered grimly what her neighbours would have said had they known that the new arrival was Robert Grimtree's wife, and wondered how Robert himself would have viewed her present surroundings, but her life in Wellington Gate seemed now so far away that it might have been part of someone else's story, never of her own. She had learned to work hard and to live hard and above all to live in the present and let the future take care of itself.

She rarely now even thought of Bill, though if occasionally she fancied she caught a likeness to him in Rosemary, she was quick to thrust it out of her mind. He was no longer in their lives.

She was searching the newspaper advertisement columns to find some possible new job when she came upon one which both interested and amused her.

'Elderly misogynist forced to seek female housekeeper who can occasionally act as his amanuensis. Almost nonexistent salary but pleasant country home and personal freedom. No one interested in matrimony need apply.'

A box number followed, and, after some consideration, Verne decided to apply. She felt that, except for the addition of Rosemary, she could fill his requirements. She was female, she could housekeep, she was a trained secretary and she was certainly not interested in matrimony!

She liked, too, his rather acid sense of humour. The thing was, would an elderly misogynist, averse to matrimony, accept a small baby as a member of his household? And if she personally vouched for Rosemary's character and behaviour, would her daughter let her down?

She wrote, however, and was candid over her position.

I feel capable of doing all the things your advertisement specifies, she wrote, but I have a child, a little girl four months old, from whom I cannot be parted. She is a good baby, and I would not allow her presence in your house to be a disturbance to you, and so long as I am

able to supply out barest needs, I shall consider an almost nonexistent
salary sufficient, nor am I in the least interested in matrimony.

She signed herself 'Verne Raydon. (Miss)', and left him to draw his own conclusions.

Greatly to her surprise, she received an answer, making no comments on the contents of her letter, but asking her to go and see him. He enclosed a postal order to cover her return fare and signed himself 'Yours faithfully, Gerald Mance'.

He added a postscript.

I shall require a personal reference. Kindly see that one is sent to me
by post direct from the referee before you come to see me.

That was a poser.

Where could she get such a thing as a personal reference? Certainly not from Mrs. Briggs-Hallet, and not from Corbett and Clark's, since she had gone there as Miss Weston and now she was Verne Raydon again.

She thought of Jeffery Templar, who had once offered to help her 'in any way he could'. Would he be disposed to aid and abet her now, with a husband in the background to whom she was only legally tied, and a faithless lover in Australia?

She decided to try him, since there was no one else, and she found it easy to talk to him, even made him laugh with her descriptions of life at High Clere, and received from him a ready promise to recommend her to the unknown misogynist.

'I don't know what on earth you can say about me that will be both true and useful,' she said. 'I'm not even respectable.'

'I think we can get over that,' he told her with a smile, and she would have been amazed at what he found to tell Gerald Mance about her.

He made no mention of the men in her life.

When, a week later, she arrived at the address in the Sussex village, she paused at the gate in sheer delight.

He had called it a pleasant home, and that was what it looked like, a small house little more than a cottage, with a timbered whitewashed front, an old thatched roof and a garden which was a riot of autumn flowers and late roses.

The door stood open, and through the opening she had a glimpse of a small square hall with a brick floor and low doorways and one or two pieces of very good old furniture.

Gerald Mance himself answered her rather nervous knock.

'Please heaven let him like me and take me on!' she was praying.

He did not look as elderly as he had stated himself to be, but was, she thought, in his early forties, a small, spare framed man with a thin, aristocratic face and keen grey eyes, his still brown hair thin on top and receding from an intelligent looking forehead.

'Good afternoon,' she said, as he looked at her inquiringly and, she thought, with an expression of faint distaste. 'I am Verne Raydon and this is Rosemary.'

'Better come in,' he said, not too graciously, though it occurred to her that courtesy was probably more natural to him than the brusqueness he had to cultivate with an effort. 'Put that down anywhere,' with a nod towards the carrycot and not attempting to look at what was inside it. As he spoke, he turned to go back into the room from which he had come, and Verne set the cot down, pausing a moment to tuck the baby in and whisper to her, 'For the love of Mike, don't cry, my pet. That's all I ask of you at the moment. Just don't cry.'

Rosemary had been slightly fractious lately, beginning to feel for her teeth. It would be just very bad luck if she chose this occasion to give voice!

She followed her potential employer into the main room of the cottage, a pleasant room, lit by latticed windows on both sides, the ceiling oak beamed, the substantial furniture of the same quality and age as the pieces in the hall, a few old Persian rugs on the stone floor, a big table drawn up near one window holding a typewriter and an untidy mass of papers.

She was wafted back for a moment to the kitchen in the flat and her own efforts with *Pantalets* of ill fated memory.

'Sit down,' he said, waving her to a chair, and she did so with easy grace and waited for him to speak.

'Can you use a typewriter?' he asked.

'Yes.'

'Can you *spell*?'

'Yes,' she said with a slight smile.

'H'm. I've never met a woman who could. Do you mind hard work? Long hours? Being alone?'

'No,' said Verne.

'How old are you?'

Twenty four,' said Verne.

'H'm. You're young.'

There was nothing to say to this, so she sat calmly waiting for him to go on. Her heart was beating fast, but she gave no indication of it.

After what seemed to her an eternity, he said, 'When can you start?'

She gave him a surprised look and caught her breath.

'You mean—I am to come?' she asked.

'Wiry not?'

'Well—you haven't asked me if I can cook, for one thing,' she said with another slight, irrepressible smile. He was quite unusual.

'Can you?'

'Pretty well, if you don't want anything too fancy. Also I can clean and wash dishes and sew, and,' with a momentary flicker of her eyes towards the garden. 'I can do a bit of gardening.'

H'm. You know I should not, in any circumstances, consider marrying you?'

She gasped, and this time managed to repress the smile.

'Your advertisement made that quite clear,' she said gravely.

'I wanted to make it clear because in the past year or two I have had a succession of females and a good many of them got ideas like that about me, goodness knows why—except that they probably thought it would be a permanency without any work to do. You'll have to work here, you know,' shooting a suspicious look at her.

'That was the idea when I answered your advertisement,' she said with composure, not trying to avoid the glance of his keen eyes.

'You know I can't pay you much? Two pounds a month.'

Less than ten shillings a week. Even after his statement that the salary would be practically nonexistent, she had not supposed it to be as small as that. Could she manage? What would there be to buy for

Rosemary? She considered her own needs unimportant. She had a fair wardrobe of workmanlike clothes, bought whilst she had been working for Corbett and Clark, and she always took care of her things.

'You would keep Rosemary and me, in food I mean?' she asked after a pause.

'Of course. Plenty of food here, fruit and vegetables in the garden, and eggs. There are some hens and ducks.'

'Do I look after them as well?' she asked, though there was the suspicion of a twinkle in her eye.

'There's an old man,' he said, and then his manner changed. He gave an exasperated sigh and ran his fingers through his thin hair, making it stand on end though it was so limp and fine that it soon settled down again of its own accord. 'Oh Lord, it's no job to jump at,' he said. 'That's been the trouble. Surprising how difficult it is to find a woman who'll work sixteen hours a day and put up with the worst tempered man in England all for ten bob a week—other than a wife, of course, who is expected to do it for nothing. Do you understand, Miss Raydon? You'll have to do everything—cook, keep the home clean, do the shopping and the mending, and in the evening type the rubbish I've written during the day.'

'And the rest of the day's my own?' asked Verne, but this time the twinkle had become an unconcealed smile.

'Absolutely,' he agreed, and this time he smiled as well. Then the smile faded. 'I can't expect you to do it, of course.'

'I'd like to try,' said Verne.

'Why?'

'In the first place, because I've got to earn my living and I don't want to be separated from my baby. And in the second. I like it here, the country, the quietness—your house. You offered a pleasant home and personal freedom. They're what I want more than anything.'

'H'm. By the way, have you any objection to calling yourself *Mrs.* Raydon? This is a village, you see, and village people talk, though probably no more, and no more maliciously then townspeople. As you have a child, it looks better and they will assume you are a widow. You're not, I suppose?'

'A widow? No,' said Verne, glad that he had not put the question in a different way. The last thing in the world she wanted was to have to tell anyone that she was a runaway wife, especially that it was Robert Grimtree from whom she had run.

'H'm,' he said again, and there was another pause.

Verne broke the silence this time.

'Am I engaged, Mr. Mance?' she asked.

'Oh yes. Yes, I suppose so, for what it's worth to you. I'm a writer of worst sellers, by the way. That's what all this mess is about,' with a wave of his hand towards the table. 'I'm half a book behind. It takes me too long to type the stuff. Can you read, by the way?'

'Oh yes,' said Verne with a little laugh she could not hold back. 'I've been able to read for some years.'

'Indecipherable handwriting, I mean.'

'I think so,' she said, remembering some of the notes Robert used to make.

'When can you start?' he asked.

'As soon as you like, Mr. Mance. Did you get the reference from Mr. Templar?'

'Yes. Well, start tomorrow. Take this for your fare,' giving her a pound note, 'and I'll send someone to the station for your luggage. There's a train that gets in about twelve noon. I don't think there's anything else—oh, you can have a look round if you like. Not much to see,' with another flick of his hand towards the door into the hall.

'I'm prepared to take it on trust,' said Verne, rising.

'All right. No fuss about a month's notice or anything like that, mind. If we don't get on, or if you can't stand the job, you just walk out. That all right?'

'Perfectly,' said Verne, hoping desperately that it would be a long time before that happened.

She liked this man who had certainly done nothing to impress or attract her. She liked the quiet old house with its ancient furniture and dim colours and atmosphere of peace, of being prepared to remain for many years ahead as it had been for centuries past, with no perceptible change. She liked the garden, the riot of old fashioned flowers which also were given 'personal freedom' and she had liked the sleepy look of the village as she had walked through it from the station which was called 'a halt'.

Here, surely, at last she would find peace and a resting place for herself and Rosemary.

She remembered Rosemary suddenly. Heaven bless her for not calling attention to her presence by so much as a whimper!

She supposed he had forgotten her too, however.

'There's Rosemary, you know,' she said anxiously.

'Rosemary?'

'My little girl.'

'Oh yes. Well, you told me about that. As long as she doesn't rush about the place and disturb me when I'm working, it won't matter.'

'It will probably be some time before she does that,' said Verne, twinkling again. 'She's only four months old.'

'Well, I don't know anything about children and don't much like them,' he said. 'Still, to get anything approaching what I want, I've got to put up with something, I suppose. Come down tomorrow. Good afternoon—er—Ms. Raydon.'

'Good afternoon, Mr. Mance, and thank you very much.'

'You're slightly premature with that,' he told her, but his face relaxed again into the smile which redeemed its lack of any good looks.

Verne took her departure and walked along the one straggling village street with the carrycot. The few people who passed her eyed her curiously and she knew she would probably be the subject of considerable speculation in most of the houses and cottages that evening.

Please heaven, she whispered to herself, that we've come to stay. Please heaven we've found some place we can begin to think of as home.

She was utterly tired of the feeling that she did not belong anywhere.

Chapter Twelve

Verne had been at Yew Cottage a month.

During that time she had learnt how right Gerald Mance had been when he said it was a sixteen hour a day job! She was seldom in bed after five in the morning, since Rosemary had to be bathed and dressed and fed and settled down before the business of the day began, and her employer liked his breakfast at seven. Throughout the day she carried out not only the multitude of jobs that fall to the house woman, but also contrived to put in an hour or two in the garden, wrestling with the weeds which grew even more luxuriantly than the flowers and were allowed by the old man, Fox, just as much 'personal freedom'. The phrase continued to remain in her mind to amuse her because the only kind of freedom she appeared to possess was the freedom to do her work as, how and when she liked, but if she had not gone on doing it through all the hours of the day, she would not have got it done at all.

In the evening, after the composite meal they called tea, she sat at the big table in the living room and tried to get up to date with the stack of hand written manuscript which had got out of the author's control, though as every day added to the stack, she felt like Penelope at her tapestry.

She had wondered what sort of books Gerald Mance wrote. She had never heard his name, and had no time to go to a library and inquire before she started to take up residence with him, and she was surprised and inwardly amused to find that they were detective stories and not of very high quality. He had described them himself as worst sellers.

'Lot of rubbish, of course,' he said to her the first evening, when they were sorting out the stack of papers. 'Still, it ekes out my income and they don't take much thought.'

Verne, typing the book, considered that certainly he did not give them much thought, not nearly enough, in fact. He slipped up in small details, and even at times in the plot itself, and she could quite imagine that avid readers of crime fiction might pick a good many holes in the methods of detection employed by a particularly irritating old man, John Stickback, who, as an amateur detective, apparently appeared in all Gerald Mance's books and consistently foiled the criminal and showed the police to be a body of uneducated nitwits who, in Verne's opinion, would have been better employed at anything rather than police work.

Since Mance did not ask her opinion, however, or offer to discuss his books with her in any way, naturally she did not suggest any interest in anything but transcribing his difficult handwriting into type.

Of one thing she was glad, however, and that was that he wrote in clear, grammatical English. He was undoubtedly a man of good education, just as she quickly realised he was also a man of good breeding and culture, though he had few friends and they were from very varied walks of life, from Sir James Gust, the local squire and his lady, to Slome, the refuse collector, coal man, window cleaner and sewage expert, known in the village as Slimy, a nickname to which he took not the slightest exception. Either of these men, or both of them, with others from all the grades between them, might be found in the garden with Mance, or by the fire in the living room, filling the place with pipe smoke and consuming vast quantities of coffee and whatever food Verne was able to provide for them.

She found that, though he did not feel himself able to pay her more than the two pounds a month, there was always plenty of food, and he told her she was to buy whatever was needed for them to live well.

And now, after the difficulties and inevitable mistakes of the first month, she felt happy in the knowledge that she had got the better of her job, and produced some sort of order in her mass of unrelated tasks, and concluded that, as Mance never complained or suggested any alteration, he was satisfied with what she did.

On an afternoon of late October, when the so far missing summer seemed fantastically to have reclaimed itself, much too late, she was in the garden digging up a plot for winter cabbage whilst Rosemary kicked her robust little limbs on a blanket spread on an old tarpaulin near by.

'Like to leave that for a bit?'

She turned with a start to see Mance beside her. He was wearing an ancient pea jacket and carried his fishing tackle and sea boots under his arm. Fishing was almost his only relaxation, and she knew that he kept a boat of some sort on the river which ran out at the little harbour some five miles away, though she had never yet managed to get as far as the sea.

She gave him a questioning glance.

'I thought you might like to come out fishing for a bit,' he said.

She glanced at Rosemary and he nodded.

'You can bring that too,' he said, the only sort of reference he ever made to the baby, whose existence he usually ignored. 'It will be all right in the bottom of the boat.'

Laughter gurgled up inside her, but she did not let it escape.

Well, Rosemary was no delicate hothouse flower, and undoubtedly she would have to take life a good deal in the raw, so why not spend an October afternoon in the bottom of someone's boat?

She nodded and smiled.

'I'd like that,' she said. 'What do I put on?'

She was wearing her oldest clothes, a tweed suit and woollen sweater, and he looked at them as if he had never noticed them before and said casually. 'They'll do. Better tie something round your head. Maybe breezy. I'll call back for you in ten minutes.'

In under the stipulated time, she was ready, with Rosemary warmly clad and tucked into the carrycot and a scarf tied gypsy fashion over her own head.

'Do we need to take food?' she asked him when he reappeared, with Slimy and his old, horse drawn cart in tow.

'No, there's stuff aboard and we can buy milk and bread on the way. Do you mind riding in this thing? It's reasonably clean. At any rate, its last load was coal which has somewhat negatived the previous one of manure.'

It was the first time he had inquired if she 'minded' anything, and she laughed and handed Rosemary up to the obliging Slimy.

'She's a proper beauty, isn't she, guv'nor?' asked Slimy.

'Who? Oh—oh the baby. Yes. Yes, of course,' said Mance with complete unconcern. 'Can you hop up, Mrs. Raydon?'

She did so, sitting on the front seat, which was a board, between Mance and Slimy.

'The boat's only down in the creek,' he said, 'but it might be a bit far for you carrying that. Can you pick us up again, Slimy?'

''Spect so, guv'nor. What time?'

'Oh—about six. That all right for you, Mrs. Raydon?'

'Yes, perfectly,' she said, thanking her stars that Rosemary was very accommodating about her meal times if one was occasionally delayed.

The boat proved to be a small cabin cruiser, actually a day boat rather than one intended for living in, but there were two narrow bunks in the little cabin which was also fitted with a lead lined sink with a cupboard over it, and a primus stove.

'It's a bit primitive, but I don't usually entertain aboard,' said Mance, who had manoeuvred the small dinghy so that Verne need not get her feet wet, and rowed them out the few yards to the moorings.

It was sunny but cold, with a breeze that freshened as they got nearer to the sea, and though he did not appear to be taking any notice of her at all, occupied with steering the boat between half submerged banks and shoals, he must have seen her give an involuntary shiver, for without turning his head, he said, 'There's an old mac in the locker in the cabin, if you like.'

She fetched it gratefully and found it an excellent windcheater, wrapping it well round her and holding it in by the belt. Rosemary was on the floor of the little cockpit at their feet, gurgling happily and fascinated by the new discovery of her own fingers.

'We'll go outside the harbour, but not too far out to sea with this breeze blowing,' he said. 'Ever done any fishing?'

'No, never,' she said.

'Not much to be got just now or close in,' he said, 'but we might get one or two stragglers ready to commit suicide. We'll keep the engine running and trail the lines today. You look after the ones on this side and I'll take the other.'

'How do I know if I get a bite?' asked Verne.

'You'll feel the jerk if you keep your finger on the line—like this—and when you do, haul in quickly or you'll lose your fish *and* your bait.'

Which, of course, she proceeded to do with depressing regularity, whilst he pulled in half a dozen good sized fish in succession.

Once, in her determination not to lose her catch, she nearly fell in, and he caught her by the legs and hauled her back with a great loss of any dignity she might have retained.

'I wouldn't do that again,' he said, 'unless you can swim. Can you?'

'No, I can't,' said Verne. 'Can you?'

'Not a stroke. Never could. In fact, I was never any good at anything requiring physical prowess even at school.'

'What did you do at school?' she asked, since for the first time he seemed inclined to talk.

'As little as possible of everything. Complete waste of my father's money, of course, but as both he and I expected I should be having a comfortable and congenial life when the family fortunes descended to me, we didn't worry. I don't know why we never reckoned on a second world war and the social revolution that disintegrated everything I had thought would endure more or less forever, but there it was. When I came out of the army, it was to a new world with nothing to recommend me to it, no money, no brains and only a very superficial education, the last my fault entirely, of course. I just float along where the stream takes me.'

He spoke cheerfully and with no suggestion of self pity.

'At least you can earn a living,' she pointed out.

He smiled.

'Yes. Suits me all right. A fire, a good bed and enough to eat. What more can anyone want?'

How well she could agree with that! After her narrow escape from getting very wet, at the least, he had decided to turn for home. They were nearing their moorings, and she had no need to reply.

Slimy was waiting for them, sitting in his cart with an old sack over his shoulders and his usual evil smelling pipe in his mouth. He waved his whip to them in comradely fashion, and they replied.

'How about a drink at the Lion before we go in?' asked Mance, during the drive home.

Instinctively Verne glanced down at Rosemary, but she had apparently decided that she had made a mistake in the time and had gone to sleep again.

'I'd like that,' said Verne, and went with the two men into the local inn. Slimy had whistled to a large nondescript dog which was strolling about outside the Lion, and told him to look after the horse and the baby.

'He's used to Nobby and Nobby knows it's more than his life is worth to move a step whilst he's sitting by him,' explained Mance. 'It'll be quite safe, and it can't fall out.'

There was a little crowd of the locals in the bar. Most of them were by now on friendly speaking terms with Verne, and to the one or two who did not know her Mance introduced her with a non explanatory 'Mrs. Raydon' and left it at that.

The village people had accepted her as they had probably accepted her many forerunners as his housekeeper, and if one or two spiteful women had suggested that she was no widow and no better than she ought to be, they were in the minority and since Lady Gust had been seen to stop to speak to her in friendly fashion in the street, they thought it best to do the same.

'Beer or a short one?' Mance asked her.

'Beer, please,' she said firmly, thinking of the comparative cost and having been taught by Bill to tolerate beer, if not to like it, and she sat on the window seat in the bar and drank it whilst the men stood and talked about fishing, the weather, the crops and the hive of bees which Mance was considering adding to his live stock, rather to her apprehension.

The local policeman, Baines, came in for his evening pint and nodded all round.

'Anybody want to be locked up tonight?' he asked. 'Because if they do, they'd better let me know. The old woman's got her washing hanging out in the lock up. Evening, Sir James. Done any more poaching lately?' at which there was general laughter.

This was an old joke that never grew stale. Sir James, having once sold part of his shoot, had forgotten all about it and gone home with a brace of pheasants which he had shot on the other man's land, hanging out of his pocket.

'I've had my pockets made deeper,' said the squire, who had joined in the laughter. 'Can I get you a pint, Baines?'

'Trying to bribe the law, are you? Thanks, sir, but Alec's just drawn mine. What about you having one on me?'

'All right. You do owe me a couple. Bitter, please. Alec—and thank you, Baines.'

The policeman moved to the bar to stand with his foot on the rail. He was officially off duty and in plain clothes, but there was no mistaking the nature of his calling, from the feet up.

'Hullo, Mr. Mance,' he said, seeing Gerald. 'How's old Stickback getting on?'

'He's just finished discovering the criminal in the Vacuum Flask murder,' said Mance. 'I nearly did an appalling thing, though. I was tempted to do him in!'

'Well, it's about time,' observed Baines amicably. 'He made a proper mess up in that one about the Blue Jug.'

'How so?'

'Well, sir, I ask you! Even a village copper wouldn't have missed those fingerprints on the telephone.'

'Good heavens, did Stickback do that?' asked Mance, shocked. 'He's slipping. But I'd probably covered up the tracks so well that there was no other way to get out of it—and at least it was the police who found the clue.'

'For once,' admitted Baines grudgingly.

Mance called through a gap in the crowd to Verne.

'We'd better watch Stickback, Mrs. Raydon,' he said. 'He's not quite as clever as he used to be, or perhaps the police are improving?'

'I never know where your particular brand of police come from, Mance,' remarked Sir James. 'All I know is that if they had to give evidence in my court, I'd have 'em up for contempt in no time!' for Sir James had been a practising barrister and, though he had officially retired, occasionally took a case of local interest.

Verne was interested to see how well Mance took the chaffing and the laughter at his expense.

'He's a good sport,' she thought, 'and I'm ready to bet he doesn't make that awful old Stickback any different either.'

It was a good day, a happy day, and it was repeated several times during the next two or three weeks, until the weather broke up and it looked as though the winter had set in.

Mance spent a good bit of his time sawing and chopping wood to increase their supply of fuel, and since he was not writing as much as usual, she sometimes had a free evening.

At first he had told her that when she was not at the typewriter, she would probably find it more comfortable to use the kitchen, which was large and pleasant, with wide windows overlooking the garden, and she did so quite happily. Now, however, he suggested that as wood did not burn very well in the kitchen range and they were short of coal, she had better share the living room with him and she found that he had brought down another easy chair from one of the upstairs rooms and put it on the opposite side of the fire to his own.

They did not talk much, but Mance read and Verne sewed or knitted, and usually the wireless was turned on without consideration of the programmes offered, but it was never loud enough to disturb either of them if they did not care to listen. Outside the wind blew and the rain lashed the window panes but there was little or no traffic in the road now, and nothing broke the quiet peace of the comfortable room with its curtains drawn and the big log fire crackling on great iron dogs in the hearth.

Every now and then Mance would give a push with his foot to a log which had burnt through in the middle, or go outside to replenish the basket, and when he did so, he would sometimes give her a half smile if she looked up, a friendly, comfortable thing.

One afternoon she heard a car stop outside the gate and, going to the window, was surprised and pleased to see Jeffery Templar getting out of it and helping out someone whom she knew must be his wife.

She hurried to the door and threw it open.

'Come in!' she cried warmly. 'Mr. Templar, how nice of you!'

He took her outstretched hand.

'We were in the neighbourhood and I remembered your address, so we thought we'd call. My dear,' turning to the quiet faced, middle aged woman with him, 'this is Verne Raydon. My wife, Verne.'

'I wondered if we should ever meet, Miss Raydon,' said Mrs. Templar, though Verne knew she was well aware of her real identity. 'This must be a delightful house in the summer, but in the winter—ugh, give me London!'

'For London, read Southport,' commented her husband with a smile. 'My wife has never become a southerner, as I have.'

Verne took them into the living room. Gerald Mance was entering it by the other door into the kitchen, his arms full of fresh logs.

'Mr. Mance, may I bring in Mr. and Mrs. Templar?' asked Verne, who had never had a visitor of her own before and wondered for an uncomfortable second whether she ought not to have taken them into the kitchen.

But he welcomed them pleasantly, pulled up the old, high backed settle near the fire, threw on more logs and asked Verne what they had in the house to drink.

'Whisky and the cooking sherry,' she said with a confident laugh, which showed Jeffery Templar at once that she was happy here and had consolidated her position.

'Well, who wants anything else if there's whisky?' he asked.

'How about you, Mrs. Templar?' asked Mance. 'Whisky, too? Or perhaps tea? I can see by your face that that's a welcome suggestion.'

'I'll make some,' said Verne at once. 'The whisky's in that cupboard, Mr. Mance,' for he rarely took a drink other than his customary beer at the Lion when he went for his evening stroll.

'I'm glad to see that Verne has settled down with you, Mr. Mance,' said Templar as his host brought the bottle and glasses.

'You call her Verne? I've never ventured to,' he said. 'We remain on very correct terms, and yes, I think she has settled down. She makes me extremely comfortable and my only fear is that she will find it too much for her and leave me. She has a lot to do, you know. I'm a lazy devil except for my writing.'

'Verne was never afraid of work,' said Templar.

'And how is the baby?' asked his wife.

'The baby? Oh, the baby,' as if for a moment he had not quite grasped the question. 'Oh, it's all right, I think. I don't see much of it, and what is more remarkable, I don't hear much of it either. It's asleep now, of course.'

'A little girl, isn't it?' asked Mrs. Templar, considering his attitude cold blooded.

'Yes. Yes, I believe it is. Soda or water, Mr. Templar?'

'Soda, please. Just a splash.'

'I see you don't approve of drowning it. Neither do I. How's that?'

'Fine,' and the two men settled down to sip appreciatively whilst from the kitchen came the pleasant sound of rattling cups which were presently followed by Verne herself, bearing a laden tray of which Mance at once relieved her.

Before the visitors went, Mrs. Templar asked to see the baby and went upstairs with Verne to the big, airy room which so delighted her, especially when it had followed immediately on her cubicle at the hostel and the absence of any room at all at High Clere.

Mr. Templar took the opportunity of discovering, in his experienced legal fashion which could achieve so much in a short time, just how much Verne had to do at Yew Cottage, and he was not too well pleased, even though she seemed happy and contented.

He was thinking of Robert Grimtree, with his wealth and his huge house and his retinue of trained servants. He had noticed that Verne's hands were roughened by hard work, that her dress had been neatly mended and that her legs were covered by cheap thread stockings.

She had not told him what Mance paid her, but he would have been appalled.

A day or two later, when Grimtree had asked him to come to his office on some business matter, be took an opportunity to introduce Verne's name, a name which had not been spoken between them for many months.

'I paid an interesting visit the other day,' he said. 'I saw a friend of yours!'

'Oh! Who?' asked Grimtree, not interested.

'Verne.'

Templar saw the other man's whole frame stiffen and his hands go taut on the papers they were holding, whilst he caught the sound of a sharply drawn breath.

'I don't know what that has to do with me,' he said at last, curtly.

'Hasn't it? She's working, Robert, and working damned hard, too damned hard. Keeping house and acting as secretary, probably almost unpaid, to a writer of very poor books.'

'I'm not interested in what she does,' said Grimtree, but, in spite of that, he added after a pause, 'What's she working for? Can't that chap support her?'

'They've parted,' said Templar. 'She's there with the child, a girl.'

Again came that stiffening of the heavy body, but as the man made no rejoinder, Templar went on calmly.

'I got the impression that the man she works for cannot, or at any rate, does not, pay her as much as she ought to have, probably not as much as she needs. She looked well—but—well, a little down at heel.'

'That's no concern of mine,' grunted Grimtree. 'She chose it.'

'That's rather a moot point. As you know, I've changed my mind quite a bit about Verne and what happened when you parted from her.'

'I'm not going to discuss that,' said Grimtree. 'If she's hard up, that's her funeral. I'm not interested.'

But after the solicitor had gone, Grimtree sat with his hands gripping the edge of his desk and, when his secretary appeared with some letters, he told him roughly to go away and wait till he was sent for.

Verne 'down at heel', shabby, needing money.

He didn't like that. It was nothing to do with him, of course, but still – he didn't like it.

He let himself remember, even though it pierced him, how she had looked at various times when she had lived with him. A gold dress in which she had looked like a flame, glowing and vital. A dress of some blue stuff, with a little tight bodice and a billowing skirt. A hostess gown of dark green velvet, dignified and sweeping the floor as she walked. Her long, lovely legs in cobweb fine stockings and dainty, high heeled shoes.

The visions maddened him but would not let him go.

He pressed the bell with quite unnecessary violence and his secretary came in with the letters.

After he had gone, the thoughts came back, and others with them.

So she and that chap had parted, had they? Well, he was not surprised. The marvel was that Verne could have stuck him at all. Not her type. Unstable. Meretricious.

He had recently learnt that word and he liked it.

Meretricious. That was what the man Trailer was.

Yet he had got Verne away from him – away from him, Robert Grimtree, important, rich, reliable, a man who would have looked after her all her life and kept her softly housed and hung with silk and jewels.

Pah!

He tried once more to lose his thoughts in business affairs, and only he and Jeffery Templar knew just how much thought those affairs demanded just now, for Grimtree was doing what he had said he would never do. He was speculating heavily, juggling with stocks and shares, even trying more than once to rig the market, obsessed to the point of insanity with the ideas of colossal wealth beside which his present fortune would be negligible.

But the thought of Verne 'down at heel' persisted, and after he had gone home that evening, he rang up Jeffery Templar and gave him specific instructions.

'Do you think you're wise?' demurred the lawyer. 'Verne would not be at all pleased if she knew. She's as proud as Lucifer and she'd think it a low down trick to play on her.'

'That's my business,' Grimtree told him harshly. 'You fix it up, and see to it that she doesn't know I've had a hand in it.'

'All right, if you say so,' said Templar.

Mr. Garret was astounded at the proposition put to him the next day by this Mr. Templar, whose name conveyed nothing to him.

'You say that your principal, who wishes to remain anonymous, really wants to buy the film rights in Lorna Derring's book, *Panialels?*' he asked. 'But—I shouldn't have said that there's anything in it that's at all suitable for filming.'

'My principal thinks there is,' said Mr. Templar calmly. 'He has authorised me to offer on his behalf five thousand pounds for them, on the sole condition that he remains anonymous. If Miss Derring will not agree to that, the deal's off.'

'Well, I am really flabbergasted,' said Mr. Garret, who looked it. 'I shall have to put it to Miss Derring, of course, but naturally she will accept it and the condition will be very unlikely to disturb her at all, though I suppose the identity of your principal will come out when the film is made?'

'Possibly, but I could not go into that at the moment,' said Mr. Templar, who knew that there was not even a remote prospect of such a film being made.

Mr. Garret was not inclined to argue the matter, since the author's acceptance of the offer would put five hundred pounds into his own pocket, and he lost no time in submitting the offer to her, sending the letter to the only means of contact he now had with 'Miss Lorna Derring', an accommodation address at a small paper shop near Beckett Mansions. By the time she left there she had given up all hope of hearing from Mr. Garret again, he having sadly assured her that *Pantalets* had now been 'remaindered' and had actually not earned the advance thirty pounds which Bill Trailer had wrung out of him.

The letter stayed there in a dusty box. Miss Derring had not called for letters for a long time and eventually, if she did not call for it, it would be sent back via the dead letter office.

Every day, sometimes more than once a day, for the first ten days or so, Robert Grimtree inquired of his solicitor if any answer had yet been received, and when the answer became monotonously a negative one, he was at first irritated and then angry.

'What the deuce does she want then?' he stormed over the telephone. 'Isn't it enough. I thought you told me she's hard up.'

'I am quite sure she is, and just as sure that it is not avarice. I gather from Garret that the only address he has is one which I should think is merely an accommodation one, though he refuses (quite rightly, of course) to give it to me. I have suggested that he should call at the address to see if she has collected the letter.'

'You don't think she has any idea that I am concerned?'

'I made that a condition of the offer, and as Garret, acting as her agent, is financially interested in putting the deal through, I am quite sure he will not risk your cancelling it on that score. I am afraid there is nothing to do but wait.'

And waiting was the very last thing Robert Grimtree was fitted to do.

'Can't you go down and see her yourself and put the offer up to her?' he asked irritably.

'I should say that she would inevitably connect it with you then.'

'Well, keep Garret at it. That's all.'

Robert would not admit to himself the root of his anger, which was a deep seated conviction, in spite of what Templar had said, that Verne knew the offer had come from him, and would die rather than accept it.

Stupid, idiotic pride! he fumed to himself. It was not every day that he was willing to part with five thousand pounds for nothing. He might as well have given it to Hermione if he wanted to chuck five thousand pounds away. Catch her refusing it!

But Garret had taken Templar's advice and gone to the address of the paper shop, to be told that the letter was still there awaiting collection, and all he could do was to leave it there in the hope that one day she would call.

It was not until a month later, however, that the letter came into Verne's hands.

Gerald Mance wanted to see his publisher, and he absolutely refused to go to London, and his publisher, an old man who had no particular reason for wishing to retain Mance on his list of authors, would not make the journey to Sedbury to see him.

'You'd better go, Mrs. Raydon,' said Mance. 'You know what I want and you can say it just as well as I can, probably better. It's about foreign and American rights, and if the old curmudgeon won't agree to my terms, go and see some other publishers. I'll make out a list of them for you.'

But for the first time, Verne was not willing to do what he asked.

'I can't very well cart Rosemary round with me,' she said, 'and I can't leave her.'

'Why the devil not? Get one of the women in the village to have her. I'll pay the few bob, of course.'

'I'm sorry, but I should be most unhappy about her,' said Verne decidedly, and they were still in the midst of an argument which was getting out of hand when the door opened and Lady Gust walked into the living room.

'I rang the bell,' she said, 'but as the door was open and nobody came, I am afraid I walked in. Is anything the matter?' beginning to realise that she had come in at an inopportune moment. Verne and Mance were facing each other like bristling terriers.

Mance told her, and she suggested an alternative at once.

'But I'll have the baby,' she said. 'I'd love to, and she's such a good pet. It's years since I had a baby to look after, and it'll be a good thing for you to have a day out of the village, Verne.'

She had taken lately to using the girl's name, a friendly gesture which Verne liked very much.

Lady Gust was a kind and very sensible woman and had brought up a family and now was hoping anxiously that she would be a grandmother. Verne could have no really valid objection to the proposal, except that she could not bear to have Rosemary out of her sight for long, and she realised that it would be churlish to refuse a kind offer so graciously made.

Once she had got over the feeling of losing an essential part of her being, however, she found she was quite glad to be in a train again, and later treading the familiar London streets.

She managed to prevail on Mance's publisher to agree to his terms, though he grumbled about it, and now she had nothing else to do.

The interview she had had, and the discussion of various publishing rights, had inevitably brought back to her mind her own single essay into authorship, and on an impulse, she rang up Mr. Garret. How she was to find any time for writing, she had no idea, but if he still thought it of any use, somehow she would find time to start on the once projected novel.

'Oh, Miss Derring, I am very glad to hear from you. Very glad indeed,' he said. 'I wrote to you some time ago. Haven't you been to collect the letter yet?'

'No, it never occurred to me,' she said. 'Does it contain some good news?'

'Indeed it does. Look, Miss Derring, most unfortunately I've got to go out of town in half an hour or so, but why not collect the letter? It tells you all I could tell you myself, and I'd like you to have time to think it over—if you need any! Will you do that? And get in touch with me tomorrow, or the next day?'

'Certainly I will,' she said, with a little thrill of excitement, for Mr. Garret's tone had been much more cordial than it had been the last time they had spoken together. There really must be good news of some sort.

But when she had collected and read the letter, she was dumbfounded.

Five thousand pounds? Five *thousand!* It seemed a wild dream from which surely she would wake, but there it was in black and white.

I am under strict orders not to put you into direct contact with the man who is making the offer, he wrote. In fact, I do not myself know who he is, except that he is some film magnate who likes to do such deals as this without having to appear in them. No doubt when he is ready to start making the film, he will get in touch with you. Meantime, I am directed to make this offer to you, and I strongly advise you to accept it. Such large sums are not often offered in this country for books which are not already outstanding successes.

Strongly advise her? Heavens, there was no need! She would clutch the magnificent five thousand and feel herself to be a millionaire.

She could not do as she would have liked, and ring up Mr. Garret at once and say she would accept, so as she now had no interest in walking about London, not even looking in the shops to start spending in anticipation some of her sudden wealth, she took the next train back to Sedbury and almost danced her way through the village.

Lady Gust was to bring Rosemary back just before six, and as it was too far to walk to The Grange, she went back to Yew Cottage.

She would have to tell Mance eventually, as such further correspondence with Mr. Garret would have to be to and from here,

225

and Mance would have to know she was Lorna Derring. Also, as she was bursting to share her exciting news with someone, and there was no one but Mance, she would tell him now. She hoped he would not feel envious, since he had never yet had one of his books filmed.

He looked pleased to see her back so early, and she kept her own news to herself until she told him what success she had had on his behalf.

'You've done very well,' he said. 'I told you you'd manage it better than I should have done. I'm flattered that you should look so pleased yourself.'

She tried to calm herself down.

'I'm pleased about it, terribly pleased,' she said, 'but—but that isn't quite all. I'm afraid I've got something to tell you, a sort of confession to make, Mr. Mance.'

His face fell.

'Don't tell me you are going to get married?' he asked.

'Oh no, nothing like that. Nothing at all like that. It's that—do you remember when I first came you said you wrote worst selling novels? Well—so have I. I mean, written one. A really worst seller. It was published before I came here, and it was a dismal failure and I decided there was nothing in writing for me, and then—today—'

'Well? Go on,' he said.

'Today—look! I've had this,' and she handed him Garret's letter, which by now she knew by heart. She had read it a dozen times coming down in the train.

He read it through twice, first at a glance and then slowly, his face inscrutable as ever, but when finally he laid the letter down, she fancied she could see a hint of regret, of some kind of disappointment, in the look he gave her.

His first words offered an explanation.

'So you're a woman of means? No longer somebody's paid employee? I take it you'll be leaving me?'

'Oh, no!' she said quickly. 'At least—not for a long time, unless you want me to?'

'Why should I?' he asked grimly. 'It isn't easy to get a slave in these days. I merely supposed that, with your feet on the ladder, you'll want time to go on climbing.'

She gave a little laugh. There was excitement in it, as if she had come alive, as indeed she felt she had. A little of the wine of success goes quickly to the head of one long used to the bitter waters of failure.

'I'm by no means sure there will ever be another rung for me,' she said. 'I've waited long enough for this one, in all conscience, and selling a subsidiary right isn't like good solid royalties from the book itself. Five thousand pounds is a fortune to me, but it won't last forever, and nobody can live even on that for long in these days. Not that I mean to spend it, of course.'

'Then what will you do with it?'

'Use it in some way for Rosemary. It will provide her with a good education for one thing, and that's always worried me. Meanwhile, I shall invest it and keep the capital intact until I have to draw on it for her.'

He looked at her curiously.

'Don't you ever want anything for yourself?' he asked. 'Clothes and things? Good holidays? Things that count as fun when one is your age?'

'Oh—in a way, yes, of course I do. But I've rather got out of the way of things like that, and with Rosemary, and my work for you, and the life of the village, I seem to have most of the things I need for contentment.'

'Bovine contentment,' he commented, and she laughed.

'Perhaps, but it suits me. I—I don't want to get out of the meadow again. I've had enough of whatever's on the other side of the hedge.'

He looked at her speculatively.

'Never told me much about yourself, have you?' he asked.

At once the mask came down over her face and he could feel her withdrawal into that place where she dwelt alone.

'No,' was all she said, and then, with a change of tone to her customary one of friendly, but distant courtesy of employee to employer, 'If you'll excuse me. I'll go and see to the supper. Lady Gust will be bringing Rosemary back very soon.'

He did not try to detain her. That, after all, was the relationship he himself had decreed, so what complaint had he?

But he sat and thought about her. He could not remain surprised at the discovery that she was a fellow writer, after all the evidence she had given him of her capabilities in that direction. In fact, he wondered it had never occurred to him. She had been too knowledgeable about the actual mechanics of writing a book for this to be her first experience of it. For a permissible moment he felt the stab of her success where he had, if not actually failed, at least never won an offer of five thousand pounds for anything he had written. Then, characteristically, he dismissed it from his mind. As she had said, it might well be a mere flash in the pan, just one of the isolated bits of luck which may come once to a writer and never again. He wished her luck of it. Though he knew nothing of her life before she came to him, he felt that she deserved a break. It was quixotic, of course, to be resolved to take none of the benefit of the money for herself but to apply it all to the future good of the child, but that was her own affair, and at least it meant that she did not intend to alter her way of life as far as he was concerned.

When, later in the evening, he discussed with her the magnificent offer for the film rights again, he gave her the benefit of his better knowledge.

'Don't write to this agent of yours until you've seen him and seen the actual proposal that has been made,' he advised her. 'Don't put anything in writing yet. There may be some snag which doesn't appear on the face of it. You may be signing away more than you ought. Go up and see him, see the draft contract and, if you feel like doing so, bring it back with you unsigned so that I can have a look at it and make sure he's not getting more than you mean to give him. Will you do that?'

She was grateful for his interest, aware of her lack of experience.

'It would mean leaving Rosemary again,' she said, 'but I don't think I'd mind asking Lady Gust. She's terribly kind and very good with babies—and I should more than appreciate your help.'

Lady Gust had already said how delighted she had been to look after a baby again, so a day or two later Verne went to London to keep an appointment with Mr. Garret, finding him much altered in manner, affable and even ingratiating.

'Since you telephoned me that you were disposed to accept this offer, Miss Derring,' he said, 'I have seen the—er—the principal's agent again, and with the exception of a few very minor alterations which he has made (most of them in your favour, as you will see!) he has agreed the draft contract. I have it here,' handing it across his table to her, 'so if you approve, I can have a fair copy made of it and you can sign it before you go.'

She took the short agreement and began to read it through, but in a few moments was brought up short by the first suggested amendment, made in the margin in a small, difficult handwriting and initialled by the writer.

She had seen that writing and those initials far too often to make a mistake.

They belonged to Jeffery Templar!

The discovery was for a moment utterly bewildering. How on earth had Jeffery Templar got mixed up in an author's contract for film rights? It was quite outside his sphere as a businessman's lawyer, an expert in company law and the usual legal complications of the city.

Then, with a sickening sense of certainty against all reason, she guessed the incredible truth. Jeffery Templar might have been disposed to give her a little help himself if she were in desperate need, a good meal, perhaps five pounds or so to help her over a difficult moment, but not five thousand pounds with a doubtful assurance of any return for it, and offered at a time when he had no reason to suppose she was in any need at all.

She looked across at Mr. Garret.

'How is Mr. Templar concerned in this?' she asked bluntly.

'Er—Mr. Templar?' temporised the agent, flabbergasted.

'Yes. I know his writing and his initials far too well to make any mistake,' said Verne with a level gaze. 'What concern is it of his?'

'He—he is acting for his principal, as you are aware,' said Mr. Garret, who felt that the mystery about this offer from the blue was deepening. 'Nothing in that, of course. I told you that the principal did not want his name known at the moment. Quite usual that. These big film people don't want to be bothered.'

'Jeffery Templar is not in the least likely to be mixed up in any way with big film people,' she said steadily. 'His business is entirely that of the city. I doubt if he even knows anything about author's rights. Mr. Garret, for whom is he acting?'

He frowned. Surely she was not going to be difficult over it? Good heavens, she was in no position to be so! Whoever was prepared to put up five thousand pounds for the chance that a mediocre book like *Pantalets* might make a saleable film, its author should jump at the chance, not begin to question the source.

'I've told you, Miss Derring. I don't know myself, and it is certainly no business of mine to try to find out. I am satisfied that Mr. Templar is in a position to carry the whole deal through and that the money will be forthcoming, and that is my only concern. Now if you will read through the rest of the suggested contract, I will have a fair copy made of it and you can sign it before you go and will have no further trouble—unless the sum of five thousand pounds (less my commission, of course) can be regarded as a trouble?' with a return to his beaming complacence.

But Verne was folding up the paper and putting it into her handbag. Her face had not changed from its frozen calm.

'I prefer to take it with me and consider it for a little while,' she said and rose.

'B—but, Miss Derring—surely that isn't at all necessary—or wise?' he stuttered, discomfited and angry, seeing his own five hundred pounds, sorely needed just now, beginning to recede from his reach. 'After all, I am your accredited agent, and I have your best interests to serve and I know a lot more about these things than you do. Believe me, five thousand pounds is a lot of money, *a lot of money,* to pay for the film rights of a book no more significant than yours, an extraordinary offer, in fact. You can have no hopes at all of getting it increased. Actually, if you delay, it might even be withdrawn. After all—'

Verne cut him short with quiet resolution.

'I quite realise that, Mr. Garret, but I still wish to take the proposals away and think about them,' she said. 'I will let you know in a few days,' and he could think of nothing more he could say to detain her.

'Blithering little idiot,' he fumed to himself as she went. 'She certainly has some opinion of herself if she thinks she can get the offer raised! More likely to lose it altogether. The man must be mad, anyway, to offer that for her piffling book which even had to be remaindered!'

Verne went steadily towards Fleet Street and Jeffery Templar's office, deciding to take a chance, rather than risk his refusal to see her.

The chance came off, for he was in and, when her name was brought to him, he sat hesitating for a moment before he spoke.

'Very well,' he said. 'You can show Miss Raydon in.'

The clerks in his office knew quite well, of course, who Miss Raydon was, but they would not be his clerks if they were not entirely discreet.

'Mr. Templar will see you, Miss Raydon,' she was told, and was conducted to the familiar office as if she did not know the way.

She did not beat about the bush, did not even return his greeting by any more than the mere courtesy of a murmur, but took out the draft contract from her bag and laid it before him.

'I want to know about this, Mr. Templar,' she said very directly.

He sighed and frowned.

'I did not wish to be implicated in it, in your mind,' he said.

'Then you should not have written in the amendments and initialled them,' she said.

'I am afraid it did not occur to me that you would see them,' he admitted with a wry smile. 'I slipped up there.'

'For whom are you acting, Mr. Templar?' she asked with her level gaze.

'Mr. Garret must have told you that I'm not at liberty to reveal that,' he said.

'He did. Is it—Robert?' she asked with a faint, discernible pause at the name.

'You know I can't possibly betray my client's confidence, whoever he is,' he said.

'Then it is Robert? All right. You need not answer that. I won't ask you to betray him. Let us merely assume that I know your client, whoever he is. Why has he made this offer to me? What does he hope to get out of it? You know as well as I do that my book was not a success, and that it is extremely doubtful, if even that, that it will make any better success as a film.'

'I am not in a position to judge of that, Mrs. Grimtree—'

'I prefer not to be called that.'

He gave a slight smile. He had always liked her spirit. He was glad to find that life had not yet quenched it.

'Verne then. I cannot express any opinion on the merits or demerits of your book.'

'Well, I can. This isn't a business offer. It's charity, and I don't accept charity from anyone.'

'But, Verne—'

'But nothing, Mr. Templar. Please tell—your client,' with a curl of her lip, 'that I do not need anything from him, not anything at all,' and she gave a scornful little push to the paper still lying on his desk and prepared to go. She had not even sat down.

He looked distressed. For one thing he wanted her to have the money and felt that she deserved it. For another, he did not relish having to face Robert Grimtree with the tale of her defiant refusal.

'Verne, do be sensible,' he began, but again she cut him short.

'It's no use, Mr. Templar. I cannot accept anything from Robert in the circumstances. My mind is quite made up and you can tell him so.'

'I shall get into very hot water for letting you know it came from him,' he said ruefully.

'You should have known better than to let him make the offer,' she retorted.

'You're a hard nut to crack, Verne.'

'You don't get far in life until you've learnt to be hard,' she said.

'Well, if I can't say anything to dissuade you from this folly, don't go off in that frame of mind. What about having lunch with me?'

She hesitated and then thought it would be silly to refuse. For one thing it was a long time since she had had a good meal not cooked by herself, and for another there was that curious, almost nostalgic feeling of contact with her husband whilst she was with Jeffery Templar.

They had almost finished the meal when Verne, sitting in a position from which she could not see the door, surprised a look, of sudden concern on the lawyer's usually unrevealing face and she turned her head involuntarily to see what had caused it.

Robert had entered the room and was coming straight towards them.

She felt the blood ebb from her face and the fork fell from her hand with a little clatter on the plate. How idiotic of her not to have foreseen that, she thought in a panic. This restaurant, with its excellent grill, was one of the places he frequented. It was he, indeed, who had introduced it to Mr. Templar long ago.

'Mind if I join you?' asked the familiar voice. 'Morning, Templar. Morning—Verne,' with just that slight hesitation over her name which told her he was not as unmoved as he wanted to appear.

Without waiting for a reply, he pulled a chair up to the table.

'I don't want lunch,' he said to the waiter who at once appeared. 'Bring coffee. Yes, for three. Cigar, Templar? And bring some cigarettes,' naming the special brand which in the old expensive days had been Verne's choice.

She could not speak and she dare not look at him. She sat staring down at her plate like a self conscious schoolgirl whilst Templar covered the awkwardness of the moment with a remark about the weather, that unfailing and useful topic to Englishmen.

At last Grimtree spoke to her directly.

'How's the country, Verne?' he asked, putting beside her the packet of cigarettes and then, on second thoughts, picking it up again to open it and offer it to her. The little courtesy, which she had taught him, affected her strangely. He had not forgotten.

'Nice, but wet,' she told him, and whilst he held the lighted match for her, she was quite unable to withhold her glance from him any longer.

What she saw in his eyes kept her own riveted there whilst the match burned down slowly, her cigarette still unlit.

She had never seen him look like that before. There was a kind of hunger there, almost an appeal, and she saw that in some indefinable way the whole man had changed, grown older, his rugged face more lined. There was almost a drooping of his heavy figure and a sagging of his shoulders. Or was it just the way he was sitting? Her imagination perhaps?

She dragged her eyes away from him, and with a little characteristic gesture of irritation, he dropped the burnt down match into an ashtray and struck another which this time he held steadily for her.

It was a moment in which nothing had really happened, and yet she drew a deep breath and felt that it had been important. Why?

He did not speak to her again but opened a discussion with Mr. Templar on some unfinished matter which did not concern her, and when they had finished their coffee, he flicked his fingers, again with a well known gesture, towards the waiter.

'The bill,' he added irritably, but Mr. Templar interposed smoothly.

'Verne is my guest,' he said, and Grimtree grunted and let it pass.

'Will you see me to my bus, Mr. Templar?' asked Verne as calmly as she could, though the blood was pounding uncomfortably in her veins.

'I'll take you wherever you want to go,' said her husband, and though she threw a look of frightened appeal towards her host, Mr. Templar did not appear to notice it but reached for his hat and umbrella.

'Mr. Templar—' she began, her breath coming fast.

But his face was wooden and imperturbable.

'I should give that scheme further consideration, Verne,' he said calmly. 'Ring me, or drop me a note, when you have done so. It's been nice seeing you,' and with a smile for her and a casual nod at Grimtree, he left them alone.

She had an instant's impulse to follow him, but she felt a hand touch her arm.

'Don't panic,' said Robert. 'It's no use,' and rather than draw the attention of the other customers in the crowded room, she walked out in front of him steadily, though she felt the floor receding from her feet.

If Johnson was surprised to see her, his face expressed nothing as he held the car door open for her and she resisted the impulse to speak to him. Robert followed her in, turning to speak to the man as he did so.

'Drive anywhere,' he said curtly, and when the door had closed and Johnson's back was visible through the glass screen, he turned to look at Verne.

'Well?' he asked. 'Surprised to see me?'

It was the old, growling tone which seemed to grudge utterance to the words.

'Was it arranged?' she asked coldly, not looking at him.

'By Templar? No. Why should it be? Templar's on your side. Always has been, though he takes my money. What were you doing with him?'

She had never been a coward, and she came straight to the point, her head high, her eyes looking straight ahead.

'I went to tell him I could not accept your five thousand pounds,' she said.

'What five thousand?' attempting to bluster.

'Are there so many in your scheme of things offered for nothing?' she asked bitterly. 'For the film rights of my book, of course.'

'H'm. How did you know? I suppose Templar told you?' sourly.

'No, he didn't. You know that he would not have done so against your instructions. As you say, you pay him to carry them out. It was not difficult for me to guess where the offer came from. I don't know anybody else who has five thousand pounds to throw away on nothing.'

'Why should you imagine I'd throw money away? I don't as a rule,' he said grimly.

'Even you can break rules. Why did you do it in this instance?'

She was finding it difficult to maintain the attitude of rigid detachment. With every moment something of the old relationship was returning, secretary and employer, or wife and husband, she did not know which.

'You're my wife, aren't you?' he grunted. 'You must have something to live on as I gather that other chap has left you flat.'

Her face flushed painfully and she sat upright.

'Not so flat that I cannot support myself—and my child,' she said. 'We don't have to rely on charity.'

'What a husband gives his wife is not charity.'

'It is when you are the husband and I the wife,' she said with spirit.

'H'm. I thought you might refuse. Your damned pride! That's why I said my name was not to appear. And why should you think it charity? You had something to sell which I wanted to buy.'

She gave a hard little laugh of derision.

'Since when has Robert Grimtree wanted to buy something which he knows to be worthless?' she asked. 'In any deal he makes, he expects to get value for money.'

'Even when it's a wife he's buying,' said Robert shortly.

'I'm afraid that was one of the deals which did not turn out very well for you, Robert,' she said in a low voice, oddly deflated now.

'One makes mistakes,' he said, and there was a change in his voice too, though she could not have defined it. 'Sometimes, though, they turn out to be quite a different kind of mistake from what first appears.'

She could not tell what was in his mind. All she knew was that in some way things had changed between them, become at once more personal and yet frightening. On what brink did they stand, and on the same side of it or separated by an impassable chasm?

'I have made mistakes in my life, Verne,' he said after that pregnant pause, his voice heavy and slow, as if he were considering every word before he uttered it. 'Some of them you know about. Some—you don't. I made one of them when I told you I didn't believe that—Adrian was my child. I never doubted that. I said it in anger.'

She drew a long, quivering breath. She knew what it must have cost him, Robert Grimtree, the proud, the self assured, the infallible, to speak those words. The fact that he had done so mattered now even more than the words themselves. She had never really believed that he had doubted his son's paternity. Her resentment and fury against him had been because he had cast such an aspersion on the child whether he believed what he said or not.

'Well?' he asked roughly, as she did not answer. 'Haven't you anything to say?'

'There isn't anything to say, is there?' she asked in a low voice. 'And whatever you believed, or pretended to believe about him makes no difference to the fact that my daughter is not yours.'

'No,' he agreed grimly, and there was a silence again until he broke it, with a shifting of his great shoulders as if seeking to throw off some heavy load.

'You say you're supporting yourself. How?' he asked.

'By working.'

'What at?'

She gave a little involuntary smile now that the tension was broken.

'Difficult to say. I'm housekeeper, cook, private secretary, gardener—the lot.'

To some man?' with a suspicious glance shot at her from beneath beetling brows.

'Oh yes, but I'm not living with him, if that's what you mean. I am a perfectly respectable member of the community—now,' her lip curling slightly.

'H'm,' he grunted. Then, 'Why won't you let me help you?'

'You need not ask that and I need not answer.'

'Meaning that you don't propose to accept something for nothing? Or let me give something for nothing? That it, eh? Eh?' with the familiar note of irritability.

'Yes. That and my pride, if I've got any left.'

When he spoke again, it was with a complete change of tone and subject.

'Like to go to a theatre?' he asked.

She looked at him in surprise.

'This afternoon you mean? Oh no, thank you, Robert.'

'Why not? Don't you like to be seen with me, eh? Eh?'

'It wouldn't be wise, of course—for you, I mean. But I've got to get back to my work.'

'Slave driver, is he?' grimly.

She smiled again.

'He wouldn't be the first one I've worked for,' she said, 'but he isn't. It's simply that I've got a job to do and I'd rather get on with it.'

'Rather than be with me, you mean?' he asked sourly. 'What's your station?'

'My station? Oh—oh, I see what you mean. Waterloo.'

He leaned forward and tapped on the glass screen. She remembered how she had tried to teach him, without success, to use the more dignified method of the speaking tube provided.

'Drive to Waterloo,' he said, when Johnson showed that he had heard.

Robert did not speak again during the short drive, but when he got out of the car with her and they were walking across the station, he asked curtly, 'Got your ticket?'

'Yes,' she said and took it out of her purse, a green ticket.

'Going third?' he asked her, looking at it.

'Naturally,' she told him calmly.

'You're a fool,' he snapped.

'Why? Because I don't travel first on a third class income?'

'For refusing the five thousand, as you're obviously hard up. I shouldn't have missed it.'

'Perhaps it would have had more significance if you had,' she told him. 'My train's in so I'll go now.'

He passed through the barrier with her, waving aside with a lordly gesture the request of the official for a platform ticket, and that individual, with plenty to do, let him go with a shrug.

'Get in here. I'll pay the extra,' said Robert testily, opening the door of a first class compartment, but Verne shook her head and walked on to one labelled 'Third'.

'There's no need,' she said. 'I'm quite used to it, not being Mrs. Robert Grimtree any longer,' and at once she wished she had not uttered the gibe. Why had she done so? Why try to hurt him? It was an odd thing to her, to know instinctively, that he *could* be hurt.

'You'll always be that,' he told her gruffly, and she did not reply.

'Er—thank you for driving with me,' he muttered when she was seated in her corner. 'You'd better take that money, you know,' not looking at her.

'I couldn't,' she said, her voice not quite steady and for a wild moment it occurred to her to say she would take it, not for her own sake but strangely, incomprehensibly, for his.

'Mean you won't,' he threw at her savagely, and he turned on his heel and left her, striding along the platform away from her.

She sat feeling perplexed and lost and lonely. His forceful personality had claimed her and surrounded her whilst they had been together just as it had always done. You could not be in Robert Grimtree's presence without that awareness of him and, suddenly left like that, she felt a strange emptiness. Was it that, once married to a man, even in such a marriage as theirs, a woman is bound by an indissoluble link? In a world where separation and divorce have become an everyday thing, did every parted couple feel like this after a casual meeting? Or was it because he was Robert Grimtree?

She closed her eyes, but opened them again because, closed, they seemed to give her an even closer vision of him. She picked up a newspaper lying on the seat of the otherwise empty compartment but could not concentrate on what she was reading.

What did politics matter? The ever present threat of a new war? Other people's exploits and troubles?

She threw the paper down again and let her mind have its way since she could not control it.

She thought of Robert.

Her husband.

He had insisted that he thought of himself still as that.

Why? Why?

Meantime, Grimtree had told Johnson curtly to drive him home instead of back to his office.

Home.

An empty, solitary place that was no more than a house.

Why had he let her go like that? Not knowing where she was going nor what she was doing, nor with whom?

This other man. Who was he? What was he? Was he in love with Verne? She with him?

He gnawed at his ringers, a trick of which he had cured himself years ago. Now he did not even notice he was doing it.

Well, he would never divorce her, never set her free so that she could be to any other man what she was to him, his wife.

His wife!

And she had gone off there, with that bright look of challenge and defiance in her eyes, that indomitable look she had always worn, gone to that unknown place, that unknown man –

He went into his library, curtly refusing Parlow's proffered drinks, and slumped down in his chair and stared at the one she had so often occupied.

He could see her now, not dressed as she had been today in the well worn grey suit, but in one of the soft, flowing gowns he had liked her to wear, silk or velvet, with diamonds flashing in her ears as she moved her head, or on her hands occupied with a book, or with the needles with which she was knitting – knitting those absurd, pitifully small baby garments perhaps.

He looked away on that thought, his hands gripping the arms of his chair, his feet shuffling in the thick carpet. He was remembering her as she had been during those few happy months before the birth of the child, when surely they had been drawing closer together, getting some better understanding of each other. He had found it possible to talk to her then, easing the tight band about his mind, taking her little by little into that secret life where the man himself had loved alone so long.

How could he have prevented the hideous thing which had happened after the death of the child? How could he have held her? If he had been able to tell her that he loved her, in so many words and not just by the gifts he bought her, would it have made any difference?

If she had stayed with him a little longer, not gone off as soon as she must have done to that lout who had let her down, would it not have been possible to recapture to some extent that understanding towards which they had groped before the birth of the child?

And what good had come to either of them? That unspeakable brute had deserted her, left her with his child still unborn, and if Robert Grimtree had needed any justification for his refusal to divorce her, he had it in the certainty he felt that, if she had been able to marry Trailer, her position now would be even worse that it was. The man would have deserted a wife as readily as he had deserted the woman who had every claim on him, who had betrayed her husband for him and who carried within her his child.

What was her position now?

He gnawed at his fingers again.

Verne could never look ill cared for or actually shabby, but she had come very near to it. He had seen her shoes when she stepped up into the train. They had been repaired. There was a tiny, very neat mend in the skirt of her suit, and her handbag was shiny with use.

Verne, his wife, actually needed clothes!

He rose from his chair and went heavily up the stairs, paused for a moment outside the door of her room, and at last brought himself to open the door and go in. He had not done that for a long time, though after they had parted he had entered the room once or twice, to stand looking round and trying to kill, through sheer pain, the aching longing for her.

He opened the wardrobes and passed his hand with a gentle, almost reverent touch over the clothes that hung there, the gleaming satins, the soft velvets. The perfume she used drifted out to him unbearably, and he turned away from these to her plainer and more everyday garments. He would not let some other man see her as he had loved her best, in the glamorous evening gowns, the silks and the furs.

Instead, he took from their hangers her street suits, tailored and very plain, and shoes that went with them, and gloves, and a handbag which had been one of his last presents, lizard skin with gold fittings. At least she could sell that for good money, he thought bitterly.

With clumsy care, he packed the things in one of his own big leather suitcases, hesitated over something which he had taken out of his wallet, a crude snapshot of himself and Verne which one of the Curloe children had taken, put the photograph back in his pocket, closed and locked the case, and then, with a sheepish grin at himself, unfastened it again, and pushed the photograph into it, and refastened it.

'At least it won't be in my pocket grinning at me all the time,' he excused himself as he did so.

It was infuriating that he did not know where to send the case, did not know where his own wife was living, but he went about his task with grim determination, lugged the heavy case down the stairs himself and told Parlow to get a taxi for him.

'Will you be away long, sir?' asked the imperturbable butler.

'I'm not going away,' snapped Grimtree.

He left the case in the Left Luggage Office at Waterloo, scrawled a note to Jeffery Templar and posted it with the receipt.

'*See that Verne gets this case. R.G.,*' was all he said and Mr. Templar, reading it the next day, wondered wryly whether any other eminent London solicitor was ever told to do the things this particular client demanded of him.

Chapter Thirteen

Once she had parted from Grimtree again, Verne felt the inevitable reaction set in. Had she been a complete fool to throw away that blessed five thousand pounds? She had wanted it so desperately, not for herself but for her beloved Rosemary, now all she had in life. Had she done the child an irremediable wrong in refusing the money which would have given her that good start in life which she, Verne, so greatly desired for her? How could she hope, by her own work, to do anything comparable to what a good education on the lines of her own schooling could do for her? Armed with that, and surrounded during her young, impressionable days by people with the way of life, the good manners and the ideals which had been inculcated in her, Verne Raydon, from earliest times, Rosemary could have faced the hard world in which she would inevitably have to make her own way.

Had she saved her own poor pride at the cost of Rosemary's whole future?

If she had, it was too late now for anything but possible regret, for she could certainly not go crawling back to Robert for the gift she had refused, even in the unlikely event of his being ready to offer it again.

Why had he offered it at all? She had not yet found any answer to that, and his own casual explanation that since she was his wife, she must have money to spend, was something to be brushed aside. It left her with no real explanation of his gesture, for Robert Grimtree never gave anything for nothing.

Nothing?

She remembered the gift which Mary Gorner had flung back at him after her husband's suicide. But had that been for nothing? Had it not been a salve to his conscience, if he had one? And in that case, had the offer made to her, Verne, also been a salve? But what had he on his conscience as far as she was concerned? Not, she was sure, the fact that he had cast off a wife he believed to be faithless. What if he no longer believed that?

She caught her breath sharply and gripped her hands in her lap. Well, even if he had come to believe her innocent at that time, she was not so now. She had lived with Bill Trailer as his wife, had borne him a child and was alone now not through any choice of action of her own, but merely because her lover had cast her off, a deserted mistress of whom he had grown tired.

Gerald Mance was at the gate looking for her when she turned into the lane. It gave her a little feeling of comfort and of homecoming, and her heart and her face lightened at sight of him.

'I hoped you would catch that train,' he said, opening the gate for her. 'I heard it come in, or imagined I did. You got some lunch, I hope?'

'Yes. A good one,' she said. 'Is Rosemary back yet?'

'No. It's still early. I've put the kettle on.'

'Good. It's a miserable day in London. Here, too, I suppose,' with a grimace at the wet garden and the dripping trees from which today's wind had stripped most of the remaining leaves. 'Somehow it never seems quite as miserable in the country at this time of year, though I wonder why?'

He gave her a quick look but did not answer, going into the cottage with her. A big fire of logs burnt in the, hearth, sending its cheerful light dancing and swaying about the room. Their two chairs were drawn up to it companionably. He had even thought of putting her slippers to warm.

'Give me your coat and hat, unless you particularly want to go upstairs,' he said, 'and change your shoes. I'll make the tea. I went down to the village and bought some scones and things, though they won't be a patch on yours.'

'That was nice of you,' she said gratefully, and accepted his thoughtfulness for her, sat in the chair whilst he busied himself in the kitchen and was glad that he had not immediately demanded to know the result of her day.

Still, it had to come, and over their tea he asked her how she had got on with Garret.

'I've refused the offer,' she said.

He set down his cup and stared at her unbelievingly.

'What on earth for? Did he make some impossible condition, or what?'

'No. There were no conditions. It's only that—I found out that it was made under circumstances which I—couldn't accept,' she said slowly, not looking at him.

'You're not going to tell me?' he asked.

She shook her head.

'Do you mind if I don't? It was—not a real offer to buy the film rights at all. No film would ever have been made. It was—just charity, and I couldn't accept it.'

'Something from the life I don't know anything about?'

'Yes.'

'I see. Well, that was a disappointment to you, wasn't it?'

'Yes, a big one. I've been spending that five thousand in my mind for a day or two,' she said, with a fugitive smile of courage.

'That's the way life sometimes has its little joke. I'm sorry, though. I wanted you to have it.'

'I know. In a way you've shared it with me and I liked it.'

'Better let's forget it,' he said practically.

'It's nice of you not to tell me I'm a quixotic fool. I've been telling myself that all the way home.'

'I should never think you are a fool. Whatever your reason, it must have been a good one.'

She gave him a grateful smile.

Thank you, Mr. Mance. I appreciate that.'

'I called you Verne,' he pointed out.

She nodded.

'I know, but it's different.'

'Because I'm your employer and about a hundred years older than you?' he asked.

'The first perhaps, but not the second.'

'It's true, to some extent. You're how old? Twenty four? Twenty five? Well, I'm forty three.'

'That's not exactly senile,' she laughed.

'No, but getting on that way, compared with twenty five. Verne, would you feel at all inclined to marry me?'

She set down her cup with a little clatter, nearly missing the saucer altogether and stared at him in blank amazement.

'Oh!' she said, and continued to stare.

'Bit of a shock?' he asked, calmly cutting open a scone and buttering it carefully.

'More than a bit,' she admitted. Then, recovering herself, 'What about your advertisement? No matrimonial ambitions, or intentions, or whatever it was?'

'Meaning that it should have worked both ways? It was meant to. Now I wish I hadn't said it, but how could I have imagined it would turn out like this, or that it should be you who answered it? Anyway, forget that. How does the suggestion strike you, Verne?'

For a moment she could find nothing to say, her mind in a turmoil of amazement, and knowing that though she hated to hurt him there was no escape.

'I'm sorry,' she said at last in a low voice.

'Meaning that you won't?'

'Meaning that I can't. You see—I'm married,' unable to look at him.

'I see. I was afraid of that. I've realised for some time that you are not in the least the sort of girl who would have had a baby without being married.'

She looked at him then, steadily, though everything within her shrank from what to her was the inescapable need to be honest with him

'Rosemary is not my husband's child,' she said. 'We had parted, but he would not divorce me. She was not born until more than a year later, but—she is not legitimate.'

'And you parted with the man as well?'

'Yes.'

Her head went up and she kept her steady eyes on his. He could think what he liked. She was not going to tell him of that humiliation.

For a long time there was silence. Then he spoke again, quietly.

'Do you think your husband would consider divorcing you now?' he asked.

'Why? Does it matter?' she asked drearily.

'Of course it does. How can we be married unless he does?'

'You still want to? In spite of what I've told you? In spite of Rosemary?'

'Why not? I've got used to her.'

'But—don't you realise that I'm not a nice person to know, now that I've told you?'

'You've been a very nice person for me to know, and what you've told me doesn't make any difference to that.'

'But why should you want to marry me? You're not—not the kind to want a wife,' colouring a little.

He smiled.

'Not just any wife perhaps, but I happen to want you. For one thing, it would tie you down so that you wouldn't leave me. I find you very useful. For another thing, I'm fond of you, Verne. I'm not the romantic sort. You know that. I can't spout poetry to you or say pretty things. I'd just like to have you for my wife.'

She could not respond to his smile. Why, oh why, had this to happen? This talk of love (if that was what he meant) and marrying— she didn't want it! Most passionately she did not want it! All she asked of life was to be left alone to work for herself and Rosemary with no man to bring in the inevitable complications.

'I'm very grateful,' she said at last. 'It's nonsense about your age. That has nothing to do with it. But I don't want to marry again. I don't want any man in my life again.'

The passion had crept into her voice. He could not fail to see how desperately she meant what she said.

'I see,' he said. 'Well, that rather sounds like that, doesn't it? If you ever change your mind, you can be sure I haven't changed mine. What about this husband of yours, by the way? Do you ever see him?'

'I saw him today,' she said slowly, looking away.

'Is he mixed up with this offer to buy the film rights?'

She shot a glance at him.

'Are you guessing, or did you know?' she asked.

'Merely deducting. If he wants to give you all that money, it looks as though it isn't finished.'

'It's quite finished,' she said definitely, and he gave a little twisted smile.

'With five thousand pounds for a bait?' he asked. 'Oh well, let's get back to normal, shall we? Do you think you could type out that last chapter for me? I'm getting so sick of old Stickback, but I'm afraid if I killed him off, I'd be killed off too. Fatuous old idiot!'

She laughed.

'You or old Stickback?' she asked.

'Both of us.'

That night, after she had gone to bed, she lay and thought inevitably of her day, of Robert who had disturbed her so that she could not keep him out of her mind, and of Gerald Mance with his astounding proposition.

Why, why, had she to inspire men with this desire for her, she who had never desired any man? Gerald had not talked of love, and yet in his own unromantic way, what he felt for her must be love.

She turned in her bed restlessly. She liked Gerald, felt happy and at ease with him. If she could give him anything in return, she might have asked Robert once more for her release, but what was there she could give other than loyal service as his employee?

Would Robert give her her freedom if she asked for it again?

The thought of being freed by him, of no longer being even legally his wife gave her a curious, twisting pain. She thought of him as he had been that day, of the look she had surprised in his eyes, of the feeling he had given her once or twice that she was in deep waters, out of her depth, drifting – where? Was there anyone in the world who had ever understood, ever known, that strange, aggressive, powerful man? What really lay beneath the strength and indomitable will? Had she only imagined that he was a haunted man, lonely and afraid? Robert Grimtree lonely? Afraid?

The memory persisted and tormented her, and when, a day or two later, the heavy suitcase with its badly packed contents arrived, she knew that she had not been wrong. Robert was still thinking of her. Needing her?

She held the crumpled snapshot in her hand and her eyes dimmed.

They had been standing in the orchard, her figure distorted as much by the camera as by her pregnancy. She was looking towards the boy who had persuaded them to let him take the picture, and she was laughing, but Robert was looking down at her, and though the photograph was a bad one, out of focus and with the light wrong, there was no mistaking the expression on his face. It was a brooding, protective look, a half smile, and though his hand had been raised to take hold of a branch of the apple tree, his arm seemed to be about her, shielding and protecting her.

She had seen the snapshot when the Curloe boy had sent it to them, but at the time had not taken much notice of it. But Robert must have kept it, and in his pocket since it smelt of his cigars.

Why had he kept it? And why had he sent it to her now?

She smoothed it out with her fingers and laid it in a drawer, but the memory of it remained with her. Anyone looking at it would think it a picture of any normal happy couple. What if it could have been like that? If he really loved her, as both Bill Trailer and Jeffery Templar had told her, what would it have meant to her to know it?

She caught her breath sharply and closed her eyes, leaning against the wardrobe which she had been polishing. To be loved by Robert Grimtree, loved with the resolution, the single minded fidelity which he gave to everything else he touched – what would that mean to a woman, to her?

That he was a man with all a man's normal passions she knew. Yet in all that time, but for that one night which now, looking back on it and with her experience of life with Bill Trailer she could understand and almost condone, he had never in any way approached her as a husband. He had gone instead to a woman whose favours he could buy so that she, his wife, could live her own untouched, untouchable life.

Why, if he had not loved her?

Gerald Mance's voice, calling up the stairs, brought her back to her normal life.

'Verne! I've got a cheque from that old skinflint, royalties on my last book. Come down and let's have a drink on it.'

He was pleased and excited and talked at length on what he proposed to do with it.

'Manna from heaven,' he said, showing her the cheque, 'and the very first thing, of course, is to give you something to make up for the miserable pittance I have been paying you. No use protesting, which I see you are about to do. I've never had a cheque this size before and it's largely through you so of course you must have your share. After that, I believe I could save something for the first time in my life!'

She was pleased, of course. It would have been foolish to refuse his offer. She knew she had earned it and, with the bouncing Rosemary's needs increasing, she was finding it very difficult to manage on her two pounds a month.

'Old Stickback's turned up trumps at last,' she said. 'I am most grateful to him, whatever I may have said about him.'

He grimaced.

'It beats me how anybody puts up with him, let alone ask for more. I've been thinking about that bit of waste land the other side of our hedge. How about my buying it? It would ensure that nobody builds on it, and we could make an orchard of it or something. What do you think about it?'

They discussed it and were in agreement.

'I know how to get hold of it,' said Mance, 'but I don't want to put the deal through with our local solicitors. Do you think your friend Templar would see to it for me?'

She hesitated. It was impossible to dissociate any contact with Mr. Templar from contact with Robert.

'It's rather out of his way,' she said. 'He might not be inclined to take on work outside London. He's a very busy man.'

'Well, no harm in trying. Write and ask him, will you?'

She had no option, but she did not make the proposition sound attractive. The reply came to the effect that if the matter could be held over for a few weeks, Mr. Templar would be pleased to go into it with Mr. Mance.

It was nearly two months before an appointment could be made, and the solicitor arranged to come down to Yew Cottage for the purpose.

Verne thought he looked tired and unusually grave but he went into the details with his usual thoroughness and then suggested their taking a look at the plot as it had stopped raining.

'Verne will take, you,' said Mance. 'I've got some infernal proofs to read before tonight's post.'

'I can do those for you,' said Verne quickly, fearing for some obscure reason to be alone with the solicitor.

'No, you go with Mr. Templar. You've been stuck in the house all day,' Mance insisted, and she went reluctantly.

They confined themselves at first to the business in hand, and then strolled along the lane which led them back to the cottage.

'I suppose you feel I owe you an apology, Verne?' asked Templar.

'What for?'

'For abandoning you to Robert after inveigling you out to lunch.'

'Was that prearranged?' she asked in her direct fashion, looking straight ahead.

'Good heavens, no. I was as much surprised as you. Did you mind very much?'

'No,' she said after a moment's pause, admitting to herself for the first time that she had not minded.

'What did you think of him, Verne?'

She looked at him, surprised.

'Think of him? In what way?'

'How did you think he was looking?'

'What are you trying to say to me, Mr. Templar? Is there anything the matter with Robert?'

'I'm worried about him.'

'Worried about *Robert!*'

She had an odd feeling of concern.

'Why so surprised if I am? I'm his friend as well as his lawyer.'

'One doesn't worry about a person who is a law unto himself in all things,' she said with a touch of tartness in her voice.

'Sometimes one's laws for oneself go wrong.'

Again she had that feeling of discomfort and vague alarm. Why should she feel jumpy about *Robert?*

'Has something gone wrong for him then?' she asked.

She felt his keen eyes on her, searching her face. She kept her voice rigidly controlled so that he should not search her mind as well. 'I'm afraid so. Quite badly wrong.'

She gave him a startled look.

'What sort of wrongness?'

'Financial.'

'Financial? *Robert!*' she exclaimed. 'How could it? He's got the earth!'

'He did have.'

'Mr. Templar, you're trying to tell me something. How could anything be wrong financially with Robert Grimtree?' she asked incredulously.

'I'd have said that once, but I find I didn't know him as well as I thought I did. Also he didn't trust me as I thought he did. He's been up to all sorts of tilings on his own and without asking my advice—or the advice of anyone reliable, as far as I can see.'

'Just what has he been doing, Mr. Templar?'

'Gambling. On the Stock. Exchange, of course, but very heavily and with too little knowledge. I could never have believed that he was such a fool, but there it is. He came to me the other day to straighten him out, but so far I've only touched the fringe of it and I don't know how far he is involved yet.'

She was lost in consternation.

'Robert? I simply can't believe it, and yet of course I must believe *you.* How long has it been going on?'

'How long is it since you parted from him?' he parried.

She drew a deep breath.

'Nearly two years,' she said, 'but—what has that to do with it?'

'Probably nothing. Possibly everything. It seems that that was when he started going into foolhardy ventures. You've heard of Cambium Incorporated?'

'Vaguely. One of those East African ventures, wasn't it?'

'West Africa this time. Some foolhardy scheme originated by some idiot and exploited by a set of knaves and unfortunately believed in by Robert. He simply poured money into it without going out to investigate it for himself, as of course he should have done—or employed some knowledgeable and honest man to do it for him. It went broke. Rather than have it generally known and his idiocy exposed, he paid up to keep it quiet and let those rascals get away with it. Several millions.'

'Millions!' cried Verne, aghast.

'That wasn't all, unfortunately. Trying to recoup his losses, he went in for other wild cat schemes, backed quite unjustifiable fancies on the Exchange without sufficient knowledge and against the persistent advice of his brokers, and never seems to have found a winner.'

'But Grimtree's itself is solid enough.'

'Quite,' said the lawyer dryly, 'but it's only Grimtree's in name now.'

'He's sold Grimtree's?' she asked, startled beyond measure.

'You know that many of his work people have got shares in it. He sold it a few months ago in order to save their holdings. It seemed to him then the only way, though if he had come to me, I'd have advised him differently—or at least have got a much bigger price for it. I can't understand him nor what got into him, but there's no getting away from the fact that during the last two years, he's gone to pieces. If I didn't know differently, I'd say his brain had given way, but he's quite sane.'

'Sold—Grimtree's,' Verne repeated, as if with the need to impress her mind with the unbelievable truth. 'I simply can't take it in.'

'Neither could I, at first. He stipulated that it should be done privately and still retain its name, and I imagine that very few people know.'

They walked along in silence, their minds heavy with their thoughts.

When Verne spoke again, her voice revealed the shattered state to which the news had reduced her.

'He must have something, of course,' she said. 'You don't mean he's actually bankrupted himself?'

'No. He's solvent, but that's about all, and now that he's brought himself, much too late, to make a clean breast of it to me, I'm making it my business to see that he keeps the little he's got left, a paltry thousand or two at best. I haven't got him clear yet, but I hope to save that much out of the wreck.'

'How is he taking it?' she asked in a low, shaken voice.

For Robert to be poor! It was inconceivable. She could not envisage it. It gave her a sudden sharp pain. That, too, was something beyond her comprehension.

'Hard to say. He's bitter, but he doesn't blame anybody but himself, not even those Cambium rogues. Says he should have known better, with which I agree, of course.'

'Better than to trust them? I wonder why he did? It's not his habit to trust anybody, not even the people he should know best.'

Mr. Templar glanced at her quickly. There had been an acid quality in her speech. Wisely, however, except for that quick, speculative glance, he let it pass.

'It's difficult to know just how much he has gone out of character,' he said, 'or how much he has been able to hoodwink us all these years. It's almost—well, I was going to say pathetic—the way he's now put himself in my hands, practically given up.'

'I can't believe that. Robert never gives up anything he's set his mind and his hand to.'

Again there was that faintly acid touch.

'I would have agreed with you there but for this business. He's gone to pieces over it. I don't know why I'm telling you all this, Verne. I had no intention of doing so when I came here.'

'I am his wife. I have a right to know.'

'You still regard yourself as that? Robert Grimtree's wife?'

'Of course. He has never divorced me. Do you think he would mind your telling me?'

'I don't think so, but I am forming the opinion that perhaps neither of us really knows him.'

'How could we? He would never let anyone get under the hard skin of him.'

They walked in silence for a few moments. Then she spoke again.

'What is he doing? I mean, where is he living? Does he go to the office still? I suppose not, if he has sold Grimtree's.'

'He went for a time, under the conditions of the sale. I don't think he does now, though. As far as I know, he's still living in Wellington Gate, but he won't be able to keep up that style, of course. We haven't got down to discussing details yet.'

She had a vivid picture in her mind of the house which had been her home, hers and Robert's, the great, over furnished rooms, the ornate decorations and fittings, all the elaborate and expensive detail, the huge staff who could never have had enough to do.

And Robert – beaten, humiliated, crushed, in the midst of all that grandeur – and alone.

Again she was aware of that pain. It was hurting her like a physical blow. Yet why should she feel anything at all? He had been defeated by the Moloch of his own making, the Moloch which was himself.

But it was that pain rather than the refutation of it which presently spoke in her voice.

'Is there nothing anyone can do?' she asked, looking steadily away from her companion.

He hesitated. He knew that, unexpectedly, he was finding himself in deep waters. His instinct, both personal and professional, was to make for the safe shore rather than attempt to plough through them to some hitherto unsuspected and strange port.

Then he looked at her again. Her face was very grave and for an instant her tongue passed over dry lips. She had plucked at a frond of bracken in the hedge and her fingers were pulling it to pieces in small jerks.

He made up his mind, for good or ill.

'There is something you could possibly do,' he said.

She looked at him sharply.

'I? But what could I do for Robert Grimtree?'

'You have quite a lot of money, Verne.'

She laughed at that.

'I wonder what gave you that idea? I have about three pounds four and sixpence.'

'You're wrong. You have over fifty thousand pounds,' he said calmly.

This time she did not laugh. She gave him an incredulous stare. Had the eminently sane Jeffery Templar gone mad?

'Don't be absurd,' she said.

'It may sound absurd, but it's true. Robert would probably slay me for this, as I know he didn't intend you to know, but he's been putting money away for you in small sums—small, that is, for him—ever since he married you and even since you parted. More, in fact, since you parted. He has put it into a banking account in your name, and no one can touch it but yourself. It now amounts, as I have said, to something like fifty thousand pounds.'

'Fifty—thousand—pounds?' she echoed, incredulously. 'But—why on earth should he have done that?'

Mr. Templar gave a little shrug.

'Who knows, except Robert Grimtree? He wanted you to be safe. Possibly even then this bug was biting him, these big speculations that have brought him down.'

'Would that money have saved him?'

'Not actually saved him, since to him it was little more than chicken feed, but yes, there was a time, a few weeks ago, when by using it, he could have staved off the worst of the ruin, managed to save at least something.'

Then why on earth didn't he take it?'

'For one thing, he couldn't touch it without your authority. It's yours absolutely, you know.'

'He must have known that I'd give it to him!' she cried, exasperated by the thought of Robert's incredible folly.

'Yes, he did know that. In fact, when I suggested that he put the matter to you and ask it as a loan, he told me that without doubt, if ever you knew you had it, you would fling it at his head! As you did that five thousand, remember.'

She gave a rueful half smile before she became grave again.

'Yes, I would have, of course. But surely he wouldn't have cared?'

'But he would. There was another reason, Verne, why he would never have asked for it back, and won't do so now. He told me that he wanted to make sure that you were all right, that you should never be in need, that you should have something of your own independent of anybody else or what you could earn.'

She was silent again. Was it true, as Mr. Templar had said, that she had never really known Robert? Her whole world seemed to be turning upside down, like a spilt jigsaw puzzle which would have to be put together again – though would it ever make the same picture?

That Robert, *Robert,* had had such thoughts! Caring what happened to her, what would happen even in the end, when she was old, alone perhaps, unable to work.

'He need not have done it,' was all she said in a low, uncertain voice. There was never any need. 'He thought there might be. As you know, he always thought in terms of money. In his view, there was nothing that could not be put right by hard cash. I did my best to persuade him to use, even as a temporary loan from you, that fifty thousand, which is not even invested but just lying in the bank, but he refused to discuss it. Said that he wanted to be sure you were never in need—if anything happened to him.'

The lawyer spoke the last words deliberately, and she caught them up at once, as he had known she would.

'What did he mean by that? If anything happened to him? What more could happen? You don't suppose he meant—?'

'That he had any idea of suicide? No, he didn't. For a moment I wondered that myself, but I realised he didn't mean that. He was thinking of the chance of death which everyone takes all the time, and also of course, the possibility that nothing at all could be saved from this wreck. No, Robert Grimtree is not the sort to end his own life. He's no coward and he's still a fighter.'

'You think it possible that he will have nothing left? Nothing at all?'

It was an appalling thought to associate with Robert – Robert whose only god was money and what it could buy for him.

'I think that's *possible,* but, as I have said, I hope to save a thousand or so for him, and on that, unless I am much mistaken, he will start all over again. He has come up the hard way once.'

'But now, when he has had so much! And when he's not young any longer!'

It was almost a cry, and again he gave her one of those quick, appraising looks which could so often wrest a secret from those who had no idea they had parted with it.

'With the fifty thousand he would not be starting so near the bottom of the ladder,' she said after a long pause, and Templar nodded.

Again there was silence between them, and then he looked at his watch.

'I suppose I'd better be getting back,' he said. 'I'll see to this business for Mr. Mance. It looks quite straightforward and reasonable.'

'Don't make your fees too high,' said Verne, and though she tried to laugh, her voice was oddly shaky. 'We're not rich people down here.'

'I'll keep it down to bedrock and make up the deficit out of my wealthier clients,' he said.

He smiled as he spoke, but she did not see the smile. She was walking along with her head bent, a look of thoughtful gravity on her face.

He was not sorry he had told her about Robert. Perhaps after all, there would be something saved out of this magnificent wreck, something which Robert Grimtree would find worth having.

Chapter Fourteen

During the next few days Verne was silent and preoccupied, doing her work with her usual efficiency but obviously not to be distracted from that communion with herself which made Mance wonder hopefully if she were giving all this thought to the matter of marrying him.

He could not know that she was absorbingly occupied with thoughts of her husband, though it did cross his mind that there might be some cause for anxiety there since in his view she was not at all the sort of person either to enter into or to break a marriage for insufficient reason.

Verne could not rid her mind of that picture of Robert, alone, defeated, in the great empty house of which he had been so proud. That would be one of the worst of his sufferings – the blow to his pride. However much she might remind herself of the man as she had known him, worked for him as his employee, and lived with him as his wife at any rate in name, she could not see him now as anything but a lost, lonely child with all its cherished toys smashed to pieces about him.

The astonishing revelation of the provision he had been making for her all this time, even after they had parted and she was living with another man, put him quite out of character for her – and yet she was remembering other things, the money he had offered to Mary Gorner in secret, the forlorn mongrel dog he had rescued and brought home, the almost ridiculous love he lavished on the adoring creature. Ridiculous – or pathetic?

Was Bunker with him now, in his hour of desolation? She fervently hoped so even whilst it hurt her oddly to think that in such an hour, all he had to comfort him and believe in him and look to him was – a mongrel dog.

She still could not understand how Robert had got himself into such a position. Always in her knowledge of him so careful, so far seeing, so suspicious of everyone and everything, how could he have let himself go like that?

Against her will, her mind fastened on one answer to that question, incredible though the idea was. Jeffery Templar had supplied it when he had told her, surely with deliberate intent, that Robert's mad juggling with his money had dated from the time they had parted.

It was a tremendous thought. If it were true, what else could it mean than that it had been a death blow to Robert to believe that she had betrayed and cheated him?

It was of no use any longer to tell herself that he had been too ready to believe ill of her, that he had put up no fight for her, that he had flung her like a discarded and unwanted parcel into another man's arms. That was too far in the past now for anyone not obsessed with vindictiveness, and there had never been anything vindictive in Verne's nature. Whatever lay in the past, it was the present that concerned her now – the present and the future.

The future?

Something in her shrank, frightened, from the thought of that, and yet even whilst she tried to thrust it out of her mind, she knew what she was going to do, what she must do.

Once she had made up her mind to it, calm succeeded the whirling chaos of her thoughts.

She asked Mance if he could do without her for the day.

'I want to see to some urgent private business in London,' she told him quite steadily. I can leave everything ready for you, of course, and I'll ask Lady Gust if she will have Rosemary again. I don't know why she's so kind to me, but thank heaven she is.'

'You're rather a kind person yourself, Verne,' he said.

'I'm not,' she snapped, and left him wondering.

She certainly had not been kind to Robert – poor Robert who had needed to be protected from himself in the earlier days, and from that terrible suspicion and jealousy winch had had its roots in an inferiority complex and had grown up to smother and choke him. She saw that more clearly now, but in order to be in a position to do so, she had had to stand a distance of two years away from it.

She had not worked out any definite plan, but when she reached the London terminus, she did not hesitate. A bus took her as near as those proletarian vehicles were allowed to approach the hallowed street, and she walked along it remembering that it was the first time she had gone there on foot.

She looked up at the tall old house. The windows were still discreetly curtained, but the steps were not as virginally white as she remembered them, nor were the brass knockers on the imposing double doors as bright.

She went up the steps and rang the bell, but no one came. Then she remembered that she had a key on her key ring. Robert had given it to her, but at the same time had requested her always to ring the bell so that a servant should admit her. Now she found it and the door swung noiselessly back into a silent hall, a silent house.

She closed it softly behind her and stood there for a moment with a queer, unexpected feeling of homecoming. Yet this house had never seemed home to her. It was too big, too quiet, too full of people whom she seldom saw but who were always there, leaving her with nothing to do, not even to take off her own coat or carry away her own hat.

An empty house, almost a house of the dead – and yet with that uncanny instinct which tells us when we are not alone, she knew that there was some other human being in it besides herself.

She crossed the hall to open the door of the library, but Robert was not there. The remains of a fire lay dead in the hearth, and no one had picked up the newspapers that lay on the floor and on Robert's empty chair. An enormous silver ashtray held the remains of his cigars, but they were quite cold.

She went through the other rooms she had known, closed the doors on their emptiness and slowly mounted the stairs. She opened the door of her own bedroom and went in. Everything was as it had always been, the white satin covers on the bed, the opulent satin eiderdown over them, the curtains drawn precisely back, but flowers had wilted in the vases and, looking at them, she knew that only a day or two ago they had been fresh.

That gave her heart a queer twist. Only by Robert's orders could those vases had been kept filled – and it was two years since she had slept there.

For two years, flowers had been placed in her room. She could not reconcile that with the man she had known – or thought she had known.

She crossed to the door which led to his own room, bat here again was only emptiness. The room was neat and the bed had been made, but a film of dust over everything told its own tale.

Where then was Robert? She still had that certainty that he was here, somewhere in the house, waiting – for what? For her?

Why, she thought with sudden bitterness, should he be waiting for her, his wife? When had she ever been at his side when he needed her? When had she not been too much occupied with her own desires and needs to give much thought to his?

The need to find him became more urgent.

The other rooms on this floor were empty and silent, but she found the service staircase discreetly hidden behind double baize doors and went up to the servants' rooms. They were deserted and left in disorder.

And at last she found him and stood in the doorway in amazement.

Had it been here all the time, this dreary little room with its narrow iron bedstead, its battered furniture, the worn linoleum on the floor and the sink in the corner?

But she gave that only a fleeting thought. Her whole being was concentrated on the man who sat there on the edge of the bed, his hands hanging listlessly between parted knees, his eyes in their sunken, dark rimmed sockets staring into space.

It was Bunker who roused him to the knowledge that she was there, Bunker who had been sitting pressed against one of the beloved's legs and who got up at sight of a friend and came to her, wagging his inappropriate tail and jumping up to lick her hand before returning to his master.

Robert stared at her as if she were a ghost, and at that first fleeting look of wild, incredulous joy in his eyes, something broke in her and she came to him swiftly and stood before him and laid her two hands on his shoulders, looking down at him with eyes bright with tears.

'Robert,' she said, choking on his name. 'Robert!'

Her voice seemed to come to him from a long way off, from the apparition his mind had conjured up, but the touch of her hands was real – real, too, their pressure and then the feel of her body, her young, strong, living body beside him, and her cheek against his own.

'Robert,' she said again, in a whisper now, and as if the mere saying of his name was all that she needed to say.

He made a blind gesture towards her, a groping, uncertain gesture which touched her almost beyond endurance.

'Verne. Why have you come?'

There was the echo of the old harshness in his tone, but now she did not mind. It was Robert she was seeking, the man himself, the man she had come to find and knew that she must find if life was to hold any happiness and peace for her again.

'Don't you want me?' she asked, and her cheek found his again as they sat side by side on the lumpy old bed of which neither was conscious.

'Verne. It's you. You're here.'

For a few moments they sat in silence, utterly aware of each other and of a nearness they had never known. Her eyes wandered round the room, puzzled. The broken bits of furniture, the cheap lace curtain, the worn linoleum partly covering the bare boards, the sink in the corner, the old gas ring – what was this room doing in Robert Grimtree's house?

Presently she asked him.

'What is this room doing here? How did it get here? What's it for?'

'I put it here,' he said in a dull voice, trying to rouse himself. 'It's the sort of thing I began with. To have it here was a sop to my pride. It made me feel what a hell of a fine fellow I was. It's where I began – and it's where I'm ending,' and, the small effort over, he let his head droop again, but this time she slid an arm about him and drew it against her breast.

She looked down at the roughened hair which now had so much more grey in it than brown, looked at the whole, drooped figure of the man whose pride had been in himself – and there came to her, flooding through her, the knowledge of that thing that had broken free in her, the thing she had refused and denied utterance for so long.

This, then, was love—this deep, overmastering tenderness, this compassion that sought nothing for itself, this overpowering urge to shield and to protect and to defend. Love was not as she had imagined it, a tiring of hot blood, of kisses and all the things that went with them, a momentary flight to some sort of heaven to which earth is very near and very accessible.

Love was a giving, a faith and belief without need for reasons, pride in nothing material but in that enduring faith. Love seeketh not itself. Where had she heard that, or read it?

Love seeketh not itself.

She drew him closer.

'Robert, put your arms round me,' she whispered. 'I need you so. We—we need each other so.'

He lifted his head and looked at her wonderingly, not believing because he dared not believe.

'How can *you* need me?' he asked.

Her eyes filled with tears again. The pain that had come to her when she thought of him as hurt and defeated was as nothing to the laceration of her spirit now that she saw him, held him in her arms. And yet only through his pain had she found him.

'I need you terribly, desperately,' she said. 'Robert—oh, my darling.'

His eyes still held hers wonderingly. He could see her tears.

'Did you say that? Did you really say that?' he asked.

'That I need you? Oh, I do, I do! I've been in the wilderness so long, too long, when all the time this was waiting for me, this—your arms— your love. Do you love me, Robert?'

For a moment she thought 'Am I wrong? Is this all a dream, a mirage? Have I just made up something because I want it to be true?'

But the look in his eyes, the sudden flare she had never seen in them before, told her that it was no dream, and through her tears, she smiled.

'Tell me,' she said.

'I can't,' he whispered. 'I've never been able to—but I have. I always have.'

'And you still do?'

'I don't change.'

This time she laughed a little, a small shaken sound.

'If you don't change, at least you hide yourself so that no one would ever know if you had changed. You've never let anybody know you, not even me—not even me, my darling.'

He moved convulsively so that his arm was about her, holding her, gripping her so that he almost hurt her.

'You said that, Verne? You called me that?'

She smiled. It was a lovely thing to see.

'Why not try saying it yourself?' she asked.

'I—I want to say it but—I've never said things like that.'

His struggle against the habit of the years was almost a physical one. 'I—I love you, Verne. I always have, you know.'

'But that's just it, Robert my dear. I didn't know. How could I when you never told me? When you hid yourself from me? When you—just cast me off with no justification. With *no* justification then, Robert. Can you believe that? I think you'll have to if this moment is going to mean anything to us.'

'I believe it,' he muttered, his voice almost inaudible. 'I've believed it for a long time,' and the shame in his voice, the humbling of himself, was an intolerable pain to her. She could almost have wished he had gone on believing ill of her than been so sunk in self degradation.

Her arms held him strongly.

'We've gone such a long way from each other, Robert. We've been such fools, such utter fools. Can we get back? Or no, not back where we were, but to some fresh place, some point of understanding and—love?'

'Love? How can you love me, Verne?'

She laughed again, but tenderly, her cheek against his rough, unshaven one.

'I don't know,' she said. 'How does anyone know that? It's just something one can't explain but it's there and there's nothing you can do about it. You're disagreeable, bad tempered, egotistical, jealous, suspicious—stuck up and filled with a sense of your own importance—so how can a woman love you?' laughing through her tears.

'Yet you do, Verne? You do?'

She nodded.

'Goodness knows how or why or even when, but I do. What fools people can be! How they can hurt one another! Kiss me, Robert. Please kiss me,' and she held up her face for his kiss and, with a strangled cry of pain and his utter need of her, he crushed his mouth down on the softness of her own.

'Verne—Verne—my wife,' he said against her lips, and when he released her, she held her head back to look at him with surprise and an odd shyness, her face flushed.

'So you do know how to kiss?' she asked him. 'Oh Robert, after all the wasted time, life's going to be fun!'

But his face changed and his arms dropped from holding her.

'Do you know about me?' he asked in the old harsh tone.

'I expect so. What in particular?'

'I'm broke. I haven't anything. I can't ask you to share *nothing* with me.'

She leaned towards him and kissed him again.

'Is this nothing?' she asked. 'As for the rest, what makes you think we're broke? We've got fifty thousand pounds.'

He threw her a look, the old familiar one of suspicion and anger, but now it had no power to harm or intimidate her.

'How did you know about that?' he asked roughly. 'Templar, I suppose?'

'Yes. Oh, he told me you'd probably kill him for telling me, but don't do it yet. Let's have a bit of fun before you're up for murder. Oh Robert, don't mind about my knowing, darling. It—touched me very much.'

'Is that why you came? To fling that back at me because I'm broke?'

She laughed and ruffled his grizzled hair.

'Do you really think that? Can't you believe in me even yet?'

'I'm not going to take it back,' he said doggedly and she laughed again.

'Alright, you great bear,' she said, 'but don't think I'm afraid of you any more. Your growls don't mean a thing to me.'

'You've never been afraid of me, Verne. That was one of the things that made me—fall in love with you.'

'I've always been afraid of you, Robert, but I'm glad of any reason that made you fall in love with me. Anyway, there are still so many things to talk about and I'm hungry. Do you suppose there's any food in the house?'

'From the bills I pay, there ought to be a herd of oxen down there, not to mention chickens and ducks and all the rest,' he grumbled, and she laughed and rubbed her cheek against his and withdrew it with an 'ouch!'

'You're disgustingly bearded,' she said. 'When did you shave last?'

'I don't know. Yesterday—the day before—I'm sorry, Verne.'

She kissed him quickly.

'Don't be humble,' she said. 'Don't ever be that. I'd rather you raved and stormed at me! Let's rout about for food and you can shave afterwards when I'm washing up.'

'*You* wash up?' he asked, scandalised.

Gaily she showed him her hands, the fine, capable hands which had worn his diamonds but which were now roughened and lined by work.

'They shan't work for me,' he said gruffly.

'That's another of the things we'll see about,' she said, and they went downstairs to find the kitchens, great vaults of places with huge tables and stone floors and high windows that let in little light.

She stood in the doorway and laughed.

'Oh Robert, how like you! Nothing so modest as a kitchenette for the great Grimtree! I don't wonder you buy your meat by the herd if it has to be cooked in a place like this! Is this the larder, do you suppose?' opening one of the several doors leading out of the huge, vault like place which smelt of mildew and mice. 'Oh no, it isn't. What a disgusting idea to have one leading out of the kitchen!' wrinkling her nose in disgust and pulling the chain before she closed the door again.

She was feeling young and gay and had never before been at her ease like this with him. He could not keep his eyes off her. He was plainly enchanted, and now that she had broken through the hard crust of him, he seemed not to mind her knowing it.

They found the larder and quantities of leftover food which she threw out in disgust, though there was a refrigerator in which she found butter, milk and eggs. She condemned, regretfully, some cold meat and a cooked chicken since she could not know how long they had been there, and there was nothing in the deep freeze.

'How long have you been left without servants?' she asked.

'I paid them off about a fortnight ago, though Mrs. Wise, good soul, insisted on staying until a few days ago, when I had to make her go, told her I couldn't pay her any more wages.'

Verne laughed.

'Isn't it amusing? The great Grimtree not able to afford even a cook? Though he's got a good one now very cheaply. There are lots of tins if you can find a tin opener, and that looks like an electric grill, though of course the Aga has gone out. Pity. I've always wanted to have a go at an Aga. We haven't got any bread that's still eatable, but there are stacks of potatoes. Do you know how to peel them whilst I sort out the tins and see how much I can do on the griller?'

'Do I know how to peel potatoes!' he echoed scornfully. 'What do you take me for? A millionaire?'

He could even make a joke of it now! It was a supremely happy moment.

'Well, that's what I really did take you for,' she agreed, 'but what I've got is a good, deal better if you can peel spuds, so get down to it. Oh, some tins of asparagus. And sausages and kidneys. I can do those under the grill if I drain off the gravy. That'll leave the top for the other things. If I had a pressure cooker, I could do quite a lot. The owner of this place has a singularly ill equipped kitchen, seeing what magnificence he's got above stairs.'

Laughing and talking, giving him plenty to do and refusing to let him relapse into despondency or self pity for a moment, she did wonders with the contents of the tins and then told him to set the table.

'Set it? Down here, do you mean?'

'But of course! Look at me, and at your own face, and if you still want to have it in style in the dining room, we can send all the stuff up in the lift, but you'll have to be pretty lively to help me stack things into it this end and then shin up to receive it at the other end.'

He chuckled, that wheezy sound which was not quite as rusty as it had been half an hour ago.

'All right, m'm,' he said. 'Down here it is, though I don't like eating with the kitchen stuff. I like solid silver.'

'Then you'll have to get used to liking kitchen stuff,' she told him. 'Here's a clean cloth, and we only want it at one end. It's a nice, well scrubbed table, anyway. I know, Robert! Let's have the best Crown Derby! It'll be so funny with the kitchen forks, and it's in that cupboard there. I saw it just now. Don't break it as it's probably worth the earth, and when we sell it, we shall want it whole.'

He paused, serious again at her gay, matter-of-fact statement.

'We may not be as poor as all that, dar—darling,' he said, gulping a little over the unaccustomed endearment.

Her laughing face grew tender.

'It's only a joke, my sweet,' she said. 'Let's keep our tails up. And we don't have to have Crown Derby to be happy, do we?'

'I wanted to give you everything,' he muttered.

For a fleeting instant she rubbed her cheek against his bristly one and drew it away again quickly.

'Ouch! I won't do that again until you've shaved,' she said.

'I'll remind you of that when I've had the best shave ever,' he told her, and began to carry the priceless old china from the cupboard to the kitchen table.

'There was no room for heating the plates,' said Verne, 'but we can't help that. How many sausages can you eat? Three? Four?' and she began to pile their plates with the sausages and kidneys, asparagus, peas, mushrooms and golden brown chips, pouring over it the thick gravy from the tin of kidneys.

It was the merriest meal Grimtree had ever had, and the best and the happiest, he thought, sitting separated only by a corner of the kitchen table from a Verne he had never known, Verne in love, and in love with him, Robert Grimtree, gay, tender, teasing by turn, and always with that look in her eyes which told him that nothing in the world had any power over him again so long as he could keep that look in them.

Afterwards, when he had insisted on helping her to wash up and had then shaved at the sink whilst she sat with a cigarette and watched him, she told him reluctantly that she must go.

'Go? Go where?' he asked.

'Have you forgotten? That I have both a job and—a child?' she asked, looking away from him.

It was a crucial moment for them both, she felt.

'No,' he said. 'I hadn't forgotten.'

'You don't suggest my neglecting—both, Robert?'

'Only the job.'

She drew a deep breath.

'You know that Rosemary is Bill's child?'

'Was. Is mine now,' he said, and she came to his arms blindly, swiftly, to be held in that close grip which needed no words. He was meeting her need at every point, just as she was meeting his.

She thought swiftly. Nothing now must break this new understanding, this groping for a full knowledge of each other, which, in spite of this evening of strange happenings, still trembled uncertainly on his mood. They must not lose each other now. She was remembering that room at the top of the house and all it represented to him – failure now, not success.

But there was Gerald Mance, who had always been good to her. And there was Rosemary, her darling.

Yet for this one night, there must be only Robert, whose need of her was greatest, who for once in his arrogant, self sufficient life was dependent on some other human being, and that human being, herself.

Still standing in the circle of his arms, she drew her head back to look at him with eyes that had never been so steady, never so loving, never more utterly honest.

'Robert, do you want me to stay with you tonight?' she asked.

'I haven't any right,' he said.

'There are no more *rights* between us. Only love,' she said. 'Do you, my darling?'

'I'd give my soul for it,' he said thickly.

'Then let me go for a moment and—I'll find you again,' she slipped from his arms and went out of the kitchen and he heard her heels tapping along the stone corridor until the double baize door shut them off.

It took some time for her to make her two telephone calls to Sedbury, one to Lady Gust, who was delighted to keep Rosemary for the night, and one to Gerald Mance, who grumbled but consented.

'You'll come back tomorrow?' he asked suspiciously.

'Yes, I will. Of course I will. But—Gerald, I'm with my husband. I'm going back to him. I'll stay with you till you get someone else, but I'm definitely leaving you.'

She could not hide from him the thrill of her happiness. He heard it in her voice, felt it across the distance, and knew that there was nothing he could say.

'All right,' he grunted after a long pause during which she thought he had hung up on her, and then she heard the click of the receiver and drew a long breath.

Well, she had burnt her boats.

She went slowly up the stairs to the room which had been hers. All the things she had left were still there, her gold backed brushes, the drawers filled with exquisite lingerie to which her body had long been a stranger.

Many things would have to be discussed with Robert, the unknown, difficult future, and the past. There would be readjustments to make, much to be forgiven on both sides if they were to start fairly with each other, but for this one night there would be nothing but the love they had found and which, please God, they would not lose.

She heard his heavy tread at last, passing her door, going into his own room, and presently she slipped out of bed and set the door between them ajar.

About two months later, Verne Grimtree stood perilously on the top of a step ladder and looked down.

'Is that the last of these boxes, Mary?' she called.

Mary Gorner emerged from the room behind the little draper's shop where she had been putting on her hat and coat.

'Yes,' she said. 'You can come down now. You're quite sure you wouldn't like me to stay a bit longer? There's still quite a lot to be done, and if you really do open the door, you may get customers in.'

'But that'll be fun,' laughed Verne, coming down. 'If they ask for things that we haven't ticketed, I'll just guess the price. Thank you a thousand times, Mary. I couldn't possibly have managed without you,' and she kissed gratefully the woman who had proved such a godsend to her during the past frenzied week.

'I think you'd manage anything, Verne,' she said, returning the kiss, 'but I must say I don't want to be here when he arrives. Be sure to give me a ring tomorrow if you want me. I shan't be going back till the end of the week.'

'Bless you,' said Verne. 'Now nip off quickly in case he comes,' and when Mrs. Gorner had gone, she pulled up the spring blind which had indicated that the new shop was not yet open, and went outside for a last look at the two small windows, one at each side of the door, which they had dressed with such care.

Over them, in modest painted lettering, were the words 'R. GRIMTREE. GENERAL DRAPER'.

Robert had had to get the permission of the firm who had bought Grimtree's to use his own name, though he had had to agree that it should be in that form and not the gilt blazoned 'GRIMTREE'S' known all over the country.

'It might have been better to start in another name,' he had told Verne, 'but I'm not going to. I've nothing to hide. I paid twenty shillings in the pound and I don't owe anybody a penny, and who knows that I shan't some day be able to buy Grimtree's back?' boastfully.

Verne had looked at him with that new tenderness that had something maternal in it. He was only a little boy, after all, a little boy who liked big toys to play with.

'I don't think I shall ever want you to, Robert,' she said. 'That's why I agreed to forget that fifty thousand and to leave it where it is and start with just what you've got left.'

'It's such a poor way for you to live, Verne. That one little shop, the little flat over,' he said wistfully.

That's the Robert Grimtree I want to live with, and that's the way I want to live with him,' she told him. 'I don't want you to turn into the great Grimtree again. I like you as you are,' but she knew that, whatever she liked or wanted, some day they would be rich again. That was the way he was made, and she could not alter it.

But for the present he was just R. Grimtree, with the one little shop in a not too fashionable suburb of a big town, and she was supposedly still at Sedbury, finishing her work for Gerald Mance until Robert had set out the shop for which he had had the goods delivered. She was to join him when he had made a start.

She was in the little room behind the shop, a tiny living room with a small kitchen leading out of it, when she heard the bell that jangled when the shop door was opened.

She looked through the glazed half of the door and saw him come in and stand staring round at the neatly arranged stock, the labelled boxes on the shelves, the stand filled with coloured cottons at which customers could make their own choice, the fittings from which gay scarves and ribbons flaunted themselves invitingly, the shining tops of the two small counters with chairs set beside them for weary housewives, the trays of 'gadgets' to tempt the coppers from their purses.

Then she opened the dividing door and came to him.

He stared at her as he had stared at the transformation she had wrought in the grimy, old fashioned little shop as he had last seen it.

'Were you looking for Mr. Grimtree?' she asked sweetly. 'He will be at home in a minute, but *Mrs.* Grimtree is at home. Is there anything I can do for you, sir?'

'Oh, Verne—Verne!'

She came to his outstretched arms, and as she did so, pushed the door shut with her foot and snapped down the spring blind which bore the legend 'closed' on its other side.

Give Back Yesterday

Helena Clurey has it all – a devoted husband, money and family. She is happy and secure, but her apparent contentment is about to be shattered by a voice from the past. Mistress she may have been, but that is not the way it is put to her: 'you were not my mistress - you were, and are, my wife.'

The Weir House

Philip wants to marry Eve. It is her way out - he is rich, not too old, and has been in love for years – but not a man she can accept. He has even secretly funded her lifestyle, such that it is. Eve feels trapped. Unlike her friend Marcia, who cheerfully accepts an 'ordinary' life without complaint, Eve has known better and wants better. A chance encounter then changesthings – Lewis Belamie pays her to act as his fiancée for a week. Adventure, ambition, and disappointment all follow after she journeys to Cornwall with him, where she eventually nearly dies after what appears to be a suicide attempt because of a marriage that has seemingly failed. However, the mysterious and mocking Felix really does love her. Just who is he; how does Eve end up with him; and what part does 'The Weir House' play in her life? Has Eve's restlessness and relentless search for stability ended?

Through Many Waters

Jeff has got himself into a mess. It is, on the face of it, a classic scenario. He has a settled relationship with one woman, but loves another. What is he to do? It is now necessary to face reality, rather than continually making excuses to himself, but can he face the unpalatable truth? Then something beyond his influence intervenes and once again decisions have to be made. But in the end it is not Jeff that decides.

Misadventure

Olive Heriot and Hugh Manning had been in love for years, but marriage had been out of the question because of the intervention of Olive's mother. Now, at last, she was of age and due to gain her inheritance and be free to choose. A dinner party had been arranged at the Heriot's home, 'The Hermitage' and Hugh expects to be able to announce their engagement. Things start to change after a gruesomely realistic game entitled 'murder', which relies on someone drawing the Knave of Spades after cards are dealt. Tragedy strikes and other relationships are tested and consummated – but is this all real, or imagined?

Printed in Great
Britain
by Amazon